Praise for
Billion Dollar Cowboy

"A real page-turner… a compelling cast of characters, the perfect country setting, and a smoking-hot romance that progresses at just the right pace, this is one story where readers won't be able to help getting swept right along for the ride."

—*RT Book Reviews*, 4 Stars

"Sizzling… Brown navigates the pair's rocky journey from friendship to red-hot sex while imbuing her lively story with lots of heart."

—*Publishers Weekly*

"Carolyn Brown delivers yet another steamy cowboy romance… witty dialogue and hilarious banter are here to be enjoyed. Once I started reading, I couldn't put it down… or keep the smile off my face."

—*Night Owl Reviews*

"Sweet and endearing."

—*Tome Tender*

"A must-read series for all lovers of Western romance."

—*Loves to Read for Fun*

"I enjoy a rich hero. I really enjoy a hot cowboy hero. Combined, you can't go wrong."

—*Dirty Girls' Good Books*

Praise for Carolyn Brown's Christmas Cowboy Romances

"Sassy and quirky and peopled with an abundance of engaging characters, this fast-paced holiday romp brims with music, laughter... and plenty of Texas flavor."

—*Library Journal*

"A sweet romance that really stresses the chemistry that builds between two highly likable characters... Readers will enjoy this cozy bright contemporary romance."

—*RT Book Reviews*, 4 Stars

"Carolyn Brown is a master storyteller! A love between two people that will enrapture and capture your heart."

—*Wendy's Minding Spot*

"Sassy contemporary romance... with all the local color and humorous repartee her fans adore."

—*Booklist*

"Full of sizzling chemistry and razor-sharp dialogue."

—*Night Owl Reviews* Reviewer Top Pick, 4.5 Stars

"This book makes me believe in Christmas miracles and long slow kisses under the mistletoe."

—*The Romance Studio*

"Carolyn Brown creates some handsomefied, hunkified, HOT cowboys! A fun, enjoyable four-star-Christmas-to-remember novel."

—*The Romance Reviews*

Cowboy seeks Bride

CAROLYN BROWN

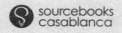

sourcebooks
casablanca

Published by Sourcebooks Casablanca, an imprint of Sourcebooks, Inc.
P.O. Box 4410, Naperville, Illinois 60567-4410
(630) 961-3900
FAX: (630) 961-2168
www.sourcebooks.com

Printed and bound in Canada
WC 10 9 8 7 6 5 4 3 2 1

Chapter 1

IF IT WAS AN APRIL FOOLS' JOKE, IT DAMN SURE wasn't funny.

If it wasn't a joke, it was a disaster.

Those five big horses complete with cowboys didn't look like a joke. Cattle bawling and milling around looked pretty damned real, too. And that little covered wagon, with a bald-headed man the size of a refrigerator sitting on the buckboard holding the reins for two horses in his hands, didn't have a single funny thing about it, either.

Haley's mouth went dry when she realized that the big dapple-gray horse was for her and that absolutely nothing in front of her was a practical joke. It was all as real as the smell of the horses and what they'd dropped on the ground.

She slung open the door of her little red sports car. The cowboys were all slack jawed, as if they'd never seen a woman before. Well, they'd best tie a rope around their chins and draw them back up because she was going to be their sidekick for the next thirty days. They could like it or hate it. It didn't really matter to her. All she wanted to do was get the month over with and go home to civilization.

"You lose your way?" The cowboy on a big black horse looked down at her. His tone was icy and his deep green eyes even colder.

"Not if this is the O'Donnell horse ranch and you're about to take off on the Chisholm Trail reenactment." She looked up into the dark-haired cowboy's green sexy eyes. "Who are you?" She planted her high heels on the ground and got out of the car.

"Dewar O'Donnell, and you are?"

Dammit! With a name like Dewar, she'd pictured a sixty-year-old man with a rim of graying hair circling an otherwise bald head, and a face wrinkled up like the earth after a hard summer, complete with a day's growth of gray whiskers. He sure wasn't supposed to look like Timothy Olyphant with Ben Bass's eyes. It was going to be one hell of a month because she wasn't about to get involved with a cowboy. Not even if she had the sudden urge to crawl right up on that horse and see if those eyes were as dreamy up close as they were from ten feet away.

"I'm H. B. Mckay," she answered.

"Well, shit!" Dewar drawled.

"I know. Life's a bitch, isn't it? But I'll be riding along this whole trip taking notes for the reality show to be filmed this summer," she said. "Unless you want to tell me that this is a big silly joke and I can go home to Dallas now."

"Can't do that, ma'am. I was expecting you to be a man, but we're ready to move this herd north so I guess you'd better saddle up. I was just about to call Carl Levy and ask where you were," Dewar drawled.

"That's the idea most people have. I guess that empty horse is for me and I don't get to drive from point to point and stay in a hotel?"

"That's the plan Carl made," he answered.

She crossed her arms over her chest. "So we are ready to go right now?"

"Unless you want to change clothes," he said.

"Hell, no! I'm wearing what I've got on, and if I get a single snag in this suit Daddy will be paying for a brand new one," she said.

Dewar frowned. "Daddy?"

"Carl Levy is my father as well as my boss."

—∿∿—

Dewar had always had a liking for redheads, but not the kind that wore high-heeled shoes and business suits. And it seemed like here lately he'd dated every redhead in the whole northern part of Texas. Because both of his brothers and his two sisters had beat him to the altar, now everyone in the family thought they had a PhD in matchmaking and had made it their life mission to get him married off.

He'd rebelled at first, but then he admitted that he really wanted to have a wife and family so he'd started looking around on his own. He hadn't joined one of those online dating services, but he had been dating a lot. Either he was too damn picky or else all the good ones were taken because very few women interested him enough for a second date.

H. B.'s eyes were a soft aqua, somewhere between blue and green like the still, deep waters of the ocean. And her lips full, the kind that begged for kisses. He felt a stirring down deep in his heart that he hadn't felt before, but he didn't know if it was anger or desire.

It really didn't matter because the whole damn thing had to be a joke. It was too ridiculous to be real. Raylen had cooked it up and paid some woman to help him pull it off. He pulled his cell phone from his shirt pocket and quickly punched in the numbers to the office of the Dallas magazine tycoon.

"Carl Levy, please."

Ten long seconds later, "Tell him this is Dewar O'Donnell and this is definitely an emergency."

H. B. shook her head and took her saddlebags from her car. "You are wasting your time, cowboy."

Dewar hooked a leg over the saddle horn and ignored her. "Carl, I've got a red-haired woman who says she's H. B. McKay. You want to verify that?"

He frowned.

"You led me to believe that H. B. was a man, sir. A woman hasn't got any business on a cattle drive."

H. B. yelled over the noise of bawling cattle, snorting horses, and laughing men. "Tell him Momma is going to throw a Cajun fit, and if he's smart he'll walk in the house with roses in one hand and an apology on his lips."

"Yes, sir, that was her," Dewar said.

She held out her hand. "Give me that phone."

Dewar leaned down and put it in her hand.

"You are going to pay for this, Daddy. I'm pissed off worse than I've ever been before in my life. I'm so pissed off that I'm not even going to talk to you about it and you can tell Joel that I know he's behind this shit and I'll get even with him when I get home."

Everything went silent. Even the cows stopped bawling.

"Stop laughing. I'll show you what I can do, but you are going to be sorry. Believe me, you are going to regret it."

She handed the phone back to Dewar. "He says to tell you good luck. You ready?"

He put the phone back in his pocket and nodded toward the dapple-gray horse. "Soon as you tie down those bags and mount up. Apache is spirited, but he's tough. You ever ridden?"

"Once or twice," she answered.

―⁓―

She still couldn't believe that she was going on a Chisholm Trail cattle run. There was no doubt that she'd aggravated her father big-time when she'd broken her engagement six months before, but she thought he'd gotten over it.

"Evidently I was dead wrong," she mumbled.

Joel was a hardworking businessman in her father's corporation, but when it came down to brass tacks, she hadn't loved the man nearly as much as her father had liked him for a potential new son-in-law. When she called off the engagement, Carl Levy sure hadn't been happy with her. Well, she damn sure wasn't happy with him today, so maybe that made them even.

Even though she wasn't marrying Joel, Carl had kept him as his right-hand man and she was sure that Joel was behind the whole idea of sending her off into the wilds on horseback, for God's sake. Well, she'd prove to both her dad and her former fiancé that she could handle the job better than either of them.

Cowboys were wonderful subjects to film. Women loved their tight-fitting jeans, boots, belt buckles, and slow drawls. But they sure weren't her cup of tea. No sir! Give her a man in a custom-fit three-piece suit any day of the week over a man who liked horses and cows better than five-star restaurants and Broadway plays. So that tall, dark cowboy with a black hat pulled down over his eyes had better lay low for at least a week. She might begin to cool off by then.

It was going to be a long month with no cell phone or even a laptop. She had to take notes by hand and give them to the cook who would send them by snail mail whenever he went for supplies.

Thank goodness she knew how to tie down a saddle-bag, even if she did have to tiptoe to get the job done. Not a single one of those cowboys hopped down off their horses and offered to do it for her, proving that she was right in her choice of men. Cowboys were only gentlemen in movies and romance books. The real thing didn't even exist. When they dropped their britches and kicked off their boots, they were just like all other men. And she didn't have time for any of them.

She stuck her high-heeled shoe in the stirrup, grabbed the saddle horn, and gave a little bounce. The slick red bottom of her spike-heeled shoe slipped in the stirrup. The foot on the ground was standing in a fresh pile of horse manure. The momentum jerked her hand off the saddle horn and she was staring with wide open eyes at big fluffy white clouds somewhere past the horses, cowboys, and even the big pecan trees. Her chest felt like it was going to explode when she finally remembered to force air into her lungs, and the smell of fresh warm horse shit hit her nose.

She quickly pulled herself up into a sitting position. Her shoes were ruined. Her best power suit was a mess. And she hadn't even gotten on that horse yet. Her

COWBOY SEEKS BRIDE 7

father had better get busy fulfilling all the things on his bucket list.

She looked up to see a hand extended toward her and she took it. A different cowboy heaved her up to her feet. He looked somewhat like Dewar, but he wasn't as tall, but then Dewar was sitting on the biggest horse she'd ever seen, so maybe he just looked like he was ten feet tall and bulletproof.

"Thank you," she said.

"Guess you didn't get a good hold on that stirrup with those shoes," he said. "I'm Raylen. Who are you?"

"Had nothing to do with my ability to mount the horse. I stepped in horse shit! I'm H. B. McKay," she said through clenched teeth.

Raylen chuckled and then roared. He wiped his eyes with the back of his hand. "I can't wait to tell Liz. Dewar, you are never living this one down."

"Who is Liz?" Haley asked.

If Liz was Dewar's wife or girlfriend, that just complicated matters even more. No woman would want her husband or boyfriend out in the wilds for a whole month with a strange woman.

Raylen didn't answer but pointed at her. "*You* are the sissified fellow my brother has been bitchin' about for two months? Now that is rich."

"Sissified!" Haley cut her eyes up at Dewar and set her mouth in a hard line.

Dewar shrugged. "How can Carl Levy be your father and your name be McKay?"

"My name is Haley McKay Levy. I dropped the last name for professional reasons. No one needs to know that Carl is my father," she said.

"What's the *B* stand for?" he asked.

"Bitch! And don't you forget it," she told him.

"You sure you don't want five minutes to change into some boots? You did bring something other than those shoes, I hope, or maybe you're planning to ride all day in your bare feet?" Dewar drawled. "I'll give you ten minutes to change. If you aren't ready to ride by then, we're leaving you behind and you can scoot right back to Daddy and tell him to send us a man who can do the job."

"I've got boots and jeans," she said from behind clenched teeth.

Did all men share DNA with jackasses, or was it just because it was April Fools' Day?

Dewar pointed toward a barn.

She untied her saddlebags and stomped off in that direction. She hadn't been on a horse since she was in college. She'd taken a riding class as an elective, but that had been eight years before. She hadn't liked anything about horses then, not the way they smelled, brushing them, or the crap they left behind. According to her professor, it was therapeutic. According to Haley, it was a big waste of her time.

But in the next thirty days she'd prove to the whole damn bunch of them that she wasn't a sissified anything. And when she got back home to Dallas, Joel had best pack his bags and catch the next flight back to Holly-damn-wood.

She'd carefully packed the saddlebags with the pair of Roper boots that she'd bought for the riding class, three pairs of jeans, four T-shirts, and clean underwear and socks plus a thick spiral notebook and several ballpoint pens. She'd gotten ready, but she still could hardly believe it was happening. She'd even prepared a speech giving her father credit for the biggest and best prank ever. Her mother had assured her every day the past week that it wasn't real, and Haley had believed her right up until she saw all those cowboys, horses, and the wagon. Wait until her mother found out that her father sent her and not Joel.

"I really, really wouldn't want to be Daddy tonight," she mumbled.

She found an empty horse stall in the barn and kicked off her smelly shoes, removed her slacks, jacket, and blouse. She jerked on jeans and a T-shirt and pulled socks from inside her boots. She cussed under her breath the whole time she put them on and shoved her feet down into the Ropers. That blasted riding class turned out to be her biggest mistake in her college years. She'd gotten a B in it—the only one on her transcript. But she was glad she'd saved the boots.

"Hey, where are you?" a woman's voice yelled.

"I'm back here in a stall," Haley said.

The voice came closer. "*You* are the reality television person?"

Haley hung her clothes on the stall door. They were ruined for sure and those shoes had only been worn once. The smell of horse crap would never come out of the leather.

"Yes, I am."

"Decent yet?"

Haley opened the stall door. "I hope I am."

She faced a short dark-haired woman wearing faded jeans and a pearl-snap chambray work shirt and a denim jacket.

"And you are?" Haley asked.

"I'm Liz O'Donnell, Dewar's sister-in-law, and you'd be the *fellow* who is going along to take notes for that reality show?" Liz laughed.

"Guess I surprised them all." Haley smiled.

"Dewar still thinks it's a joke that Raylen has pulled on him. I'd love to be a fly on the tree bark when he figures out this whole thing is real and my husband did not play an April Fools' joke on him," Liz said.

"I'd love to be a fly on the dining room table tonight when my momma figures out that Daddy sent me on this trip. There might not even be a Dallas after tonight," Haley said.

Liz pulled off her denim jacket and handed it to Haley. "Put this on. I bet you didn't even bring a jacket and it's still cold in the mornings. You'll need it."

She slipped it on over the T-shirt. "You sure? I didn't even think of a jacket."

Liz stepped back and pulled off her well-worn straw hat. "Fair as you are, you'd best have this too."

"Why are you doing this?"

"Because Dewar deserves it. I wanted to make this trip, but oh, no! A woman could not go. It was boys only, and girls were banned," Liz said.

"That's ridiculous!"

Liz giggled. "That's exactly what I told him. I'm hoping you give him grief all month. Think you can do that?"

"You bet your sweet ass I can." Haley nodded.

Liz led the way out of the stall with Haley keeping step right beside her. "They've all been crowing all week about spending a whole month out in the wide open spaces without a woman to nag, whine, and bitch. This is just too sweet."

"They haven't seen bitching yet, but it's coming," Haley said.

Liz handed her a fist full of rubber bands from her pocket. "That hair is going to be so tangled by the end of the day that you won't be able to do a thing with it, so take these so you can braid it startin' tomorrow morning."

"I packed a brush, a bar of soap, and a couple of headbands, but I didn't think I'd really be doing this," Haley said.

"What else have you got?"

"Two pair of jeans, shirts, and underwear. I barely got it all in the saddlebags."

"You'll be all right."

"For thirty days?" Haley asked.

"Did you pack toilet paper?"

Haley groaned. "Daddy said I couldn't have a laptop or a phone because the batteries wouldn't last and there was certainly no electricity. I thought that was a death sentence. I didn't even think about toilet paper and using the bathroom in the woods."

"Just hope that you can find woods or bushes or even mesquite trees. Some of the land where you are going is flatter than a pancake. You'll be lucky to find a tumbleweed to squat behind," Liz said.

The door was in sight, but Liz detoured to a tack room with a small bathroom and handed her a roll. "Shove it down in your duffel bag and don't share."

"I can't believe you are helping me," Haley said.

"The paper won't last thirty days, but by the time it's gone you'll have your bluff in on them, and Dexter, or

Coosie, as he insists everyone calls him on the trail, will be more than glad to pick up some for you when he buys supplies. I'm just evening up the playing field. I can't wait to see the reality show that comes out of this. Did you know they filmed part of that noodlin' show not far from here?"

Haley frowned. "Noodlin'? Oh, you mean hand fishing?"

"Yeah, that's it, but the folks in this area call it noodlin'. Looks like it's time to mount up. Don't worry about your shoes and suit. I'll take care of them and they'll be ready when you come back."

"Who are all those cowboys? Tell me their names. I've done my research, so I know that Coosie is the nick-name for the cowboy who drives the chuck wagon and who does the cooking," Haley whispered as they walked toward the horses.

"The one on the ground is Raylen, my husband. He's not going with them. Dexter, I mean Coosie, is driving the wagon. Buddy is the middle-aged man who stutters. And then Sawyer, Finn, and Rhett are O'Donnell cous-ins. They would have made a man prove himself on this trip, but they sure didn't plan on *you*, so go strike a blow for women."

Haley settled the hat down better on her head. "You are scarin' me a little bit, but don't tell them I said that."

She marched right up to the horse named Apache with new determination, stuffed her roll of toilet paper into her saddlebag, jammed her scuffed-up work boot down into the stirrup, grabbed the saddle horn, and threw a leg over the horse. It was like riding a bicycle and it all came back to her, right along with the reasons that she didn't like that class all those years ago. Her butt hit with a thump and the jar traveled up her backbone with enough force to make her wince before the horse took a single step.

"You ready?" Dewar asked.

Haley nodded.

She had a hat and a jacket.

She had toilet paper.

It didn't transform her into a cowgirl, but by damn, those cowboys didn't know that.

"I can take notes and send back to Carl. You don't have to go," Dewar said.

"Oh yes I do," Haley said. She'd show her father that she was as tough as any field reporter on his payroll.

Dewar inhaled deeply and yelled, "Head 'em out!"

He rode ahead of the whole crew, slapping his hat against his thigh to start a hundred head of cattle moving out of the pasture and across the two-lane highway. Four other cowboys did the same, with the chuck wagon bringing up the rear. Haley wasn't sure what she should do, but finally she and Apache fell in behind the whole affair. In an hour her butt was asleep, her legs felt like they'd never be straight again, and the bagel she'd eaten early that morning had vanished.

She urged Apache on to a trot and rode along beside the cows so she could see Dewar better. He sat loose in the saddle, his back ramrod straight, and his long legs didn't look like they hurt like hers did. An image appeared in her head of him riding strip stark naked like the hero in the Cheryl Brooks book she'd heard about from a friend who worked on the *RT Book Reviews* magazine.

Cheryl wrote amazing erotic paranormal fiction. In

a recent interview she'd described the beginning of her new book. Just reading the interview had given Haley hot flashes and had been the primary reason she called off the engagement with Joel. If her fiancé couldn't make her as hot as a book teaser, then there was something wrong with the relationship. She couldn't very well tell her father such a thing, but it was the truth.

She'd imagined Joel sitting on a horse with no clothes on and all it did was make her giggle. She'd imagined him doing the things to her body that Cheryl's heroes did to her heroines and not one faint little shiver of anticipation tickled her backbone.

But imagining Dewar sitting all straight and tall and *naked*, now that was a different matter and it scared the bejesus right out of her. She'd only just met the man and he could be married or engaged or in some kind of a relationship. Surely someone that sexy wasn't single, so she had no right to be drawing mental pictures of him naked.

Hmmm, if that's against the rules, then he can keep his hat and boots. Oh, my! That even presents a sexier picture, she thought.

She leaned forward for a better view through the cows, and when she sat back a fresh stab of pain hit her tailbone. She wanted to cry, but she'd be roasted alive over a barbecue pit in the devil's backyard before she complained.

Her stomach grumbled, but she kept a death grip on the reins and fell back far enough that she couldn't see Dewar so plainly. She would definitely slide right off Apache if she kept leaning to one side to get a better virtual vision of him wearing nothing but boots and a hat.

Her stomach growled again. Were there chocolate cookies somewhere in that wagon? In her research cowboys ate a hell of a lot of beans on the trail, especially if no one killed a deer or enough rabbits for Coosie to fry up for supper. The reality show would have a helluva time getting seven cowboys and as many cowgirls to do a Western reality show if all they got was beans and wild game on the whole trip. Or would they? That big payout at the end of the trip in Dodge City would bring contestants out by the droves.

Next week, while she was gone, the committee would begin throwing around names for the show and that's where she wanted to be. It had been her idea from the time she heard about the *Hand Fishin'* reality show, and it wasn't fair that she couldn't be sitting behind her desk fielding ideas. Just because Joel was Carl's golden-haired boy wonder at the office, he got to stay in an air-conditioned office while Haley got bunions on her ass and a nose full of fresh cow-shit scent with every foot that the cowboys herded the cattle through the mesquite.

Who would have believed that cows could crap so much and just keep walking the whole time? Or that it took five cowboys and a chuck wagon to herd a hundred of them to Dodge City, Kansas?

She rode along behind the wagon and talked to herself, wishing that she could write down ideas and ride at the same time. "We've got to cross the Red River, and I bet there's no way that egotistical cowboy is going to use the bridge. I wouldn't on the reality show. It's too great an opportunity for things to go wrong, and that's what makes a good show. Note one when we stop tonight: first there's going to be saddle-sore tempers at the end of the day, and the Red River will have to be crossed, so get the cameras rolling from the other side. Fall off the horse and it's an automatic point deduction. Let a cow get away from you and it's more deductions. Fall into bed with the trail boss and you get fifty extra points."

She looked around to see if anyone was listening, only to find a straggling old black and white cow staring at her. Haley stuck her tongue out at the heifer and she looked the other way.

"One cow down. Six cowboys to go. Wonder if I stick my tongue out at them if they'll back down and leave me alone?" she mumbled.

Dewar led the way across the Red River at a narrow place with sloped sides down to the water's edge. The clay-colored water flowed gently that morning and barely skimmed his horse's belly. Only the bottom of his jeans and the soles of his boots were wet when the cattle reached the other side.

The horses pulled the chuck wagon across without a problem. Haley made mental notes and hoped that when her contestants crossed the river that it was rolling and much deeper.

They would begin filming in late summer. She planned on having the season ready to roll by spring of the next year. If pretty boy Joel hadn't gone back to his precious West Coast by then, he could just stand back and know that she had as much film smarts as he thought he had. The first season wouldn't be prime time, but it did have a pretty good chance at a slot on Sunday afternoons, and reality shows had better ratings if there was danger.

It was a probably a good thing that her father had sent

her on the trip. Joel, bless his heart, would have died of acute nose snarling the first time he got a good solid whiff of cow shit. And his delicate skin would break out in hives for sure if he had to wear tight-fittin' jeans.

On the Oklahoma side of the river they passed through several acres of mesquite before coming out in a flat pasture between the ghost town of Fleetwood and Terral, a small town located to the west of them. Haley could hear traffic passing on Highway 81 even though she couldn't see anything except patches of mesquite, tractors stirring up dust in fields, and pastureland.

Haley read that the Chisholm Trail came out in Indian territory right across the river. In one account, it said that cattle were so thick at times in the river crossing that a cowboy could walk across the river on their backs. She looked for the places where her research said that there were still signs of a million cattle being herded, but she only saw green grass.

The wagon pulled up under a big pecan tree and stopped. As if they knew it was midday, the old long-horn bull who'd been leading the herd came to a halt. He bawled out a message to his followers and they all lined up around a farm pond for a drink before they started nibbling on the green grass.

Haley tugged on Apache's reins. "Whoa, boy!"

When the cowboys dismounted, she slung a leg over the side and stepped out of the stirrup only to get a charley horse in her calf. She sucked air, stomped it out, took a step, and looked down at her bowed legs. If her knees ever touched again it would be a sheer miracle. She would have to wear long flowing skirts for months to cover up the effects of riding every day.

"Little sore, are you? It will get better every d-d-day. I'm Buddy," the cowboy stuttered.

"Pleased to meet you, Buddy. I hope it gets better real soon," Haley said.

Buddy was taller than she was, but that couldn't be counted as bragging about much since she barely tipped the charts at five feet three inches. He had arms as big as hams and a belly that hung out over his belt. Haley didn't figure anybody would ever mess with him, not even with a stutter. His thick hair was brown, and his eyes were the same color. His face was round and kind looking, and she'd guess him to be somewhere in his forties. His boots were scuffed and his jeans worn, and his confidence said that he knew everything about riding, camping, and herding cows.

The man on the chuck wagon hopped down and extended his hand. "You shocked us so bad we weren't even polite back at the house. My real name is Dexter but on the trail I'm Coosie and I run the eatin' part of this trail ride. Every time a cowboy calls me anything different than Coosie he gets his pay docked by a dollar at the end of the line. Since we didn't have breakfast there were no leftovers to use for dinner, so I've got bologna sandwiches and chips today, but that's a treat we won't be gettin' very often."

Haley shook hands with him, her small hand dwarfed by his. "I'm glad to meet you, Coosie."

He should have been one of those huge football players that ran a couple of steps and blocked anyone trying to get past him to the ball. He was somewhere around Buddy's age but twice his size. His arms were enormous, and his big round head was shaved smooth as a billiard ball. His eyes were gentle and his smile genuine, but Haley sure didn't want to ever get on his bad side.

One of the younger cowboys spoke up, "And we're the O'Donnell cousins. Dewar's daddy had three more brothers. We each belong to one of those brothers. I'm Sawyer. This here"—he pointed to his left—"is Rhett, and that would be Finn." He pointed to his right. "We weren't expecting a woman on the ride, but if you'll keep up, we won't hold the fact that you're a girl against you."

"Hell, we might even convert you to a real cowgirl by the time the trip is over. You might get a tat on your neck and learn how to two-step," Rhett said.

"Don't bet on it," she said.

Tat, her ass! Two-step? They could all go to hell. She might have a hat and a pair of boots, but she couldn't wait to get back to her high heels and power suits.

It was easy to tell that they were all kin to Dewar. They had the same thick black hair. Sawyer had almost black eyes that looked right into her soul when he nodded. His skin was that lightly toasted color that said there was some Hispanic in his genes. Finn had clear blue eyes, light-colored skin, and a tight smile that said he kept his thoughts close to this heart. Rhett sported a tat of a longhorn on his upper bicep and wore his dark hair pulled back in a short ponytail. Obviously the rebel cousin, his green eyes glittered when he shook hands with her.

Dewar rode up and expertly slid off his horse. His knees weren't bowed in the least and for that Haley could have choked him and enjoyed watching him turn blue.

"You ready to go back yet? My cell phone still has enough battery power to call Liz, the woman you met back at the ranch. She'll come rescue you. I still think this is a prank Raylen and Liz is pulling on me because I wouldn't let her come on the trip with us," he said.

"Why didn't Raylen come with you?" Haley asked.

"Because he wouldn't if Liz couldn't." Rhett chuckled.

Haley cocked her head to one side. "And why couldn't she come? She rides and I bet she cooks."

Sawyer laughed out loud. "She rides, but she doesn't cook. We got Coosie to do that for us anyway. We don't need a woman to cook for us on the trail, and I'm willing to bet a hundred-dollar bill that you don't last a week before you call your people to come get you."

"I don't cook either, so if anything happens to Coosie, don't expect me to do his job. And honey, don't bet money you haven't got because I will take it away from you with a smile on my face," Haley said.

"We planned on this being a…" Dewar stopped without completing the sentence.

"A boys' clubhouse with no girls allowed?" Haley asked.

He held out his phone. "Something like that."

Haley's chin jacked up a full inch. "I'll stay."

"Well, you got until tomorrow morning. That's when I reckon my cell phone will go dead, lady. What does that *B* in your name really stand for anyway?"

"I told you, it stands for bitch," she said.

Sawyer chuckled. "I believe it and that bet is still on, lady. You leave, you shell it out. You stay all the way up to the time when you get back in that cute little sports car and I'll hand it over."

"I asked a simple question. What's the *B* for?" Dewar said.

Her skin tingled just listening to Dewar's deep twangy drawl. Sawyer's was just as deep and twangy, but it didn't send the vibes to her soul like Dewar's did.

"And I answered it, Mr. O'Donnell." Haley pointed at Sawyer. "Bet is on, darlin'. But let's make it interesting. Let's up the ante that says you can't run me off."

Sawyer shook his head. "Hundred dollars is enough of a bet for me, lady."

Dewar took a step closer to her. "Name is Dewar. Mr. O'Donnell is my granddad on my father's side."

"Well, I don't like Dew-Are so I'm going to call you Dewy. It sounds like someone is trying to ask for Scotch whiskey to me. Why would your mama name you after something that comes in a liquor bottle anyway?"

"If you call me Dewy, there will be a war and, darlin', I will win. My mama named me that because she's real fond of Dewar's White Label and it's a good old Irish name," he growled.

"I wouldn't call him that if I was you," Rhett drawled.

Haley turned her head slightly to look at him.

"I heard about this guy who came on to him in a bar and called him Dewy Darlin'." Rhett grinned.

"That never happened. It's just a rumor." Dewar blushed.

Haley turned back to Dewar. "Leave me alone about my middle name and I'll call you Dewar and I'll even say it right."

Dewar stuck out his hand. "Deal."

The effect of his bare skin touching hers sent shock waves through her body. It really was going to be a helluva long thirty days, and she was going to have to curb her imagination because that tingle was exactly what she imagined the heroine in Cheryl's book feeling like when the hero touched her.

Chapter 2

DEWAR RAISED A GLOVED HAND AND CALLED A HALT to the ride as the sun drifted toward the treetops on the western horizon. The cattle and horses had free rein in a sixty-acre pasture split down the middle by Flat Creek. It was little more than a shallow gully filled with spring rainwater, but it would water the livestock and it wouldn't be too tough to cross the next morning.

Haley slid off the horse and untied the saddlebags.

"Let m-m-me help you," Buddy said.

"Thank you." Her voice sounded tired even in her own ears.

Together, they removed the saddle and blanket from Apache's back, brushed him well, and turned him out to graze with the cattle.

When they finished she turned around to find that the cowboys had already staked out a claim for bedrolls and settled their saddles at one end to use as a pillow. She looked around at the circle they were making around the campfire. Coosie and Buddy were on the east side with the foot of their bedrolls toward the fire. The chuck wagon was on the south, and the O'Donnell cousins were lined up on the west. Dewar had rolled out his bed under a weeping willow at the edge of the gully on the north side of the camp.

The aroma of whatever Coosie was cooking caught up in the evening breeze and floated right to Haley's nose. According to what she'd overheard the guys talking about, they were only a couple of miles south of Ryan. She pushed her hat back and looked toward the west into the setting sun. Was it really the twenty-first century? She felt as if crawling up on Apache's back had triggered a time lapse. She had settled into the saddle and in that instant, she was suddenly thrown backwards more than a hundred years. Should that be a tagline for the reality show? Can today's people endure what their ancestors did right after the Civil War?

She heard a rumbling off to the west and squinted into the setting sun. She didn't see a single cloud, so where was the thunder coming from?

"It's not thunder. It's the trains traveling north and south on the tracks parallel to Highway 81," Dewar said.

How had he known what she was thinking? Lord, if he could read her mind, she ought to put a hood over her head with only slits to see through.

"Sounds like thunder," she said.

"Sure does. Made me check for lightning too."

Thank God! She wasn't looking forward to a hood, and yet there was no way she could control her crazy thoughts.

She nodded. Day one of thirty was finished. She wondered what the reality crew would do with that first day. Would they all be moaning and groaning about sore butt muscles and legs that didn't want to straighten out? She tried to imagine the contestants going about driving a herd of cattle with cameras pointed at them.

"What are you thinking about? Where to throw that bedroll?" Dewar asked.

"No, I was thinking about the first day of the reality show."

"They'll be thinking they were crazier than drunk roosters to sign on for such a trip. I can't begin to imagine this trip with all the lights, cameras, and action stuff," he answered.

"Me either." She pointed toward the ground. "Is this spot taken?"

"Yes, it is."

"Not the one where your bedroll is but this one I'm standing on. You got a problem with me being this close to you?"

"I snore," he said.

"So do I." She threw her bedroll down and paid careful attention to the way it was tied and rolled so she could put it back the same way. Buddy had helped her unsaddle Apache and in his slow stuttering way had refreshed her lessons the riding coach had given her all those years ago.

"Is every day going to be more just like this one?" she asked.

Dewar nodded. "If you are lucky. After the excitement of getting started wears off, your contestants will be bored. Put that in your notes. Fightin' boredom was a problem during the real Chisholm Trail days and it will be with your fake one. It's another twenty-nine days and they'll all be basically just alike. I can't imagine how you're going to keep the viewers entertained for a whole season. Only exciting thing I can think of is that you'll face coyotes, snakes, and rain that swells the rivers and makes crossing tough," he answered.

"During the real trail drive there were saloons and brothels along the way," she reminded him.

"Good luck finding even an old empty building where those were. Of course, you could get the film crew to come on ahead of you and build a movie set with a brothel or a saloon," he said.

"Sounds like a great idea, but we really want this to be as real as possible, so I don't see that happening. Wouldn't it be something if I did find an old brothel still standing, though? Or the building where an old saloon once stood? Man, that would make for some real good footage." She pulled a notepad out of her saddlebags and started writing.

———

Using his saddle for a pillow, Dewar leaned back and stretched his long legs. The woman was crazy if she thought she could control coyotes and rattlesnakes so her reality show would be more exciting. Those things just happened and were totally out of her control no matter what she wrote down.

He could imagine her writing that the first few days would be getting used to the saddle. Coyotes would appear pretty early in her notes. Rain would pour down in buckets at least once, even if it was hot summertime. Hell, she might even think she could make it snow right there in August just by writing it down. Boy did she have a lot to learn about nature.

How could he have been so stupid not have asked to talk to H. B. on the phone? If he'd heard her smooth southern voice, he would have known he was talking to a woman. There wasn't a man alive that had a voice like hers. But nothing could be redone and everything was in motion. He didn't have to like it, but he did have to put up with her because her father, Carl Levy, was footing the bill for the whole trial run.

Earlier in the year he had scouted the route as near to the Chisholm Trail as possible, gotten all the permissions to cross landowners' property, and cut fences where he had to, and figured out where the best places to make camp were located. Not one single time had he thought about taking a woman with him.

When she had fallen flat on her back, he figured she'd dust off her ass, get back in that cute little car, and throw her smelly shoes out the window, but something changed when she went into the barn to take off that fancy black suit. She'd left a businesswoman with an attitude; she'd come back a woman with a purpose and that was by far scarier than a woman with an attitude.

He slid a sideways glance toward her, sitting not six feet from him hunched over a spiral notebook, pen in hand, and writing as fast as she could. When had she braided her hair? She had arrived that morning with it floating on her shoulders and now she sported short braids with hair poking out at every twist. Her jeans were fairly new and hung low on her hips. The jacket she'd worn out of the barn was tied around her waist by the arms. A knit shirt stretched tightly over a big chest. Not Dolly Parton style, but top-heavy on that small frame. Her face was round and reminded him of someone.

Surely he hadn't met her. She'd been surprised when she looked up at him sitting on his big black stallion and he'd damn sure never forget a redhead that looked like Haley. But there was surely something familiar about that face. His brow furrowed into deep lines and he shut his eyes tightly trying to remember where he had seen her.

Instead of an instant memory of having seen her at a rodeo or in a bar, a song played in his mind—Jo Dee Messina singing "Because You Love Me."

"That's it!" he said.

"What?" she asked.

"Nothing. I was just thinking," he said without opening his eyes.

Her face was a little rounder, the planes on her cheeks not nearly as defined, but the eyes, the mouth, the smile, and the hair color were very similar to Jo Dee's. He wondered if Haley had a singing voice. He sat up with the song still running through his mind on a continuous loop and glanced at her. Yep, she might not be Jo Dee's sister, but she could definitely pass for a cousin.

"What's for supper?" she asked.

"That's up to the cook. Coosie makes whatever he feels like cooking and we eat it. That's the way of the job. It's plain trail food, nothing fancy. You sure you're up to a whole month of it?" Dewar asked.

"Why did you hire Coosie to do the cooking, anyway?"

"Because until Lucy went to work over at the Double Deuce Ranch he was the cook and he's good at what he does. You won't starve," Dewar said defensively.

She put up a palm, pen stuck between two fingers. "Hey, I'm not bitchin' so don't attack me. I'm just asking, making conversation I guess. I can't remember the last time I spent a whole day without saying ten words to anyone."

"You said more than ten words to me at dinnertime," he told her.

She narrowed her green eyes into slits and set her wide mouth into a firm line. "Why are you fighting with me? I'll stay out of your way and keep my notes. I'm a big girl. I can take care of myself."

"Just make sure that you do."

"Oh, honey, you don't have to worry a bit about me getting in your way."

He detected a bit of a different accent. Not totally Texan, southern, but not Deep South. "Where are you from?"

"Dallas."

"Originally? Were you born there?"

"Yes, I was, but my mother is from Louisiana. Down in the Cajun country," she said.

Before he could say anything else, she uncrossed her legs, rolled up on her knees, and slowly stood up. Her walk as she headed toward the chuck wagon was positive proof that she wasn't used to riding all day. It was far different than the cute little wiggle she'd had when she stormed off to the barn to change clothes earlier that morning.

Sawyer squatted down at the edge of Dewar's bed and groaned. "Damn! I'd forgotten how much it hurts the first day."

"So did I," Dewar said.

"You tell her that?"

Dewar chuckled. "I did not! You notice the difference in the way she's walkin'?"

"Oh, yeah. Pretty woman. Sexy walk any way she does it. Little too old for me or I'd be doin' some sweet-talkin'. Is that what you were doin' before she left?"

"Not me. She's not ranch material and I don't waste my time on hard-core businesswomen. Work and pleasure don't mix, anyway. I'll find a woman when I get back home. I'm ready to settle down, but it won't be with a big city gal."

Sawyer stood up and moaned again. "Hurts sitting. Hurts standing. I'll have blisters on my ass by the end of the week."

"You aren't getting any sympathy from me, feller," Dewar said.

"Maybe I'll go see if Haley will feel sorry for me."

"If I remember right your woman wasn't so happy about you being gone for a whole month. You want to tell her all about that redhead massaging your sore ass when you get home?"

Sawyer chuckled. "She *was* pretty pissed. There's something about goin' back in history to herd cattle and eat trail food that a woman just doesn't understand. She'd throw a tantrum if she knew a woman was on the drive. I swore to her that it was for guys only."

Dewar nodded seriously. "Amen to women not understanding. I'm not so sure I would have taken the job if I'd known H. B. was a woman."

Coosie rang the dinner bell and everyone gathered around the back of the chuck wagon. While everyone else took care of cattle and horses, he'd set beans to boiling, made biscuits, and fried an enormous skillet of potatoes. He handed each person a tin plate and a spoon and set a tub of soft margarine and a jar of plum jelly on the worktable that dropped down from the back of the chuck wagon and propped on a single leg.

Sawyer stepped aside and motioned for Haley to go first.

"Thank you," she said.

Dewar watched her expression when Coosie removed

the lids and carried them to the wagon. She didn't flinch
or snarl her nose, which was a good sign. She broke a
biscuit in half, dipped the ladle deep into the pot, and
covered her bread with beans. Somewhere in her background there were country people who had been raised
on a farm or a ranch. City slickers did not eat their beans
like ranch hands.

Haley sat up so quick that it made her dizzy. If the
wind rustled last year's leaves lying on the ground, she
heard it. If one of the cowboys groaned in his sleep, she
thought someone was breaking into her apartment. She
tuned out the hoot owls and strained her ears toward
the cattle.

It wasn't bawling cows or even a disgruntled rangy
old bull that had awakened her that time. It was voices—
low whispers just across the barbed wire fence to the east
of the campsite. She pulled on her boots and cocked her
head to one side. There were people out there among the
cows, and she intended to find out what they were doing.

Dewar had set his rifle against the tree behind their
bedrolls when he tossed his saddle down for the night.
She eyed it for a split second before she picked it up
and eased through the mesquite until she saw the pickup
truck with a cattle trailer behind it on the other side of
the barbed wire.

She had no idea if the rifle was loaded or not. The
only gun she'd ever shot was her cousin's BB gun, and
that had been twenty years before. But by damn, she was
the queen of bluff and those sneaky little shits were not
stealing one of their cows. There were two of them, a tall

one with blond hair that shined in the moonlight and a shorter one with dark hair and a white T-shirt that glared just as brightly as Mr. Blond's hair did.

"How many you think we can get?" the taller one asked.

"Two or three anyway, and I got a kid over in Grady who'll buy them from us for a hundred dollars apiece," the other one answered.

She popped the gun up on her shoulder like she knew what she was doing and said in a loud voice, "You boys really want to try that?"

Their hands shot straight up in the air and they fell down to the earth on their knees in the middle of the milling cows. She hoped they were on the verge of pissing their pants when she stepped out into the moonlight, rifle still on her shoulder.

"Don't shoot. Please don't shoot! You might kill a cow."

"I'd rather kill a rustler," she said.

The tall one stood up and took a step toward her. "It's a girl, man. She won't shoot us. I bet she don't even know how to take the safety off that gun."

"Don't test me, son," she said.

The other kid stood up. "Take it away from her and let's get out of here."

She aimed above the cows. Dewar would make the phone call himself and send her back to Dallas if she killed a cow. She could see him tying a bologna sandwich in a hobo bag, pointing her in the right direction, and telling her to walk if she shot that old bull that led the herd. She closed her eyes when she pulled the trigger. The first sound was a loud crack, the second was a zingy noise when it ricocheted off the trailer, and the third was a hissing like one big-ass snake.

When the crack sounded, the rifle kicked her shoulder. When the zingy noise hit her ears, she was falling backward. The hissing noise covered up the yelp she let out when her ass hit the hard ground. The rifle went scooting between the cows' legs and both her hands came to rest in fresh cow shit.

"Run," the short one said. "She's a crazy bitch, man."

"Daddy's goin' to kill me when he finds a bullet hole in his trailer."

The cows began to bawl and move restlessly in a circle. The old bull lowered his head, raised his tail, and let her know his opinion about being disturbed by dropping at least a quart of warm shit right in front of her.

"Dammit all to hell. I'm going to kill you both, you little shits!" She jumped up, grabbed the gun like a billy club, and took off after them.

The boys dodged between the cows with her right behind them, screaming so loud that the cows parted like the Red Sea and let her through. The guys grabbed the barbed wire fence, squealed like little girls when the barbs bit into their hands, and bailed over it, landing on their butts. But their fannies didn't stay on the ground long enough to flatten the grass. When she reached the barbed wire, they'd gotten up and were diving through the windows into the cab of the truck without even opening the doors.

"You come back here and take your medicine like men," she yelled.

The pickup engine roared to life and the trailer weaved all over the pasture as they drove away. She slammed the gun down on the ground and the damn thing fired straight up into the air. She stomped and cussed, sending another cow pile flying all the way to her knees.

"What the hell is going on?" Dewar yelled.

She looked up to see all the cowboys running toward her, every one of them barefoot. They'd better keep their mouths shut or she fully well intended to hug every blessed one of them, starting with Dewar.

"What have you done to my gun? Shit, Haley!"

"Exactly. You get an A, Dewar O'Donnell. It is definitely shit."

"Don't you have a lick of common sense? You could have killed a cow, damn it. What were you thinkin' firin' a weapon out here in the middle of the herd? It's a wonder you didn't set off a stampede." Dewar flapped his arms around as he threw a fit.

"Better watch where you are stepping, boys. My cows knew I was protecting them. They weren't going to run away from their savior. There were rustlers out here trying to help themselves to a cow or two. You should be kissing my feet instead of hollering at me."

They didn't need to know that the bull had protested or that the cows probably did need Prozac ground up in their watering tanks.

She picked up the gun by the stock and handed it to Dewar. "Here's your precious gun—unless you want me to take it down to the watering hole and clean it up when I wash all this shit off me."

He snatched it from her. "You don't clean a gun in water, woman, and those cows do not think you are Jesus. You're just lucky they didn't stampede and stomp you to death. And it's a good thing those rustlers were amateurs and didn't have a weapon themselves. Lord, Haley, you could've been killed!"

Haley sniffed. That wasn't a "thank you," but at least he was worried about her safety. "I'm going to get cleaned up and y'all really better watch where you are steppin', boys. And you'd best not be coming down to the watering hole while I'm cleanin' this shit off me either." She stuck her nose in the night air. They could think she was uppity if they wanted. Truth was, she just wanted a whiff of clean air.

The cowboys shook their heads in unison as they headed back to the campsite, but they stepped so gingerly that she bit back a giggle.

She made her way through the cows to the watering hole. And be damned if right at the edge of the water she didn't slip in yet another pile of cow droppings and land square on her ass in knee-deep water.

"Shit! Shit! Shit!" She slapped the muddy water and it sprayed up into her hair. "Damn it all to hell! Now my hair has shit in it. Daddy, I only thought I was pissed before. You'd best head for the hills before I get home."

Chapter 3

EVERYONE WAS TUCKED DOWN DEEP IN THEIR SLEEPING bags when Haley awoke the next morning. She checked her watch with a tiny flashlight hooked on her spiral notebook. Four thirty. That meant Coosie would soon be up and the rest of the crew would stop snoring and start rounding up horses. Dewar had said that they'd be in their saddles no later than seven, and Coosie had said that he'd be up by five to start cooking.

She eased out of her sleeping bag, crammed her feet into her boots, and quietly removed a plastic bag containing deodorant, a washcloth, and a bar of soap from her saddlebag. The water wasn't clear but it was wet, and she could wash up even if she did have to wear the same clothes another day. She walked up the creek several yards from where the cattle watered and found a spot where she couldn't see a single cow or the wagon. She quickly pulled her shirt over her head, did a quick sponge-off, applied deodorant, and re-dressed.

She heard someone whistling and knew Coosie was awake, so she hurriedly jerked down her jeans and underpants. She'd been taught how to pee outdoors years ago by her older cousin when she and her mother visited Louisiana. She remembered the instructions well. Squat down, hook your thumb in the waistband, and hold your britches out to keep from getting pee on them.

She was feeling smug right up until she looked down

and saw the huge spider sitting in the crotch of her black lace panties. She couldn't yell or the cowboys would all come running, so she clamped her mouth shut tightly and didn't move a muscle. Her legs cramped. Her toes ached. And the spider acted as if it intended to take up homesteading right there in her panties.

"Shooo," she whispered through clenched teeth.

It hopped up to her thumb. She let go and sat down with a thud, kicking and flailing around like a dying fish out of water. Boots, jeans, and underpants flew through the air as she came out of them and tried to brush the feeling of a thousand imaginary vicious spiders from her legs at the same time. When she was absolutely certain that the big, brown-striped spider was gone, she shivered and realized that she was naked from the waist down.

She located her panties in a blackberry bramble and tore the lace getting them away from the evil clutches of the stickers. She checked every square inch for the spider and then stepped into them, feeling a little less vulnerable with something covering her bare butt. Her jeans had landed against the tree and the spider was sitting on the pocket like the king of a major world-power country. She found her boots near the water's edge, snuck up on the creature, and swiftly executed him, leaving a smudge on her jeans. She wiped that away with her washcloth and then went back to the creek to clean it again.

"So much for your expert advice," she fussed at her cousin who'd taught her to squat behind a tree on the banks of a Louisiana bayou. "Rustlers and spiders right here at the beginning. It's not fair."

Yeah, but just think what a neat thing that would be on the reality show, her cousin's twangy Cajun voice said so close that she checked to see if Michelle was really there.

She folded her washcloth and stuffed it back in the ziplock bag with her soap and started back up the slight embankment when a hand appeared right in front of her. She took it without even thinking and her whole body warmed. When she looked up she was staring right into Dewar's mesmerizing green eyes.

He pulled her up and said, "Mornin'."

"Good morning," she said.

"Ready for another day?"

"Do I have a choice?" She was surprised that her voice didn't quiver after the incident with the spider and then the shock of his touch.

"Phone still has lots of juice. I'll be glad to call Liz to come get you."

She did a little "Hummmph."

"Guess that means you are a sucker for punishment."

"Get it through your thick head, Dewar O'Donnell, I'm not going back. I'm staying with this to the bitter end, no matter how much you don't like a woman in your man-world," she said.

"Okay then, get your bed tied down and your horse saddled up. Breakfast is almost ready and we'll move out as soon as we've eaten. But remember, Haley, once the cell phone is dead you'll have to hitchhike back because I'm damn sure not stopping this cattle drive to take you home."

"I'd crawl on my hands and knees before I'd ask you, but I'm not going anywhere."

He disappeared into the wooded area without another word.

She'd show him, by damn. And at the end he could eat a big helping of crow right along with the other cowboys. She might want more fizz than Joel had to offer, but she damn sure did not want it with a cowboy from Podunk, Texas. She would show them all that she could ride as long, complain less, and eat whatever was offered without bitchin'. Liz had told her to go stand up for womankind and she intended to take that job seriously, but it did not mean she was going to convert to cowgirlism!

Back in college she'd enrolled in the riding class to impress a cowboy. When they broke up her heart had been broken to the point that she'd vowed she'd never get involved with anyone who had any dealings with a farm, ranch, or even planted a vegetable garden in the backyard. Just because Dewar's touch gave her hot flashes did not mean she was ready to break that vow.

And just because he reminded her of a mix of the lead male stars from *Justified* and *Rookie Blues* did not mean a blessed thing. They were characters and he was the real thing. The writers could change characters; she had a feeling that nothing or no one could change Dewar O'Donnell.

She stuffed her meager bath supplies inside her saddlebag and carefully rolled up her bed. The first time it looked entirely too loose so she undid it and started all over.

Dewar deftly whipped the edges of the tarp around his sleeping bag, tucked the ends over like a burrito, and tied it all tightly.

"Not bad for a second try," Dewar drawled.

"I don't do this for a living," she smarted off.

"Well, I don't either. I raise cattle and horses. I ride horses every day and I work the land. But at night I sleep in a house in a king-sized bed. I'm not a professional cattle driver either. Think of this as a vacation for me and the guys," Dewar said.

"You're not doing the reality show next spring?" she asked. "Didn't my father hire you to head up the show? He talked about it at one of the meetings we had."

"Hell, no! Me and the boys are having lots of fun. We ain't got any plans of doing the real show," he said.

"But you didn't figure on a woman crashing your little boys' clubhouse, did you?" she asked.

"No, we did not! But you did fairly well for a woman on the first day."

Her eyes flashed anger. "A woman! I did as well as any one of you egotistical male cowboys."

"Let's just say that if you do as well as you did yesterday, we might not let the bobcats drag you off into the mesquite and eat you alive," he said.

A chill ran up her backbone. Bobcats? "You tryin' to scare me?"

Dewar's eyes glittered. "I'm just statin' facts. Watch out for the varmints and remember, I've still got cell phone power for a little longer. Oh, and I reloaded my gun with real bullets instead of buckshot, so if you steal it, you might remember that."

"If a big cat comes lookin' for me, I'll convince him that I'm too tough to eat and send him over to you. I don't need a gun for that." She hoped her voice carried more bravado than she felt. Honestly! Bobcats?

Coosie rang the breakfast bell. The bedrolls had been rolled up for the day and all that was left was flattened green grass where they had been.

"Ham and eggs and biscuits," Coosie said.

"Coffee?" Haley asked.

He poured a cup from an enormous blue granite pot and handed it to her. "Water is in the dishpans on the table over there, so wash your dishes and stack them up when you are done."

Haley normally ate breakfast on the run. Usually it was a bagel to go with her Starbucks latte in the mornings. If she was running late it was a granola bar from her desk drawer sometime in the morning when she had time to chew and swallow between meetings. Her first thought was that she'd eat a biscuit and call it a morning, but the scrambled eggs and ham slices looked so good that she piled her plate full.

She looked around at the cowboys to see how they managed to balance a plate, a coffee cup, and eat all while standing up. They were carrying their food toward the back side of the wagon and using a fallen tree for a bench with their plates balanced on their knees.

Dewar motioned toward the end of the line right beside him. "Got enough room for you right here."

She backed up and sat down easily. Too far back and eggs would go flying. Too far forward and she'd slide right off the slick old tree trunk and land smack on her butt for the second day.

"It won't bite you," Sawyer said with a twinkle in his near-black eyes.

"But it might buck me off. I never was too good on a mechanical bull," she answered.

"Aha, Haley has been to Billy Bob's," Sawyer said.

"No, she has not," she said quickly.

"Well, where did you ride a mechanical bull?" Dewar asked.

"At the Texas State Fair." She set about eating without another word.

"First one I ever rode was at a fair," Rhett said. "Spent twenty bucks before I tamed that long-horned critter."

"First one I ever rode was at Billy Bob's. I won a six-pack for staying on it with a beer in my free hand the whole time," Sawyer said.

"Yeah, well, you been ridin' the real bulls since you was in diapers," Rhett told him.

"And drinkin' beer nearly that long," Finn added.

Haley tucked away facts as she ate. That evening she'd write down everything she could remember because it could make a difference on the reality run. One thing for sure, after one day on the trail, she would not be coming back to help direct the reality show. Her father could fire her and she'd flip burgers at McDonald's before she traveled the historic Chisholm Trail again. Let Pretty Boy Joel live in the wilderness for several weeks. By damn, that ought to send him back to his precious Hollywood with his tail tucked between his legs.

Her hips felt as if they'd been torn from the sockets. If she had a floor-length mirror like the one on the back of her bathroom door, she was sure she'd see purple bruises on her butt cheeks. And if she didn't have the makings for skin cancer with all the sun exposure by the end of the month, it would be a pure damn miracle. And that wasn't even taking into account that her skin would have holes eaten in it from salty sweat. How did pioneer women ever survive without moisture cream or hand lotion?

A soft moan escaped her lips.

"What?" Coosie asked.

"Good food," she mumbled.

Coosie smiled. "Thank you, Haley. We'll be havin' more of that ham today so I'm glad you like it. We'll have leftover eggs and ham stuffed in biscuits for lunch and then for supper we're havin' it fried up with potatoes and onions."

"Sounds yummy," she said.

"Don't be sarcastic. When we slice into a salt-cured ham, we have to use it all or it will spoil."

She pointed her fork at him. "I was not being sarcastic. I love ham. It's one of my favorite foods."

"Oh, yeah. Well, enjoy it because when it runs out we'll have to live off the land. You ever eaten wild game?" Dewar asked.

She glared at him. "Of course."

"In Dallas? Come on. You have not!" Dewar said.

"Squirrel, rabbit, or venison—I've had them all, along with nutria and every kind of fish that came out of the swamp in Louisiana when I went to visit my cousins. So don't be calling me a liar," she said.

Coosie chuckled. "Guess that disgusting look on your face means you ain't too partial to it, though, doesn't it?"

"Does Dewar like wild game?" she asked.

"Yes, I do. Coosie can fry rabbit and squirrel so tender you think you are eating chicken," he answered.

"If you eat it, I'll eat it. Whether I like it or not doesn't really matter. Just like my reality crew. They'll eat whatever is provided for them and if they bitch about it they'll lose points and get the honor of being the first ones kicked off the show," she said.

Buddy chuckled and looked at Haley. "I'm goin' to saddle up. I'll get yours, M-m-miz Haley."

"Thank you. Let me watch so I can do it tomorrow morning." She quickly ate the last bite of her biscuit and followed him to the dishpans.

They washed, dried, and stacked their plates, spoons, and cups at the back of the table and moved to one side for Dewar and Sawyer.

"You don't have to saddle or unsaddle. We can do that for you," Finn said.

Haley was close enough that she could see the tiny gold flecks in Dewar's eyes. Her answer to Finn's offer was a test and she'd pass it or die trying.

"I need to learn as much as I can so I can help when it comes time to put the show together. The contestants will all be even greener than I am and they'll have to learn," she said sweetly.

"Green? Lord, girl, I believe you could saddle the devil and ride him right through the Pearly Gates." Dewar laughed.

She smiled. "In high heels if I don't step in a fresh cow patty. Now you are getting to know me, cowboy. Thank you for the compliment."

"It was not a compliment," he mumbled.

"I'll take it however I want," she said.

Buddy led Apache up to Haley and handed her the reins. He set the saddle on the ground, rubbed Apache's back to make sure there wasn't a bit of dirt or a burr in his hair, and then tossed the blanket across the middle of his back.

Haley kept a loose hold on the reins and started around to the other side, but Buddy shook his head. "This side, m-m-ma'am. Don't never go on that side."

She nodded and watched carefully. Buddy eased the

stirrup and cinch over the blanket and explained that was to keep from hitting the horse and scaring him. Then he lifted the saddle high and gently lowered it onto the horse, telling her that was to keep the flaps from hitting him. After that he checked the blanket all around the saddle to be sure the saddle didn't rub sores on him.

He explained that the fork should rest neatly over the withers and she should always lower the right stirrup and cinch and not just give them a toss because they might slap Apache. After that he lifted up on the front part of the saddle pad to create an air space between the blanket and the withers. He talked about the cinch, the latigo, and the rigging ring next and how to be careful that the cinch wasn't twisted. She glanced over at Dewar, who was busy performing all the same steps without even thinking about it. Would she ever remember everything and be as comfortable doing it as he was?

"I'll help you tomorrow m-m-morning," Buddy said.

She patted him on the shoulder. "It might take a few days for me to get the hang of it."

"That's okay, m-m-ma'am." He grinned and whistled shrilly. His big buckskin horse trotted over to him and Buddy rubbed his nose.

"You're a good boy, Major," he crooned. "You're going to d-d-do alright, old boy."

Haley rubbed Apache's nose but she couldn't make herself talk to him. Maybe by the end of the trip she'd like the horse, but right now it was the cause of her legs aching and her tailbone feeling like it was poking through her skin. And if she said anything to him, it would probably be peppered with enough cuss words to scorch the hair out of his ears.

Dewar and the other three cowboys were already in the saddle and rounding up a herd of mixed breed of cattle with the one rangy old brown and white mottled longhorn bull. He reminded Haley of the king of the mountain game she and Michelle played with the Cajun cousins. He meandered along ahead of the rest of the herd showing the whole bunch that he was the leader and the rest of the stock had best be walking behind him at least two steps.

"Kind of like Dewar," Haley mumbled and quickly looked around to see if anyone heard her.

She checked the ground for fresh horse manure, got a good foothold in the stirrup and a handhold on the saddle horn, and mounted up for the day. Shooting pains went from her fanny to the top of her head when she plopped down into the saddle. Her inner thighs felt like a dock hooker the morning after a ship of sailors came in from a six-month sea tour. She wrapped the reins around the saddle horn and jerked on her gloves. They weren't made for riding but for driving and she hoped they lasted a month.

She'd put the next expensive pair on her expense account right along with the price of her fancy shoes and suit if Liz's cleaners couldn't get the stains and the smell of crap out of them. Oh yes, sir, her father was going to rue the day that he sent her on this trip.

Chapter 4

IF YOU ARE NOT THE LEAD DOG, THE VIEW NEVER CHANGES.

By mid-morning, Haley had decided the person who came up with that quote was the smartest person since Einstein and deserved a Pulitzer Prize for writing the single sentence. She'd seen nothing since she'd saddled up the day before but the south ends of northbound cattle, and the view was not a pretty one.

If she had a lick of sense, she would take Dewar up on his offer to use the last of his cell phone battery to call Liz to come get her. With what she already had to contribute to the reality show, she might be forgiven for not lasting until the end of the cattle run. But that would make her unworthy of the straw hat and denim jacket. Liz had entrusted her with both and they'd already become the equivalent of a queen's crown and velvet robe. Giving them back without finishing the drive would be like giving up a Miss America title.

If only she hadn't read that excerpt from Cheryl Brooks's upcoming book, her thoughts might not keep going to Dewar's sexy green eyes or the ripped abs she imagined underneath his shirt. She vowed to read nothing but sweet romances from that day forth.

She shut her eyes tightly and tried to remember the last book she'd read that had no sex. It had to have been back when she was still in grade school because in junior high she found her mother's stash of Jude Deveraux and Bertrice Small novels and from then on she was hooked on hot, steamy romances.

A blush reddened Haley's face when she looked up and saw Dewar riding toward her. A sudden picture of him tangled up in the gold sheets on her bed fixed itself firmly in her mind. Candlelight and the color of the sheets brought out those little gold flecks in his eyes. His dark lashes lowered as he moved toward her and then those hot, sexy lips would meet hers in a clash that would blow out every candle in the room.

She sighed. "So much for sweet romance books."

Lord, have mercy!

She needed something to do other than sit on the back of a horse and let her imagination run wild. He herded a cow back into the herd and turned that big black stallion of his around to go back to the head of the pack without even a sideways glance her way. But just being there in close proximity had already set her mind into a tailspin.

It was all because there was nothing else to think about. She made a few mental notes along the way about the reality show, but that didn't take up nearly enough time. So there she was, time on her hands, and Dewar looking like a cross between her two favorite television characters. What was she supposed to do? A ninety-year-old nun would have trouble keeping her thoughts pure with that man around to tempt her, and Haley McKay didn't have a holy cell in her body.

"You talkin' to me?" Coosie asked.

"No, I was talking to myself. It gets lonely out here, don't it?"

He nodded.

Thank God that Coosie couldn't see inside her mind.

"Is it just day after day of the same thing? Or is there something exciting coming up?" she asked.

"You got it, darlin'."

"But surely something happens," she said bleakly.

"Nope, it's the same thing every day. Get up, eat breakfast, herd cattle until noon, and eat dinner—that's the noon meal out here and supper is the evening meal. Then we get back on the trail, stop for supper, and go to bed. Don't know how in the world they're goin' to make a *Survivor* thing on the television with this to work with," he said.

"Oh, they'll glamorize it all to the devil and it'll be the next big thing. Think about that one about grappling fish. It had millions of viewers."

Coosie's big head barely tipped forward. "Boys have been doin' that for years in our part of the world. Never even heard of it being called hand fishin'. Even Lucy got all involved with that crazy show."

"Lucy? Is she your wife?"

Coosie shook his head that time. "No, ma'am."

He didn't appear to be much for talk.

Talk!

That was a great idea for the show. Who could tell the best story? After a hard day they all had to come up with a story to entertain everyone around the campfire. The public could call in their vote and the contestant who got the least votes would have to go home the next week. She'd already decided that there would only be three guys and three women at the end of the journey and they would bring the herd into the feedlot at Dodge City in a big season semi-finale. Then the public would vote on the best cowboy and cowgirl of the finalists, which would be announced at the finale. Those two would get the big bucks.

Haley was bored out of her wits so she pushed on, "Is Lucy your daughter?"

Coosie shook his head. "She could have been if I'd have got an early start with a family, but I didn't. No, Lucy is just Lucy."

"And she cooks at the ranch where y'all work."

"She cooks at the ranch where Buddy and I work. Dewar lives on another ranch, and the other O'Donnell cousins live on still another one."

Haley felt like she was pulling teeth. "Tell me about her."

"Like I said, Lucy is Lucy."

"You don't talk much, do you?"

"Ain't got much to say."

Haley's curiosity was piqued. "Why don't you want to tell me about Lucy?"

"You want to know about Lucy, you ask Lucy."

"Then tell me about you," she said.

"Ain't much to tell that would interest a television person like you."

"Come on, Coosie, I'm just asking for a story to make the time go by. Anything to beat looking at cows meandering ahead of us at a snail's pace. I'm not taking notes and I'm not interested in writing your personal stories. I just want someone to talk to me. I'm used to dozens of people around me all day and the buzz of several conversations going all at once."

"Get unused to it, Miz Haley. All you're going to get is cows bawlin' and cowboys cussin' out here."

"If you don't want to talk about Lucy, then tell me about Dewar."

"You want to know about Dewar, ask him. You want to know about Finn, ask him. You want to know about Rhett…"

She held up a hand. "I know, ask him. This morning I want to know about you. Tell me something, anything. Talk to me about the wagon or the horses or how you got roped into this job."

"Didn't get roped into jack shit. I volunteered for it. Me and Buddy both. We had a lot of vacation time that we ain't never used because we get a week a year and we ain't never took any of it, so we asked our boss, Ace, and he said that his brothers could help out on the ranch this month. So here we are. So I chose this vacation. I wasn't roped into it, not like you were."

"Is Ace Lucy's daddy?"

"No, Ace is Lucy's boss."

Haley was thoroughly confused. If Lucy was just a working woman, then why did Coosie's eyes go all soft whenever he talked about her?

"What do you do on the ranch?" she asked.

"Anything Ace wants me to do, now that Lucy is doing the cooking. Me and Buddy grew up on ranches so we know what needs to be done and we do it."

"And this wagon? Is it rented or what? Can we rent it for the reality show?"

"Hell, no! It's my wagon. I built it from the ground up. Took me two years to get it designed and built just like I wanted it, and it's damn sure not for rent."

"Would you show my team how to build one?"

"Be easier to buy one. Big shots like y'all should be able to find places to buy them on the computer."

Haley sighed. So that was the problem? Coosie viewed

her as a big shot, not as a bored-to-tears woman already tired of the long ride and wishing to hell she was back in Dallas.

"Then tell me what we should look for when we go shopping," she said.

"Look for one that has a Studebaker design. Mr. Goodnight chose that design for a reason. It's sturdy and it'll hold up over the rough rides for many years."

"Who is Mr. Goodnight?"

"He was the one who designed some of the first, if not the first, chuck wagons. You can't talk to him about it though because he did all his work way back during the Civil War days."

They rode along in silence as she made mental notes about the chuck wagon. It would play an important role in the show because it would carry the food supply and not a single contestant would stick around if they weren't fed.

"Do they come in different sizes?" she finally asked. Coosie nodded.

"Like small, medium, and large?"

"I have no idea. I just patterned mine after the Studebaker. It's ten feet long by forty inches wide with the bentwood bows of a traditional covered wagon. The canvas that is tied down over the bows is waterproof because you can bet your redheaded fanny that it will rain sometime while we are gone. Like Goodnight, I added a chuck box to the rear of the wagon."

"A chuck box?"

"Yes, it's the thing that looks like a desk with cubbyholes to hold spices, bakin' soda, and such to help with the cooking, and it's got a hinged lid to serve as a worktable. And there's a boot underneath the wagon for extra storage for my pots and pans," he said.

"What's inside?"

"Food, lanterns, kerosene, a spare wagon wheel, rain slickers."

"For a whole month for all seven of us?" she asked incredulously.

"For a few days. We can buy supplies along the way and we refill our water barrel when we can if it don't rain enough to catch water that way."

"Oh, then, we get to shop?" She could hear the excitement in her own voice.

"I shop. You and the guys will take care of camp. You aren't here for a good time. You are here to take notes and learn all about how to herd cows so your show won't be a big flop."

You sound like my dad, even if you don't look a damn thing like him.

"What kind of food is in there?"

"That is my business. I am the cook so I decide what's in there and when it gets used. And at night I turn the wagon's tongue toward the North Star so the trail boss, that would be Dewar, has a compass direction in the morning."

She giggled. "Really, now."

"This is as authentic as we can make it, lady. You might want to remember what I'm telling you because it might come in handy. You want those city slickers to get turned around and waste a whole day going the wrong way?"

It was thirty minutes before she could think of another question, but one finally came to mind. "Is the Studebaker design the only one out there?"

Coosie shook his head.

"What else is there?" she pressed on.

"The Studebaker is my favorite, but there's also the Springfield Wagon, Old Hickory Wagon, Moline Wagon, and the Mitchell Wagon Company."

"This one doesn't look a thing like the ones in the old Western movies. Which one did those folks use?" she asked.

"They used the Conestoga, but it was for the movies, not for real life cattle drives."

"Why?"

Coosie inhaled deeply.

Haley didn't care if she was bugging him. She needed to know for the show and she wanted to know because it beat ambling along behind cows.

"It's too heavy and bulky. It just looked good for the movies. Kind of like your reality people. They'll look good but they won't be the real thing."

The cattle stopped as if on cue and Coosie pulled up on the reins. He hopped down off the wagon and lumbered around to the end where he pulled down the lid, propped it on the single leg, and started preparing dinner. Dewar slid out of his saddle and walked to the creek where he counted the herd. The rest of the cowboys all grouped around Coosie and waited.

Haley took a few squares of her precious toilet paper and made a fast trip to a mesquite thicket. When she returned Coosie was handing out biscuits stuffed with eggs and ham. A big community bag of barbecue potato chips was opened on the table and everyone helped themselves.

Buddy pointed to the water barrel attached to the

side of the wagon. "You'll need to fill up your canteens. Coosie is going to refill when we go through Comanche. There's a gas station there on M-m-main Street and they got a water hose."

Haley washed her hands in the dishwater and dried them on the seat of her jeans, picked up a handful of chips, and reached for a biscuit. Dewar grabbed at the same time she did and their fingertips brushed. The sizzle startled them both and they jumped like they'd grabbed hold of a rattlesnake.

"Excuse me," Dewar drawled.

"Quite all right," she said.

"Coosie said you were full of questions this morning," he said.

"I just wanted to know what kind of chuck wagon we needed to buy for the reality show," she answered.

"You won't ever find one as neat as his. He built it from the ground up and made adjustments until he got it just right."

She bit into the biscuit. "That's what I hear."

Dewar carried his food to the other side of the table. "Coosie, did I hear you say we had enough clean water to last till Comanche?"

Coosie nodded. "Just like the plans you drew up, it's goin' to last until then. Miz Haley, you write in your notes that it might not last that long if the show people are going to make this trip in the summer. It all depends on how hot it is."

"Why?" She had already fetched her notebook and paper and was writing as fast as she could remember while she ate.

"Because," Finn answered, "if it's hot, they drink

more water. If it's nice like it is now, they won't need quite as much."

"It's goin' to get hot. You sure you don't want to give me that hundred dollars now and go on back to the comforts of air-conditioning and long, lazy baths and ice in your water and…" Sawyer teased.

Haley butted in before he could go any further. "I'll take these cows in by myself if you want to go on home to your jealous girlfriend. I've been razed by specialists, Sawyer, and you ain't nothin' but an amateur."

"Whew!" Rhett wiped his forehead. "Looks like you done met your match, Sawyer. How'd you know about his girlfriend, anyway?"

She smiled and kept writing. "Tell me those kinds other than Studebaker again."

Coosie rattled them off so rapidly that she had to write fast.

"And you are sure you won't rent us yours?"

"D-d-don't nobody touch his wagon," Buddy chuckled.

"I didn't build it so someone else could ruin it. Better quit your jawin' and start your chewin' 'cause the nooner don't last half the afternoon."

Dewar set about eating like nothing at all had happened when their hands touched. Maybe he had a woman back in Ringgold. No one as handsome and sexy as he was could possibly be single. He had to be close to her age and that would put him at thirty or a little more.

She shut her eyes and visualized the file that Carl had on Dewar back when they first came up with the idea of the cattle drive reality show. He was part owner and operator of a cattle-slash-horse ranch and that he could easily get a crew of six and a herd of a hundred cows together for the reenactment. It didn't even have a place for married, single, or divorced.

"Shit!" she mumbled and quickly jerked her head up to see if anyone heard her.

He was probably engaged and that was the underlying reason that he did not want a woman on the drive with him. If she was his fiancée, she'd be on her way to drag his sexy little butt right back to Ringgold, Texas, as soon as the gossip hotline told her that H. B. McKay was not a stuffy, middle-aged man.

Chapter 5

DEWAR WAS SITTING STRAIGHT UP WHEN HE AWOKE. Nerves on the back of his neck prickled and his heart thumped around in his chest like it was looking for an escape route. He quickly turned his boots upside down, shook any possible bugs out, and jammed his feet down into them. A lonesome coyote yipped in the distance, but he didn't get an answer. Crickets and tree frogs chirped away. Still, something wasn't right. He could feel it in his bones and they never lied to him. He quietly unsheathed his rifle and held it beside his leg.

He scanned the campsite. Buddy even stuttered when he snored. Finn mumbled in his sleep, and Sawyer rolled from one side to the other, trying to get comfortable. The fire crackled in the moonlight, but everything and everyone looked all right.

Until he turned around and realized Haley's bedroll was empty. His gun was still standing beside the tree, which meant she hadn't gone to check on rustlers again. Dear God! Someone had kidnapped her for a ransom?

"Not without a fight from that redhead," he mumbled. "She'd be pitching a screaming hissy fit."

Lord, why did H. B. McKay have to be a woman!?

Everyone along the trail knew they were bringing a hundred head of cattle down the old Chisholm Trail. It would be easy to back a trailer right up to a gate on the far side of the pasture and drive off with a straggler or two or even half the herd. He could imagine a dozen places where it could happen that very night.

He leaned against a scrub oak tree, keeping himself out of the moonlight as he scanned the area for stealthy rustlers. He felt a presence behind him, spun around, and whipped the rifle up to point right at Haley's heart.

"Shit! It's me. Haley. Don't shoot." She grabbed her chest with one hand and held up her palm.

He quickly lowered the rifle. "What in the hell are you doing out here?"

"I might ask you the same thing," Haley smarted off right back at him.

"Trouble is brewing," he said.

"How did you know?"

"It woke me up. Now you? What were you doing out here?"

"I woke up and went down to the creek for a bath. When I came back you were gone and I came to see what you were doing sneaking around out here. We got more of them pesky kids trying to steal cows?" she whispered.

The aroma of sweet-smelling soap wafted across the night breeze to his nose. At the same time a slinky, low-to-the-ground movement near the mesquite trees at the far fence line caught his attention.

He pointed. "It's probably a bobcat or maybe a mountain lion. Wind is blowing away from us right now or he would have picked up our scent and run away before now."

The longhorn bull put his head down and let out a low bawl that sounded like a warning. The cows moved restlessly behind him.

"Shoot 'im?" she asked.

"Not unless I have to. It would spook the cows, maybe cause a stampede, and definitely wake everyone up. Walk with me." Dewar's voice was barely above a whisper.

Chill bumps chased down Haley's backbone, not from fear of danger but from his voice at that timbre. It was so damn sexy that it brought all kinds of naughty images into living high-definition color.

He moved across the pasture in long easy strides with her doing double time to keep up. Finally, he reached down and took her hand in his. She wasn't even a bit surprised at the warmth spreading through her body.

Before they got around the herd, she heard a deep-throated growl and another shadow ran back into the woods in a lope. Dewar turned to look at the bull that was already trotting back to his herd with his head up.

"That bull thinks he's the big hero," she said.

Dewar turned around but he didn't let go of her hand. "He's a good leader and he probably would have stood his ground, but I'd hate to lose him."

"You think he would have lost?"

"Coyotes run in packs. Those were just the two out scouting for a midnight snack."

"I'll make a note of that for the show," she said.

"Hey, why do you go by H. B.? And what's the big deal about letting folks think you are a man? There are women correspondents in war zones. And last I heard women could even vote these days," he changed the subject abruptly.

"My whole name is Haley Belle McKay Levy. McKay was Momma's maiden name. Momma is half Irish-Cajun. The Levy name is Jewish."

"Does you mother have red hair like you?"

"Oh, no! She's got all the Cajun features. Dark hair. Dark eyes. Just like her momma. Daddy is the same. Dark hair and dark eyes like Grandpa. I was named after my grandmothers. Mahalia on Cajun side. Isabelle on the Irish side. Think about it," she said.

He frowned.

"Think harder."

He shrugged.

She squeezed his hand. "In grade school they called me hay bale. That could ruin a serious businesswoman."

"Kids can be cruel, can't they?" He grinned.

"How'd you get a name like Dewar? It sounds like something out of a historic romance book. I bet people mispronounce it all the time and call you Dee-War instead of Dew-Are," she said.

"Folks probably don't even know how it looks on paper. When I'm introduced they just say Dew-Are and that's the way they remember it. My folks are both Irish and Dewar is an old family name, but I never got teased until Sawyer came up with that stupid Dewy Darlin' story."

"Now that we understand names, what do you do about the big cat or coyote problem? I need to know for the show."

"Either stand watch at night or buy a donkey."

"A donkey?"

"They are natural enemies for coyotes and wild cats."

"Okay, I vote for a donkey, but it'll be more dramatic if we make the contestants stand watch. How do they do that?"

He started walking back toward the camp. "Four-hour shifts. What time are you calling it a night on the trail?"

She fell in beside him. "Ten at the latest, but I suppose there'll be some love interests like on all reality shows and the couple who can't keep their hands off each other will do some sneaking into the night."

"Then someone watches from ten to two and someone else from two to six. Rotate the guards so no one loses two nights' sleep in a row. Someone will be grouchy on the days that they have to stand watch. Or you can just send one of them to buy a donkey the next day after a coyote or mountain lion becomes a threat. It's a lot easier than a bunch of grumpy folks."

She shook her head. "I'll put that in my report, but I like the guard idea better. But who knows what the producers will like? How does a donkey fight off coyotes and cats anyway?"

"Donkeys will bite and stomp them to death. They get along fine with cattle and they'll protect them, but coyotes and big cats are a different story. I hope I can find a rancher willing to sell me one—hopefully tomorrow. I should have thought of that before we even left."

"Did they use them on the real Chisholm Trail rides?" she whispered as they neared the camp.

"I wouldn't know, but I'm going to buy one as soon as I can. Starting tomorrow night we'll stand watch until I can find one."

"We don't need to do watch tonight?" She didn't realize he'd stopped until she took two more steps and collided with him, breast to hard muscled chest. And then his arms were around her to keep them both from tumbling to the ground in a heap.

"Whoa!" she gasped and looked up.

His eyes went soft and dreamy and were half-shut

as his lips came closer and closer. Her pulse raced as she rolled up on her toes. His thumb grazed her jawline and traced the outline of her lips. Her eyes fluttered, half-open, half-shut. She moved a hand away from his chest to his neck.

Just before his lips met hers, his eyes popped open for just a second. She'd never seen such raw hunger before. Her eyelids slowly drooped shut and his mouth landed on hers in a kiss that raged through her body like a Texas wildfire coming over the plains with a good strong tail-wind. She tangled her fingers in his hair, holding his lips on hers. She couldn't think of anything but putting out the fire as his tongue flicked through her lips and she tasted heat and desire rolled into a long, lingering kiss.

His hands moved to her back, drawing her closer to his chest, as if he wanted to melt the two of them into one to ease the blistering hot flames that had him instantly ready for sex.

And then he broke the kiss and stepped back.

"I'm sorry," he said.

"Why? Are you engaged or married?"

"N-n-no!" He sounded like Buddy.

"Then there's nothing to apologize for. Good night, Dewar." She walked away without looking back, sat down on her bedroll, kicked off her boots, and crawled into her sleeping bag.

—⁕—

Dewar could not sleep. He looked in her direction but her back was to him and all he could see was a mop of still-damp red hair. What would it feel like to have that thick hair splayed out over his chest when he woke up the next morning? Or tickling his nose as she kissed him awake?

The visions did nothing for the semi-arousal, so he turned his back to her and forced himself to think about plowing a hay pasture. He always listened to country music when he was in the tractor, so one song after another played in his head, but each one turned his thoughts back to the woman barely six feet away with the sweet-smelling soap aroma still hanging on the night breezes.

Finally, he slept only to dream one erotic scenario after another, with Haley the center of each one. He awoke to hear the rattling of pots and pans and Coosie whistling "Oh What a Beautiful Morning." He threw back his sleeping bag, dug his toothbrush from his saddlebags, and stuck it in his shirt pocket. Maybe if he brushed his teeth and got the taste of Haley's kisses away from his lips, he'd forget all about how they felt.

He forgot all about brushing his teeth when she sat up, rubbed the sleep from her eyes, and finger combed her hair. He rolled his bedding slowly so he could watch her deftly twist her hair into braids and secure the ends with rubber bands she pulled from her shirt pocket. Her jeans were tighter and darker than the pair she'd worn the day before; the shirt long sleeved with buttons and two pockets bulging over those big breasts that had poked into his chest the night before.

"Good morning," she said.

"What's so good about it?" he grouched.

"It's not raining and I smell breakfast cooking. Two good things," she said.

He did a half snort, half humph and tied the rope

knots around his bedroll. "We've got the Comanche thing today."

"What's that?" she asked.

"Didn't Carl give you an itinerary?"

She shook her head. "He said that I didn't need anything that would cloud my ideas. I did do some extensive research back when I came up with the idea. Aren't Comanches Indians?"

Coosie laughed as he flipped plate-sized pancakes in a big cast-iron skillet. "Comanche is a town probably about eleven or twelve miles north of where we are right now. We'll be doing a parade through the town in the middle of the afternoon since it's one of the big things on the historic Chisholm Trail. The newspaper folks will take pictures and maybe even corner one of us for a few quotes. *My* main concern is getting to the service station with a water hose so I can fill up the barrel. We're getting low and it'll be a while before we are in another town."

"Oh, I remember now. It was called Tucker at first and the town site was north of where it is now. Are we going through town? Won't that take us off the real trail? Is there a possibility there's an old saloon or bank or something still standing that was built during the cattle run days?" she asked.

"So you did some homework," Dewar said.

"Had to in order to make this all happen to begin with," she said.

Dewar glanced at Haley. Had he dreamed the kiss from the night before? "The town is real big on being part of the Chisholm Trail and they've asked for a parade. When we move the cattle out of the fields and start up the highway, you'll ride point with me. Coosie will bring up the rear in the chuck wagon. Buddy and Sawyer will herd from the east side and Rhett and Finn from the west side. If we all keep in our place it should be fairly easy traveling."

"Why do I ride point?" she asked.

"Because the people in town are all going to want to see the person responsible for bringing a reality television show through their town. Think of it as being the queen of the rodeo," Dewar said.

Coosie slapped a pancake on a plate and handed it to Haley. "Syrup, butter, and sausage patties are on the table. Help yourselves."

"So why all the worry about going through town?" she asked.

Rhett raised his hand. "I'm done with breakfast. I'll answer that one. We've got one rangy old longhorn bull that hates loud noises and ninety-nine more head of cattle that could stampede at the drop of a hat. Think about glass window fronts, the sides of the street packed with people watching the trail run. Now add in a lot of yelling kids, dashing out into the street to see if they can touch the horns on our big bull. It could go smooth. It could be a total disaster."

"Ah, the stuff reality shows are made of," Sawyer said. "You going to finish the drive if you get a broke leg in a stampede?"

"I'll finish it if I have to ride on the horns of that bull," she smarted off. And by golly, she would, too.

───⁓───

Haley snuck looks toward Dewar as he ate that morning. She'd awakened with a smile and touched her lips to see if they were still as warm as they'd been when she went to sleep. He'd awakened grouchy. Did that mean he was sorry he'd kissed her?

She hung back when they started out.

Coosie looked straight ahead and didn't offer anything at all. It looked like another long morning with nothing to think about but the kiss, and that was dangerous territory.

"Tell me about you and Buddy. Are y'all brothers?" she finally asked.

Coosie flicked the reins to get the horses to move along a little faster. The land had more rolling hills than the day before and they weren't too keen on pulling the wagon up the steep sides.

"We might as well be brothers, but we ain't. We was born down around Bowie the same year and started to school at the same time. Buddy stuttered from the time he could say his first word and the kids, well, you know how mean kids can be. I was always the biggest kid in class, so that first day when someone picked on him, I whooped the snot right out of that kid. Every time a new kid came to town they had to get their whoopin' before they understood that nobody picked on my friend. Buddy might stutter, but he's real smart, so he helped me with the learnin' and I helped him with the bullyin' kids."

"What'd y'all do after you graduated?" she asked, since he was evidently in a much more talkative mood than the day before.

"We signed up for the army and wound up in the Gulf War. Said if we ever got back into Montague County we'd never leave it again. This is our first time to break that vow. Oh, we scoot around the north part of Texas on Saturday nights doin' some two-steppin' and pool shootin' at the bars, but we stay pretty close to home, which is the Double Deuce, where we both work for Ace Riley."

"Married?" she asked before he could barely draw another breath.

Coosie shook his head. "Hadn't found the right woman yet, but neither one of us is dead yet either, so there's still a chance. You'd be amazed at how many women think that stutter of Buddy's is cute. He says why settle down with one heifer when he can have a whole herd."

Haley laughed and asked, "So you came home from the army and went to work at the Double Deuce?"

"Yep, Ace's granddad hired us and we been there ever since. We were both raised up on ranches, so we knew about cattle and tractors. Looks like Dewar is calling a halt and the sun is straight up, so it must be dinnertime."

"What are we havin' today?" Haley asked.

"Beans. I set them to soakin' last night and boiled them an hour this morning while I was makin' flapjacks. Got some leftover spoon bread to go with 'em and I made too many pancakes on purpose so we could roll them up around some honey and peanut butter for dessert."

Dewar kept his distance while they ate dinner, barely even acknowledging that she was part of the crew. Damn his sorry old cowboy hide anyway! His kiss made her want more, lots more, and he acted like it never even happened.

Haley had had relationships, but never before had a kiss created such a hot spot of lingering liquid desire. And the man who'd delivered the hotter'n hell's blazes kisses was over there acting like he didn't even know her.

Well, if that's the way he wanted it, he could damn sure have his aloofness. She wasn't interested in anything past a diversion from the boredom of a month on a cattle drive anyway. So there, Dewar O'Donnell with the sexy strut and the hottest kisses in the whole universe.

She turned her attention to the cattle lined up at the edge of Cow Creek. Getting them from Ringgold to Dodge City was the issue, not whether Dewar could set her ablaze with his kisses. When that was done, her job was over and Joel could do the actual reality show. And she'd be damn glad to have him out of the office and out of her hair for the weeks that he was out in the woods. And she was not sending a single roll of toilet paper with him, either.

After dinner they moved on north through the rolling hills again, keeping the herd going through long stretches of pastureland, sometimes through gates, across a section line road, and through another gate. Sometimes they had to cut a fence. Then Buddy and Finn hung back to repair it and catch up later.

In the middle of the afternoon Dewar steered the cattle to the west. Haley could hear the traffic before she actually saw a vehicle. The first one was a white pickup truck speeding down the road toward the south. The next was a pretty red sports car that made her long for her own car. Dewar rode toward a wide gate opening out onto the road and opened it. The cowboys flapped their hats and headed the big longhorn bull through the gate with the rest of the cattle following along behind, then yee-hawed them into a ninety-degree turn back to the north with the chuck wagon bringing up the rear.

"Y'all ready?" Dewar yelled.

"Might as well be," Sawyer hollered back.

He crooked his finger. "Haley?"

She slapped Apache's neck with the rein and he trotted right up the right edge of the cattle formation to Dewar. "So I'm the rodeo queen, right? Do I have to wave at the crowds?"

"The *Comanche Times* newspaper has already done this big spread about Carl Levy sending H. B. McKay up here to check things out for a reality show. Since you are H. B., then yes, you are the rodeo queen. They're having this big sidewalk sale and the ladies are setting up tables with food to sell. It's a fundraiser that'll bring in folks from all around."

She grinned. "Ahh, shucks. I forgot my diamond hat band and my hair spray to get my hair all big and fluffy."

"You'll do." He quickly scanned her from boots to hat. "If the cattle start to get restless, we'll hurry them up a bit. If they get too wild, you might have to help corral them. Think you can do that?"

"I can do anything I set my mind to do," she said. "You aren't much for compliments, are you?"

"What?" His dark brows became one long line across his green eyes.

"Nothing. Let's get through this," she said shortly.

Sure enough more than one little boy darted out to slap a cow or a bull on the rump and then ran back to the safety of his parents. Cameras were out by the dozens, maybe even hundreds, to record the modern-day cattle drive through the small town. A pay phone attached to the side of a convenience store caught Haley's eye and she entertained notions of making a call to end the whole thing. But that kiss kept her moving.

If it was a spur-of-the-moment thing, then the second one wouldn't fry holes in the toes of her socks.

If it wasn't, she was in big trouble.

She pulled up reins at a mailbox on a corner and dropped an envelope in it with all her notes for the past two days. It might be a week before her father got another letter, so he could just chew on her discoveries up until then. Besides, he didn't deserve news more than once a week. Until she could mail him another batch of notes, he could be looking for a chuck wagon, preferably a Studebaker, and he could be thinking about buying a donkey right along with a hundred head of cattle.

Something whirred beside her ear, and she jerked her head around to see a blur that looked like a baseball or a rock. It hit Apache square on the flank and he reared back on his hind legs. The first crazy thing that went through her mind was "Hi Ho Silver." His front feet came back down, hitting the ground with enough force to jar her teeth.

Suddenly, the saddle felt like it had been greased down with Coosie's bacon grease. She was cussing and screaming at the kid who was running like the devil poking his butt with a pitchfork. Apache threw his head back, and his mouth opened and screamed right along with her. The cows joined in the concert, and the old bull lent his deep voice to the mix.

Cows were on both sides of Haley and it definitely was not like the running of the bulls. Apache got ahead of the whole herd and led the charge, like General

Custer himself, right down the sidewalks festooned
with merchandise for the annual spring sidewalk sale.
The horse sideswiped a table of leftover valentines,
and paper goods went flying through the air. The bright
red tablecloth landed on Apache's saddle horn and the
old bull must've thought Apache was a bona fide bull-
fighter, because he gave a bellow, lowered his head,
and charged.

One of the bull's horns caught on a straw hat and the
other one snagged a lady's black lace camisole. Apache
veered to the left with the bull so close behind him that
Haley could feel his snorts. Two cows managed to get
flannel nightgowns over their heads in such a way that
only one wild eye was visible and they were giving the
bull a real run for his money.

Hell's bells, the running of the bulls didn't have a
thing on a stampede in southern Oklahoma. A lady was
cornered between a rack of jeans and the door into a
store by a big heifer that still had horns. The woman
was shooing at the cow with her handbag. The cow
tossed her head back and bawled, then stomped through
a round rack of blue jeans and one of bras. She went
tearing down the street with a hot pink bra strap stuck
firmly on one twitching ear.

Women were screaming like wounded coyotes and
fighting so hard to get their kids to safety inside stores
that they were stampeding worse than the cattle. Haley
saw the whole thing in a blur of flashes as Apache ran
full out ahead of the whole herd. Lord, what a show it
would make, but nothing could ever be staged to look
like the real thing.

The red tablecloth flipped up over Haley's eyes about

the time that the stampede reached the edge of town, so she couldn't see what was going on when Apache came to a long greasy stop. She tumbled out over his head to land right in the middle of a table full of cupcakes. The table collapsed and cupcakes went sailing through the air like miniature Frisbees. As luck would have it, she landed smack in the middle of dozens of chocolate cupcakes and the red tablecloth floated right down on top of her. She fought her way out, slinging chocolate every which way. Once she was free, she found Apache nibbling away at the cupcakes, with chocolate icing in his teeth.

Haley licked chocolate icing from her fingers, remounted, and gave thanks that she'd landed in that rather than shit—for a change. She slapped Apache on the rear end and they raced on ahead, this time behind the herd instead of in front of it. The cowboys were all still working their asses off trying to turn the bull and cows around. If they could get the first ones turned and head back toward the rest, the oncoming cows would slow down and they'd stall out the stampede.

Dust boiled up all around her, but she and Apache kept to the side as the cattle finally came to a stop half a mile out of town in the middle of a corn patch. A withered-up little old man with a shotgun trained on Dewar's chest stopped cowboys, cows, bulls, and even Apache quicker than six cowboys on horses had been able to do.

"You the revenuers?" he asked.

He had wispy gray hair that the wind blew every which way. His overalls were unbuttoned on the sides, and from Haley's vantage point, it was evident that those and a pair of scuffed-up cowboy boots were the only things the man wore.

"No, sir. We just drove this bunch of cows through Main Street and we had a stampede."

"Smart-ass kid threw a rock and hit my horse and the little shit caused the whole thing," Haley said.

The shotgun lowered and the old man grinned. "I keep tellin' Mama that folks don't raise their kids right no more. I swear to God that I'd kick that kid from here to next week if I caught him. Damn kids ain't got a lick of sense. It all comes from all them damn things that they keep plugged in their ears. God only knows what the hell they're listenin' to…"

A voice from the house shut him up. "Clovis, shut up your bitchin'. I got two big pans of corn bread cooked up and my bathtub is full of moonshine. If that damn sheriff comes out here, and you know he will to see if any of them crazy fools got hurt in town, he's going to put us both in prison. So bring them people in here and I'll give them a chunk of fresh corn bread and a jar of shine to take with them."

"I made that to sell, not give away," Clovis yelled back at the little house with peeling paint.

"You'd try to sell a coffin to a dead man. It won't be worth a damn if we're in prison and can't spend the money. Get them people on here to help me get it in jars. Miz Gertrude just called and said the sheriff is on the way. He was down near Terral, so he'll be a little bit makin' his way up here."

Coosie drove the wagon up into the yard, heard the last of the conversation, and said, "Y'all dismount, tie your horses to the wagon, and get on in there."

"Well, hell!" Clovis dug a cell phone out of his pocket and listened for a minute, jammed it back in the bib pocket, and yelled, "Momma, grab a jar of that shine and hide it in with your under-britches. Lawman is comin' from the north to help put things to rights. He ain't but five miles up the road. Pull the plug on the tub."

The gun went back up. "I oughta make y'all pay for that shine."

"We didn't cause it. That red-haired kid did," Haley said.

The gun lowered again. "Red-haired? 'Bout ten years old?" He squinted against the sun and pulled his brows down over his deep-set eyes.

She nodded.

"Yep, that'd be the preacher's kid. Mean little shit. Well then, I'll just tell the police and they can go fuss at the preacher for raisin' up a kid like that. I bet they can take up an extra offerin' this Sunday down at the church to pay for the damage done in the town and for my shine that's goin' down the drain."

"You ought to fix up an underground cistern in the backyard and let it drain into it if you nearly get caught again," Haley said.

"Smart girl. Mama, bring on out that corn bread. Police car is pullin' into the drive right now," Clovis yelled.

A rotund woman opened the door and handed Coosie a paper sack, already showing grease marks where she'd slid a whole pan of corn bread into it.

"Thank you, ma'am," Coosie said.

"They're calmed down enough to move them on out of here now," Clovis said. "And y'all ought to thank that little lady for your hides tonight. She's the smartest one in the whole bunch of y'all. Movin' cows through town. What the hell was you thinkin'?"

Haley breathed a sigh of relief when they headed back to the west and out into the open ground. The bull had shook free of the black lace teddy, but he still trotted along with his straw hat impaled in a jaunty slant on one horn. The flannel nightgowns on the two cows had flown off into the ditch, but the old horned heifer still sported her pink bra proudly. Haley swiped a finger across a chunk of chocolate on her shirt and licked it from her finger.

She turned to say something to Dewar and a woman in a little red pickup truck pulled up beside Dewar's horse.

"Hey, Dewar, darlin', you ready for a party?"

Didn't the broad know that they'd just survived a stampede and a double-barreled shotgun? She should be whispering, not yelling. Damned idiot! If those cows stampeded again, Haley hoped that they ran right over her big hair and flattened those enormous boobs.

Dewar grinned and waved at her. "Not today. Got cattle to herd."

Leave it to a man to eat up all that attention.

Apache snorted and Haley wished she had the energy to do the same.

"Come on, now! Betcha I can stay on that bull at the club down at the Resistol Rodeo longer than you can. Winner gets the prize. I'll be callin' you when you get home," the woman hollered.

"I'll look forward to it," Dewar answered.

"Just how far does your reputation as a ladies' man go?" Haley asked.

"We are only about forty miles from Ringgold," he said.

"Who is your bull-ridin', prize-winnin' woman?" she asked.

"Jealous? And we hardly know each other," he teased.

She glared at him. "No, I'm not jealous. I just wasn't prepared for the way the women act when they see cowboys. I'll have to put that in my notes. The contestants will love it, and if there's already a little love interest between a couple, then jealousy can be played up when they parade through Comanche."

Dewar threw a hand over his heart. "I'm hurt. I thought that kiss meant you were madly in love with me."

"I kissed a jackass once on the ear. It didn't mean I was madly in love with him."

"Four-legged or two-legged?"

"Four, but I have kissed two-legged ones as well. Neither one gave me the instant desire to look at wedding dresses and white cakes."

"You are a tough cookie, Haley."

"Yes, I am, Dewar, darlin'!" She drug out the last word until it became *darrr-lynnn,* like the hussy on the side of the road had done. "Now who was she?"

"That, Miz McKay, is not a damn bit of your business. Who she is or what she is to me has no bearing on your reality show. We're going to open that gate up there and run the cattle back close to the original trail before we turn north. Get them off this main road and away from traffic. You can stay with me or fall back. As Rhett said in the movie, 'Frankly, my dear, I don't give a damn.'"

She stayed behind the chuck wagon the rest of the day. To know that line meant that Dewar had watched *Gone with the Wind* and that made him a romantic.

Rugged good looks and a soft romantic core? It's a wonder all the women in Texas weren't laying bets about who'd drag him to bed and hopefully down the aisle. That shrill cowgirl on the side of the road might have even put up the most money.

When they stopped that night in a cottonwood grove, her rear end had stopped aching and gone into the absolutely numb stage. She slid off Apache, loosened the bedroll, and carried it over toward the place where she and Dewar had already thrown down his gear. Coosie was setting up his irons to cook supper. Buddy hustled firewood. Cattle were lining up at Claridy Creek to get a drink.

She rolled out her bedroll on the ground under a big tree and walked down to the edge of the creek, stuck her hand in it, and groaned. It was clear water, tumbling over a rocky bottom and would have made a lovely place to take another bath. But it felt as if it was coming straight off an ice-capped mountain in Wyoming.

"Probably spring fed," Dewar said at her elbow. "You brave enough to take a bath in that?"

"Not me. I had one last night that'll have to do until we get to something warmer. I can use the dishrag to wipe the remaining chocolate from my shirt."

"Then if you'll stay at the camp, me and the boys will get washed up," Dewar said.

Her eyes snapped open so wide that she could almost hear the pop. "You are kiddin' me."

"No, ma'am, I am not! You might offer to stir the stew for Coosie so he can get a bath, too. It's been a long day. I reckon one of our longest since we managed eighteen miles and put on a parade to boot."

Haley nodded and went back to the camp. Any man brave enough to shuck his clothes at the first of April and take a bath in ice water was a tougher cookie than she ever thought about being.

Chapter 6

SHE WAS DREAMING OF DEWAR WRAPPING HIS ARMS around her and drawing her close to his chest as they slept. His warm breath caressed her ear and the heat it generated felt like warm butter in sharp contrast to the chill of a spring morning. She didn't want to open her eyes and leave the dream behind, so she reached up and her fingertips grazed his face, feeling the bristly growth of a day's beard.

That wasn't a figment of a dream. It was damn sure real! She popped her eyes wide open and crimson filled her cheeks. His face was so close to hers that she could count his eyelashes one by one.

"Don't move a muscle. It's curled up behind you," he whispered softly.

"What?" She stiffened.

He eased an arm over her curled up body, sending tingles down her spine as his hand brushed against places he'd set on fire in her dreams.

"A huge rattlesnake. I didn't want to shoot it and scare you. I want you to lie very still and not move. Whatever you do, don't roll over. And don't say anything else. You might wake him up."

Every nerve in her body itched. Her muscles tensed so tight that they throbbed. She was afraid to blink and her eyes hurt with want for moisture. If he was teasing, he was a dead man. If he wasn't, he might be anyway.

He eased a pistol up over her, covered her ear with his hand, and pulled the trigger.

Her scream would have curdled fresh milk and it brought every other cowboy to a sitting position so fast they looked like a blur. She threw both hands over her ears, shut her eyes, and tried to rip her way out of a zipped sleeping bag.

"Be still and let me help you," Dewar yelled.

His mouth moved, so he was talking, but all she heard was the roar in her ears. She looked away from him and there it was, still coiled up but without a head, as big as King Kong and wicked as Lucifer. She shivered so hard that she feared her toenails had fallen off inside the sleeping bag.

Chilly wind circled her when Dewar finally got it unzipped to let her out. She wiggled free of the entanglement and danced around, swiping at her arms and neck worse than when the spider crawled inside her lacy underwear. Snakes! Spiders! She was throwing in the towel and going home to Dallas as soon as she found a pay phone. She didn't care if her father fired her ass. She'd stand on the street corner with a soup can and beg for nickels before she ever got one mile away from civilization again.

Coyotes and bobcats at a distance were one thing. A snake slithering into bed with her was a whole different ball game. Yes, sir, she was going back to Dallas as soon as she could find a phone. And she would never again go anywhere that did not have hot and cold running water, toilets, and hair spray.

Coosie picked the snake up by the tail. It was as long as he was tall, even without a head, and its body was as big as his arm.

"Supper!" He grinned like he was right proud of the dead critter.

"You are shittin' me," she yelled.

The guys all laughed and she glared at them. There was not one thing funny about a damn snake snuggling up next to her or the roar in her ears. They could have the next one for a bed partner. She wasn't sticking around to see if there was anything worse than rattlesnakes and panty spiders.

From the way they used their hands to talk, she guessed the breakfast conversation centered around who'd seen the biggest, baddest snake in the world. Sawyer made a hacking motion like he'd killed his trophy crawling varmint with a shovel or a hoe. Finn must've gotten his with a knife, and Coosie used his thumb and forefinger to show them how he'd shot one. To Haley's way of thinking, there wasn't a wrong way to kill a snake, so they were all heroes.

The roar in her ears continued while they saddled up and got under way after breakfast, but by midmorning it had toned down. She and Apache brought up the rear of the whole herd, each minute lasting a whole hour.

Boredom was what would send the contestants packing. Not snakes or bugs. It would be the pure boredom of day after day looking at a cow's ass while their own rear ends turned into one big callus.

Dinner was held on the banks of Stage Stand Creek and consisted of cold biscuits stuffed with sausage and pepper jack cheese. She was glad that she could finally hear enough to listen to the stories the guys told about rattlesnake hunts down around Ringgold. She couldn't believe any fool would actually go out and hunt those things. And Coosie must have been serious about eating the thing because Buddy asked him if he was going to use cayenne pepper in the cornmeal when he fried it.

She'd said that she'd eat anything and there wasn't a doubt in her mind that they'd hold her to her word. But rattlesnake? Maybe they were teasing. She could hope so. Beans again or even peanut butter sandwiches sounded like gourmet food compared to snake. She wouldn't even make her contestants eat snake.

Dinner was over too quickly. She'd make a note later to let the contestants draw out the dinner hour occasionally. That's what she desperately wanted to do that day. Anything beat getting back on the horse and riding another five or six hours.

She'd barely settled back into the saddle when Apache's muscles tensed and his front feet were suddenly fighting the air. She slid backwards, the saddle catching her before she scooted right off his backside and onto the ground. She glanced down to see where she was about to fall and a snake slithered by like it had all day to crawl away into the brush. With a force that jarred her teeth, Apache's front feet came down, hitting the snake right behind its head.

And then the horse snorted and took off in a dead gallop. It was all she could do to hang on until he reached the edge of the creek and stopped so fast that she had to hug him like a brother or she would have shot right out over his head into the cold water.

One minute she was moving forward. The next she was jerked back. And then strong arms reached up and hauled her off the horse. Dewar set her firmly on the ground and held her close to his chest. She was amazed that his heart was speeding every bit as fast as hers. She looked up into his worried eyes, but before she could even thank him, cowboys came running through the trees. Buddy was stuttering and stammering and the rest of them weren't doing much better.

"You okay, M-m-miz Haley?" Buddy spit out.

She nodded.

Coosie patted her on the shoulder. "You done good, girl. Any other fool would have fallen off that horse right on the snake. Now we got enough meat for a real meal tonight. I'll skin this one and then we'll get back on the trail."

"I'm fine," she said.

"You ready to make that phone call? I think Dewar's phone has a little bit of power left," Rhett asked.

She shook her head and said, "Hell, no!"

Where had those words come from? She wasn't that brave, that mean, or that crazy. She wanted to go home to air-conditioning, exterminators, and a real bed with no varmints.

Dewar took his phone from his pocket and handed it to her with a wide grin and a twinkle in his sexy eyes. She flipped it open to see one bar left. She flipped it shut and handed it back to him, crawled up on Apache's back, and rode him up over the embankment and back to the campsite where Coosie was busy skinning the second snake of the day.

Her granny Mahalia Jones always said that bad things came in threes. Well, she'd faced all three of hers in less than a week, so the rest of the journey should be smooth sailing. One mean old spider and two damned miserable rattlesnakes. Thank goodness she'd squashed the spider with her boot or Coosie would be rolling it in cornmeal and frying it for supper too.

She shuddered at that idea!

In no time he'd cut the snake into edible pieces and tucked them away inside the chuck wagon. Then they were right back on the boring trail. She wanted to get Coosie to talking about something… anything… to make the day go faster, but the only thing on her mind was having to eat that snake.

By evening she had convinced herself that she could eat it. If she could eat nutria down in Louisiana, then she could eat snake. She'd pretend like it was fried fish or chicken and eat one tiny little piece. Buddy helped her unsaddle Apache and she gave the big gray horse the usual thorough brushing before she turned him loose to graze on the spring grass.

She watched him romp around in the pasture like a young colt, thankful to be free of rider and saddle. She could understand his feelings. She'd be glad to be free of horse and saddle and get back to her life, hectic as it was. Apache rolled over a couple of times in the knee-high green grass and then stood up and started eating.

Haley's stomach growled and she laid a hand on her midriff.

"Guess we are both hungry. I'll trade with you. I'll eat your grass if you'll eat my piece of snake," she muttered.

Someone touched her on the shoulder and after a day of thinking about spiders and snakes, the adrenaline rushed through her body so fast that she doubled up both fists, spun around, and was instantly ready to do war.

"Hey, I didn't mean to startle you. I just wanted you

to know I was here. I rolled out your bedroll for you," Dewar said.

"Sorry, but after today everything is scary," she said.

"I expect it is, but wait until you taste the supper. Hush puppies, baked beans, and fried rattlesnake. It don't get any better than that." Dewar grinned.

"Rib eyes, baked potato, and fresh green salad," she said.

"I didn't think you'd be brave enough to try fried snake," he taunted.

"Oh, you didn't, did you? Well, you better guard your plate with both hands, mister, because I'm hungry." She wished for the second time that day that she could reach up into the evening breeze, snatch the words before they hit his ears, and cram them back in her mouth.

The first bite almost gagged her, but once she got past the idea of what she was eating, she had to admit it was delicious. Like mild-flavored fish with a nice spicy cornmeal coating that was very crispy. It was much better than the calamari that Joel ordered when he took her out to his favorite restaurant for dinner. And it was one hell of a lot better than that sushi stuff that Joel thought was the best shit since ice cream on a stick.

"Haley provided supper tonight. What are you fellers going to do to beat this kind of meal?" Coosie asked.

"I shot that snake," Dewar argued.

"But you couldn't have shot it if it hadn't been on her bedroll, so it was her snake," Coosie said.

"Squirrel tomorrow night," Finn said.

"Young enough to fry? Won't have time to boil one tender for dumplings if it's an old one," Coosie told him.

"Young enough to fry and maybe two or three old

ones to boil after supper for dumplings for the next day," Finn said.

Coosie pointed at him. "I'll hold you to it."

Dark clouds covered the moon and the stars that night soon after supper, bringing on nightfall a full hour earlier than usual. Coosie was the first one to turn in, followed by Buddy and then Finn. Sawyer yawned a few times and then he and Rhett were snoring.

Dewar had thrown out his bedroll closer to Haley's than the previous nights and after they were tucked in he whispered, "You goin' to be okay?"

"I'm fine," she said. In reality she kept hearing slithering noises and her eyes darted from one side of the tarp to the other constantly, but she would rather fight another spider attack as admit it to him.

"I can sit watch four hours so you can sleep," Dewar said.

"I said I'm fine!"

"Okay, then. You ready for squirrel tomorrow night?"

"Of course I am. This idea of wild game will make my show even better than the one about grappling catfish out of the Red River. The contestants' faces will be priceless when they see wild game on the supper table. What makes you think Finn will get enough for supper anyway?"

Dewar laughed softly. "He was a sniper in the army."

Chapter 7

HALEY'S GRANDMOTHER, ISABELLE, USED TO SING A song while she was working in the flower gardens that had a line asking for one day at a time, sweet Jesus. Haley awoke to those words playing through her mind.

They were camped south of a town called Ninnekah up next to a farm pond that watered cattle but was useless for bathing with all the mud around the rim. Dewar had ridden away before they turned the horses loose for grazing and returned with a dark gray donkey before suppertime. The silly animal bypassed all the cattle and stood right beside Haley when Dewar herded it into the camp at dusk. And now, it stood only a few feet from her bedroll, looking right at her.

"Friday. What kind of trouble will happen for the contestants tomorrow?" she whispered.

The donkey brayed loudly and pawed at the ground as if answering her question.

"What do you know about my reality show?" she asked him.

It brayed again and pawed.

"I think he's talking to you," Dewar said.

She looked over to see Dewar all sleepy-eyed and propped on one elbow. She really, really needed to stop being so damn stubborn and take him up on that phone call. Every time she looked at the man she wanted to go to bed with him and that wasn't even a possibility.

"Why?" she asked.

"The lady I bought him from said that he was hell on wheels when it came to coyotes or anything that threatens the herd, but he's a big baby. Her granddaughter raised him from a baby and the granddaughter has red hair. Guess that's what draws him to you," Dewar said.

"You bought a crazy jackass knowing he'd plague the hell out of me because of my hair?" she asked.

"You are so welcome," Dewar said.

"Oh, hush!" She looked away from him and back to the donkey. His eyes looked like his feelings were hurt that she'd say a thing like that about him. "Okay, I'm sorry. Stop pouting. With that hangdog expression, you look like Eeyore."

"That's what the lady said his name is. I figured we'd just call him Jack," Dewar said.

"No, he is definitely an Eeyore," Haley said.

The donkey nudged her hand as if he was accepting her apology.

"See, he likes you." Dewar rolled up his bed. "He can be your pet. Bet you left a cat behind, didn't you?"

"No cats. No dogs. Never had a pet."

"Well, looks like you got one now," Dewar said.

The animal stood watch over her all night, waited the next morning while she rolled up her bedroll, went with her to breakfast, and stood beside her while she saddled up Apache.

"Looks like that jackass has done beat all you cowboys out for the lady." Coosie laughed.

"They didn't have a chance anyway," Haley said. "I'll take a four-legged jackass over a two-legged one any day of the week. They don't break your heart."

It was another parade day, basically forced upon them by an interstate highway that they couldn't cross. They had to take the cattle through Chickasha, Oklahoma, using an underpass. Dewar said this time wouldn't be as big a deal as the Comanche parade but that it might take longer. They herded the cattle out onto the access road in the middle of the afternoon with Haley, Dewar, and Eeyore riding point.

The cowboys and cattle came in behind them and when they passed a Walmart store over to the east, Coosie pulled into the parking lot and tied his team to the cart station. Haley noticed a man picking up trash in the parking lot and would have traded places with him for fifteen minutes in the Walmart bathroom. She longed to stand in the middle of the ladies' room and just look at toilets, sinks with running water, and hand driers.

They made it through the underpass and back into the wilderness without any fanfare. No sexy women to yell at the cowboys and no kids dashing out to slap a cow on the fanny or touch the old rangy longhorn. Even though the town was much larger and she'd spotted such luxurious places as Holiday Inn and McDonald's, it was rather anticlimactic after the Comanche welcome.

From her research, she knew that Chickasha wasn't even a town during the cattle trail days, but she wondered, since it was located near water, if there weren't a few brothels and saloons situated close by. She imagined a fine-looking trail boss like Dewar giving a few of his cowboys the evening to go blow off some steam and flirt with the barmaids.

Jealousy flashed through her heart like lightning. "For cryin' out loud, there's not even a saloon around here.

But I'd love to be a barmaid if he did swagger through the doors of my saloon. Just call me Miss Kitty," she whispered with a grin.

For the better part of an hour they meandered east to get back on the trail with Coosie catching up and falling into place a little after they'd turned back to the north again.

She rode up to the front of the line where Dewar was and said, "Tell me a story."

"About what?"

"Just a cowboy story."

"And how does just a cowboy story start?"

"Like all good stories, once upon a time. Tell me about a cowboy."

He smiled and began, "Once upon a time a cowboy wished he could go back in time. Just get on his horse and ride out across the pasture and when he got back home everything would be way back in the past. So he got this opportunity to play like he could do that for a whole month. The End."

"That's not long enough," she grumbled.

"It is for Rachel."

"And who is Rachel?"

"Rachel is my niece and she likes once upon a time stories, but I've learned to keep the beginning and end close together. So that's my story and I'm stickin' to it." He laughed.

"Okay, then question time. Why did the cowboy want to go back in time anyway?"

"Because he always thought he'd been born in the wrong century. You ever feel like that, Haley?" Dewar asked.

"Not in the wrong century. In the wrong place maybe."

"And where would that be?"

"Dallas, Texas. I always liked the wild freedom when Momma and I went to visit the Cajun cousins down on the bayou in southern Louisiana. Have you always lived in Ringgold? My Granny Jones lives in a little bitty community outside of Jeanerette. It reminds me of Ringgold."

"I was born in the Bowie hospital and brought home to the ranch. It's where I've lived my whole life and I love it there. It's home and I wouldn't want to live anywhere else. I've got friends and family everywhere and I'm doin' what I love. Granny O'Malley says that makes a man a success."

Sawyer whistled loudly and Dewar left her side to go round up a couple of strays that wanted to turn around and go back south. Haley fell back to travel with Coosie, who was ready to talk about the store and what all he'd bought. Evidently, shopping for flour and sugar loosened up his tongue.

They camped that evening on a flat piece of ground with nothing but dirt and sky as far as she could see. Another farm pond provided water for the cattle and her new best friend, Eeyore. It wasn't fit for bathing, so she made do with her washcloth and soap and a pan full of water that she carried under a weeping willow tree and pretended that the drooping branches were the walls of her bathroom in Dallas.

Time on the trail was like time in a hospital. It was all out of kilter, going as slow as a lazy snail, and then suddenly the whole day or night had passed. She couldn't believe that she'd survived six whole days, and who would have guessed she would be washing up under the semi-privacy of a weeping willow tree and enjoying it? When did she stop hating the trip and enjoying it, anyway?

The twang of guitar music floated across the pasture and she cocked her head to one side. Surely she was imagining such things. Music in the middle of nowhere? She buttoned her shirt and peeked out between the thick tree branches. Coosie stirred a pot of stew and the warm night breeze carried the aroma straight to her nose. Sawyer, Finn, and Rhett lazed on their beds and Buddy sat on an old stump not far from the campfire.

Dewar strummed the guitar, frowned, and tightened up a couple of strings. To be just a plain old cowboy, he sure had a lot of surprises up his sleeve. He strummed again and then broke into a guitar medley. She recognized "Bill Bailey" and "Red River Valley," but that was all.

"Sing something," Coosie said.

Haley dropped the tree branch, combed her hair with her fingertips, and dumped the water. She didn't want to miss hearing Dewar sing, not even if he was off-key and it had the coyotes howling at the moon.

"What do you want to hear?" Dewar asked.

When Haley parted the willow limbs and started toward the campsite, Buddy motioned for her to take his tree stump for a chair. She thanked him and shook her head.

"I'd rather sit on the ground after riding all day. Does he really sing?" she whispered.

Buddy backed up and sat back on the stump. "They all d-d-do."

"All of them?" She nodded toward the other three O'Donnells.

"All," Buddy answered.

Dewar's fingers picked out a prelude to Ricky Van Shelton's old song "Simple Man." When he began to sing, Haley's breath caught in her chest. His voice was deep and pure and goose bumps popped up on her arms. He'd be an instant star in Nashville with his looks, his voice, and his ability to make that guitar do everything but talk.

The lyrics said that he was a simple man and he wanted a place to lay his head and three squares in a frying pan. Heat shot up from her neck to her cheeks when he sang about wanting a soft woman and warm bed. Dewar O'Donnell was certainly not a simple man. He was very complex, and just when she did think she had him all figured out and wasn't even going to think about him again, he showed her another side.

He finished that song and went right into another Ricky Van Shelton song, "Statue of a Fool." It was a sad song about a man who felt like a fool for letting love slip through his hands. Haley was a city girl and loved the bright lights of Dallas, but she'd cut her teeth on country music from her father's side of the family and zydeco from her mother's side. So she'd heard both songs and knew the lyrics by heart.

Finn stood up and dusted off his jeans. Dewar put the guitar in his hands. His voice wasn't quite as deep as Dewar's but had a haunting sound as he sang "Don't We All Have the Right."

It was about a man who laughed it off when his woman left him because he thought she'd come back again. He sang that in love there was two ways to fall.

Dewar took two long strides to where Haley sat and held out his hand. "May I have this dance, ma'am?"

She stared unblinking up at him. "You dance?"

"The question is, do you?" He smiled.

She put her hand in his and he pulled her to her feet and into his arms. One of her hands went around his neck and one of his rested on her lower back. Two-stepping on grass by the light of a campfire with a cowboy whose touch made her insides sizzle was a heady experience.

"Which way is best?" she whispered.

"What?"

"Which way is best to fall in love?"

"Which two ways are there?" Dewar asked.

"In and out," she said.

"I'd think the in way is less painful," he said. "You ever been in love?"

"Thought I was."

"And?"

"I wasn't, so I didn't have to fall out of love because you got to be in love to fall out," she said.

Finn went from that song into another Ricky Van Shelton tune called "Somebody Lied."

It was an old beer-drinking, two-stepping song about a man having trouble getting over a woman. It didn't apply to Haley, but tears welled up in her eyes at the way Finn delivered it, as if he felt the words rather than just sang them. Had he left behind the love of his life when he was deployed and she left him?

Sawyer was the next entertainer and he veered away from Ricky Van Shelton to Mark Chesnutt's "Goin' On Later On." It was too fast to two-step to so Haley stepped back, did a wiggle, and fully well intended to do some fancy footwork to the song, but Dewar grabbed her hand and showed that he was as adept at swing dancing as he was at two-stepping.

She was out of breath when the song ended, but Sawyer chuckled and went straight into "Come on in, the Whiskey's Fine." It was something between a country swing and two-stepping and Dewar didn't miss a single beat when he swung her out and back to his chest, all the time singing right along with his cousin.

Sawyer sang about it being hotter than two rats in heat inside an old wool sock. Haley threw back her head and laughed when Dewar swung her out again. It felt like the lawn parties they had down on the bayou in Louisiana where there were no walls to hold in the giggles or the loud music from the band.

Haley giggled. "You are makin' me hotter than that rat that he's singin' about."

"Weather-wise or otherwise?" Dewar flirted.

"What do you think?"

Sawyer's next choice was "If the Devil Brought You Roses." The lyrics asked if the devil brought her roses and a bottle of red wine would she be an angel and take him back to heaven one more time.

Dewar twirled Haley and brought her back into his arms for a fast dance step around the grass.

"Would you?" he asked.

"What?"

"Would you take me to heaven if I brought you roses and wine?"

"How do you know you wouldn't end up kissin' the devil smack on his forked little tail instead of an angel and winding up in hell rather than heaven?" she asked.

"Well, guess I'll save my red roses and wine if there is that possibility," he said.

Sawyer handed the guitar off to Rhett, who decided

to sing Travis Tritt's songs beginning with "Best of Intentions," a nice slow ballad.

Dewar and Haley swayed to the music, barely moving their feet at all. She wondered what words would be written on Dewar's heart if she could read it like a book. Were there women who had left tears on the pages of his life? Did he take someone for granted and found out later that he had really loved that woman?

Rhett took the guitar from Sawyer and strummed the first chords of "Love of a Woman."

She looked up at Dewar and asked, "Do you go crazy trying to catch your feelings like the song says?"

"Always," he answered. "Do you stand beside your man even when he is wrong like the song says?"

"Never have, but then I've never loved anyone that much," she said.

"Married to your job, are you?"

"Pretty much."

"Your turn," Rhett called out when he finished the last of the song.

Dewar bent Haley back and whispered, "Thank you for the dances, ma'am."

"Thank you," she said.

"I don't know about the rest of you, but I'm ready for bed," Coosie said. "Saturday on the trail don't mean sleeping in an extra hour."

Rhett handed the guitar to Buddy, who carried it to the chuck wagon and stowed it in the right place.

"Thanks, guys," he said.

"It was fun. Maybe we'll do it again at the end of next week," Rhett said.

"Why wait until the end of the week?" Haley asked.

"You tell her, Dewar. I'm sleepy." Rhett yawned.

"Gives us something to look forward to at the end of a long week," Dewar said. "Wouldn't be special at all if we had music every night. You might keep that in mind for your reality show."

His hand brushed against hers, but he sidestepped a little to keep it from happening again instead of taking it in his. That confused her to no end. He'd held her tightly when they danced. He'd flirted and his eyes had said that he liked holding her close and now he didn't even want to touch her?

She wanted to drag him under the weeping willow tree, strip off naked, and make wild passionate love with him until daybreak, and he didn't even want to grasp her hand. When they reached their sleeping bags, he nodded at her, sat down, and tugged his boots off. She did the same and slipped into her bag, zipped the side, laced her hands behind her head, and stared at the stars.

The cowboy was getting under her skin and it was driving her totally insane with desire, want, and need all balled up together.

Chapter 8

HALEY AWOKE ON SATURDAY MORNING TO EEYORE braying right outside the campsite and Coosie telling him what a good boy he'd been. She sat up so fast that her head spun around like it was suffering from an acute hangover. She squinted against the very first signs of the sun peeking over the eastern horizon.

Coosie looked her way and pointed to Eeyore, who had a dead coyote at his feet.

"Your new little friend is earning his keep," he said. "I can't believe the critter got this close to the camp. Must have been hungry."

Haley shook her boots to make sure no spiders had taken up residence deep in the toes and crammed her feet down into them. She went straight to the donkey, rubbed his ears, and told him what a good boy he'd been to save the cows from that mean old coyote.

"Please tell me we aren't having that thing for supper," she said.

Coosie laughed. "Be like eatin' dog. I ain't never been that hungry yet."

"We had snake and we had squirrel, which isn't anything but a glorified rat with a fluffy tail," she reminded him.

"But that ain't dog. Don't think my stomach would handle dog or cat very well. We'll leave him here for the buzzards. They deserve something for taking care of roadkills for us," Coosie said.

The morning lasted six days past eternity. After a night complete with dancing, a woman ought to at least get a good-night kiss at the door, but Dewar rolled over with his back to her and promptly went to sleep. And that morning he acted like she had the damn plague.

She and Eeyore brought up the rear for a while and not one time did Dewar ride back to check on the herd stringing along back there. Before noon they came into El Reno and had to herd the cattle through the Interstate 40 underpass. A police escort led the way down two lanes of the highway with another black and white car bringing up the rear. Two of the policemen tried to flirt and one even asked for her phone number. Fat lot of good that would do since her phone was in her car back at Dewar's ranch. She wished Dewar would show her a fraction of the attention they did.

Eeyore didn't like the cars, the town, or the traffic on the other two lanes and he brayed all about it the whole hour that it took to get through town and back into the pasture. Too bad it didn't look like it did way back when it was a wild Chisholm Trail town. Eeyore would have been a lot more comfortable with horse-drawn buggies than fast cars.

That evening, Dewar ate and made an excuse to check the cattle, since they'd been on the trail for a week. He crawled into his sleeping bag before anyone else that evening and was snoring before Haley took out her notebook.

The next day wasn't any better. Dewar didn't speak to her all day and had very little to say to the rest of the crew. She made notes that night about the trail boss being a total jackass and that it should be worked into the reality show. Everyone could wonder what they'd done wrong to put him into a black mood after the night of singing and dancing.

That night he and the boys washed up in Buggy Creek and then sat around the campfire talking about horses, cows, and ranching. She spent an hour at the creek taking a cold bath, shaving her legs in cold water, washing her hair, putting on clean clothing, and washing her laundry. She hung it, panties and all, on a line she stretched from the wagon to a mesquite tree and dared Dewar to make a comment about it.

But he didn't.

Sunday she awoke to a cloudy day, but at least her laundry had dried through the night, so she packed it away in her saddlebags and got ready for the second week of the drive. She'd dropped more notes in the mail in El Reno and hoped that Joel was having fun getting the reality show details together from her notes because he was the one who'd be sleeping on the ground pretty soon even if he didn't know it just yet.

She giggled when she thought about him sleeping in a hayloft or a chasing a spider out of his underpants. She'd never have to worry about him running roughshod over her again when that happened because he'd throw up his hands and die right on the spot. He might have wormed his way into the family business, but he didn't have the backbone or the fortitude to last the whole time on the trail.

Thinking about Joel and what he'd endure on the trail didn't help that evening when they made camp. She felt like she'd been on a first date, kissed so passionately at the door that her knees buckled, promised a call later in the week, and then nothing, nada. No flowers, phone call, not even a friendly nod at the water cooler in the office. Trouble was that on a cattle run, there was no place to get away from the sorry SOB who'd led her on with all those sweet songs and two-stepping and a kiss that was better than sex with most men.

Clouds as black as Haley's mood covered the sky the next morning. The air was pregnant with the promise of rain, and the cows all faced the southwest. Even Eeyore kept his head down as if he was getting ready for the onslaught of a heavy rainstorm. Coosie fried up extra sausage and bacon for breakfast, made three times the usual biscuits, and removed the lid from the water barrel.

"It's a comin', no gettin' around it," he said while they ate that morning. "I'll get the slickers out of the wagon. You might just as well go ahead and put them on."

"But it ain't rainin' yet," Buddy said.

The first big drop hit him on the end of his nose. "Guess I was wrong."

Dewar jogged over to the wagon, pulled up the canvas cover, and grabbed the yellow slickers. His hand brushed against Haley's and the heat was still there. He cut his eyes around to stare at her for a split second, and the longing in his eyes said he felt it too.

"Thank you," she said curtly.

"You are welcome," he answered formally.

The first big drops of rain hit as she slipped her arms into the sleeves and pulled the hood up over her hat. She was glad she'd saddled Apache while waiting on breakfast because the rain got serious, falling in waving sheets that left her vision limited. She put a boot in the stirrup and grabbed the saddle horn. Her right foot slipped on the wet grass and she was grabbing at air when strong arms grabbed her from behind and set her upright. She turned quickly, expecting to see Dewar but looked into Coosie's smiling face.

"'Bout took a second tumble there, kiddo. Try again and get settled. Can't have a broke leg. You will need to help keep the strays rounded up today. Rain makes them crazy sometimes," he said.

"Thank you," she said. The second time she got a better footing and slid right into the wet saddle. She'd barely gotten her gloves on and the reins in her fingers when Dewar rode up on his big black horse.

"Your job is to keep an eye out for strays at the back of the herd. Can you whistle?"

"Why do I need to whistle?"

"If you can't herd a stubborn cow back into the herd in the rain, whistle and one of us will come help," he said.

"You do whatever the trail boss does. I can do my job just fine," she said. "I hope it rains just like this for my television show."

He rode away without even a nod.

Dewar gripped the reins so tight that his hands ached as much as his clenched jaws. It had nothing to do with the pouring rain and everything to do with that woman. He'd known she'd be trouble when she drove up into his yard in that fancy car, but he'd expected it to be whining, bitchin', and being a general pain in the ass. He didn't expect her to learn the ropes, stay out of his hair, and crawl into his heart.

He'd thought his older brother, Rye, was crazy as a drunk rooster when he fell ass over belt buckle in love with Austin Lanier. Not that Dewar was admitting anything near the *L* word, but he did understand Rye's dilemma much better. He was attracted to Haley, plain and simple. But he was determined to nip it right in the bud before it got a better foothold, because the only end game held too much pain and heartache. Sure, he'd been looking for a woman for a few months. Hell, he'd gone a step further than just looking; he'd been seeking diligently for someone to fill the void in his heart. But Haley wasn't the one. No, sir! It was just one of those physical attractions that happened because she was the only woman around. When he got back to Ringgold all the women at the church, the café, and ranch in the whole area would be looking for a woman to hook him up with and any one of them would do better than that red-haired piece of sass.

"Move 'em out," he yelled and rode up to the front of the herd to ride point with the big longhorn bull right behind him.

Going was slow that morning and the rain poured relentlessly. At noon there was no break in the sky, no way to heat up a pot of coffee, or even a place to get dry. They kept moving instead of stopping and picked up biscuits from Coosie when they had time, eating them in a hurry before the rain turned them into a soggy mess.

They traveled through unfenced territory that day, so Dewar made wide loops around the herd to check several times to make sure the cattle weren't straying off in the storm. Before they made camp, they would be back in pasture roped off with barbed wire. But right then Dewar was glad they didn't have to work their way through gates or cut fences and mend them in the pouring rain.

It wasn't uncommon to get hard rains in April, especially around Easter time, but it made for slow going. Thinking about Easter brought on thoughts of the ranch and what had gone on there on the Sunday before. There would have been a big family dinner. All his siblings and their mates would have been there, and pictures would be taken of the little children. The next generation was coming on strong. And he'd missed it all to herd cattle in pouring down rain! He should be back at home seeking someone to *ride the river with*, as Grandpa called it. Not just any woman would do. It had to be someone very special because the river Grandpa talked about was the river of life.

He rounded the back of the chuck wagon and saw Haley and Apache keeping the herd moving forward. Her shoulders were hunched against the north wind. Cold water dripped off the end of her nose, and what hair had escaped from under the hood of the bright yellow slicker hung in limp strands around her face.

Dewar wanted to take her to the nearest motel, spend an hour drying every inch of her body, and then make love to her the rest of the afternoon. He could visualize her curled up naked in his arms and kissing her awake when the first afterglow dimmed.

He shook the picture from his head. But with silent catlike stealth it snuck right back in. In the vision, he brushed back her freshly washed and dried hair and kissed that soft part of her neck as he whispered sweet love words in her ear. The rain pounding on the roof of the old fifties motel and slapping against the window-panes was romantic instead of cold and miserable. The cotton sheets were warm and soft against their skin.

"Dammit!" he mumbled.

"She's gettin' under your skin, isn't she?" Finn said.

Dewar turned his head to see outside the wide hood. "Where'd you come from and who is getting under my skin?"

"Well, I'm damn sure not talkin' about the weather, although it is getting under my skin. Sinking right into my bones and chilling them since the wind shifted. I see a gate up ahead. Guess we'll be back in fenced land again?"

Dewar nodded. "For several days."

"Any chance this is going to let up or are we going to have to break out the tents for tonight?"

"Don't have a weather channel on my saddle. You got one?"

Finn chuckled. "Wish I did. Now let's talk about that woman."

"Let's don't," Dewar said.

"I figured she'd be a city slicker that whined and moaned at every turn, but she's shaped up pretty damn good. Coosie is taken with her, and Buddy thinks she hung the moon. Lucy might be losin' her place."

"Those two might like Haley, but they love Lucy and after this is over, Lucy will still be there for them. Haley will be gone, never to be seen again."

"That what's got your mind in a twist?"

"She's got a fancy office, wears fancy clothes, and you saw what she drives. Her daddy owns a television station or two or maybe a dozen. She's going right up the success ladder and I'm just a cowboy. Oil and water do not mix."

"You got that right," Finn said through clenched teeth.

"Want to talk about it?"

"Wouldn't do a bit of good. It's over and there's more than a television station and a hundred miles of highway between us," he said.

"Someone over there?" Dewar asked.

"She was our translator's sister. I asked her to come home with me but she wouldn't. Her family would disown her and family was everything to her. Like you said, oil and water don't mix. Our hearts didn't know about religion, skin color, or even family ties, but in the end the heart took a backseat."

"I'm sorry, man. Have you heard from her at all?"

"Buddy of mine sent a note a month ago. She and her brother were on their way to the base one morning and hit a land mine. It was instantaneous and neither of them suffered. I'm working my way through the bitterness of it all and this trip is helping. You are the first person I've told. Even my folks don't know."

"Talk helps and I'm here," Dewar said.

"Thanks. And I mean it. Now about those tents?"

"We're in luck tonight. Rancher has an empty barn with a big corral out back at the far end of his property. We'll have to ride an hour longer, but we're already wet so don't guess it'll matter. We can herd the livestock into the corral, pull the wagon inside, and bed down in the dry."

"Sounds better than the Waldorf Astoria right now," Finn said.

Dewar went on ahead to open the gate into a wide flat

pasture. When the cows had passed through and headed on north with their heads down against the bitter wind, he rode back to shut the gate.

"I got it!" Haley yelled over the roar of the wind and rain.

She leaned to one side and fastened the gate without ever getting off her horse. She had come a long way in a short time. Too damn bad it was all for a television show and had nothing to do with him.

Chapter 9

AFTER RIDING ALL DAY IN THE RAIN THE WEATHERED gray barn was a beautiful sight. Haley pulled up on her reins and stared at it as if it would disappear if she blinked. Eeyore left her side and marched into the corral with the last of the herd, and Finn fastened the gate shut with a piece of baling wire. Coosie pulled the wagon right into the barn through the big double doors, and Buddy rode in behind him to help unhitch the two horses and put them into a couple of the stalls inside the barn.

Dewar raised his voice above the rumbling thunder. "Hey, you got enough sense to come in out of the rain, don't you?"

She shot him the meanest look that she could conjure up. "I thought it was a mirage."

"It's real, so come on inside so we can shut the door, feed the cattle, and dry out."

She nodded and urged Apache on forward. *Dry out!* Two of the sweetest words she'd ever heard. The slicker had helped keep her dry, but it didn't cover from the knees down. The rain had even blown into her boots and her socks were wet. Since the wind had shifted, it was a cold, miserable feeling. She didn't care if she had a bite of supper; she just wanted to curl up inside her sleeping bag and get warm.

The other cowboys had already unsaddled, slung wet blankets over the stalls along the west side of the barn, and had claimed stalls for their horses. Ten stalls, eight horses, hay to feed the cattle, and even some food for the horses. It looked entirely too perfect to have just happened on a fluke.

"So you arranged this?" she asked Dewar as they slung saddles off their horses at the same time.

"Not exactly. In the real Chisholm Trail run there were families who lived on the trail and sometimes the cook bought food from them. When I talked to the fellow that owns the property we're crossing he told me about this old barn, said there was hay leftover from last year, and he'd put some oats in here for the horses just in case we wanted a place to hole up for a day or two," Dewar explained.

Her heart jumped around like a hyperactive child who'd just gotten out of the classroom and turned loose on the playground. "So we're staying more than just tonight?"

Dewar shook his head. "We've been traveling slow enough and there's been enough pasture grass that the cows aren't losing weight, so we'll go on tomorrow morning."

Her heart fell into her boots. She slid the wet blanket off Apache's back and slung it over a stall, led him into it, and brushed him down before shutting the door. Now it was her turn and she was almost too tired to even take off her wet clothing.

Dewar leaned against the stall where his big black horse, Stallone, was happily eating from a feed trough. "Loft is yours. We'll spread out over the bottom here and Coosie already claimed one of those last stalls as his."

She picked up her saddlebags. "Good night."

"Supper in an hour. Coosie has dug out a fire pit over there." He nodded toward the far end of the barn, "and opened that door enough for the smoke to escape that way. He's got a pot of stew going and says he's frying doughnuts tonight because after today we need something to pep us up."

She looked at the ladder leading up to the loft, slung her saddlebags over her shoulder, and grabbed the first rung.

"I'll bring up your bedroll," Dewar said.

"Thank you," she mumbled.

The area wasn't half as big as her bedroom in Dallas. Loose hay was scattered on the rough wooden floor, half a dozen hay bales were stacked against the south wall, and a lantern hung on the north wall.

"Does that work?" she asked.

"If it's got kerosene in it, it probably does, but you'd have to be careful. As dry as this hay and wood is, if you knocked it over the place could burn to the ground in a hurry," Dewar said.

He untied her bedroll and unfurled the whole thing with the expertise of a true cowboy. "There you go. I'll yell when Coosie has the food ready."

"Thanks again." She opened one of her saddlebags and removed a notebook and pen, sat down on a bale of hay, and started writing ideas.

If it rains, keep going. Bring whatever equipment you'll need because it's a real test to stay on the horse without even stopping for lunch. She scratched out the word *lunch* and wrote *dinner. They wouldn't call it lunch and dinner; it's dinner and supper on the trail. Check with the owner of the barn north of El Reno to*

*see if the television show could use it to sleep in one
night. Would make a wonderful filming area with the
horse stalls and the hayloft. Throw in a barn rat to test
the bravery of the ladies. And if it's raining or lightning
it'll make for more drama.*

She looked up at the rafters above her and scanned the
whole loft for rats. She'd only thought that a downtown
Dallas office was drama prone. Riding the trail with six
men brought about the real, honest-to-God stuff, not just
the watercooler kind of shit where someone was whining because they didn't get flowers or a call after that
one-night stand.

Put them out here in a *Survivor* world with a hundred
head of cattle, a rangy old bull who thought he was the
boss, and a donkey that was fast becoming her personal
sidekick. Take away their laptops, mirrors, makeup,
Prada shoes, power suits, and their cell phones and after
a month, ask them how much that watercooler gossip
was worth.

Haley carefully put her notes back into the saddlebag
and removed a whole new set of clothing. She tugged
her wet boots off and set them to one side, hopefully
to dry before morning, hung her wet socks over a hay
bale, and peeled out of her jeans, shirt, and underwear,
spreading them out flat so they'd dry. Then she removed
her washcloth from the baggy and opened the window in
the big doors and held it out to soak up enough rainwater
to wash.

Goose bumps popped up on her body from the tips of
her toes to her scalp, but she could endure the cold long
enough to cleanse her body before she put on clean clothing. It took a while to wash, rinse, clean the washcloth,

and re-dress, but the warm feeling afterwards was well worth the time. If it hadn't been so damned cold and there hadn't been six men in the barn, she would have taken a rain shower. She threw back the saddlebag flap and took out her notes.

If it rains, have the women on the trail take showers in the rain. It'll make wonderful footage but remember to be discreet. This will be a family show.

"Still writing?" Dewar's head popped up through the hole in the floor.

"Writing again. Supper ready?"

"It is. And you changed," he said.

"Yes, I did, and I'm not putting those wet boots back on tonight," she told him.

"We've got the chores done and we're in our dry sock feet also. Coosie is dipping up stew, and the boys are askin' for your portion if you don't want to eat."

Her stomach growled loud enough that he heard it. "Guess that means you aren't giving away your supper?"

"It does. Back down off my ladder and I'll come claim my food. You did say we were havin' doughnuts?"

He grinned.

She wished for the thousandth time that he wasn't a real cowboy. If only he was a Texan who liked boots and Stetsons, but went to work in an office every day, then she'd gladly go on and fall for him. But like he'd said, he'd never be content in the city.

The fire pit threw off heat that felt as good to her skin as the stew did to her insides. Six weeks before she would have bought a straitjacket for the person who said she'd be enjoying hot, thick beef stew ladled up over cold biscuits in a metal plate. But that night, as the rain continued to pour, the wind howled, and the cattle lowed in the corral on the other side of the thin wall, it was right next door to heaven.

She remembered an old Travis Tritt song, "It's a Great Day to Be Alive." He said that it was a goofy thing, but he had to say he was doing all right. He thought he'd make him some homemade soup, and even though there were hard times in the neighborhood, it was a great day to be alive.

Nothing could be goofier than sitting in an old horse barn eating plain stew and enjoying the experience. She glanced around as she ate and wondered if they appreciated a nice, warm barn as much as she did. Finn, the quiet O'Donnell with the haunted eyes, she had no doubt he'd have her back if she got into trouble. Heaven help a coyote or a bobcat that tried to harm her. Finn would shoot it without a second thought. Then there was Sawyer, the noisy boy of the lot. Always a smile and always had something to say, and that boy could sing like a Nashville star. Rhett was the rebel with his tattoo and blond ponytail. Buddy and Coosie were two overprotective uncles. That left Dewar sitting to her right. She slid a sidling glance toward him.

After only a week she already knew the six men better than she did the office staff she'd known for eight years. There was just something about the honest openness of the whole bunch that touched her heart and put a tear behind her eyelashes as she ate the stew and listened to them.

"That's a hell of a bull you picked out," Sawyer said.

"He showed leadership skills in the pasture, so I figured he'd do all right on the trail," Dewar said.

"Too bad he'll probably be ground up into hamburger," Finn said.

The little tear dried up instantly. "What are you saying?" Haley asked.

"What do you think happens to the cattle that go to Dodge City to the feedlots?" Dewar asked.

"I never thought about it," she answered.

"They fatten them up and sell them to slaughterhouses. The hamburger you buy in the grocery store was once a critter on four legs."

"And you'll let them take your lead bull with those gorgeous big horns and make steaks out of him? He's breed quality, Dewar. You can't let them kill him."

"If he was breeding quality, I wouldn't have made him walk over four hundred miles to a feedlot," Dewar argued.

"And my donkey?" she asked. "Is he going to be hamburger?"

"No, probably cat food," Sawyer teased.

She spun around to glare at him. "Eeyore is not for sale."

"How do you suppose you're going to get him back to your apartment in Dallas?" Dewar asked.

"How are you getting these horses back to Ringgold? Are we riding all the way back?" she asked.

"Hell, I hope not," Rhett said.

Coosie held up a hand. "There will be a semitruck to take the chuck wagon home and a horse trailer to take the horses back. If you want to keep Eeyore, then he can ride home with the horses."

"Thank you." She had no idea what on earth she'd do with a donkey in a fifth-floor apartment complex in

Dallas, but she'd cross that bridge later. Could she leave him in her parent's backyard?

Hell, no! That's an exclusive gated community that doesn't even allow clotheslines or the garage doors left open in the daytime. There's no way they'd let a donkey through the gates, even if he is better trained than some of the people who live there.

"Well, now that the fate of the donkey is taken care of and you two have stopped bickering, it is time to fry doughnuts," Coosie said.

Haley polished off the last of her stew and then mopped up the juice with another biscuit. She watched Coosie flop a mound of bread dough out on the make-shift worktable and roll it out. Using a sharp knife, he cut the dough into rectangles and laid them on a big flat pan. He carried it to the fire, dropped the pieces into the boiling grease a few at a time, flipped them when they floated, and took them out as soon as both sides were brown. Then he took them back to the table where he spooned a brown sugar glaze on the tops and motioned for Buddy to come get that trayful while he worked on the next one.

Haley groaned when she bit into the first maple long john. "God, this is wonderful. Why aren't you running a bakery?"

"Because you and Dewar would kill each other if I wasn't here to keep you apart." Coosie was already frying a second round. "Eat 'em up because they get tough when they're old."

"I'd eat bugs with this icing on them." Haley reached for her third one. "How come you haven't made these every night?"

"Same reason we don't have singin' and dancin' every night," Coosie said. "Put it down in your notes that after a week on the trail, the cookie should make doughnuts to keep up their morale."

"Cookie?" she asked.

"That's what the Chisholm Trail cook was called. Either that or Coosie, like me. I liked Coosie better than Cookie. It sounds tougher, don't you think? And he was almost as important as the trail boss. He was the dentist, the doctor, and the cook. So when you choose that person for your reality show, make sure he can do the job."

"I'll tell the directors to make sure of that," she said.

She and Dewar both reached for the last pastry on the tray at the same time. When their fingers touched, they jerked back and Buddy grabbed the long john.

"That'll teach the whole bunch of you not to fight." He laughed.

"You are mean!" Haley said.

"But I got the d-d-doughnut," he stuttered.

She slapped him on the shoulder. "Yes, you did, but you'd better eat it in a hurry or I'll bite your fingers tryin' to get at it."

Dewar got the first one of the second tray and it was so hot that he had to jiggle it between two hands while he ate. "I'd live like this forever if you'd make these once a week, Coosie."

"I imagine after a month of this life, you'll be ready for a soft bed and your old lifestyle and wouldn't be no doughnuts in the world that would put you back in the saddle during a cold rainstorm," Coosie told him. "How about you, Haley?"

"These are delicious, Coosie, but darlin', I wouldn't trade my soft bed and lifestyle for a hundred of them," she answered.

Chapter 10

IT WAS ALREADY DARK WHEN SHE TOLD THE GUYS good night and climbed the ladder to the loft. Since the very first day, she'd been without privacy unless she awoke early and snuck off to the creek for a quick washup or back behind the trees to take care of personal matters. And now that she had it, she hated to leave the guys behind.

She picked hay from her socks and slipped into her sleeping bag, all dry and warm even though it was still pouring rain outside. A loud clap of thunder startled her and she sat straight up. A rat the size of a possum ran across the end of her sleeping bag, through a hole down into the floor, and she could not stop shivering no matter how hard she tried.

"Scared you, did it?" Dewar asked.

"Where did you come from?" she gasped.

"That hole in the floor that the ladder comes up through." He pointed.

"I didn't hear you."

He chuckled and sat down on the edge of her tarp. "You was busy watchin' that rat run from you. Not too fond of them, are you?"

She slowly shook her head. He'd kissed her, danced with her, whispered sweet songs in her ear, and then avoided her like she had eaten garlic, wallowed in cow crap, and had the plague all rolled into one.

Now he was sitting beside her talking like they were old buddies.

"What is this, Dewar?"

He held out an ink pen. "You had this tucked behind your ear and dropped it when you left."

She reached out and took it, not surprised in the least by the effect his touch had on her skin. Anger and indifference did not stop physical attraction any more than it could make it happen if it wasn't there.

"Thank you. It's my favorite, but that's not what I'm talking about. You haven't said two words to me in three days. We had a kiss that lit up the sky like the Fourth of July and those dances that were fantastic, and then you avoided me like I was a skunk. And now out of the clear blue sky you bring my pen up here and want to talk?"

He reached over and pushed a strand of hair away from her cheek. "I'm lonely. The guys all were snoring by the time they zipped up their sleeping bags."

"So I'm going to be your pal when you are lonely and other than that I'm going to be treated like a leper?"

"Okay." He inhaled deeply. "I'm attracted to you. I've always had a thing for redheads and you are sexy as hell. But we both know this won't work, Haley. Like you said down there while we were eating, you wouldn't trade your way of life for anything, not even a hundred of those doughnuts. Me, I'd go back in time to a more primitive era if I could. I love ranching, cows, horses—all of it. I'd never be happy in the city. So starting something would be downright crazy."

She sat up and unzipped her sleeping bag. "I agree, Dewar. We aren't relationship material."

"Do I hear a *but*?"

She shook her head. "You don't hear a *but* or an *and* or even a *however*."

"Friends for the duration of the trip, then?"

She sat up and took two steps on her knees, stopping when she was close enough to feel the heat between them in the darkness. She would have liked to see the expression in his eyes when she reached out and un-snapped his shirt in one long popping motion. She did hear him gasp when she put both palms on his chest and tweaked his nipples with her thumbs.

"My turn. What is this, Haley?" he drawled.

She slung a leg over and sat in his lap. "This is what it is. What do you want it to be?"

～

He groaned and wrapped his arms around her. "I want it to be more than it can ever be."

"I bet you say that to all the sexy redheads that grab your attention," she whispered.

"I said I was attracted to redheads. Not that many have gotten my attention," he told her.

He buried his face in her neck, drinking in the soft-ness and the smell of perfumed soap. That much had him fully aroused and ready, but it had been a long time since he'd held a woman and he wanted the whole package, not just a slam-bam-thank-you-ma'am bout of sex.

He traced her jawline with his fingertips and bent to kiss her. Her lips were moist, her tongue ready to do a sizzling mating dance with his. Her kisses tasted like brown sugar and hot black coffee, the combination as heady and sensual as her full lips on his.

Haley tangled her hands in his dark hair and kept his mouth on hers for more and more. He could almost hear her body purring as he slipped his hand under her shirt and slowly ran it up her backbone.

He pulled her so close that her breasts were smashed against his chest, but the material of her shirt kept her from feeling the soft hair, so he leaned back, pulled it over her head, and tossed it toward her boots. He fumbled with the hooks on her black lacy bra and finally had it dangling to her sides as he massaged her back from the waist up.

"God, that feels so good." Her voice was throaty.

"Yes, it does," he whispered softly.

Chill bumps popped up under his hands.

"Cold?"

"Hot as hell," she said.

"Good, because I am too."

She reached between them and unbuckled his belt, unzipped his jeans, and ran her hand inside to grasp his erection.

He gasped. "Your hands are cold and that feels so good."

"So do your hands," she whispered.

He slipped a hand up under the wires of her bra and cupped a breast, brushing the nipple with his thumb until it hardened in anticipation.

"You are so damn sexy," he whispered.

"And you are so damn big." She squeezed.

"Think so?"

"Oh, yeah!"

The bra came off and dangled on her wrist because she wouldn't pull her hand out of his jeans.

"Dewar, this is getting uncomfortable. Take it all off and we'll use the sleeping bag for a cover."

She shifted to one side, put her bra on top of the saddle-bags, and wiggled free of her jeans and panties. She was about to remove her socks when he reached down and took them off for her, kissed each toe separately, then strung kisses from her feet to her belly button.

"God almighty!" she said.

"He must be because He made you," Dewar said when he left her midriff and kept traveling to her breasts.

She'd been kissed before. She'd had sex before, but nothing prepared her for the sheer fire that turned her into an absolute yearning hussy craving his hands to touch more and more.

———

Haley inhaled deeply and arched against him, wanting to get on with the show and yet not wanting the foreplay to end. She'd never known such searing heat and was afraid to let go of the feeling for fear it would never come around again. It was the most delicious thing she'd ever felt, and she looked forward to the ultimate climax. It could easily blow the top of her head right off if the foreplay was any indication of what the sex would be like.

He left her breasts and latched on to her lips, nibbling and teasing her soft mouth open and then starting another mating dance even more provocative than the last one. All the air escaped her lungs and they burned as hot as the rest of her body before she remembered to inhale again.

"Dewar, please," she said.

"Are you sure? I can play all night," he said.

"Darlin', I do not doubt your ability, but I'm about to turn into nothing but ashes. Please."

The first thrust took her from earth to the clouds. She floated higher with every rocking movement, arching tighter and tighter toward him, wrapping her legs around his midsection and purring deep in her throat with the pleasure of it all. He was multitalented, able to kiss, touch, and keep up a steady motion all at the same time. And each one drove her completely wild with desire.

"I've never felt like this," she gasped.

"Me either," he said.

His hands moved down her sides, touching places that she'd never even thought about being erogenous zones. Lord, after that night she'd be able to write erotic romance or at least an article for those women's magazines about the ways a man can please a woman.

The next thing she knew he'd lifted one of her hands and was licking the inside of her wrist. The thought was silly but the feeling was purely sexual, his tongue tickling the soft skin. Dammit! If a bracelet did that to a woman's wrist, there'd be a run on every jewelry store in the whole world.

She clasped her legs tighter. The thrusts became shorter and faster and she clamped on to his neck with her mouth to keep from screaming out. He slipped his hands under her bottom and with one final thrust, he collapsed on top of her with a throaty groan.

"My God!" he mumbled.

"Oh, yeah!" she whispered and straightened out her legs.

"That was... wow!" he said.

"I know," she agreed.

He held her tightly in his arms as he rolled to one side, her skin bringing the plastic-coated tarp with her. He deftly peeled it back and tucked the edge of the sleeping bag around them, wrapping them in a cocoon of pretty sparkly colors dancing around the hayloft.

"Am I dreaming or did we just have mind-boggling sex?" she asked.

"You ain't dreamin', darlin'," he assured her.

"Don't leave me, Dewar. Stay with me," she said.

"I will until I have to leave," he promised.

She snuggled close to his chest, using his arm for a pillow. The pretty colors faded and the afterglow dimmed. She shut her eyes and slept.

––––⁓––––

Dewar slept for a while but, when the rain stopped, he awoke. The clouds shifted and the moon hung in the loft window as if it were dangling from a string. Stars popped out around it like diamonds on black velvet.

Haley slept soundly, her snores more like the purrs of a baby kitten than the full-fledged man-snores sneaking up the ladder from the men below. Dewar was not a virgin. He'd had women. He'd had a few real relationships. But nothing had ever prepared him for what had happened between him and Haley. It must be what sent his older brother into a tailspin of love-drunk blues when he'd met the woman who was to be his future wife.

Things had worked out for Rye because Austin had inherited a watermelon farm right across from his ranch in Terral, Oklahoma. Haley didn't have a square foot of land anywhere near Ringgold, so she had no reason to stick around once the trip was finished. Besides, miracles weren't a dime a dozen and all four of his siblings had already dipped deeply into the miracle trough.

"Miracles are all used up and nobody left one for me," he whispered.

She muttered and turned over with her back to him. He carefully moved away from her and wrapped the sleeping bag more firmly around her body before he dressed. He crawled silently down the ladder and was sleeping in his own bed when Coosie started rattling pots and pans at daybreak.

"'Bout a noisy cook, aren't you?" Dewar grumbled.

"Time to rise and shine. Look at that sun peeking over the horizon out there. We got miles to go and cattle to herd. Kick them cowboys out of those warm beds and let's get started," Coosie said.

Dewar would have rather had a big king-sized bed with Haley curled up with him all day. Just thinking about the positions they could get into in a big bed like that aroused him to the aching stage. He sat up and made himself think about shoveling horse shit from the stalls at the ranch to take away the pain.

"Good morning!" Haley said from the ladder.

She wore the same jeans she'd thrown in the corner last night, but Dewar knew now what was underneath that shirt and those jeans. He knew how she tasted, what she felt like, and how she responded to his touch, and even shoveling horse shit didn't work.

"Good morning. Looks like the rain stopped," he said.

Finn sat up and kicked back his blanket. "Rain wasn't as uncomfortable as a sandstorm, but I'm not complainin' about it bein' over."

"Me either." Sawyer yawned. "What's for breakfast, Coosie, or do you want us to call you Cookie from now on?"

Coosie shook an egg turner at him. "I told you last night, Coosie sounds tougher than Cookie and that's what you will call me or you'll be eatin' a lot of burned food. We're havin' fried potatoes, ham, and scrambled eggs."

"Biscuits?" Rhett asked.

"Every morning that I can make them, that way we got part of dinner fixed at the same time," Coosie said.

"When we get back home, I'm callin' you D-d-d-dexter," Buddy said.

"At home I am Dexter. On the trail I'm Coosie."

Haley wandered through the back door and out to the corral where Eeyore came trotting right over to the corral fence. He stuck his big, long nose out and she scratched his ears.

Dewar jerked on his boots and said, "I'll check the cows."

He walked up behind her in time to hear her say, "They're not making fancy cat food out of you, sweetheart. I'll find a place to put you even if I have to pay a boarding fee."

"Guess you could board him at my horse ranch. I don't reckon he'd eat a lot of grass and he could protect the new colts from coyotes," Dewar said.

She almost spun around and kissed him hard right there in front of the cowboys and Eeyore and even that longhorn bull, but she checked herself just short of doing it. "What would this boarding fee cost me?"

"Not a thing. Like I said, he'll pay for his keep by

protecting my colts. I don't have time to mollycoddle him, so you'd have to come up to the ranch and see him if you want him to have attention."

"Oh?"

Dewar shrugged. "Or you can find a boarding place closer to your apartment in Dallas."

She whispered, "I reached for you this morning and was disappointed when you weren't there."

"Yeah, well, I expect there'll be fewer problems if the rest of the crew doesn't know."

"You are probably right, and thank you for offering to keep my donkey. I appreciate it and I'll be glad to pay you," she said.

He chuckled. "Just don't go chargin' me a fee for every coyote he kills."

Would a stubborn gray jackass be enough to make her learn to love his way of life? Maybe there was a miracle left in the trough for him after all and its name was Eeyore!

Chapter 11

THE SUN WAS OUT WHEN THEY TURNED THE COWS AND Eeyore out of the corral and started north again. Haley intended to act like the night never happened, but she couldn't keep the crazy grin off her face. Dewar did a much better job, but maybe she hadn't made him as hot as he did her.

"Well, that must have been a mean thought," Coosie said.

"What?" Her neck popped when she twisted it too fast to look at him. She hadn't even realized that she'd ridden up beside the wagon and wasn't riding behind it anymore.

"You were all smiles and your eyes were sparkly at whatever you were thinking about and then boom! Everything in your expression went black as sin. Looked like an angel that got kicked off a big old fluffy cloud in heaven and landed smack on the devil's pitchfork."

Haley smiled at the description. "That bad, huh?"

"Oh, yeah, must've been a terrible thought."

"It was, but it's gone now. Talk to me," she changed the subject.

"About what?" Coosie asked.

"Tell me about Dewar's brothers."

Coosie shook his head. "You want to know about Dewar's family, you ask him, not me. Or better yet, ask them."

"They aren't here right now," Haley said.

"Then you'd better talk to him about them."

"Please! Tell me about Rye. He's the oldest one in the family, right?"

Coosie nodded.

"And his wife is?"

"Her name is Austin and they have two kids. Rachel and Eddie Cash."

"So is she from Ringgold?"

"No."

Lord, getting Coosie to talk about the O'Donnells was worse than trying to pull hens' teeth, as Granny McKay used to say.

"And Dewar's momma and daddy raise horses?" she asked.

Any minute now he was going to get started and keep her entertained all the way up to dinnertime.

"That's right."

It damn sure wasn't that minute.

"If you want to know about Dewar, ask him, child," Coosie said.

"I'm not a child."

"You're acting like one. You want me to tell you all about his family when it ain't my place."

"That don't make me a child."

Coosie laughed. "No, it makes you a manipulative woman. And it doesn't become you. Let's talk about cows or donkeys or even what I'm cooking for supper because I'm not going to tell you the O'Donnell family stories."

"You are mean."

"Yep, I am." He chuckled. "I will tell you that when Rye went all love drunk over Austin that we all knew it before he did. Happens that way sometimes."

"Love drunk?" She frowned.

"That means that he couldn't think of another thing but her."

"Oh," Haley said flatly.

Was she love drunk? Did one fantastic night of sex in a hayloft with rain beating down on the tin roof make a person moonstruck? Was there a cure for it? Was Coosie telling her that he saw something between her and Dewar that morning?

Before Coosie could say anything else, Dewar rode up and motioned for Coosie to pull up reins. "We've got a railroad track up ahead about a quarter of a mile. I'm going to get the cattle across and then send Finn and Buddy back to help you with the wagon. Might need some muscle to get the wheels over the tracks."

"Guess we'll have a late dinner because you'll want to get the cattle a mile or so down the road from the track before we stop, right?"

"Why?" Haley asked.

"Because if a train comes past, the noise could spook them into a stampede." Dewar turned the horse around and rode away. His back reminded her of where her legs had been the night before and how broad and muscular it had been when she raked her nails down across his shoulders.

Dewar rode back toward the front of the herd without so much as a wink or a word.

"Austin makes watermelon wine," Coosie said out of the clear blue.

Finally! A statement without her having to pry it from his lips.

"Watermelon wine?"

"Yep, Austin uses her granny's recipes and has a pretty damn good business with her wine making."

"Is it good? I've never had watermelon wine before."

"You'll have to ask her to let you sample it sometime."

He didn't venture forth with anything else and she couldn't think of another question that he would answer, so she dropped back behind the wagon and herded a heifer that was trying to veer off to the west back into the herd. When they finally reached the train tracks, she pulled up reins and watched the process. Coosie crawled down off the buckboard and gave the reins to Finn, who led the horses from the front. Then Buddy and Coosie eased the front wheels over the first rails. Finn clucked his tongue and the horses moved a few feet. Coosie and Buddy pushed the wheels over the second rail and the back ones bumped up over the first one. It looked easy but that wagon was loaded and heavy. Haley had a whole new respect for both Coosie and Buddy by the time Coosie was back in the seat and they were rolling along again.

"Tell me about Dewar," she said. If she could catch him off guard, he might talk for a couple of hours.

"He's a real cowboy. Not a fake one. But I think you know that, Haley. You been lookin' at him like you could eat him up ever since that first day."

"I have not!" she declared.

Coosie chuckled down deep in his chest. "I see the cowboys are letting the cattle have a drink out of that farm pond up ahead. I reckon that's where we'll be stopping for dinner."

She carried her dinner to a fairly large-sized scrub oak beside the pond and sat down with her back to the tree bark. Haley had turned thirty the previous January. Her mother kept telling her that her clock was ticking loudly, but she hadn't even made up her mind to have children. That had been a very small part of the problem with Joel. He wanted one child to carry on the name and inherit all of the Anderson oil money but no more. Haley had wanted either two or none. Being raised alone was no fun.

Dewar sat down beside her. "Penny for your thoughts."

"They'd cost you far more than a penny."

"Dollar for your thoughts."

"I was thinking about babies."

Dewar choked on a sip of black coffee and sputtered until he finally got control. "You are on birth control, right?"

"Yes, I am."

He exhaled loudly. "I didn't even think to ask last night and I damn sure didn't bring condoms. I wasn't planning on…"

She giggled. "I hope not."

He cut his eyes around to glare at her. "What's that supposed to mean?"

"Look around you, Dewar. If you'd been plannin' on sex, it wouldn't have been with a woman. I'm glad you are straight."

Dewar chuckled. "Okay. But why were you thinking about babies?"

"I'm thirty and I'm trying to decide if I want any."

"I thought all women wanted kids."

"I'm not all women and I haven't made up my mind."

"Well, I want half a dozen. I don't care if they're boys, girls, or a mixture. I love my nieces and nephews and all my friends' kids and I want some of my own to love and spoil," Dewar said.

"And what happens when you find the right woman, fall in love, and can't live without her? She just wants to be in love with you and have this amazing life with you without kids," Haley asked.

Dewar didn't answer for five minutes. "I wouldn't fall in love with a woman like that."

"Why?"

"When I'm an old man, I want to put my grand-children or even my great-grandchildren in the wheel-barrow and give them a ride out to the horse stable. I want to put them on their pony and lead them around the corral before they're old enough to ride a big horse. And I want to see my wife's smile, her pretty eyes, or maybe her attitude in those kids. To know that she lives on and on in the children that our love produced and the life that we shared. That's why I want children."

One of those sentimental tears formed and found its way down her cheek. She wiped it away in the ruse of swiping at sweat. What Dewar said was the most beauti-ful thing she'd ever heard and touched her heart deeper than the most elegant poem in the world.

"So why don't you want children?"

"I didn't say I didn't want them. I just said I didn't know if I did."

Coosie yelled across the campsite, "Y'all about through jawin' over there? It's time to wash up your plates, and get a move on it if we're going to have sup-per at a decent time tonight."

Dewar stood up and held out a hand. She slipped hers in his and he pulled her up to her feet. For a minute, she thought he'd kiss her, but he just winked and walked away.

Chapter 12

HALEY HAD LOOKED FORWARD TO A BATH ALL DAY. Not just a pan of water, her washcloth, and soap, but a flowing creek where the water was at least semi-warm that she could sit down in and it would come up to her waist. Where she could wash her hair and shave her legs and wash out her dirty clothing.

But Kingfisher Creek was barely deep enough to water the cattle and entirely too muddy to take a bath in. Apache was unsaddled, brushed, and let loose with the cattle to graze on the spring grass in the pasture where they were camped. Coosie was fussing about with a pot of something that smelled wonderful. The rest of the crew had already unfurled their bedrolls and were stretched out with their hats over their eyes blocking the evening sun as it set in a glorious array of colors.

Haley's bedroll could wait until later. She pulled a few sheets from her diminishing roll of toilet paper and headed for the trees lining the creek with Eeyore trotting along beside her.

"Not just every man on the trail gets to go to the bathroom with me," she said to the donkey as she looked for a secluded spot and checked for spiders and snakes before she dropped her jeans.

Eeyore stood watch ten feet from her. The creek barely moved. Cows lined the edge with some wandering right out into the ankle-deep water.

Haley finished and joined Eeyore, slung an arm around his gray neck, and hugged him. "I wanted a bath tonight, but look at that water. Evidently they didn't get the rain we did or the creek would be running beautiful."

She sighed and scratched the donkey's ears before going back to camp. When she emerged from the trees the cowboys were gathering around the supper pot, plates in hand.

"What smells so good?" she asked.

"Quail that Rhett shot today with some dumplings and potatoes thrown in the pot," Coosie said. "We're gettin' thin on supplies so I'm going make a trip into Kingfisher soon as we eat. That's why I didn't unhitch the horses yet. Way I figure it is we're only about a mile from town and Walmart shouldn't be far from any place I come out on the road. If anyone is in need of something, make me a list."

Haley dipped up a plate full of food and sat down on her bed. "Thank you to whoever fixed my bedroll."

"That would be Dewar. That old donkey follows you around like a dog," Finn said with a motion toward the herd.

Eeyore hung back with the cows, but he kept a steady eye on Haley.

"Never had a dog, so I wouldn't know," she said.

"Never?" Sawyer asked.

"No, or cat or anything that had fur. Only time I got to play with kittens or puppies was when Momma took me to Louisiana to visit our relatives," Haley said between bites.

"Why?" Sawyer asked.

"Daddy is allergic to dogs, cats, hamsters, gerbils, and

any fur-bearing animal like horses and cows. He never went to Louisiana with us because all Momma's folks have animals. They live out of town near the bayou and there's dogs and cats everywhere on the sugar plantation."

Coosie hefted himself up into the buckboard. "Anyone got a list? I'm leavin' in two minutes. Soon as I get this rig turned around and headed west."

"I need a roll of toilet paper," Haley said.

Coosie was gracious enough not to chuckle.

"I want a big old fat chocolate candy bar. I'm not even particular about what kind. I didn't realize I was addicted to a candy bar in the middle of the afternoon until we started this trail run. Lord, I miss 'em," Rhett said.

Buddy raised his hand. "M-m-me too. I want a candy bar."

Coosie pulled a piece of paper from his pocket along with the stub of a pencil and wrote down those items. "TP for Haley. Candy for Rhett and Buddy. Anything else? Speak up or hold your peace because this is the last trip I'll make for a whole week."

Finn held up a hand like a little boy in kindergarten and said, "Twenty-two shorts. One box will do fine."

Coosie looked at Sawyer and then at Dewar.

"Beer. I want a beer. If you got two six-packs we could all have one and draw straws as to who got the others," Sawyer said.

Dewar wanted lots of things but they all had to do with Haley. A dozen bright red roses would be a good starter. "I expect you'd best just buy us all a candy bar and maybe toss in a big bag of pretzels or peanuts to go with the beer."

Coosie added that to his list and flicked the reins

against the horses, turning the wagon toward the west and the road leading into Kingfisher.

"Why is he taking the wagon? Couldn't he bring back what he needs on a packhorse?" Haley asked.

"It would take three or more packhorses. He might as well take the wagon and load it up to suit himself," Dewar explained.

Haley looked around at the five cowboys left. "Are y'all in agreement that you aren't running me off after ten days has passed?"

Dewar cut his dark green eyes around at her. "Why are you asking that?"

"Well, if I've proved up my ability to keep up then I'd like to get to know y'all better. I thought maybe we could swap stories."

"What if we ain't got stories?" Finn asked.

Haley looked him right in the blue eyes without blinking. "You are the quietest one of the bunch. You were in the army and you were a sniper. Your smile is tight and I wouldn't play poker with you. I'd say you've got stories."

Finn set his plate down. A grin turned up the corners of his mouth but just slightly. "You are driven by your job and demand the same dedication that you give. You've had a recent upset in your personal life that bleeds over into your business life and that confuses you."

Haley sputtered, "How did you know that?"

Finn shrugged. "I can read people too. And FYI, I wouldn't play poker with you, either."

"Speaking of playing poker," Sawyer said.

Haley threw up a hand. "Whoa! I want more out of psychoanalyst Finn here."

Finn finished his coffee and tossed the grounds left at the bottom onto the ground. "You're proving something to your father, probably that you can do this job even though he should have sent one of the men from the reality committee. You are mad at him for letting someone else sway his thinking. The only thing that would put a wedge between you two is something personal and it's got you in a twist. Which means it's probably got to do with a marriage, a divorce, or an engagement. How close am I? You've mentioned your mother being a force to deal with so it could be that your father had an affair and/or is thinking of leaving your mother. If you take her side then you could be without a job so you have to prove that you are mean and tough."

Haley's laughter echoed out through the flatlands and Eeyore trotted over to the edge of the campsite to make sure she was all right.

"So?" Dewar asked.

Using the back of her hand, she wiped at the tears, glad that she wasn't wearing her usual mascara and eyeliner. "Part right. Mostly wrong."

"Explain?" Dewar's eyebrows shot up.

"Okay, you did real well right up to the time you brought Momma into the picture, Finn. I was engaged to Joel, who wormed his way from a minor player in a Hollywood television station to my father's right-hand man. I thought I loved him and then one day about six months ago I woke up to realize that I didn't. So I ended it. Daddy did not like it one bit. I think Joel was relieved and had come to the same conclusion I had, so it was a friendly breakup, but he played up the part of the hurt ex to Daddy and now they are big buddies and I'm the one sleeping on the ground and taking baths in creeks."

Sawyer smiled. "And your momma?"

"She told me to follow my heart and not think I had to marry Joel to please my father. And honey, if Daddy ever cheats on Momma, he'd best get ready to like the feel of swamp water all around him. She's Cajun and she wouldn't bat an eye at giving him a water burial and putting a curse on his soul for all eternity to boot," Haley said.

"So which one are you like?" Sawyer asked.

"My mother," Haley said without a moment's hesitation.

"But you went into the media business like your father?"

"I like what I do. At least I did until Daddy hired Joel."

Dewar raised an eyebrow. "Why?"

"He's egotistical, thinks his way is the only way, and since he lived in Holly-damn-wood, he thinks he knows all about the film industry and I'm just a country bumpkin."

"That man ever seen you run off a bunch of cattle rustlers single-handed?" Finn asked.

Dewar chuckled.

She pointed a long, slender finger at him. "Don't you laugh at me. Wait until you meet him. You'll think I was being nice."

"What does your mother do?" Sawyer asked.

"My mother is the head of the accounting department for the whole conglomerate. She has a staff of dozens and her word is the law. If she says we don't buy out this company, Daddy listens to her. She's got a head for business. He's got a head for making a business work. They are a team."

"Hey, your donkey must've decided we weren't killing you. He's gone back to the cows." Sawyer pointed in that direction.

"You see what he did to that coyote? You'd better think twice before you attempt to kill me." She laughed. "Now it's your turn to get under the spotlight, Finn. What made you decide to be a sniper?"

"I didn't."

"Then who did?"

He sighed. "I don't like to talk about it."

Sawyer poked him on the arm. "It might do you some good."

"Okay," he inhaled deeply and started, "I've always been good with a gun." He hesitated for a full minute before he went on. "I went into the army right after high school to get away from the ranch. Swore when I saw the place in my rearview mirror that it was the last time I'd feed cattle in the cold winter or bale hay in the hot summertime. First time on the shooting range they thought I'd cheated some way so they pulled me out of my bunk in the middle of the night, gave me night vision glasses, and made me shoot again. I did even better and with that many soldiers surrounding me, they knew I didn't cheat."

"Go on," Sawyer said.

"So they put me through the psych evaluation and I passed that with no red flags. They put me with a spotter and trained us, sent us over there, and we did our jobs. Trouble is when you come home, it's still there and it's not easy to forget."

"Kind of like Haley having to work with Joel, right? When she goes back to Dallas, Joel will be there," Sawyer said.

"Little more intense," Finn said.

Haley refilled her coffee cup. "I'd say a hell of a lot more intense. What you're going through makes my situation look like a drop of rainwater in the ocean."

"Thank you," Finn said. "They gave us a target and we worked well together. We had a ninety-eight percent effective rate and they offered both of us the moon and half the stars to reenlist."

"What was his name?" Haley asked.

"Who? My spotter?"

"Yes, what was his name? Do you ever go see him and talk about what all went on?"

"No, and it wasn't a him. It was a her and her name is Callie."

"A girl?" Sawyer's eyes popped wide open.

Finn looked his way. "A pretty woman with black hair and dark brown eyes."

"Go on," Sawyer said.

"Nothing there. I was in love over there but not with her."

Dewar inched over closer to Haley and whispered, "Want to take a walk down to the river?"

"Not now. Finn needs to talk."

"Might as well tell the whole story," Dewar said.

Finn opened up and told them about the young woman he'd been in love with and how she'd refused to come to the States with him. "And then she was killed," he ended his story.

"I'm so sorry," Haley said sincerely.

Sawyer patted his shoulder. "Man, that's a tough break."

"Too bad, m-m-man," Buddy stammered.

Rhett slowly shook his head from side to side. "I'm sorry, Finn. That's just not right. Us O'Donnells are a passionate lot and when we fall, we fall hard and usually only one time in our life, so that's plain old wrong."

Finn's smile was still tight but his blue eyes weren't as haunted. "You know, it does help to talk about it."

"I want to know why you came back to ranching." Haley said.

"I needed peace," Finn told her.

They heard Coosie fussing at the horses and saw the light bobbing up and down from the dangling kerosene lantern long before the wagon pulled into the center of the campsite. Buddy jumped up to help Coosie unhitch the horses, brush them down, and turn them out to the thick green pasture.

Haley could hardly believe that more than two hours had passed since he left or that her heart felt lighter than it had in months. She wondered if talking lifted a brick from Finn's heart too. Did the cowboy group session do him as much good as it had done her? She hurried back to her bed, found her notebook, and started writing. The contestants should have one evening when they all bare their souls.

Dewar sat down beside her. "What are you doing?"

"I got an idea for the show."

"Is that all you think about?" he asked grumpily.

"Right now it's what I'm thinking about." She kept writing.

He got up and went over to the wagon where Coosie was untying the flap on one side. She should say something, but she had to get this brilliant idea on paper. It was one that she'd fight for when they started putting the details into the day-by-day planning for the show. Every contestant should keep one thing about themselves a total secret until the night they told all. Maybe at the halfway mark into the season would be a good time, so it would be a great teaser for all the viewers.

She looked up when she closed her book to find Buddy leaning on a tree only a few feet away.

"D-d-dewar likes you," Buddy said softly.

"I like him too. I like all of you. I didn't at first. I only liked you, Buddy, but now I do." She smiled.

"But D-d-dewar likes you m-m-more than that," he spit out in a hurry.

"What makes you think that?"

She'd gladly sit through the stammering for an answer.

"I just know," he said and walked away.

All of the cowboys, including Dewar, had gathered around the wagon. Coosie handed Sawyer a bag and Dewar a six-pack of beer. He pulled one free of the plastic tab and handed it to Rhett and kept on until there were only two left. Sawyer gave Dewar two candy bars from the bag and he tucked them into his shirt pocket.

He carried them over to Haley's bed and sat down on the tarp. "It's not champagne and roses, but here you go."

He pulled the tab on a beer and handed it to her, then fished the two candy bars from his pocket. "You choose first?"

They were both Snickers.

She deliberately brushed her fingers against his palm when she picked one up. "This is even better than champagne and roses. I never thought I'd look forward to beer and chocolate."

"Never miss the water till the well runs dry," he said.

"That is true in more than beer and candy." She tore into the candy with her teeth, afraid to set the beer down for fear she'd knock it over, and she wasn't wasting one drop.

Chapter 13

A QUARTER MOON HUNG IN THE SKY AND STARS DANCED all around it. The night air had turned chilly when the sun took its warmth away. They were in flat country again where trees were scarce and the land stretched out on all sides to meet the blue sky. A few scrub oaks and willow trees lined the edges of Little Turkey Creek, and the spring rains had given the creek enough water to make it flow along gently as if it had nowhere to go and all summer to get there. Even though it wasn't even lukewarm, after the guys were all asleep Haley stripped down naked and eased herself into the water.

She held her breath until she got used to the water and then quickly bathed, shaved her legs by the light of the moon, and washed her hair. She'd gotten out of the water, shivered as she dried off on her shirt, and had clean underwear in her hand when Eeyore snorted.

She jumped and tried to cover herself with the shirt.

Dewar chuckled and stepped out from behind a tree.

"Good evening. You are beautiful in the moonlight."

"How long have you been there?" she gasped.

"Let's just say your guard donkey didn't tell on me for a long time. It's pretty sexy watching a woman wash her hair in the creek by moonlight."

"Any woman or this woman?" she asked.

He pushed away from the tree and walked toward her. "I'm talking about you, Haley."

His voice was deep and husky, want and desire coating every word. He scooped her up like a bride and carried her back into the shadows of the trees, sat down on a quilt with her in his lap, and brushed her damp hair away from her neck. He started a string of hot, passionate kisses right below her earlobe. The next one landed on her eyelids, and then his lips found hers in a scorching clash that tightened every nerve in her body. The heat surrounding them warmed her quickly and fried every sane cell in her brain. One moment she was sitting on the quilt with Dewar kissing her, the next they were lying down. Like magic he flipped the edge of the quilt and they were encased in it like it was their own private cocoon.

The kisses grew hotter and more demanding as his hands roamed her body. She arched against him, felt stiff denim in places where she wanted bare skin, and without breaking the sizzling kisses, she undressed him. One shirt button at a time, taking time to run her hands over his broad muscular chest before she unbuckled his belt, unzipped his jeans, and released an erection that throbbed in her hand.

"Your hands feel like cool silk against me," he murmured in her ear.

"And this," she squeezed, "feels like hardened steel."

She flipped over until she was on top and then rose up, a knee on each side of his body. She guided him inside and then put a hand behind her on his thigh and started a slow motion.

"God, Haley…" he groaned.

"Even though I like the idea of you thinking I'm a god or goddess, I'm not, darlin'," she said.

His hands circled her waist. "Right now you couldn't convince me of that."

"Do you like this?" she asked.

"Oh, yeah," he said.

She bent forward to taste his lips and he rolled to one side with her, taking over the thrusts and turning up the heat level of the kisses from sizzling to searing. She opened her eyes and the stars were like lightning bugs dancing around the moon.

"Dewar, this is spectacular," she whispered.

"And so are you." His face had a full day's dark growth on it, just enough scruff to tickle her cheeks, and then he whispered, "You are so sexy I can't keep my eyes off you in the day and I dream about you at night."

No one, not even Joel, ever talked to her during sex. There was foreplay in varying degrees, sex, and then snoring. She shouldn't compare, especially in the middle of the most earth-shattering sex in the world, but she couldn't help it. She kept expecting the moon to fall right out there on the other side of Little Turkey Creek and the stars to follow, landing like the burnt-out ends of a Fourth of July sparkler on the water and sizzle as they drowned.

"Lord help us," she mumbled.

Dewar lowered his lips to hers. "I don't think even He has that much power."

The whole world, complete with thoughts, disappeared as she gave in to her body's needs and let desire take over. At the climax, the stars all exploded, creating the most gorgeous array of sparkle she'd ever seen.

So that's what it's supposed to be like, she thought as she fought to regain her breath.

"Age-old question? Was it good for you?" he gasped.

"Yes, sir, it was very good for me," she said.

Somehow he'd moved and she was snuggled up against him. It had to be the magic that had re-situated him without her even knowing.

He flipped the edges of the quilt up over her and hugged her tighter. "We can sleep for a while, but it would probably be best if they didn't…"

She covered his lips with her finger. "I understand, Dewar."

He kissed her fingertips and buried his face in her hair.

She shut her eyes but the beautiful warm feeling still lingered. Would it go away when they peeled back the quilt? That was the question on her mind as she dozed off into yet another dream about Dewar.

Eeyore nudged her back and awoke her an hour later. She quickly looked at the horizon to see if the first signs of the sun coming up heralded a new day and squirmed out of Dewar's tight embrace.

"Don't go," he whispered.

"I've got to go rinse off and get dressed or else I'm going to smell like sex all day." She giggled.

He threw the quilt back and carried her to the creek. He sat down with her in his lap with the cool water rushing around them. He bathed her with his hands and rinsed the soap away with double hands full of water.

"I've heard that a woman never believes anything a man says when he's having sex with her so I want to say something," Dewar whispered.

"And that would be?"

"You are so beautiful that you make my brain go to pure mush when you are near me. All I want to do is drag you off to a private place and make love to you all day and night," he said.

She was speechless. Nothing anyone had ever said to her had been so simple and yet the depth of his words were so romantic.

"Well?" he asked.

"Are you sure?"

He nodded. "I just don't know where it can possibly lead, though. We're almost half-done with the trail run and what happens when it's over?"

She kissed the scar on his cheek. "Let's don't borrow worry from tomorrow. We'll just enjoy the miracles of today."

He cupped her cheeks in his hands and brought her lips to his.

"You make me hot as hell," she panted when he broke the kiss.

"Yes, ma'am, and you do the same to me." He laced his fingers in hers and led her back to their cocoon quilt. He helped her get her clothing on before he quickly dressed himself.

One of a kind, she thought. *There will never be another real cowboy in your life, so you'd best cherish every single memory.*

She flipped the quilt over to the dry side and sat down, reluctant to let the night come to an end. He sat down beside her and ran his fingers through her hair, combing out the tangles gently. Then he deftly French braided it, weaving wildflowers he picked from around the quilt into the twists and turns.

Her scalp tingled at his slight touch and she would have given her job to a beggar on the street for a mirror to see what she looked like with Daisy Mae braids complete with wildflowers. When she looked at him, he smiled and she could see herself in his eyes. With no makeup, no fancy haircut, no high-dollar stiletto shoes, and not even a mist of exotic perfume, he thought she was wonderful. And it felt right.

———

Eeyore snorted and started back toward the camp.

"I know," Dewar told him. "We can't stay here until daybreak."

He'd never known a woman as strong, as determined, or as willful as Haley. Not even his red-haired sister, Colleen, and she was a force. But sitting there with her eyes shut, half her face in shadow, the other half illuminated by the moon, she looked soft and sweet. She had two sides, his Haley did.

My Haley! Whoa! Hold the horses. She's not mine and probably never will be. But there will never be another woman who'll make me feel as alive as this one.

Eeyore snorted again.

"Okay, I hear you. It's time, isn't it?" He moved away from Haley and together they gathered up her things.

She wrapped her arms around his neck and mumbled, "I'd rather stay here and be in trouble. I was dreaming about you when Eeyore woke me up."

"What was happening?" Dewar asked.

"If I tell it before breakfast it will come true and that's one dream I do not want to come true," she said.

"You are superstitious?"

"I come from Cajun background. Of course I'm superstitious. How long until daybreak?"

"Two hours tops. Coosie will be up puttering around in an hour."

"Where did you get this quilt?" she asked.

"Are you always full of questions?"

"Seems that's the way I'm made."

Dewar chuckled softly as they tiptoed toward the chuck wagon. "From the wagon. It's for emergencies. Guess last night was an emergency."

"I don't imagine he was thinking of using it for what we did," she said.

Eeyore followed them and waited a few yards back until Haley was safely tucked into her sleeping bag before he went back to the herd.

Dewar kissed her on the forehead. "I swear he is just like a dog."

"And he's going to have a wonderful life at your ranch," she said.

Would I have a wonderful life there or would I grow tired of it after the glow wore off? she wondered.

She was already sleeping when he returned from putting the quilt away. He laced his fingers under his neck and wondered what she'd been dreaming.

It seemed as if he'd just shut his eyes when he heard Coosie cussing the donkey.

He sat up and glanced over at Haley to see her rubbing the sleep from her eyes.

"What's happening with Eeyore?" She yawned.

"Damned critter, wakin' me up before I was ready to get up. Just come right up to my sleeping bag and commenced to snortin'. I thought a coyote was about to bite my ear damn near off, but it was just your jackass," Coosie fumed.

Dewar bit back the chuckle. The damned jackass was probably tattling about what he'd seen down at the creek the night before. Thank God Coosie didn't understand jackass lingo.

Haley stretched, reminding him of the old momma cat out in the horse stables when someone stroked her back. She wiggled the kinks out of her. "What makes everyone think that critter belongs to me alone? Evidently he loves you too, Coosie. He didn't want you to oversleep."

"First time he's ever done that and it better be the last. I swear he scared the hell out of me. First thing I see is his ugly nose when I open my eyes. My soul shot right out of my body like a bottle rocket."

"Did it go up or did it go down?" Haley giggled.

Coosie grumbled as he flopped the morning biscuits into the top part of the Dutch oven and hung it above the fire. "You are too damn happy to be just wakin' up. You must've had sweet dreams about somebody and I bet it wasn't that pesky jackass."

"No, it wasn't and yes, I did, and, no, I'm not telling what my dreams were. Is that sausage I smell?" Haley changed the subject.

"Yes, it is. Gravy can boil and thicken while the biscuits cook. Coffee is ready, so get up and help yourself. It looks like another rainy day so you'd best be gettin' the idea in your heads. I'd forgotten about the spring rains in this season." Coosie cocked his head to one side and drew his eyebrows down when he saw the flowers in her hair. "You goin' to a dance or something?"

Dewar caught the look Haley flashed him when she realized the flowers were still woven into her hair and graced her with his most brilliant smile.

Haley touched her braids. "No, just thought I'd put a little sunshine in your world this morning. You like my new hair decorations? Since we don't have a hairdresser out here, I had to make do with what was available. I had a bath in that creek last night after everyone was asleep."

"Bet the water was cold," Dewar whispered.

"Don't pay no attention to him," Coosie said. "He's always grumbling about something. That's the way of a trail boss. I think they look almighty fetching and it's nice to see a woman takin' care of herself. Just don't go braidin' flowers in that damn donkey's tail."

"Yes, sir." She whistled shrilly and Apache came trotting across the field to her side.

Sawyer sat up and grabbed his head. "That's a hell of a way to wake a man up. Reminds me of that damned alarm clock Momma sent to college with me. First time it went off I thought a freight train was coming right up the middle of my bed."

Finn rose up on an elbow. "Is it morning? What's our job assignment today, Callie?"

Rhett dug his fists into his eyes. "Sorry, cousin. You're in a different type of war zone this morning. That wasn't a bomb threat. It was Haley whistling for Apache. I didn't know a girl could do that."

Dewar looked up to see Stallone trotting across the field. "You told me you couldn't whistle."

"I did not. You asked me if I could whistle and I asked you why I needed to. I didn't want to or need to until now."

Dewar frowned. "Well, it looks like she's done called all the horses up. You been holdin' out on us, girl. Where'd you learn to whistle like that?"

"From my Cajun cousins," she said with a shrug.

"What else did those wild cousins teach you?"

Haley rubbed her hands across Apache's back and removed one small burr, tested again, and tossed the saddle blanket across him before hefting the saddle up. "They taught me lots of things, but I'm not telling all my secrets. Apache and Eeyore and I keep some things real close to our hearts."

Chapter 14

THE MORNING HADN'T STARTED OFF LIKE FRIDAY THE thirteenth. Haley had awakened to the sounds of Coosie cooking, the fresh aroma of sausage frying, coffee boiling in the blue granite pot, and Eeyore standing under the tree a few feet away, keeping watch over her.

She had looked across six feet of spring grass to see Dewar propped up on one elbow, a grin on his face, and the sun rising behind him. In the soft golden glare she barely caught the slow wink, but the blush that it caused burned her cheeks. Dewar could relay more with a wink than some men could with a candlelit dinner for two in a fancy restaurant.

Breakfast was over, dishes put away, and the campfire stomped out when she whistled for Apache. And that's when the day went to hell in a handbasket. She barely got him saddled when the dark clouds rolled over the beautiful sunrise and thunder rolled over in the southwest. Lightning streaked through the sky, and Eeyore snorted disapproval.

"It's all right, boy. We've ridden in rain before and it didn't melt either of us. I don't suppose it will this time, either, but nothing says we have to like it, does it?"

She finished saddling Apache, put her slicker on, and settled into the saddle just as the first big drops of rain splattered against the yellow slicker.

"Worked the sore out yet?" Coosie asked from the wagon.

"Pretty much. After two weeks, it should be gone, shouldn't it?" she asked.

A loud clap of thunder made them both duck their heads.

Coosie laughed out loud. "That one parted my hair."

Haley looked at his big round bald head and cracked up. "I think it scared any hair from growing for the next ten years."

"It faded the red in yours." Coosie still laughed.

She stuck her tongue out at him. "Since it's raining and you made fun of my hair, you have to talk to me to atone for your sins."

"Well, it is redder when the sun shines on it and sayin' so is not sinnin', young lady. So start with the questions and we might find something I'll talk about, but then again, maybe we won't. I'm not telling you stories that you should be asking Dewar about. And besides, you should be riding up front with him and talking to him all day anyway, not lingerin' back here with the old chuck wagon driver. I bet his feelings are hurt."

"Why would you say that?" she asked.

"Well, honey, any old cowboy worth his salt can see that you two got a thing for each other and if you really want to hear about him and his family, then spur that horse and ride up there beside him where you belong."

The cows moved slowly in the rain and nothing the cowboys could do hurried them. The old longhorn bull decided the pace would slow down and by damn, it did.

After the first few huge drops, the rain settled into a soft drizzle. The lightning passed over them, taking the thunder with it to rattle its way toward the northwest. From what Dewar said that morning, they were moving southeast of Enid that day.

Enid was one of those towns that had been settled during the Oklahoma Land Run long after the railroads had put an end to cattle runs, but since it was so flat, she could well imagine that during the cattle trail days there would have been a store sitting just over there. It would sell basics for the cowboys like tobacco and whiskey.

Mercy, but she was glad that Dewar didn't chew. She hated the smell of any kind of tobacco. A good shot of whiskey on his breath wouldn't be bad, but her nose snarled at the idea of chewing tobacco.

"Well, why aren't you up there with him?" Coosie asked.

"I haven't been invited," she said.

"Can't see a headstrong redhead like you waitin' for a formal invitation. Guess I was all wrong about you havin' a backbone and bein' sassy."

"No you weren't," Haley said quickly.

Coosie chuckled. "I heard that you got Finn to open up some the other night. That's a good thing. Man needs to talk that kind of experience out of his soul or else it will eat him alive and leave nothing but a hollow shell of a man."

"He's a good man and he was doing his job. I think losing that woman that he loved was as hard as the job," she said.

"Probably so. So did Sawyer tell you all about his woman or did Rhett talk about that sissified ponytail?"

"They did not," she said.

Coosie smiled. "Well, then you better get your

questions lined out for another night if you want to get inside them boys' heads and get them to talkin'."

"Come on, Coosie. You talk to me. I'm bored."

"Girl, you'd best not be sayin' that too loud out here on the cattle drive. It'll come back around and bite you on the butt real quick."

"What does that mean?"

"It means that you'll have your hands so full you'll wish for a nice quiet ride without no problems. You ever think about gettin' a cowboy for Christmas, Haley?"

She was glad for the slicker hood and hoped it covered the burning crimson filling her cheeks. "Of course not. What would I do with a cowboy?"

How in the devil did he tell so little and suddenly have a dozen questions of his own, anyway?

"Any chance when you sit on Santa's knee this year that's what you'll be thinkin' about?" he asked.

"Christmas and Santa are both a long way down the road, Coosie," she said.

"Well, it'll sneak right up on you so you'd best be thinking about it. And while you are thinkin', if you ain't goin' to do right by him, don't do at all. He's a good man. I'd hate to be in your shoes if you break his heart."

"What's that supposed to mean?"

"Just what I said. His sisters are pretty damn protective of him and I'd sooner face off with a mountain lion as those two, especially if they gang up on you. Gemma rode broncs professionally and Colleen used to crawl up on a bull's back pretty often."

"You tryin' to scare me?"

"I'm just telling you that you need to be careful. Toyin' with a cowboy's heart can get yours broken in the process."

Haley let that sink in as she rode along. What would Dewar's wife be like? Would his sisters like her or would they hate her?

A brilliant shade of jealousy replaced the scarlet in her cheeks. The idea of another woman touching him, holding him, making wild love with him, or worse yet—the very thought of him braiding flowers into another woman's hair—that was just plumb downright damn wrong.

An airplane flew over their heads and she was amazed for a few minutes until she remembered that she really did live in the modern world where jet airplanes and even little biplanes like the one right above them existed. The days of the cattle trail drives from southern Texas to the railroad in Kansas had long since passed and what they were doing was just the forerunner of a reality television show.

An old Western movie on television had started this whole thing. When the credits rolled after the show, she wondered if modern-day cowboys could stand up under the pressure of the primitive lifestyle. Would they be able to give up the real world where airplanes took people all the way across the country in half a day? Could they learn to live in a world where traveling involved going thirteen to fifteen miles in a day that lasted from sunup to sunset?

The rain stopped as suddenly as it started and the sun popped out from behind the clouds. She shed her slicker and handed it off to Coosie without getting out of the saddle. And the next phase of Friday the thirteenth went into effect.

The airplane had made her homesick for her office, for her friends, and for her family. She wished she was on it and headed back to Dallas to a civilized lifestyle. She sighed and argued with herself. One old gray jackass did not a ranch make! She and Dewar were as different as night and day in the real world. Sure, they were hotter than a wildfire coming across the plains when it came to sex; however, wildfires burned down everything in their pathway and then died. Even knowing that, it was still impossible to walk away from Dewar and too late to stop her stupid heart from wanting him.

Dark clouds covered the sun and lightning zipped through the sky. The thunder was loud and shrill and the cows picked up their step to a faster walk. Eeyore brought up the rear, urging the cattle along with his snorts. A slow drizzle started again and another flash of lightning ripped through the sky and met the ground in a crackling pop.

The hair on Haley's neck tingled and her toes felt heavy. She rode up beside the wagon and Coosie handed her the slicker without a word. She donned it but left the hood back, waiting for the rain.

Dewar and Stallone looked like a black and yellow flash as he rode hell bent for leather from riding point to the rear of the drive. "Everyone all right back here?"

"We're fine," Coosie said. "That last lightning gave us a start. Landed right over... huh, oh!" he said.

Dewar's eyes went in the direction that Coosie pointed.

"Did it hit a cow?" Haley asked.

Dewar slid out of the saddle.

He pulled Haley off the horse and held her. "It hit your donkey. Thank God it didn't hit you."

She heard him loud and clear.

Eeyore was dead.

But the only thing that registered was the hoarseness in his voice when he said he was glad it hadn't hit her.

"We can't leave him in the pasture like that." Her voice sounded like it came from a long dark tunnel.

"It's raining," Dewar said.

"But we can't..." she started.

Dewar stepped back. "You are right. We'll dig a hole and bury Eeyore for you, Haley."

Buddy took first shift with the shovel and dug down about six inches in the mud before handing it off to Coosie, who hit dry dirt in another inch. After that Finn took over and the rain completely stopped and the sun came out again. He removed his slicker and put his back into the work. By the time Dewar took the last turn, the hole was big enough for the six of them to push Eeyore's body off into it. But when they pushed the donkey gave a heave and rolled his eyes around trying to focus.

"Holy shit!" Haley spit out.

"He was stunned! Anyone think to touch him to see if he was breathing?" Coosie asked.

All six of them shook their heads. Haley dropped down beside the donkey and hugged him tightly. "You aren't dead. It must've hit close to you and didn't actually get you."

Dewar picked up the shovel. "We should've thought to check him for burns at least. Looks like we've got a hole to fill in."

"I'm glad he's alive," Buddy said.

"Don't get too happy just yet. He hasn't stood up yet and bad as I hate to be the party pooper here, we might have to put him down," Finn said.

Haley hugged him tighter. "Come on, Eeyore. You

were shocked but it didn't kill you. Stand up. Somebody go find a coyote so he'll have a reason to stand up."

The donkey quivered from nose to tail, but he didn't make an attempt to get up on his legs.

"You rascal. If you don't stand up I swear I won't even let them put you in that hole. I'll let the damned coyotes gather round your body and eat you for supper. That would be poetic justice for you not even trying," Haley yelled at him.

Eeyore flopped his head into her lap and snorted.

"No sass. I mean it. Either you get your little gray ass up or the coyotes can have you," she said.

He held his head up.

Dewar chuckled.

"I'm not carrying you. You've got four feet and you can walk on them," she said.

Eeyore's eyes stopped rolling around and he looked up at her.

Dewar swore he saw the damned jackass smile.

"Get up!" Haley yelled at him.

Eeyore heaved a huge sigh and stood up, wobbled for a few seconds, then shook it all off with one terrific shudder. He walked around the hole that had been dug for him and then trotted to the cattle and started nibbling on the green grass.

"Ain't never seen nothing like that before," Rhett said.

Buddy took the shovel from Dewar and filled in the grave, mounding it up and patting the dirt when he was done.

"I knew she could m-m-make him get up," he stammered.

"Well, thank you for the vote of confidence." Haley smiled at him.

"Okay, now let's have some dinner since we're stopped and then we'll herd the cattle into the next pasture. Do you remember if we stay on this man's land until supper, Dewar?" Coosie asked.

"Yes, we do. We'll be camping at the far end of it near a farm pond. Hopefully it won't be a muddy mess," Dewar answered.

"Sun's coming out. Got all afternoon to dry up," Finn said.

Dewar and Haley lingered behind. Haley watched Eeyore to be sure he was all right, and Dewar watched Haley.

"I heard that lightning hit the ground and I was terrified that it had hit you," Dewar whispered.

Haley wanted to hug him but she couldn't. "It was pretty fierce and Coosie and I heard the sizzle, but it didn't even shock me."

"You were lucky. Another fifteen or twenty feet and it would have been you lying out there on the ground instead of that donkey."

Haley cocked her head to one side. "Never thought of that."

Chapter 15

AT FIRST HALEY THOUGHT THE NOISE WAS A HELICOPTER and looked up to see if she could spot it in the sky. Then she figured it was a train rumbling off in the distance, but it kept getting louder instead of fainter.

Then the cows all looked toward the west where the sun was putting on a spectacular show of color as it finished its day's work. And Eeyore trotted right into the middle of the campsite to stand at her side.

She slung an arm around his neck and scratched his ear. "It's not thunder, old boy. You aren't going to get zapped again."

"He's going to be a psychotic mess when it really storms again. Think he'll need to see a jackass therapist?" Finn asked.

"If he does I'll damn well hire one for him. You want me to make an appointment for you?" she asked.

Sawyer held up his coffee cup. "Touché, Haley."

"Hey, you don't get to say that. You haven't bared your soul yet. It's not until you tell us all your story like Finn did that you get to say something like that," she told him.

"Touchy tonight, are we?" Rhett asked.

"Eeyore took the lightning hit for me. If we'd been a few feet on up the road it would have hit me and believe me, if it had I would have been real bitchy tonight instead of just mildly irritable," she answered. "What is that noise anyway?"

"Four-wheeler," Coosie said.

He'd barely gotten the words out of his mouth when the machine came to a stop beside the chuck wagon and two people crawled off. A short round man wearing bibbed overalls and a red plaid shirt, a baseball cap, and work boots, and a woman three inches taller than him in jeans, a chambray shirt, baseball hat with a salt-and-pepper-colored ponytail hanging out the hole in the back, and cowboy boots.

"Hello, the camp," the man yelled.

"He's always wanted to say that. He's jealous as hell that he's not doing a trip like this and he just had to come out here and see y'all." The woman's voice had the gravel qualities of a long-time smoker.

"If I hadn't lost my mind and married you forty years ago I'd be on a run like this," he grumbled.

"If you hadn't lost your mind and married me, you'd be a dead fool instead of a common old breathing and snorting fool."

Coosie laughed. "Y'all must be the ones who own this land. Thanks for letting us stop here for the night and for the grass our cows are eating. Come on into the camp. Would you like a cup of coffee? I'm Coosie, the cook. This is Dewar, the trail boss." He pointed as he introduced all the crew.

"I'm Raymond and this is my mouthy wife, Loretta," the man said.

"He's full of shit, but I love him," Loretta cackled. She looked over at Haley and said, "I thought me and you might ride back to the house and leave these men to their war stories."

Loretta edged closer and whispered just for Haley's

ears, "I got a bathroom with a tub and some sweet-smellin' bubble bath."

Raymond had found a seat next to Buddy and all the men were already deep in conversation about the lay of the land, cattle, and how much further it was to Dodge City. Haley tied up fresh jeans and underwear in a clean shirt and followed Loretta to the four-wheeler with Eeyore right beside her the whole time.

"Looks like that donkey has taken a liking to you," Loretta said.

"He got stunned by lightning today, but he's always been my buddy," Haley answered.

"They're like that. Take up with one person pretty often. We got one on the place to take care of the coyotes. He don't like me a bit, but he follows Raymond around like a puppy. Here, I'll get on first and you sit right behind me. It's not a whole lot different than ridin' a motorcycle except it's got four wheels and don't go near as damn fast. Raymond won't let me have a motorcycle anymore since I wrecked the last one. It was his fault. He made me so damn mad when he flirted with that big-boobed motorcycle momma at a rally that I couldn't even see the damned road," Loretta said.

"When did that happen?" Haley asked.

"Oh, 'bout six months ago," Loretta cackled. "I just barely got this thing broke in. Hang on tight. We'll see how fast it can go."

Five minutes later they parked in front of a big, white two-story house with a wide front porch. Two dogs came out to greet them and a couple of gray cats peered through the railing posts. Haley felt like she'd been thrown headfirst through time, air, and space.

God almighty, Loretta must have souped-up that four-wheeler to make it run like a bat out of hell.

"Little faster than a horse, ain't it?" Loretta crawled off the machine and led the way to the house. "Don't mind the critters. They're nosy, but they don't bite. I've got a loaf of fresh baked bread, some whipped honey, and a chocolate sheet cake for us to nibble on while we talk, but first you're having a long bath."

"What did you do to that machine?" Haley asked.

"I tinkered around with it a little. Scared the hell out of Raymond first time he rode back behind me. That'll teach him to flirt with big-boobed women. Course, now he won't let me drive if we go on it together," she cackled. "Now you scoot on upstairs and get a bath and then we're going to visit."

"Thank you," Haley said as she looked around the wide foyer just inside the front door. An antique buffet with a mirror back sat to her left and a staircase went up at a steep angle on her right. Ahead she saw a door that opened into a living room with lots of big windows facing the east. She imagined sitting on the big, deep blue sofa with a cup of coffee in the morning and watching the sun come up.

Loretta waved her arm in a circle, taking in the whole place. "I was born in this house. My folks gave it to me and Raymond when we married and they moved into a smaller house. We raised all six of our kids here. They're all married and scattered seven ways to Sunday now, but they come home for Thanksgiving every year. Bathroom is at the top of the stairs. You go on and don't rush. Use anything you need and if you want something you don't see holler right loud and I'll try to find it for you. I'll get the coffee going. Bet you haven't had a real bath since you left Texas two weeks ago," Loretta said.

Haley shook her head. "Creeks and rivers. This is a treat, ma'am."

Loretta shook her finger. "Don't you be calling me ma'am. You're about the same age as my youngest daughter and I'd shudder to think about her out on the trail with all those cowboys, not a woman to talk to, hell, not even a cell phone, and no bathroom. Go enjoy and don't hurry a bit. Raymond will talk those men's ears plumb off and fuss because we didn't stay gone any longer."

Haley smiled. "I can vouch for the fact there's not a big-boobed woman out there."

"I wouldn't have left him if there had been." Loretta laughed.

Haley started water running in a deep claw-foot bathtub, poured in some vanilla bubble bath that had been sitting on the vanity, and quickly undressed. She sunk down into the water while it was still only a few inches deep and rolled the kinks from her neck. And then she settled her neck on the sloped back and shut her eyes in deep appreciation. Never again would she take something as simple as a bubble bath for granted, or for that matter, warm water.

The shampoo smelled like vanilla beans and lathered up so well in her hair that she almost swooned. After her bath, she wrapped a big fluffy yellow towel around her body and sat on a vanity stool while she towel dried her hair. She finger combed it and was about to get dressed when Loretta's voice floated up the stairs.

"Go ahead and help yourself to the hair dryer and

curling iron if you want to. It and the hair spray are under the vanity."

"Thank you," Haley yelled through the door.

Electricity. Curling irons. Prune skin. A steamy mirror above the vanity. She'd died and gone to heaven and while she was there she fully well intended to float among the clouds as long as she could. Forty minutes later when she came out of the bathroom, she felt like a brand new woman.

"Come on in here and pull up a chair," Loretta yelled when she heard the stairs creaking.

Haley followed her voice through the door at the back of the foyer into a great room that housed the living area, kitchen, and dining room, separated by rugs on the hardwood floor and a bar in the kitchen.

"This is beautiful," she said.

"It didn't always look like this. We had it redone after the kids all left home so we'd have more room when they came back. Raymond says kids are like momma cats. They leave for a while but they come back and bring more with them." She laughed and motioned toward the bar where she was sitting. "Pull up a bar stool and we'll have some coffee. Tell me, do you think your reality girls would like a stopover at my house since it'll be about halfway through their journey? I'd be glad to offer it for them to have a bath."

Haley's mind went into overdrive. "What a wonderful idea, Loretta. We could have a contest and the one that got the most points could get to go inside a real house and a real bathroom. But," she leaned forward and whispered, "do you think Raymond will flirt with them?"

Loretta giggled. "Probably, but that'll give us a good

reason to argue. You do know what happens after you argue, don't you?"

Haley tilted her head to one side. "What?"

"You have the best damn sex in the world."

High color filled Haley's cheeks.

"And that's even better than a fast four-wheeler," Loretta said. "Now let's talk about those cowboys. Good Lord above, I haven't ever seen such handsome fellows in my life. Well, four of them are sexier than movie stars. That big old cook fellow kind of scares me and the one that stutters is sweet, but he's not sexy."

"Coosie and Buddy are sweethearts, but you're right, they aren't sexy." Haley smeared whipped honey on a slice of home-baked bread and bit into it. "Oh my God, this is so good."

"Thank you. Momma taught me to make bread. I bet it's the trail boss that's took your eye, right? Those other three are pretty boys, but he's about your age and rugged enough to make a woman's under-britches crawl down to her ankles, right?"

Haley laughed. "He really is that sexy and he has a heart of gold and is so kind it's scary."

"Did you know him before you agreed to go on this crazy trail drive with him?"

"Oh, no! I thought the whole thing was an April Fools' joke and that my daddy, who owns the company that's sponsoring this thing, would tell me to come back home and we'd have this big laugh. I guess Dewar thought his brother was playing a joke on him too. Only it wasn't a joke and here we are two weeks into the trip."

"So you live in the city? You did know how to ride a horse, didn't you?"

"I live in Dallas and I'd taken a few lessons in riding way back when I was in college, so I knew how to get into the saddle, but that's about all. I swear, I have calluses on my butt and it was so sore those first few days that I thought I'd die."

Loretta nodded. "I can well imagine. You didn't whine or let on though, did you?"

Haley shook her head. "Not one time. They weren't about to know that I had trouble keeping up."

Loretta slapped her thigh. "Good girl. Give 'em hell out there for all us women. The reality show won't be near as interesting to me as your story because those women will have each other to whine and bitch to and you're out there making the path for them to go on all by yourself."

"Well, thank you." Haley grinned.

"Just stating the hard, cold facts. Here, have some more of this bread. You going back to Dallas when this is over or are you and the trail boss going to reach an agreement? Y'all would make some pretty babies together and there could be a reality show after first one showing what happened to the contestants."

Haley almost choked on the next bite. "I'm going home. But he's going to keep my donkey and let me come visit him when I have time."

"Well, praise the Lord, it's not over when it's over, is it?"

"Time will tell." Haley sipped coffee. "This is so nice. Getting to talk to a woman and having coffee out of a glass mug in a real kitchen."

"Things we take for granted, right?" Loretta said. "How'd you come by that donkey? Did it start out the trip with you?"

Haley shook her head and told the story of the mountain lion or bobcat in the shadows, stalking the herd.

"That the first time y'all was alone out there?"

Haley nodded. "Yes, it was."

"And the last time?" Loretta asked.

Haley blushed scarlet.

Loretta laughed. "You don't have to answer that. I'm prying and putting my nose in where it has no business. We live so far out that I only get to visit with other women on Sunday at church and on Wednesday nights at our quilting bee. And besides all that, after raisin' up six daughters, I'm just naturally nosy."

Haley didn't even think before she spoke. "You remind me of my mother. Sometimes I tell her something before I even realize it's out of my mouth. But no, it's not the last time we've been alone."

"You ever see that movie *Steel Magnolias*?" Loretta asked.

"It's one of my favorites."

"Remember the scene in the beauty shop when she says she and her boyfriend did things to frighten the fish?" Loretta's green eyes glittered.

"I do and yes, ma'am, we have. But it's a secret. I sure wouldn't tell it in the beauty shop."

"Neither will I or at the quilting bee, but I will tell that he looked at you all wistful when we left the camp, like he was afraid you'd never come back. And that when we returned, his eyes lit up like a Christmas tree," Loretta said.

"That's embellishing the story," Haley said.

"No, darlin', that's telling it just like it happened. You didn't see his eyes but I did and when we get back, if they don't light up, I'll give you that four-wheeler back there and make Raymond walk home. And you can scare the shit out of him when you take him for a ride." Loretta laughed again.

Chapter 16

DEWAR HEARD THE FOUR-WHEELER BEFORE IT APPEARED out of the darkness. He'd met with Raymond when he made the trip and got permissions to go across various landowners' property, but he didn't know the man or his wife well enough to let Haley go off into the night with Loretta.

Raymond fit right into the group around the fire and after hearing about poor old Eeyore's plight that day, they told stories about lightning hitting the flat land and bouncing like big round balls. Dewar laughed at the right times and nodded when he was supposed to, but his ears kept tuned to the sounds of the darkness. And he could have shouted when he heard the four-wheeler.

For a minute he thought Loretta was going to drive that damn machine right into the fire, but then it came to a long, greasy stop, sending tufts of grass flying every which way. He'd been away from machinery too long or else that was the four-wheeler from hell.

"Loretta likes to tinker with engines. I don't know what she did to that thing but it'll go like a scalded hound set loose from the devil's furnace. She must like you, little lady, to let you drive it," Raymond said.

That was when Dewar realized that Haley was driving and Loretta was behind her. Did she have a death wish, driving like that?

"If I buy one of these, will you come to Dallas and soup it up for me?" Haley asked Loretta.

"Damn straight I will. You got my phone number, darlin'. Just give me a call and we'll do some business."

Haley's hair had been let down from its normal braids and shined like copper pennies when she drew close to the fire. Something wonderfully exotic wafted out from her that smelled good enough to eat. His eyes caught hers and she dropped one eyelid in a sexy, slow wink that instantly aroused him. Loretta whispered something and Haley smiled.

All Dewar caught was something about Raymond not having to walk home when she laid a hand on Raymond's shoulder. "I know you done talked these fellows deaf and they have to get back on the trail to-morrow morning, so we'd best go on home."

Raymond put his hand over hers. "And I bet that pretty filly has listened to you asking questions until her head is plumb spinning."

"You got that right, and she's going to see about letting one or more of the reality show girls come to our house for a bath while you spend some time with the guys."

Sawyer chuckled. "You mean the men on the reality show don't get a bath?"

Loretta shook her head. "They can have a bath if they want in any creek betwixt Texas and Dodge City. Boys don't set such store by a real bathtub as girls do. I raised six girls. I know."

"You going to jaw with these boys all night or take me home?" Raymond teased.

"I'll drive," Loretta said.

Raymond stood up and slung an arm around her shoulders. "If you are, I'm walkin'. You done broke me from suckin' eggs the last time I rode behind you, woman."

They were still bantering back and forth when they roared out into the night and the last thing Dewar heard was Loretta's giggles fading away.

Dewar patted the place next to him in the grass. "Guess you had a real bath?"

Haley smiled. "Yes, I did. And I had several thick slices of homemade bread with something she called whipped honey. It looked like butter and tasted like honey."

"Haven't had that in years," Coosie said. "My momma used to whip up real butter with honey until it looked like whipped cream and we'd slather it on fresh-out-of-the-oven yeast bread."

Sawyer slapped a hand on his belly and moaned, "I'm jealous."

"You should be. It was delicious, but it was nothing like that warm bath in a big old claw-foot tub," she teased. "Now I understand why the cowboys who ran the cattle back in history couldn't wait to get to Dodge City and into a bathhouse."

"They still got bathhouses?" Rhett asked.

"They call them hotels now, cousin," Finn told him.

"And we're staying at least one night in them, right?" Sawyer looked at Dewar.

He held up two fingers. "If it all goes as planned, we'll get into Dodge City sometime up in the evening. We'll help load up the horses and get the chuck wagon ready to go home and then we'll check into a hotel. There are several so you can choose wherever you want to stay. Next day you can do some sightseeing or sleep all day in a real bed. It's up to you. The day after that, Haley's dad is sending a charter plane for us. It will take us to the little municipal airport over in Nocona and there'll be family there to take us back to the ranch."

"And from there we'll split seven ways to Sunday," Sawyer said.

Dewar nodded, not wanting to think about that day when seven ways to Sunday meant that Haley would be going to Dallas. Not even Eeyore could hold her attention long enough to come back to the tiny town of Ringgold very many times.

"It's past our bedtime, folks, even for Friday night," Coosie said.

"Guess we'll have music tomorrow night." Finn yawned.

Dewar took off his boots and set them beside his bed. He laced his fingers under his neck and inhaled deeply. In among the night smells of wet dirt and grass and cows, the night breezes carried to his nose that sweet, erotic aroma of whatever Haley used in her bath. He shut his eyes and a vision appeared of her in a claw-foot tub like his grandparents still had in their house. Her red hair was piled up on her head with strands sneaking out to stick to the wet skin on her neck. In the picture, she crooked her forefinger, motioning for him to join her.

Eeyore's snort erased the image in an instant. His eyes popped open to see the donkey standing between his bedroll and Haley's. Her eyes were wide open and a smile played at the corners of her full mouth as she stared at him from under the donkey's belly.

"Guess he missed me," she whispered.

Dewar propped up on an elbow. "I missed you too. It wasn't smart of me to let you go off like that."

"I'm a big girl. You didn't let me do anything. I went because I wanted to go with Loretta and I'm glad I did. It gave me another idea for the reality show. And that woman is a hoot, Dewar. I want to grow up and be just like her."

"A ranchin' woman?" he whispered.

"No, but a sassy one," Haley said.

"Honey, you already got sassiness cornered," Dewar said.

Eeyore moved back to the herd, taking time to sniff the air several times on the way.

"Guess he's going to trust me with you. I really was worried when you rode off with her," Dewar said. "But not as worried as I was when I thought you were going to drive that four-wheeler right through the fire."

"Honey, it goes so fast that if I had, it wouldn't have even left the smell of smoke on my boots. Truth is, I didn't apply the brakes soon enough and the four-wheeler slid the last several yards. Don't worry about me, Dewar. I can read people pretty good. Loretta and Raymond are not serial killers," Haley said. "And Eeyore doesn't trust you with me. He's just telling both of us that he's mad because strangers came into our midst and didn't even take time to pet him. He's a selfish jackass, not totally unlike some two-legged ones I've known."

"Don't be slinging mud," Dewar said.

"Don't be taking what I said personally. When I call you a selfish jackass, you'll know I'm talking to you because I will use your name," she told him.

He sat up, pushed back his cover, and in two long strides was beside her. She threw back her cover and he slipped into her bedroll, wrapping her into a fierce embrace.

"You smell like heaven and sin all mixed up together. I've wanted to touch you ever since you came back," he whispered.

He ran his fingers through her hair, picking up strands of the silky red tresses and letting them float from his hands to fan out around her face.

"So soft," he murmured.

Haley curled up in Dewar's arms, fitting there as if she was born just for that purpose. His hands in her hair set every nerve in her body to purring. His breath on her neck as he whispered something about sin and heaven all bound up together ignited a fire that liquefied desire into an aching pool.

She ran a finger down the faint white scar, following his cheekbone across the deep cleft in his chin and up the other side to his hair. She clasped a fistful of his near-black hair and brought his lips to hers in a hard kiss. Tongue met tongue in a hunger that left them both breathless.

"We can't, not here," she whispered.

"I want you, Haley, but…" He let the sentence dangle as he sought out her lips again.

When he broke away that time, she touched the scar again. "I know. There's not even a mesquite tree in this godforsaken flat land. And you can bet either Eeyore or Coosie would wake up if we breathed much harder than we're doing now."

"Tomorrow night we're camping beside Pond Creek and there's a thick stand of trees. I'll be miserable all day with wanting you," he said.

She stifled a giggle. "I'll be plumb bitchy after all this making out. I feel like a sophomore in high school."

She wiggled away from him just slightly so that she

could see one Dewar and not a blurry vision of two. "Where did you get the scar anyway?"

"Talking won't make us less hot for each other."

"I know, but it'll take my mind off stripping you down naked and having wild passionate sex with you like a couple of rats in heat inside an old wool sock, like Mark Chesnutt sings about," she whispered.

He kissed her on the tip of the nose. "Does feel kind of like that all stuffed under this sleeping bag together, doesn't it?"

"The scar?" Anything to get her mind off what she wanted to do.

"I was fifteen and busting a bronc out in the corral. It was an offspring of Glorious Danny Boy and a particularly mean old mare. She had good lines but she was a real bitch of a horse. Anyway, this stud got his momma's meanness and it took a long time to saddle break him. He'd bucked me off several times, but I could feel that he was getting tired, so I went back one more time. I broke him and we were riding around the corral when he gave one more buck just to test my mettle. I wasn't ready for it and I flipped out over the corral fence and hit a post my dad had tossed a bunch of barbed wire around. The wire cut my cheek."

"How many stitches, and was your momma mad?"

Dewar kissed her on the forehead. "Twelve and how'd you know that Momma was so mad at Daddy for putting that barbed wire there that she didn't speak to him for a week?"

"If it had been my handsome son, I wouldn't have spoken to him for a month. Did the girls all come around and feel sorry for you?"

"Hell, no! They all thought Rye was the handsome one anyway and Raylen was the cute one. I was the one with the scar down my cheek," he said.

She planted twelve soft kisses down his jawline. "One for each stitch. And honey, I've met Raylen. He is cute. Don't know about Rye, but there's not a cowboy on the earth more handsome or sexier than you."

"Ah, shucks, ma'am." He grinned.

"Don't give me that line. I figure you've run from women so long that you've got the race down to an art. You ever plan on slowing down and letting one catch you?" she asked.

"Do you?" he answered her question with one of his own.

"No, I don't plan on a woman catching me." She giggled softly.

Coosie mumbled something in his sleep. Buddy's and Rhett's snores sounded like they'd synchronized them with their watches before they shut their eyes. Haley held her breath, expecting one or all of them to wake up and catch Dewar in her bed.

"Scared you when Coosie talked in his sleep, didn't it?" Dewar whispered.

She nodded.

"To answer your question honestly, I'd love to settle down and raise a bunch of kids on the horse ranch, Haley, but a woman would have to take me like I am, just a cowboy with no thoughts of changing me into something I'm not."

Anyone who had a crazy notion of changing Dewar had cow shit for brains. And he was much, much more than just a cowboy. He was a real cowboy: honest, loving, and kind, and it would be so easy to fall in love with him. But that would mean instant heartache. He'd just stated his position and it couldn't be clearer. He wanted a ranching woman.

Haley was a businesswoman. She thrived on deadlines and researching great stories. She could not even begin to imagine herself living on a horse ranch in a place like Ringgold with a population of a hundred people. After the blistering hot sex played out, she'd be miserable.

But who says it would ever play out? that niggling argumentative voice in her head asked.

Nothing lasted forever. Not even the most fantastic sex she'd ever known could last that long. After a few years the flames would wan and then she'd be dissatisfied. Dewar O'Donnell deserved better than she could ever give him.

He sighed and relaxed.

Her head rested on his shoulder. His right arm was thrown around her, his fingers splayed out on her back. She thought she'd shut her eyes just for a minute and then she'd wake him up and send him back to his own bedroll.

When she opened them again, Eeyore was standing at the foot of her bed staring at her with those big old soulful eyes. Coosie crumbled sausage into the heavy iron skillet. Sawyer let out a shrill whistle for his horse. Finn and Rhett looked toward her as they rubbed the sleep from their eyes with their fists.

She sucked in a lung full of air and slowly turned over to wake Dewar, but he wasn't there. All the air left her lungs in a whoosh as she sat up and looked around to see him beside the back of the chuck wagon. His sleeping bag was already rolled up and he had a cup of coffee in his hands.

"You going to wake up this morning," he asked, "or did that bath turn you into a pansy? Boys, you think she'd better ride in the buckboard with Coosie today? That bath might have made her too much of a lady to sit in a saddle all day."

"For a bath in a deep tub, I'd ride on the buckboard," Finn said.

She stuck her tongue out at Dewar. "All that bath did was wash away the grit. I can ride better and longer now than any of you. Buckboard, my ass!"

"Your ass is not riding on the buckboard with me. I don't care if he did get shocked by lightning." Coosie cracked up at his own joke.

"Well, I see you are all in a fine mood," Sawyer said. "While we're talking about asses, your ass killed another coyote last night. It's layin' out there by the fence on the far side of the herd. I'm surprised he didn't wake you up snorting and bragging about it."

"I'd say that Haley has a good ass, then." Dewar laughed with Coosie.

"Oh, hush!" She stomped her feet down into her boots and went to pour a cup of coffee. "I'd like to know what exactly y'all talked about with Raymond that's got you so spicy this morning."

"Good coon hunters don't tell what they talk about," Finn said. "What did you and Loretta talk about?"

"Good women don't repeat what's said in the kitchen over a cup of coffee and fresh bread from the oven," she shot right back at him.

Chapter 17

CLOUDS HAD COME AND GONE ALL DAY. THE LAND WAS still flat and Haley wondered if there was really a creek up ahead with a dense growth of trees on the side. They crossed a railroad track that day and had to cut their way through two fences that Finn and Rhett hung back to fix. They herded the cattle through one gate, up a section line road a quarter of a mile, and through another gate on the other side, with the old longhorn bull arguing with them every step of the way.

Trees beckoned to her from the far horizon in the middle of the afternoon and she sent up a silent prayer that the clouds wouldn't bring rain. All she'd thought about from the time Dewar teased her at breakfast that morning was how much she wanted to feel his naked body next to hers and she was plumb giddy with desire.

When they finally reached Pond Creek, the sun was slipping toward the western horizon where freshly plowed dirt met the blue sky. The cows eagerly lined up for a drink in the creek. It wasn't decent enough for bathing, but it was lined with beautiful willow and scrub oak trees that would serve as bedroom walls later that evening.

Coosie and Buddy started a fire and hung a pot of stew on the andirons to boil while they set about taking stock of what was in the wagon and what they needed. The rest of the crew unsaddled horses, brushed them good, rolled out bedding, and stretched their tired bodies out for a few minutes before supper.

Sexual electricity practically crackled and popped in the short distance between Haley and Dewar's bedrolls. She sat with her knees drawn up, arms wrapped around them, and her braids falling forward. He lay flat on his back, one arm thrown over his eyes to block the sun, the other arm tucked up under his neck. It all looked innocent, but the energy surrounding them was alive with anticipation.

"Coosie going to town tonight?" Haley asked.

"No, tomorrow night. We'll be close to Medford and there's a store there where he can refill the water barrel and replenish supplies. You got time to think about what you want him to bring back for you."

"I need another notepad. Think he could get that and mail my ideas?"

"Sure," Dewar said. "What kind of ideas did you come up with today?"

When she didn't answer he moved the arm over his eyes and sat up. He looked across the grass and she winked.

That one gesture sent his imagination into overdrive.

"Oh, really?" he whispered.

"Yes, sir!" she said.

"Really what?" Sawyer asked.

"We are really having some music tonight. Dewar promised me a dance or two," Haley said quickly.

"That's not fair. He monopolized your time last weekend. I think we should all get to dance with you while he plays the guitar tonight," Sawyer said.

"Sounds like fun to me. I get to dance all night that

way. How about a dance for each of you and then Dewar can dance the last one while you play the guitar and sing?"

"But that's not fair, Haley," Finn protested.

"Why?"

"Everyone knows that the cowboy who gets the last dance takes the girl home," he answered.

"Well, he sure won't have far to take me, will he? It might be ten feet back there to my bedroll. I don't reckon there's much unfair about that," she said.

Buddy laughed. "That's v-v-very funny. I d-d-don't care who you are!"

"And that is Larry the Cable Guy's line from his comedy routines," Finn said.

"You like that?" Haley asked.

"Love it. You ever watch it?"

"Yes, but I liked Ron White better," she said.

"Aha! I knew you had a bit of redneck in you," Dewar teased.

"Not a single drop, but I love his stories. Especially the one about them throwing him out of the bar. You ever been tossed out of a bar?" She looked at Dewar.

Finn threw back his head and laughed.

"What?" Dewar looked innocent.

"I could tell Haley here some things that would make Ron White's tales look kind of mild," Rhett said.

Dewar felt the hot flush climbing up his neck and was glad that the sun was throwing red rays across the land.

"Coon hunters and cowboys don't tell everything they know," he said.

"I wasn't going to tell. I was just going to make Haley wonder if the right cowboy was going to walk her all ten feet from the dance floor to her bedroll to-night," Rhett said.

"I expect supper is ready if you boys will stop flirting with Haley," Coosie said.

"Yes, daddy," Sawyer said and then roared.

Coosie drew down his eyebrows. "Boy, you don't want me to be your daddy."

Sawyer sobered right up. "You got that right. And I'm hungry, so let's eat."

After supper, Dewar got the guitar out of the wagon and tuned it. He started off the music with an old Waylon Jennings tune, "Mommas Don't Let Your Babies Grow Up to Be Cowboys."

She listened to the lyrics as Buddy sashayed her around the campfire and Joel came to her mind. Dewar sang about not letting babies grow up to pick guitars and drive them old trucks. He said to let them be doctors and lawyers and such. Joel fell into the *such* pile since he wasn't a doctor or a lawyer. He didn't pick a guitar and he damn sure wouldn't be caught dead in an old pickup truck. And he didn't do a thing to set her heart to racing like Dewar O'Donnell did. Not once in their engage-ment did she think about him all day long, imagine him sitting at his desk with no clothes on, or even have a desire to sneak into his office and kiss him so hard that it made her knees weak.

Looking back at the engagement and her relationship with Joel, it would have been a business marriage. Both of them were a force in the office, but in the bedroom it had been more than a little bit blah.

She and Dewar were exact opposites. She wouldn't know a ten-year-old nag from a show horse and yet in the bedroom, they were one hot couple. She inhaled deeply just thinking about the way one of his kisses could set her whole body to quivering.

She danced with Coosie next to a Marty Stuart song, "The Whiskey Ain't Workin' Anymore." The timbre of Dewar's tone changed as he sang about needing one good honky-tonk angel to turn his life around and that he was looking for a woman warm and willing.

Well, she was damn sure warm and willing but she'd never be a honky-tonk angel, so if that's what Dewar was looking for, then she was left out in the cold. Hell's bells, not just out in the cold, but standing in six feet of snow in her underpants.

But I could be a honky-tonk angel in the bedroom, couldn't I? That's where Dewar and I seem to have the strongest connection, so I could be anything in the bedroom. Warm and willing or hotter'n hell and crawling his frame every night. Maybe even at noon and before supper, too.

She scolded herself for even thinking such a thing could work as she danced with each of the O'Donnell cousins. Then Dewar handed the guitar off to Sawyer who, with a twinkle in his eye, sang "Do You Wanna Go to Heaven," a T.G. Sheppard song from years before.

Dewar held her tightly to his chest, one arm out, the other on the small of her back, as Sawyer sang about taking his hand and he'd lead her to heaven. Haley remembered the comment Dewar had made the night before about her being heaven and sin all twisted up together. Well, she damn well felt the same about him as they danced.

Sawyer went straight into "Heaven's Just a Sin

Away." By the time he finished, Haley had adopted the song as her theme song for the whole trip. The lyrics said that heaven was just a sin away and that way down deep inside she knew it was all wrong but the devil had her and she thought he was going to win.

"Is it? Is heaven just a sin away?" Dewar asked as he swung her out and brought her back in a flourish.

"Oh, yeah!" she said.

When the song ended he bowed and she curtsied. He crooked his arm and he led her to her bedroll.

"Thank you for a lovely evening, Miz Haley," he said loud enough for everyone to hear.

"Ah, look at 'em," Finn said. "Their first date and he's walked her right up to the door."

"No good-night kiss?" Rhett teased.

"She didn't even invite him in for a drink." Sawyer loosened the strings on the guitar and handed it to Coosie to put away.

"First dates don't warrant drinks or kisses." She kicked off her boots and sat down. "Good night, boys. Thanks for a lovely evening."

~~~

She waited until the guys were all asleep before she put her boots back on and headed toward the creek. She'd barely gotten away from the campground when two strong arms reached out and picked her up. Her feet dangled as Dewar's lips found hers, cold from the night air, but it only took one kiss to warm them right up to the blistering stage.

"I thought they'd never go to sleep and then I was afraid you had," he whispered.

He carried her to the quilt laid beneath an oak tree. A bouquet of wildflowers lay in the middle, the stems tied together with a piece of twine from the chuck wagon. When he sat down with her she picked them up and held them close.

"Flowers on a first date?" she said.

"You deserve orchids, m'lady."

"But I love these. They're wild, like you."

"I'm the good son. Rye and Raylen were the wild ones."

She cupped his face with her hands and kissed him with so much raw passion that he gasped. "Darlin', I flat out do not believe you."

"You just ain't been with a real cowboy before," he argued.

She kissed him again. "I'm not here to talk, cowboy."

"You're the wild one." He laughed.

"Not me. I'm the hardworking, career-minded businesswoman."

"Must be the full moon then," he said as he unbuttoned her shirt, taking time to taste her skin and smell the remnants of that exotic stuff she'd bathed in the night before.

"Lord, Dewar, you are making me crazy!" She tugged at his buttons until she could wiggle next to his chest and her bare skin could touch his. "I've thought of this all day long and prayed that the clouds would go away and it wouldn't rain."

"You never did it in the rain?"

She looked up at him and shook her head. "No, I have not. But if it *had* rained I would be losing my rain virginity right now because I couldn't go another day without this."

She pushed the bouquet to the side of the quilt and started humming the song about heaven being just a sin away as she removed the rest of her clothing and then started on his, tugging his boots off, then peeling his jeans down from his slim hips.

"Heaven and sin," he murmured.

She stretched out on top of him so she could feel skin against skin all over her body. "Yes, darlin', and I'm about to have a taste of both."

Most of the time Dewar liked the foreplay almost as much as he liked the sex, but that night he had to have her and she was more than ready for him by the time they were both undressed.

He rolled on top of her and with a powerful thrust began a rocking motion that carried them both away to either heaven, sin, or a nice big helping of each. She arched against him and dug her nails into his back. Her imagination had not disappointed her as she reached first one climax and then two before he finally buried his face in her neck and said her name in a hoarse drawl.

"Dear Lord," she gasped.

"Must have been heaven and not sin," he said hoarsely.

He rolled to one side and she nestled down into the crook of his arm. He kissed her eyelids, her forehead, and then her mouth with all the fervor of the first time and then began to tease her body back into a frenzy for the second round.

She nipped at his earlobe. "And now sin."

"Oh, yes, and now sin," he agreed as she rolled over on top of him and settled him inside her for round two.

"Do you want to go to heaven?" she singsonged as she began a steady rhythm.

"Just lead me on," he whispered.

"Can you feel that feeling?" she sang softly.

His smile parted the clouds above them.

It was the smile, she decided right there in the middle of the hottest sex in the world. Dewar's smile could melt steel. Lord, it could make a nun throw her habit in the trash and offer herself to him. And Haley was not a nun or made of steel!

Chapter 18

COOSIE AND BUDDY DROVE OFF TOWARD MEDFORD FOR supplies, but before they left, Dewar untied bamboo poles from the side of the wagon. Haley didn't need a manual to know what the poles were for and what they'd use for bait to go fishing. She'd been fishing dozens of times with her cousins in the Bayou Teche.

"We need grasshoppers or worms?" Sawyer said.

Finn grabbed the shovel and an empty bean can. Sawyer and Rhett followed him to the edge of the pond where the soil was moist.

"Do only guys get to fish?" Haley asked.

Dewar handed her a pole. "I got five poles ready. You can't write home about it if you don't do it. You can use it for your reality show."

"Never thought of the reality contestants fishing," she said.

"We're up for supper tonight," Sawyer said. "While you were gone Coosie said so."

Haley looked over at Dewar.

He shrugged and headed toward the back side of the pond. "We're supposed to catch the fish, have them cleaned and ready to fry when Coosie and Buddy get back."

Cattle lazed in the green pasture, some chewing their cud, others just happy to be still after fifteen miles of constant walking. They'd drunk from the pond on the south side and left a muddy mess in their wake. However, on the north side there was a grassy bank and a couple of big shade trees where the fishermen could be comfortable.

"What do you expect to catch?" She kept in step with Dewar even though his stride was longer.

"Farmers stock their ponds with bass and catfish. I got permission when I scouted the area to fish in this pond and for your reality team to do the same if you want to use that for a scene."

The whole episode played out in her mind. The contestants would be tired and cranky and fishing would be a good diversion at the end of a long day.

Finn turned over a shovel full of dirt and Sawyer fetched several big fat earthworms. Rhett removed one, laced it on the hook at the end of the line on his bamboo pole, and tossed it out into the water.

"Contest don't start until we all got a line in the water," Finn said.

"What contest?" Haley asked.

When Dewar graced her with his brightest smile, her imagination kicked into overtime. She could see the two of them skinny-dipping, body parts slithering around each other until the whole pond began to boil like a hot tub.

"Haley, are you listening?" Dewar asked.

"I'm sorry. My mind was on those worms," she lied.

"I said that the contest is whoever catches the most fish doesn't have to cook tonight," he said.

"Coosie isn't going to cook?" she asked.

"No, Coosie is bringing back a pound of bologna in the ice chest. If we don't have supper ready then we eat sandwiches. If we do, then we have the sandwiches tomorrow at lunchtime."

"And what happens to the person who catches the least fish?" she asked.

"That person cleans and cooks the fish. What do you think of that for your reality show?" Dewar answered.

"Sounds like a wonderful episode." Inwardly she shivered. She had no idea how to clean a fish or cook one and she'd never live it down if she admitted it.

"You know how to bait a hook?" Dewar asked.

"Of course," she said.

Dewar passed the can of worms to her. She reached in and grabbed one at the same time Eeyore let out a bray right behind her. She jumped, dropped the worm, and it began to work its way right back into the soft earth.

"Oh no you don't!" She grabbed it by the tail and pulled it right back out without popping it in half.

"Good work," Dewar said.

She held it tightly in her hand while she unwrapped the line from around the pole. Then she laced the worm onto the hook.

She watched Dewar flip the hook out into the water and she followed his lead. When he sat down on the grassy bank, she did the same.

"Now we wait," he said.

"For what?"

"See those little red bobbers out there?"

She nodded. Of course she saw the bobbers. It wasn't her first fishing rodeo.

"When one goes under, jerk it up and hope there's a fish on the end."

Finn and Sawyer put at least two dozen more worms

into the can, baited their hooks, and found a place to sit. No one said a word for the longest time and Haley could hardly endure the silence.

"You sure there's fish in here?" she asked.

"Shhhh," all four of them hissed.

"Don't talk. It'll scare them away," Dewar whispered.

Haley had been fishing with her cousins too many times to remember and the Louisiana Bayou folks took their fishing very, very serious. Yet, not a one of them said anything about scaring fish with talk. It must be a cowboy thing.

"You are shittin' me?" she whispered.

"Shhhh," was all she got for an answer.

She glanced sideways at Dewar, who had leaned back against a rock and had his eyes shut. No way could he watch the red bobble that way. He must be depending on feeling the rod jerk. She looked back at the red ball dancing around on the water and unfocused her eyes. It became a beach ball that she and Dewar were batting around on the white sands of a Florida beach.

He wore a cute little Speedo. No, that wasn't right. Dewar wasn't a Speedo man; he was a cut-off jeans man and they rode low on his hips. She could see that fine line of dark hair that feathered from his chest downward inside the band of the jeans. That wasn't right either. It was her visual so she could imagine him anyway she wanted, even naked. His tight little rear end was white against a bronzed chest, and the scar on his jawline was a faint white line against his rugged face. They tossed the beach ball to the side and waded out into the cool salty gulf water and he picked her up like a bride, her naked skin resting against his chest. She'd never made love in the ocean before, but she was damn sure game to give it a try.

Her fishing pole jumped in her hands and the beautiful vision disappeared. She refocused on the bobble as it went completely under the water and she had to grip the pole to keep from losing it. This would be a great episode for the reality show.

"I got one. What do I do?" she yelled.

"Jerk him in," Dewar told her without opening his eyes. "Getting one to bite isn't the trick. Bringing him to land is what's important. And stop talking!"

She shot him a dirty look. She reached out with one hand and grabbed the line, then laid the pole on the ground. Inch by inch she worked until the head of the fish showed. She continued to pull until the big catfish was flopping around on the ground at Dewar's feet.

"Your hands all right?" he asked.

She looked down at the bright red lines crisscrossing her palms. They weren't bleeding, but she'd be really glad for her gloves the next day because they'd be sore.

"Now what does a silent cowboy do?" she whispered.

"Looks like it'll weight about eight pounds," Dewar said. "If you want to let it stand at that and hope no one beats your record, then you take a nap. But first you take that hook out of his mouth and sink a bigger one through him that's tied up to that stake over there and toss him back."

"Like this?" She deftly removed the hook she'd caught the fish on, secured another one into his gills, and put him back in the water.

"You been holdin' out on me. This is not your first fishin' trip," he said.

"You didn't ask me if I'd been fishing, did you?"

He handed her the can of worms and sat back down. "What else are you keeping secrets about?"

"Shhhh," she said loudly. "You'll scare the fish."

Sawyer caught three small bass. Rhett caught three sun perch. Finn brought in a catfish, but it was smaller than Haley's, and Dewar caught a bass, but it, too, wasn't as big as Haley's fish.

She was glad that she didn't have to scale or cook the fish. Her granny had insisted that she clean a sun perch one time but she'd done such a poor job that there had only been one single bite of fish worth frying when she was finished.

"Who caught the biggest fish?" Buddy hopped off the wagon seat with the agility of a teenager.

Haley held up her hand. "I did and I talked and they all shushed me and I still got the biggest one, so I don't believe that bullshit about not talking because it will scare them."

Buddy laughed. "Smells v-v-very good!"

"Yes, it does," Haley said. She'd watched Dewar prepare the cornmeal that Coosie had left behind. He'd added salt, pepper, and a teaspoon of red cayenne pepper.

"And since Haley caught the biggest fish, she gets the first pieces that float." Dewar used long-handled tongs and fetched out several pieces that came to the top of the cast-iron cauldron filled with boiling oil. He laid them on a plate and handed it to Haley.

She broke a piece off and blew on it before she popped it into her mouth. "H-h-hot!" she said.

"Fire or pepper?" Coosie asked.

"Both," she gasped.

He popped the ring from the top of a can of Coors beer and handed it to her. "That's why I brought cold beer. Hot fish, hush puppies, and cold beer. Don't get no better than that."

Haley sipped the beer but she disagreed with his last statement. The fish was good but that beach scene she'd played out in her mind was a helluva lot better.

———※———

Her intentions were to stay awake until everyone went to sleep that night and then slip into bed with Dewar. Even if there weren't trees to produce bedrooms or even a remote area where they could find privacy, she could still feel his arms around her. But two seconds after she shut her eyes she was asleep.

She dreamed about falling off Apache's back right into a bed of hungry fire ants. They were all over her, biting and making red marks that itched so bad that even clawing couldn't bring relief. She awoke sitting straight up, whining and scratching her ankles so hard that they had red stripes on them.

Dewar unzipped his sleeping bag and walked across to her on his knees. "Haley, what is it?"

"Ants. They're biting me."

He shined a small flashlight on her feet. "There's nothing here. Were you dreaming?"

"Fire ants and they're still biting me," she said.

He looked again and went back to his bed, opened his saddlebags, and brought out a bottle of clear fingernail polish. "It's not ants. You've got a bad case of chiggers. Hold this flashlight for me."

"Painting my toenails isn't going to help."

"But painting theirs will." Dewar chuckled.

She held the light and he began to put one drop of nail polish on every red dot he could find. He blew on each drop until it dried. She wasn't sure if the polish stopped the itching, or if the warmth of his breath creating a fire in her gut made her forget about it, but something worked.

"There's one on my thigh," she whispered.

"Take off your jeans. Looks like I need to check you for ticks." He smiled.

"I thought you said chiggers. Is that some kind of evil ticks from hell?"

"No, chiggers are little red bugs that get on some kinds of wildflowers and grasses. They bury into your skin and itch like hell, but the polish suffocates them and they die. I was making a joke. Brad Paisley has a song out about checking his girlfriend for ticks."

"Honey, you can check me for anything you like as long as it stops itching." She kicked off her jeans and peeled her knit shirt over her head. "Check away."

He pulled up the leg edge of her lacy panties, applied three drops of fingernail polish, and again blew on the tender skin until it dried.

She managed to keep the moan soft. "Do you know what you are doing to me?"

"I've got a very good idea because it's making me pretty hot doing it," he said.

He found two more under her bra strap on her back and one an inch from her nipple. "Put that in your reality show notes."

"Bring fingernail polish and don't ask why," she said.

"Clear fingernail polish or someone might look like

they've got measles," Dewar said. "Now let's get you dressed and I'll hold you until you fall back to sleep."

"I'd rather get all the way undressed and take care of a deeper itch," she said.

"So would I, darlin', but there is no privacy at this place. Unless you want to go up on the other side of the pond."

She shivered. "No thank you. That's where chiggers live. Damn their sorry hides, anyway."

He helped her re-dress and then stretched out beside her. "I love the way you fit in my arms."

"Me too. Like I was made special for that purpose," she said sleepily.

Chapter 19

Monday morning dawned without a cloud in the sky. The sun came up in a big orange blaze of glory with the promise of a warm day, and the cows were eager to move out of the pasture, across the gravel section line road, and into the next phase of the journey. Even Eeyore had a little extra spunk in his usual ho-hum, head-down walk.

The fingernail polish had been passed around before they left that morning and Haley had found two more places right below her belly button where a couple of slow climbers had buried in. She'd escaped behind the wagon and threatened the whole bunch of cowboys with justifiable homicide if they so much as peeked while she painted the red dots.

And now they were back in the saddle for another day herding cattle north toward Dodge City. Dewar had told them at breakfast that morning that they'd probably cross the state line that evening and her heart had stopped beating.

"That only means that we're more than halfway there," Coosie had said.

Her heart settled into a regular routine as he explained they'd still have about thirteen more days until they actually sold the cattle to the feedlot Dewar had picked out.

They'd only been riding an hour when they passed

a cemetery. It didn't cover acres like the ones Haley had seen in Dallas, or even the ones in Louisiana where her grandfather was buried. It was small but well kept with flowers on the grave sites, freshly mown grass, and tombstones of all descriptions shining in the morning light.

It reminded her of the brevity of life and how she should be reaching out to grab opportunities while they were at hand instead of waiting until they were miles down the road. Was Dewar the opportunity of a lifetime? Or was he a plaything for a month? She had never in her entire life started a relationship of any kind after only knowing someone for a week. She'd certainly never even thought about falling into a pile of leaves with a cowboy.

The faint noise of a train rumbling down the tracks to the west drew her thoughts away from the cemetery. She'd researched what seemed like a lifetime ago on the Internet and found it was the trains that brought an end to the trail drives. When the railroad put tracks closer to their ranches, the need to drive the cattle all the way to Dodge City disappeared.

What would it take to change her? And at the age of thirty, could she even make changes or was she so set in her ways that it would be impossible? She pondered on that the rest of the morning. Would Dewar like her if she became a ranching woman or would her decision make her such a different person that he fell out of love with her?

Love! She sputtered without even saying the word. He'd never uttered such words, never even mentioned them after sex or during sex when men will say anything.

Not Dewar; his words were always well chosen and so sweet. But if he did fall in love with her, would he fall out of love with her if she changed? That was the question.

At noon she was downright grouchy because of un-answered questions. Coosie laid out bologna, cheese, to-matoes, and everything to make Dagwood sandwiches. She slathered mustard on one slice of bread and folded it around one piece of bologna.

"Chigger bites still bugging you?" Finn asked.

"They're fine," she said.

Rhett raised dark eyebrows over his green eyes. "You sick?"

"Nope, just not too hungry. Ate too much breakfast," she explained.

"Well, I'll tell you one thing. If I'd known them damn chiggers were taking up homesteading on my legs I would have never gone fishing. The fingernail polish stuck the hair down flat and every time I move it rips out another hair. I swear, Haley, I don't know how in the devil you girls get your legs waxed," Sawyer said.

That brought out a weak giggle. "Boys ain't as tough as girls."

Dewar smiled.

"What's funny?"

"You said ain't instead of aren't. You're beginning to talk like a redneck. Be careful or they won't let you back into that fancy office down there in Dallas," he said.

Daggers shot from her eyes. "It's living around the bunch of you that causes me to swear like a sailor and..." She stopped herself before she said, "think about having wild sex with you all day."

"And what?" Dewar pressured.

"And use the word *ain't*. Momma will throw the whole lot of y'all off the roof of the office building if you do much more damage," she said.

"We still got almost two weeks to ruin you, girl," Rhett said. "You may go home with a tat yet."

"Hmmph," she said and bit into her sandwich.

When it was time to pull up reins that night they were back in a flat area with no trees, not even a sapling beside Bluff Creek. There was no more than two inches of water in the bottom of the creek; barely enough to water the cattle. Not nearly enough for a real bath or washing clothes.

"So we're in Kansas?" She removed the saddle from Apache and carried it to the spot where her bedroll was lying.

"We are," Dewar said.

She went back to her horse and took off the blanket, brushed him well, and sent him out to graze with the cattle. Coosie was already working on supper, and the smell of fried chicken permeated the evening air. Buddy was busy brushing down the two horses that pulled the wagon. The cousins were making out their beds and griping about the water being low in the creek.

"This has been fun, but I wouldn't do it again for all the money in that damned reality show," Sawyer declared.

"Why?" Buddy asked.

"I didn't realize how much I'd miss a bath at the end of a long, hard day. I don't mind getting dirty and sweaty. But when the day ends, I like to be clean and…" He paused and looked at Haley.

"Finish your thought. Don't hold back on my account," she said.

"Go to bed clean and naked, instead of wearing everything but my boots and not having a real shower or even a creek bath," he said.

"Nothing like the feel of cool sheets on a naked body," Dewar said.

Haley's imagination picked up speed so fast that she could almost hear the gears grinding. Dewar, tangled up in sheets, his head on a pillow, and not a stitch of clothing between him and her fingers. There he was in her mind's eye propped up on an elbow smelling all woodsy and sexy, his hair wet with a fresh shower and his body ready and willing.

"How about it, Haley?"

"What? No, I am not getting a tat. Momma would throw me in the Bayou with the gators and Daddy would disown me," she stammered.

"Wasn't me talking." Rhett chuckled.

"It was me—I asked if you miss a bath every night," Sawyer asked.

She nodded and gulped, glad they couldn't read minds. "Oh, yeah, I damn sure do! So you wouldn't be interested in being the trail boss for the reality show, Sawyer?" She changed the subject.

"Your daddy hasn't got enough money for me to do that job."

"Not even if the women contestants looked like Dallas Cowboy cheerleaders?" she asked.

"No, ma'am! When I get to that hotel in Dodge City, I may have room service brought into the bathroom and not get out of the tub for two whole days. When I get home, my girlfriend isn't going to want a man that smells like a boar hog," he said.

"How about you, Finn? You want to be trail boss for the reality show?"

He slowly shook his head. "Not me. This has been a good run, but I'm ready to go home and buy my own place and get settled into life."

Dewar looked up. "How remote are you willing to go?"

"For what?"

"A ranch?"

"Why?"

"Well, I heard from a friend that there's a ranch out in the Palo Duro Canyon that's been for sale for more than a year and the folks are itchin' to sell," Dewar said.

"Don't say yes, man!" Sawyer said. "I went back in there to look at a place one time and believe me, it's way, way back in the sticks."

"Sawyer ain't tellin' the half of the story," Coosie said. "Only thing that lives in that place is rattlesnakes and lizards."

"Y'all stop it," Dewar said. "My friend thinks it's paradise."

Finn looked at Dewar. "Sounds like something I'd sure be interested in looking at."

"I'll call him when we get back home and he can set you up with the realtor if it's still for sale," Dewar answered.

"What are you two going to do when this is over?" Haley asked Sawyer and Rhett.

Rhett loosened his ponytail and shook out his hair. "Get a haircut and find a job. You need help at the horse ranch, Dewar?"

"Always got a job for you there, cuz," Dewar said.

"Might talk to Aunt Maddie about that," he said.

Sawyer held up a palm. "I'm going home to my woman and never leaving her again. I'm going to use the money I make on this trip to buy a diamond ring and propose to her. I like ranchin', but I want to live close to a town. It don't even have to be a big one but it's got to be big enough for at least one good decent honky-tonk so I can shoot some pool and have a beer."

"Think you're going to do that when your woman gets that ring?" Rhett asked.

"She's a good woman. She won't mind me going into town and blowing off some steam on Saturday night."

"Ain't no woman worth havin' that good, cuz," Dewar told him.

"And why would you say that?"

"What's she going to be doing while you are shootin' pool and havin' a beer at a honky-tonk filled up with women wanting to dance or take you home for more than a dance?" Dewar asked.

Haley's head slowly moved from side to side.

"What? You don't agree with me?" Dewar asked.

"About the woman part? Yes, I agree with you. Sawyer, you'd best think twice about an engagement ring if you aren't through with partying. I was shaking my head at the idea of that canyon. I've been to that place. There is nothing out there for miles and miles and it's all flat land and then boom, it's like a big bomb blew a crater in the earth. Pretty land but desolate," she said.

"And you couldn't live there?" Dewar asked.

"I could, I suppose. I wouldn't though. I need people and civilization around me."

Coosie called supper before she could say anything more and Dewar was quiet the rest of the evening. When she tucked herself in that evening, she looked over at him only to see his back. Was the short-lived relationship over because she didn't want to live in a godforsaken canyon? She'd never sleep without an answer, so she threw back the side of her sleeping bag and padded across the grass in her sock feet.

She snuggled up to his back and nibbled on his earlobe. "Wake up and talk to me."

"What's there to talk about, Haley?"

"Quit pouting. You are mad at me because I said I needed civilization, aren't you?"

"I'm not mad and I'm damn sure not pouting," he said.

"I am who I am, Dewar. You knew the day I drove up on your ranch. You are who you are. I don't ask you to change so don't ask me to."

He rolled over and kissed her with so much tender passion that it brought tears to her eyes.

"And what do we do about that side of it?" he asked.

"What side?"

"The one that can't stop thinking about you. The one that wants to touch you every minute of the day and listen to your voice and hear your giggle. Who loves just to watch you pet that damned old donkey. What do we do about all that, Haley?"

"We face it head-on and make decisions later. Right now we've got cattle to get to the feedlot and a reality show to plan," she answered.

"And when it's over, can you walk away without looking back?"

She shivered. "I don't know, Dewar. I guess we'll wait until it's over and see what happens."

He pulled her close to his body and wished that he was naked and they were in a bed with sweet-smelling sheets. She deserved that much. Hell, she deserved more than that, but like he'd told her repeatedly and from day one, he was a plain old cowboy. He could give her all the love in the world, all the security in the world, and promise to be faithful unto death. But he couldn't change any more than she could. Once they were back in their separate and opposite worlds, love, security, and faithfulness might not be nearly enough.

Chapter 20

HALEY WOULD HAVE BEEN MUCH MORE COMFORTABLE if she'd been wearing her business suit and high heels when she opened the door to the *Caldwell Messenger*, a small weekly newspaper in Caldwell, Kansas. But those things were half a lifetime in the past and she needed to talk to the person in charge of the newspaper.

"Hello, could I help you?" a woman asked.

Haley removed her dusty cowboy hat and held it to her side. "I'm H. B. McKay."

The woman extended a hand. "I'm Dorothy Amos. We were hoping you'd come by and visit. It'd be a big thing for us to have your people come through our little town and set up shop for an episode. We are very proud of our Chisholm Trail heritage around these parts."

Haley shook it firmly. Usually a woman with a gift of gab, Haley was eager to get out of the office and back with the drive. Apache, her horse, was hitched to a porch post, but the cattle would be coming along any minute and the people were gathering to watch the sight. A little boy was out there eyeballing the horse and after the fiasco in Comanche, she damn sure didn't want him to turn her horse loose.

"I appreciate that," Haley said.

Dorothy brought a pen out from the gray bun on top of her head. "I've got the questions right here if you don't mind answering them. Number one is: What's it like, being the only woman on a drive like this?"

"It's been an experience that has given me a lot of ideas for the show. Ideas that I would have never thought of if I hadn't come along for the ride," Haley said.

She could see a little boy messing with Apache's reins. If that horse got loose, Dewar would never let her live it down.

"I bet it has. We've got a man out there taking pictures. He just sent a couple back to the computer. Good-lookin' cowboys for the most part."

"Yes, ma'am. Did he get a picture of Coosie, our cook?"

She nodded. "That man looks like he should be playing football for the Dallas Cowboys, not cooking for a cattle drive. Do you miss your modern conveniences?" she asked.

"Of course, and so will the contestants. That'll be part of the intrigue of the show."

"How about the contestants? Will you be interviewing them when you get back to Dallas?" Dorothy asked.

Haley nodded again, eager to get out of the shop and back outside before that child turned Apache loose in a hundred head of cattle. "That process is going on right now. Anyone who is interested should be contacting the 800 number at Levy Enterprises."

"I think that's everything. We'll use your quotes and write up our own story. Want me to send a tear sheet down to your business address?" Dorothy smiled.

Haley nodded. "That would be very nice, and thank you for your time. If I'm going to head up the drive, I'd best be going now. And whoever is in charge of the show will drop by when it comes through Caldwell."

"Am I right? Dewar is the one heading up the cattle and Coosie is the one driving the wagon at the rear?"

"That's right."

"And the other ones? I'd like to get their names right when I do the article for today."

"Dewar O'Donnell's three cousins who are also O'Donnells: Finn, Sawyer, and Rhett. And then there's Buddy."

She pointed at a picture on her phone. "He's this man?"

Haley pointed to the picture. "That's right. Dewar is this one."

She could hear the cattle bawling and the cowboys whistling at them as they came into town. "Got to go. Any other questions, just send them down to Joel at Levy Enterprises and he'll answer them. I just wanted to stop by and pave the way for the reality crew."

"Nice to meet you, H. B. Frankly, I was surprised to see that you are a woman. I figured you'd be a man." Dorothy followed her to the door.

"Most people make that mistake." Haley stepped out into a brisk south wind that brought the smell of cows and horses right along with it. Would she feel as caged as she had in the newspaper office when she returned to her own world? Had days on a horse and nights under the stars turned her into an outdoors woman? Would life ever be the same?

That ornery kid looked at her, grinned, and slapped Apache on the rear end. Evidently he'd already untied his reins because Apache took off into the traffic running like the wind right up the middle of the street. All she could do was run like the dickens and whistle for him to stop and come back to her.

Cars and trucks were on both sides of him, and a stray dog jumped between the vehicles and snapped at his heels. Horns blared and people leaned out of trucks to tell her to get her damn horse off the street. Apache finally heard her whistle and stopped dead, stirrups flapping against his side and cars still breezing past him at twenty-five miles an hour.

Then suddenly the cars all pulled over to the side like a funeral procession was coming up the street. Only it wasn't a hearse, it was a rangy old bull. And the procession wasn't a string of cars with their lights on; it was a line of cows. The stray dog slunk back down a side street with his tail tucked firmly between his legs. He wasn't nearly as mean when it came to facing off with a big black bull as he was chasing a running horse.

Haley picked up a rock and slung it toward him. The dog picked up speed and darted under a parked car.

"Get on out of here and leave my horse alone, you mangy bastard," she screamed.

The cows looked from one side to the other as if they were disappointed that there wasn't a sidewalk sale going on. Haley just hoped that that little boy had run all the way home and wasn't brave enough to slap a cow. Lord, she'd done already had enough stampedes to last a lifetime. She was totally out of breath and heaving until her sides ached when she finally caught up to Apache. She reached for the reins and looked up into Dewar's twinkling eyes.

He handed her the reins. "Lose something? Want me to go back and get that dog so it can be your second pet? Poor little bastard looked lonesome, didn't he?"

"You bring that dog to camp and I'm tellin' Eeyore

that it's a coyote. One more kid touches my horse, throws a rock at my horse, or sticks his tongue out at me, or tries to steal one of our cows, I swear to God, I'm going to chase him down and…" She tried to think of something horrible enough to do that wouldn't land her in jail.

Dewar threw back his head and laughed. "Does that mean you don't want a dozen sons?"

"Right now you'd have to pay me big bucks to even consider a sweet little daughter."

<center>~~~</center>

Dewar pushed them past the usual mileage that day, especially on a day when they had to go right down Main Street of a town. Haley began to think she'd grown fast to the saddle and it would be stuck to her butt forever. Even Coosie was cranky when they finally stopped a hundred yards from the Chikaskia River.

"You ran at least five pounds off those cows today," he told Dewar.

"They'll gain it back with good fresh water and all this green grass. I wanted to reach the river so we could clean up, so stop your whining."

Coosie narrowed his eyes. "Don't you talk like that to me, son. I could take you down with a broken arm and the other tied behind my back."

"Are we m-m-mad?" Buddy asked.

"We are tired. Y'all are getting potato soup and corn bread for supper. I'd planned on doughnuts, but it ain't happening tonight," Coosie snapped.

The saddle didn't stick to Haley's butt like she'd feared, but it was a hell of a lot heavier than it had been that morning. By habit, she'd dropped her bedroll six feet from Dewar's and then lugged her saddle over to the same spot. Apache waited patiently for her to come back, remove the blanket, and brush him. Finally, she finished taking care of her horse, unfurled her bedroll, placed the saddle at the top end, and stretched out, surprised as hell when she lay down that with her bowed legs she didn't look like she was rigged up in the stirrups at her gynecologist's office.

As tired as she was, the idea of stirrups conjured up a vision of sex with Dewar in that position and she had to hold back the giggles. In her Dallas corner office she damn sure wouldn't be entertaining thoughts of sex in stirrups with a cowboy. She'd be all about the business, the next conference, and the next big thing on television. She hardly even knew this new wanton hussy that had taken over her body. Were the Cajun genes surfacing? Granny would be tickled, but her father would be mortified.

She shut her eyes and the next minute someone kicked her boot. "Hey, supper is ready."

She didn't want to wake up. The dream had been good. She and Dewar were in a nice restaurant with a candle in the middle of the table and she was all dressed up in a cute little dark green dress that showed off her cleavage. Dewar laid his big hands over her small ones and squeezed gently.

She opened her eyes reluctantly to see Rhett standing at the foot of her bed, a smile on his face. "Is Coosie in a better mood?"

"Hell, no! I am not!" Coosie said from the campfire.

She sat up. "Is the potato soup burned?"

"I don't burn food just because I'm pissed at the trail boss for making us do a parade and extra miles."

Dewar yawned and stretched. "You'll feel better with some food in your stomach and a good bath."

Coosie pointed the soup ladle at him. "Way I feel right now I might drown your sorry ass."

Haley fished the notebook from the saddlebags and wrote:

We're more than halfway through the cattle drive and we pushed on to a record amount of miles after running the cattle through downtown Caldwell. Stopped at the newspaper and talked to the lady editor who is running an article this week and very interested in the reality show. Tempers are getting edgy and Coosie, who's usually calm about everything, is cranky as hell. Tonight the guys are taking a bath in the Chikaskia River and then I will take one. Think pushing the contestants to the limit today just to see how they react.

"You going to write in that thing all night or eat?" Coosie asked.

She slipped the notebook back into the saddlebag and stood up. "I was just waiting for you guys to get your soup first because I'm hungry and what's left belongs to me. I can eat while you are getting cleaned up, and then I can get my bath."

Coosie handed her a bowl and the ladle. "That's a lot of soup you plan on eating."

She looked into the pot. "That is potato soup?"

"Lucy calls it potato chowder since it has got bacon and sour cream in it. Ice is about melted in the chest so I needed to use up the sour cream. Fried enough bacon this morning to use in it," he explained.

"Well, it looks delicious," she said.

The scowl on his face softened.

"Don't you dare get it all. I'm coming back for seconds. My belly feels like my throat has done been slit," Sawyer yelled.

"You better hurry. Boss man has done kept us all in the saddle so long today that we're all hungry," Haley said.

"I got so hungry I almost ate my ponytail," Rhett said.

"Hey, I meant to ask and forgot. Why did you say you were cutting your hair when you got home?" Haley asked.

"Because summer is coming and it's hot. I thought maybe you and I'd go get our hair cut together. You can get a spike and a tat, maybe of a set of bull horns on a pretty heart that has initials in the middle." He wiggled his black eyebrows.

He was waiting for her to ask what initials, but she shoved a spoonful of soup in her mouth and said, "Mmmm, delicious, Coosie."

"Thank you," he said.

"Is the water clean?" she asked Dewar, changing the subject even more.

"Not as much as I'd like," he answered.

Rhett finished his second bowl of soup and followed Sawyer and Finn to the river. Buddy left next and then Coosie, leaving her and Dewar at the camp alone.

"Confession," she said.

"Me or you?"

"Me. I felt cooped up in the newspaper office today and it scared me."

A grin curled the scar on his jawbone even more and the dimple in his chin deepened. "What do you figure that means?"

"That I've been in the saddle too long."

"What're you going to do about it?" he asked.

"Get over it, I guess. I got over the measles when I was a kid. I guess I can get over this. You going to take a bath?"

"Oh, yeah. Want to take one with me?" He flashed the most brilliant smile she'd ever seen on his sexy face.

"You ready for the whole world to know about us?"

"Are you?"

She slapped his arm. "Do you ever answer a question?"

"Do you?"

He carried his dishes to the pan at the back of the chuck wagon, washed and dried them until they were squeaky clean, and picked up his clean clothing. "Guess that means I'll be washin' up all alone."

"Guess so, trail boss," she whispered.

"Hey," Finn yelled from the tree line. "The water is okay to take a bath in but don't think about washing your dirty clothes in it. Have to see if Coosie will let us have a panful from the barrel for laundry."

Haley yearned for the washer and dryer in the utility room of her apartment. She might even hug them when she got home. She'd finished her dinner, wrote some more in the journal about the grouchy mood that had hit the whole crew and how that could be played into the show, and then it was her turn for a bath. She gathered up her clean clothes and headed through the trees with Eeyore following behind her.

"I don't think there's coyotes or mountain lions out here in this flat world," she told him.

He wiggled his big ears and kept pace with her.

She stripped down to bare flesh, picked up her soap

and washcloth, and sat down at the edge of the water. The cold water made goose bumps pop up all over her skin, but washing away the grime of the day felt really good.

She had just leaned back and dunked her red hair into the lazy river when Eeyore let out a bray that brought her straight up to a sitting position, eyes wide open and wet hair plastered to her neck and back.

His eyes were set across the narrow river and he took off in a fast trot, the water splashing up to his belly as he ran. She looked toward the other bank to see a coyote. The stupid thing had the audacity to wade right out into the creek and growl at Eeyore, who never slowed down. They clashed in the middle of the creek like a hurricane colliding with a class five tornado. The coyote tried to latch onto Eeyore's legs, but they were moving too fast. Eeyore kicked and snapped at wherever he could find a chunk of hair.

The coyote figured out pretty quick that he'd bitten off more than he could chew but he couldn't get away from the jackass so he put up a hell of a fight. Mud and water shot up like a geyser all around Haley. She threw her bar of soap at the coyote and screamed, "Get the hell out of here, you mangy bastard. Eeyore, go back to the bank and give him some space."

Neither animal listened. All the frantic carrying on soon churned the creek up into a muddy mess. Haley looked like she'd been a contestant in a mud-wrestling contest—and lost. She had waded right into the middle of the fight, kicking the coyote and trying to separate them.

She didn't even see all six cowboys coming at the creek in a dead run. Until Dewar waded right out into the water in his sock feet, kicked the shit out of the coyote's ribs, and removed his clean shirt all in one motion, she wasn't aware of anything but protecting her donkey. When she came to her senses she was covered in mud, wearing Dewar's red and black plaid shirt, and five cowboys were staring at her from the edge of the creek.

The coyote finally got loose from Eeyore and took off whining with his tail between his legs. Eeyore brayed a few jackass cuss words at him and calmly walked over to see about Haley. She tugged the edge of Dewar's shirt down over her butt and kissed the donkey smack between the eyes.

"Good boy," she said. "You showed that mean old coyote who was boss, didn't you?"

"You scared the living shit out of me," Dewar gasped as he pulled her close to his chest. "I thought that damn coyote was eating you alive."

"We'll be getting on back to camp," Coosie called out.

"Oh my God!" Haley clamped a hand over her mouth. "Did they see me naked?"

"Honey, you're so covered up with mud and there was so much fightin' goin' on out here that I don't think they saw very much." Dewar grinned. "It looked like a spewing volcano raining down mud and cuss words. Damn, I didn't know a girl could use that many bad words in such a short time."

Haley's cheeks were so hot that the mud covering her face felt like it was drying and cracking. "I can't ever look them in the eye again," she whispered.

"They're going to tease you for sure."

She stepped back, grabbed at the edges of the shirt, and pulled it around her naked breasts then realized it was Dewar's shirt. "Oh, no! Your clean shirt. I'm so sorry. And you're all dirty just from touching me."

"Don't be. It's worth getting it dirty to see you unhurt. I do think you should go on up the creek a little ways and get cleaned up again. I'll go back to camp, wash the mud off, and you can…" He grabbed his ribs and laughter rang out across the land.

"It's not funny," she said.

Eeyore let out a long pitiful bray and Dewar laughed even harder. "Even he thinks it is."

Haley fished her soap out of the water, stomped out of the creek, picked up her clean things, and held them out away from her body. "I'll see you both after a while."

Eeyore dropped his head and followed her up the creek, braying the whole way.

She glanced over her shoulder when the laughter died down. Dewar was on his way back to camp where he'd wash up in a basin of water. Damn that coyote anyway. If it showed its face again, Eeyore would have to stand in line behind her to even get a single kick in.

Dewar was finishing up his laundry when she got back to camp. He reached for the dirty shirt she had in her hand and grinned.

She whipped around and faced the whole bunch of grinning cowboys. "Okay, get it over with and then I don't want to hear any more about it the whole trip."

Finn held up a hand. "I just want to say that we thought you were dyin' and we didn't even know that you mud wrestled. Guess it shouldn't surprise us after the way you tried to kill a couple of kids with buckshot."

Sawyer went next. "I wouldn't wrestle you, the way you and Eeyore put the fear of a jackass and a redhead into that coyote. Poor thing probably didn't even go home to his wife and kids, he was so embarrassed."

"Okay, Rhett," she said when he didn't chime in with a comment.

"Ma'am. I just got one thing to say. You'd do to ride the river with if you can whoop a mangy old coyote."

"Buddy or Coosie?"

They both shook their heads, but the way Coosie bit his lip, she knew he was barely keeping the laughter inside.

Dewar motioned for her to toss her things in with his and the instant that her hands joined his in the soapy water, she knew she'd made a big mistake. She blushed again when their slick hands kept getting tangled up together. By the time their clothes were hanging from the only empty bow on the chuck wagon, she was eyeing the trees and hoping that Dewar didn't fall asleep too quickly that evening.

The evening wore on and on and she thought the cowboys would never stop talking and go to sleep. Then they fussed around and fidgeted in their sleep forever before they settled into that deep, snore-producing sleep that she wanted to hear. Crazy how Joel's snoring about drove her crazy and yet she couldn't wait to hear the cousins, Coosie, and Buddy's rattling that night.

She heard Dewar moving about even though he was as quiet as possible. She saw him go to the chuck wagon and pick up the quilt. Then his shadow melted into the trees. She carefully pulled her boots back on, holding her breath when her foot made a thumping noise as it hit bottom, for fear it would wake someone up. She slipped away so quietly that Eeyore didn't even follow her.

She found Dewar sitting on the quilt staring up at the stars.

"I keep saying that you are beautiful, but it's the truth. I can't keep my eyes off you in the daytime, but at night with the moonlight shining in your hair, you take my breath away," he whispered.

"Even with mud caked all over my body and screaming like a banshee?" she asked.

"Yes, ma'am, even when..." He grinned.

"The boys were nice about it."

Dewar reached up and grabbed her hand. "Honey, they were afraid you might tie into them like you did that coyote and if you did, your jackass would join in the fight and they'd lose face when you two whooped them."

"Thank you, sir. You want a lap dance tonight?" She started humming a country ballad and unbuttoning her shirt in her first striptease. His green eyes were hungry with want as he watched her.

He reached for her. "I want you tonight. I've wanted you all day, Haley."

She stepped back. "Not tonight, darlin'. Tonight I'm a stripper and you are a paying customer. You cannot touch me." She ran her fingertip down his jawline and made a couple of circles on the dimple in his chin.

She straddled his lap and ran her hands through his thick dark hair, then she unbuttoned his shirt, one slow button at a time, and brought his nipples to hardened attention with her lips.

"Lord, Haley, I can't take much more of this!"

"What do you want to do?"

"Touch you. My hands hurt for wanting to touch you."

"Only paying customers get to touch the merchandise," she teased.

"Name your price."

"Two nights in the same room at the hotel."

His hands left his side and slid down her back, unfastening the bra hooks on the way. "You got it, darlin'."

Before she could jerk his jeans off, he had already thrown her bra into the pile of clothing at the end of the quilt and was working on taking her underpants off with his teeth, tasting every sweet, clean inch of flesh as he drug them toward her toes.

"You taste wonderful," he said.

"So do you." She latched on to his neck and remembered just in time not to suck a hickey there.

His lips found hers at the same time her back arched toward him, inviting him to do more than sample the goods. Her legs parted and then were around him tightly. He took her with a firm thrust as his tongue and hers met in a sweet fiery kiss. The combination was so heady that she moaned.

"What? Did I hurt you?" he asked hoarsely.

"No, it's the fire in the sex and the sugar in the kiss. They work together to set my whole body to blazing."

He smiled. "Yes, ma'am. It sure does."

The first time was fast, furious, and wild. She was panting so hard when they tumbled over the edge into a big black hole called sexual satisfaction that she couldn't even breathe. The second time was slow and deliberate, so much so that she felt as if Dewar was making love to her rather than having sex with her.

It brought tears to her eyes.

Chapter 21

DEWAR GOT THAT ANTSY FEELING DOWN DEEP IN HIS soul that said something wasn't right. He turned around in his saddle and checked what cows he could see. They were all following the longhorn just like normal. The feeling stayed with him so he motioned for Buddy to ride point and he rode back along the herd. Finn, Sawyer, and Rhett were all bored but fine so he kept riding toward the chuck wagon.

"How are things going back here?" he asked Coosie.

"Cattle is moving right along, but I lost that dumb jackass and Haley back there about a quarter of a mile. She said she was going to ride through that little cemetery we passed by and the donkey stayed with her."

"Well, shit!"

"I told her not to stay too long and to ride out before she lost sight of us," Coosie said.

Something about that little cemetery had intrigued Haley. When she rode back to look at it, she found one of those historical markers that Oklahoma is so famous for, affixed to a metal post just outside the cemetery. She slid off Apache's back and read that the house was an old saloon, and had been added to the national register of historical homes and places fifty years ago. It had played a big part in the Chisholm Trail cattle runs, and was now a museum for pieces donated from that time period. Down below it was another little sign, not nearly as fancy, that said the museum was open by appointment only. No admission fee. Donations accepted.

Haley led Apache and read the names on the stones and wooden crosses as she meandered. They were the strangest tombstones she'd ever seen, bearing names like Sassy Sally, Sweet Jane, Jewel, Katy, and Pretty Inez.

She'd stopped to look at one that said Big Joy on it. The stone was bigger and fancier than all the rest. She was so intent on studying it that she didn't hear a thing, but she sure felt the barrel of a gun when it was stuck firmly against her backbone. She slowly raised her arms and said softly, "I'm not armed and I'm just looking around."

"Museum is closed up tight today so get on your horse and get on out of here," a thin voice said.

Haley looked over her shoulder. The woman holding the gun was frail and tiny, but there was a look on her face that said she'd shoot now and ask questions later.

"I'm with the cattle trail run. I just stopped to look around, honestly," Haley said.

"That television shit they been talkin' about on the news? You part of that? What are you? The camp whore?" The gun lowered a few inches.

Red-hot heat flushed Haley's face and she stammered, "No, ma'am. I'm the one that takes notes to send back to the television station that's going to produce the reality show."

A smile twitched at the corners of the old lady's mouth. "Well, I'll be damned. They let women folks really do that, do they?"

"Yes, ma'am."

She sat down on Big Joy's tombstone and propped the gun beside her. "Put your hands down, girl, and sit down here beside me. Y'all goin' to bring that show right through here?"

Haley obeyed. "Yes, ma'am, we sure are."

"And you plannin' on stoppin' at my museum?"

"We could if there's something interesting in the old saloon."

The woman cackled and slapped her thigh. "If I don't shoot you, can I talk on your show?"

Haley swallowed hard. "It could be arranged."

The old woman stuck out her hand. "We'll shake on it. Woman's word is good as a signature in blood, I always did say."

"I'll shake if you don't shoot me," Haley said.

"You drive a hard bargain. I figured you for some-one who'd be casin' my cemetery for crosses to take home and hang on her wall. They're the big thing now, you know."

"I wouldn't rob a historical landmark," Haley said.

The woman cackled again. "Historical, my ass." Then she really did laugh.

Was the old girl daft? Had she lost her mind completely?

"What do you want to tell on television?" Haley asked.

"My name is Sadie and I'll be the last one buried in this cemetery someday. I'm the last living whore that ran the biggest whorehouse on the Chisholm Trail. Miz Big Joy right here was the first one who set up shop. And them dumbass politicians need to know what a dumbass thing they've done. Nobody has ever listened to me. No sir, but if I was to tell it on television, why, they'd have to admit they made a big mistake. I betcha it was one of them pork barrel things or some shit like that. If somebody found a historical site then somebody would donate a million dollars to a fund." She laughed again.

Haley didn't want to get entangled in a political war about historical sites on her reality show, but Sadie had sure piqued her curiosity.

"It goes like this," Sadie said. "The first whore, that'd be my five or six times back great-granny, set up the original house for the cowboys on the Chisholm Trail. She had a daughter that she intended was going to be a doctor and she sure was a great one. Delivered more babies around these here parts than anyone and cured all kinds of sickness. Came home to die, though. She's probably the only one should have a cross in here, girl. That'd be Katy over there." She pointed.

Haley gasped. "You mean this is a prostitutes' cemetery?"

Sadie slapped her leg again. "Damn sure is. Ever one of them 'cept Katy is a whore that is buried here. I tried to tell 'em fifty years ago when they got a bug up their ass and put that fancy sign out there callin' my house a saloon, that it was a whorehouse and there was a difference in selling whiskey and sex."

"But…" Haley looked around at the graves.

"But oh, no, they declared it a saloon and made it into a museum. Then they hired me to come down here and babysit the place two hours a day when somebody makes an appointment. Give me a good salary to do it even if they wouldn't listen to me."

"And you want to broadcast *that* on national television?"

Sadie nodded. "Before I up and die, I want folks to

know that I am the last living whore from a long line of businesswomen that started back more'n a hundred years ago. It's something to be proud of, darlin'. That's why I keeps the grass mowed on a cemetery full of women with names that don't make a bit of sense."

Dewar found her at the back side of the cemetery. Her horse was tethered to the top rail of a fence and she was sitting on the porch steps of a weathered old two-story house. An elderly lady sat in a rocking chair under the shade of the wide porch and the two women were deep in conversation.

"Haley?" he called out.

"Get off that horse and come on up here. You've got to meet Miz Sadie. I found it, Dewar. Never thought I would, but I found a brothel right here on the trail."

"Brothel my ass, girl. Brothel is just a fancy name for a whorehouse," Sadie said loudly.

Haley smiled at Dewar. "Okay, then it's an old whorehouse and Sadie is going to tell my contestants all about it on my show. It might be the only one left between Ringgold and Dodge City."

Dewar slid out of the saddle, tied his horse to the rail beside Apache, and brushed the dust from his shirt.

"So this is the young man." Miz Sadie smiled.

She looked like a dried-up potato with thin wisps of hair that had been pinned up on top of her head. Her hands were almost skeletal, and she wore a calico dress that reached her ankles. Bright blue eyes twinkled in a bed of deep wrinkles, and when she smiled, the whole porch lit up.

"This is Dewar, and Dewar, this is Sadie."

"Dewar is an Irish name, right?" she said.

"Yes, ma'am. And you live here?" Dewar asked.

"No, you sexy thing." She winked seductively. "I live a couple of miles from here. I'll be going home here in a few minutes. This here is the last whorehouse still standing and be damned if them ignorant politicians didn't call it a saloon. In spite of that sign out there, it needs to be remembered for what it was. I bet all them whores out there in the cemetery is turnin' over in their graves. Hell, they was paid to pleasure a man, not whet his whistle."

"So it closed down fifty years ago?" Dewar asked.

"That's right, but there's some good stories I can tell your people about it while it was still up and going strong. Stories they won't see in all that junk they call museum pieces inside the house. Why, back in 1920, a tornado come through here and picked up the out-house and slung it right through the parlor. Shit flew everywhere and covered the walls of the parlor and the tornado had picked up some chickens along the way and pitched them right into the parlor with the outhouse so there was bird feathers stuck to the wall with all that mess."

Haley giggled. "Please remember that story and tell it."

"I sure will if you'll put it right on the television set. I'll make us up some sweet tea and tell you stories that are real, not a crock of shit about a saloon, and I'll even put on my fancy dress I wore back in them days. I might have to take it up a little here and there because I was a bigger woman. It's red satin with black under-drawers."

"That would be great," Haley said. "Did anyone get hurt when the outhouse blew into the parlor?"

"Granny said that the madam was the only one hurt. A chunk of the outhouse hit her right square between the eyes and knocked her colder'n clabber. Her workin' girls thought she was dead for sure but she come around and told them to get the house cleaned up and ready for business."

"What else happened?" Haley wished she had a tape recorder to tape what Sadie was telling.

"The flu epidemic come around right after World War I, and that's when the cemetery came into being. They was the ones that have died while in business right here at this house. I remember some of them and some of them I'm related to. I done got my stone bought and it's got *Sweet Sadie, the last one standing* engraved on it. Don't need to know when I was born or when I died, just that I was."

"Thank you, Sadie," Haley said.

The lady grabbed the arms of the rocker and hefted herself up. "If I was a younger woman I might open it up again just to take you upstairs for a poke, Dewar."

Dewar turned fifty shades of red and Haley giggled.

She picked up her shotgun and headed around the house. "A man that can still blush. He's worth his weight in gold, Haley. You might want to hang on to him."

In a few minutes they heard an engine start up and then a four-wheeler shot past the end of the house going almost as fast as Loretta's had. Sadie stuck one hand up in a wave as she went by.

"Wow!" Dewar exclaimed.

"I've changed my mind. I want to grow up and be like

her." Haley stood up and brushed the dust from the back of her jeans. "So, cowboy, you've come to my house of sin. What's your pleasure today?" she teased.

"What do you do and how much do you charge?" he played along.

"According to my research the going rate was a dollar and…"

He picked her up and tossed her over his shoulder. "Darlin', I'll take a hundred dollars' worth of whatever you're selling."

She giggled. "You think you can stand that much? Where are you taking me?"

"I'm putting you on your horse. Much as I'd like to give you all my money, I figure in about five minutes Coosie will stop the drive and come looking for us," he said.

"Well, shit!"

"Say good-bye to your whorehouse, Haley," he said as he plopped her down in the saddle.

"No, I hate good-byes. I'm not ever saying good-bye to you, Dewar. We'll just have to agree to walk away and not look back when the job is finished." She bent down and kissed him soundly. "And I mean it."

"Me too! I hate good-byes worse than anything in the world. Both my sisters live in the Texas Panhandle. When they come home, I make an excuse not to be there when they leave."

"I'm not your sister."

"Darlin', that's one thing I'm sure of and I'll hate telling you good-bye even worse than I do them," he said.

That night she could hear the faint drone of traffic out on Highway 160, far enough away that they couldn't even see headlights, but the noise seemed strange to Haley's ears after eighteen days of very little but crickets, tree frogs, and cows at night.

She was curled up on her side when she felt Dewar mold himself around her.

"You okay?" he asked.

"I'll get it sorted out," she whispered.

"We'll get it sorted out together, Haley. I've never felt like this about another woman. Fate has sure played a trick on both of us, hasn't it?"

"Damn straight. I didn't even like you sitting up there on that horse when I drove up into your yard. I thought you were the most egotistical fool I'd ever seen."

He brushed her hair back and kissed her neck. "Well, I never thought you'd be able to ride a horse even one day. You proved me wrong too."

"Guess the April Fools' joke was on both of us. Our hearts didn't get the message that we aren't compatible except in bed," she said.

"We haven't even been to bed." He chuckled. "We've been to quilt and leaves and even water, but not to bed. Won't know about bed until we try it."

She giggled. "I damn sure intend to try it when we get to Dodge City."

"If we make it through the bed test, would you consider going out to dinner with me when we get back home?"

"Where?" she asked.

"I'll drive to Dallas or you can come to Ringgold. Got a nice little country restaurant up the road from the ranch called Chicken Fried."

"A real date?"

"Yes, ma'am, with flowers and a walk under the stars afterwards."

"And a trip to your bedroom?"

"Not on the first date. I've never gotten lucky on a first date."

She giggled again. "Your luck could be changing, honey."

On the nineteenth day of the trip they pulled up at noon beside the winding Chikaskia River again. Haley could see the steeple of a small church to the west and when she'd eaten a biscuit with ham and leftover eggs stuffed inside it, she started walking in that direction. It didn't look to be too far because she could make out the individual red bricks.

"I'll be back by the time y'all pull out," she called over her shoulder.

She'd only gone a few yards when suddenly Dewar's fingers laced in hers and he slowed his stride to match hers.

"I can feel their eyes on our hands," she said.

"I reckon it's all right since we are going out on a date in a couple of weeks."

The church was red brick with a tall pointed white steeple topped with a cross that reached so far up that it looked as if it touched the clouds obscuring the sun that afternoon. The arched windows in the front of the church matched the windows flanking it on either side.

"Are you Catholic?" he asked.

She shook her head. "Baptist when I go. Momma's people are Catholic down in Louisiana. My granny is Catholic. My dad is Jewish."

She sat down on the porch steps and pulled him down beside her.

He untangled their hands and threw an arm around her shoulder. "My Irish ancestors were Catholic but the little church where we go in Ringgold is Baptist. In my opinion God doesn't have to be confined to a building."

"It's peaceful here, isn't it?" She leaned on his shoulder.

They had a date so it wasn't the end of the road when they got back to Texas. But would there ever come a time when her father walked her down the aisle toward Dewar waiting at the front of a church?

Lord, where did that thought come from? I can well understand seeing him naked on the horse after reading Cheryl's romance books or even all the other wicked imaginations that have popped into my mind, but him as a groom. That would be stretching things to the breaking point.

"What were you thinking about? You suddenly went all stiff," Dewar asked.

"I was wondering if God would strike us dead for making out on the steps of a church this old."

Dewar tilted her chin up with his forefinger and kissed her passionately. "Don't guess He will," he said when he broke away.

She pulled his lips down to hers for another kiss right there in broad daylight.

"Wow! Your kisses are just as hot in the daylight as in the night."

He grinned. "And so are yours."

"So we might be compatible in the daytime?" she asked.

"Looks like it, darlin'. Ready to go back to the camp? It's about time to move out again," he said.

"No, I'd like to sit here and kiss you all afternoon."

Dewar pointed toward the clouds that were growing blacker by the minute. "That might lead to something that would get us struck by lightning and those clouds are lookin' pretty dark."

"Looks like we might have to get out the slickers," she said.

A few drops hit them before they got to the campsite where Coosie waited with two yellow slickers held out toward them. Dewar helped Haley into hers and then got his on and into the saddle before it got wet.

Coosie raised an eyebrow at Haley. She winked and mounted up for the afternoon ride. A jackass might not make her a rancher, but she had an invitation to dinner at a café called the Chicken Fried and no amount of gloomy weather could take that away.

That evening they pulled the wagon under a thick pecan grove. It was still drizzling rain, but the thick foliage offered enough protection that Coosie could make a small fire and scramble sausage and eggs together for supper. A trip down to the edge of East Sand Creek for some serious lovemaking wasn't even an option. Haley and Dewar snuggled down into their sleeping bags and were asleep before Coosie snored the first time.

The next day the skies were still overcast but the rain had stopped. Coosie and Buddy rolled the canvas back from the chuck wagon and fastened the wet sleeping bags to the bows with old-fashioned wooden clothespins so they would dry as they traveled.

She'd written in her journal that morning and told about sleeping in the rain and the water dripping on her from the tree leaves. The end of the journey didn't seem

so formidable anymore and she actually woke up looking forward to the finish.

What would her father think of Dewar? Her mother
would think he was handsome, but she'd just see a
plain cowboy. Granny Jones down in Louisiana would
love him.

"So?" Coosie asked.

"So what?" Haley asked right back.

"We saw Dewar holding your hand. In Texas that
means something. I like Dewar. He's a good man. You
wouldn't hurt him, would you?"

"What makes you ask that?"

"He'll do right by you. He's that kind of man. But
you two come from two different worlds. When did all
this start anyway?"

"A while back. I don't want to talk about it right now.
You won't tell me about his family. Will you tell me
about him? Stories you know about him growing up and
things like that?"

"Nope, that's his job. How long have you two been
makin' moony eyes at one another and talkin'?"

"A while," she admitted.

Coosie nodded seriously. "I knew it. You can't keep
nothing from old Coosie. He sees everything."

Haley bit the inside of her lip. "I knew you'd figure it
out. Now tell me a story, please."

He grinned. "Once upon a time a spoiled princess met
just a plain old cowboy."

"I am not spoiled and I'm damn sure not a princess.
Just ask my Cajun cousins. They'll tell you I'm a hellcat
on wheels."

Coosie threw back his head and laughed. "I'd say it's

your job to make a story with or without him. You can do your own detective work on that story, missy."

"He asked me out to dinner when we get back," she said. "What if he don't like me in my high heels and fancy clothes?"

Coosie laughed again. "Way he's been lookin' at you I don't reckon you've got a lot to worry about. Darlin', the heart, it don't have ears or eyes, but it does know what it wants. And once it feels something that is its soul mate, then it don't rest until it has that person for all eternity."

"You think Dewar is my soul mate?"

"Hell, honey, I don't know. Ask your heart. It'll tell you right up front. Trouble is when you ask and it tells you, then you'll have to do something about it or be miserable as hell the rest of your life."

"Are you speaking from experience, Coosie?"

He blushed so red that if he'd fallen off the wagon he would have started a grass fire in the wet grass.

"That's a story for another day," he said softly.

Chapter 22

HALEY WAS SO EXCITED THAT SHE COULD HARDLY SIT still on the wagon seat. It must be what the pioneer women felt like when they got to go to town once or twice a year. She would never be able to put into words the anticipation of walking through a Walmart store again. She'd even tucked her credit card in her hip pocket for a new bar of soap. Hers was nothing more than a thin sliver and wouldn't last another week.

The wagon bounced up and down over rolling hills for the better part of an hour through a pasture with both Black Angus cattle and black iron oil wells with their arms slowly pumping up and down. Dewar pulled up the reins and hopped down from the buckboard to open a gate, and Haley could see the highway right there in front of her. White lines and concrete had never looked so beautiful.

A rusty old pickup truck rattled past when Dewar crawled back on the seat and flicked the reins. When the horses were through the gate, she jumped down on her side and quickly pushed it shut and threw the barbed wire loop over the fence post to secure it.

"Thanks," Dewar said.

"You are so welcome. I still can't believe that Coosie let us go into town for supplies."

"He doesn't think anyone can roast a turkey without burning it," Dewar said.

"I've never eaten wild turkey cooked over an open fire," she said.

"It's pretty good if it's done slow and done right. Coosie didn't trust any of us, and besides, he winked at me when we drove away. He thinks this is a date situation. It is Saturday night, you know," Dewar said. "Maybe you can use the idea in the show. Send two people off to the store for supplies. Let the public vote on which two should go. It might surprise you who they choose. It could be the two who hate each other or the two who've been slipping down to the river at night for hanky-panky."

"I don't hate any of the guys," she said.

"But you aren't a contestant with her life being filmed on the trip."

She adjusted her hat. "I like the idea. It's a way to keep the public involved. They could call in their votes about who got to go to town in what's the name of this place again?"

"Spivey, Kansas," he answered.

"Okay, three weeks into the trip, two people—one guy and one lady—get to go to Walmart for supplies. I guess he'd best be able to control the wagon and the horses."

"Or maybe she'll be the cowgirl who does the driving," Dewar said.

Her eyes glittered as they clipped along faster on the paved road. "That part could be up to the public too. Whoever gets the most votes that week gets to do the driving."

A pickup pulled around them and sped on down the highway. Seventy miles an hour looked like a lightning streak from where she sat. From her calculations Dodge City was less than two hours away going at that speed, but it would take them another week to get there.

"Sometimes I feel like I'm in a time travel machine," she said.

"That's the way it's supposed to feel. We've gone back more than a hundred years to when they really ran cattle up the trail."

"Making the contestants feel like this will be the trick, won't it?" she asked.

He nodded. "There it is."

She looked up and saw a sign that welcomed them to Spivey. She expected to hear more traffic and see the glow of the Walmart parking lot lights up ahead, but everything was quiet in Spivey for a Saturday night.

"Just how big is this place?" she asked.

"It's got two churches and they turned the old school into a convenience store. That's where we're going to refill the water barrel and get supplies," he said.

Her heart tumbled down into her boots. "Are you teasing me?"

"No, ma'am. This is Spivey. I made arrangements with the store owner to order extra things this week and paid for them in advance. He is expecting us either tonight or tomorrow night."

"But Coosie always goes to Walmart for supplies," she said weakly.

"Until this time," Dewar said. "Oh! Haley, I'm sorry. You thought you were going to a big store."

"Don't be. This will be a great scene for the show.

The two contestants will be all fired up and happy and then we'll see their expressions when they pull up in front of this place."

Dewar touched her shoulder. "But you wanted something more, didn't you?"

"I wanted a bar of soap, Dewar. The rest can wait."

"Whoa!" Dewar pulled back on the reins and the horses came to a stop not far from the two gas pumps.

"Guess we won't need to fill up with that," Haley said.

"No, we run on grass and water." He slid to the ground and held up his hands. She scooted across the seat and he grasped her slim waist in his hands, picked her up like she weighed no more than a feather pillow, and set her on the ground.

"That part of going back in time, I do like," she said.

A bell at the top of the door jingled when he opened it and stood to one side. A middle-aged man looked up from the cash register. "Y'all are the cattle run folks?"

"Yes, we are," Dewar said. "We preordered supplies and we'd like to fill our barrel with water."

"Hose is right out there at the end of the store. Help yourself. Supplies are in the box by the door. I'll get the meat you ordered out of the refrigerator. You got an ice chest, right?"

"We do and we'll need two bags of ice for it. While you do that, we'll look around the store. We aren't keeping you open too late, are we?"

"No, we don't close shop for another hour." He disappeared into a room toward the back of the store.

Haley wandered up and down the few aisles and picked up a bar of soap. The DJ on the radio playing beside the cash register said that the next two days were going to be sunny and bright in southern Kansas with no rain in the forecast.

"And now it's time for more of your favorite country music and the five for five contest. At the end of the five songs we're about to play the fifth caller who knows all five songs and the artist who sang them will get two tickets to the Boot Hill Museum in Dodge City. So get out your pencils and paper, folks, and write them down if your memory isn't good. Starting right now we're playing five for five."

At the first strum of the guitar strings, Dewar said, "I wouldn't have nothing if I didn't have you."

She turned so quickly that she dropped the soap.

He bent down, picked it up, and handed it back to her. "That's the name of the song that Randy Travis is about to sing."

"How'd you know that quick?"

"I've played it dozens of times." He hummed along as Randy sang that he counted his blessings and prayed every night that the Lord let him keep her just one more day.

"Do you?" she asked.

Dewar removed two six-packs of beer from the cooler and set them on the counter. "Do I what?"

"What you are humming?" she asked.

"I'm humming along with that song and yep, I do. Just one more day," he said.

"For real?"

"Oh, yeah." The song ended and the next one began as soon as the last note faded away into the far corners of the tiny store.

"And this one is our song. It's the Kendalls singing about heaven being just a sin away. Do you still believe that?" he asked.

"Oh, yeah!" She smiled. "You are definitely the devil with a halo."

He chuckled.

The fellow who ran the place came out of the back toting a heavy cardboard box. He set it on the counter and said, "There you go. Y'all find anything else you can't live without out there on the trail? Looks like the little lady needs some soap and you've got some beer and what else for you?"

Haley laid seven candy bars and a big bag of pretzels, plus a whole bag of popcorn and a roll of toilet paper on the counter. "We'll be needing these too."

"You realize that's not microwave popcorn." The man laughed.

"Our microwave got hit by lightning," she said with a serious face.

He laughed harder. "She's a keeper, mister."

"Yes, she is." Dewar pulled out a bill to pay for the extra things.

The fellow made change and picked up the heavy box. "I'll help y'all get this all out to your wagon and show you where that water hose is located. We're all excited around these parts about the idea of a reality show coming through our town. As you can see we're about dried up to nothing but dust and oil wells, so it'll give us something to look forward to."

"And we'll look forward to doing business with you," Haley said. "Where's the nearest mail drop?"

"Post office shut up last year. You got something you

want mailed I'll be glad to put it in my mailbox and the rural carrier will get it tomorrow," he said.

She pulled a thick envelope from her back pocket and handed it to him. "I appreciate that."

"No problem. Be glad to do it," he said.

Twenty minutes later they went through the gate separating present from past and headed back to the camp. Haley expected to be disappointed on the return trip but she wasn't. She was eager to get home to the cowboys and hand out beers and candy bars after a supper of wild turkey and fried potatoes. She was impatient for the evening to end so she and Dewar could slip off to the river and cuddle on the quilt.

"There was a pay phone there. I should have told you so you could talk to your momma," Dewar said.

"It's only a few more days," Haley said.

When she had slipped from the past back into the present, she'd talk to her mother every morning in the conference room. Would it be as difficult to climb into the time machine and go forward to the present-day scene as it had been on April Fools' Day to fall backwards in time?

Dewar reached across the distance and held her hand. "Sometimes I envy those Amish folks."

"You haven't had enough of this?" she asked.

"Have you?"

"Are we back to the questions?" she asked.

One side of Dewar's mouth turned up in a crooked grin. The dimple in his chin deepened and his eyes locked with hers. "I'll be ready to go home, but I won't be ready for you to go home. I meant it when I said I wouldn't be nothing if I didn't have you."

"What exactly are you saying?" she asked.

He let go of her hand and wrapped his arm around her shoulders. The smile faded and his eyes went soft and dreamy as his mouth met hers in the sweetest kiss she'd ever had in her life. No tongue, just the promise of what would come later in the brush of two people exchanging a chaste kiss.

"I'm saying that I'm very, very glad that our relationship isn't ending when we leave Dodge City."

"Me too." She laid her head on his shoulder.

Chapter 23

THEY FOLLOWED THE RIVER ALL DAY SUNDAY, MADE good time, and camped early. Coosie had pulled up right at the river's edge where there wasn't a tree in sight, so the quilt wouldn't leave the wagon that night.

"Dammit!" she grouched as she removed Apache's saddle and turned him loose in the narrow fenced pasture. Coosie couldn't get to sleep the night before and had carried on about leg cramps until she and Dewar finally gave up on taking their nightly trip back into the trees and now there were no trees so tonight was going to be another lonely one.

"What's your problem?" Finn asked.

"Ready to call in that bet we made at the first of this trip?" Sawyer asked. "You can give me the hundred dollars, and I'll ride over to the phone for you."

"Oh, hush, Sawyer. That's my hundred-dollar bill, and it'll teach you not to bet with girls. Finn, I was looking out over the land and now I understand why a tornado could pick Dorothy up in this place and carry her all the way to Oz," she said.

"Never did understand the fascination with that story. My sister loved it, but us boys hated it when it was her turn to choose the movie on Saturday night," he said.

"Saturday night?" she asked.

"Momma and Dad's date night. They got a cousin to watch us and they went out. They still do, only now they don't have to hire a babysitter. Sometimes it's a movie and dinner. Sometimes it's a rodeo or just a stroll on the River Walk."

"You live in the San Antonio area?"

Finn nodded. "Little town down south of there. They usually drive into town on Saturday night. But I hated it when we had to watch the Dorothy movie."

"I loved it, but I always wondered how a tornado could carry a girl so far. Now I know. It's this flat land. A good gust of wind can blow a tumbleweed from here to the gulf," she said.

"Where's a tumbleweed?" Dewar asked.

"Nowhere. I'm just bitchin' about this flat land."

"Ain't it great! We make really good time when it's flat like this. I can imagine how much the cattle drivers loved it," Sawyer said. "And just think about those folks who were riding in a covered wagon going to California during the gold rush days. I bet they were so happy to see flat land."

"Stop being so happy. I'm grouchy as hell and I've grown rather fond of my mood the past two days," Haley said.

"What put you in a cranky mood?" Dewar asked.

She shot him a dirty look.

Sawyer grabbed his chest. "That mean look bypassed him and shot me right through the heart. I may not live to get my hundred bucks, guys. If I die, you can have it, Rhett, to pay for your haircut and get another tat."

"You are not funny," Haley said.

"I thought he was doing a pretty good job of it," Coosie said.

Dewar raised an eyebrow.

She shook her head.

She couldn't tell him that she'd been in a funk since the night they went into Spivey for supplies. Nothing had gone wrong on the way back to camp that evening except that Coosie couldn't sleep. They'd had the whole evening together, so that wasn't really the problem. But then Sunday stretched out forever and today wasn't a helluva lot better, not when they'd stopped at a site with only one blackberry bush up next to the river for her to squat behind.

If she was totally honest, it was the end of the trip looming up ahead that scared her senseless and put her in the grumpy mood, but she didn't want to think about that. So she blamed it on the weather, on the boredom, or on the fact that she hadn't gotten to make out with Dewar in two nights.

"Poker or dominoes?" Coosie asked as he set up the fire for cooking.

"Poker and whoever loses the most money has to buy the first round in Dodge," Finn said. "You playing, Haley?"

She was kneeling beside her bed, getting the plastic tarp under it straightened out just right and sleeping bag stretched out perfect. Never before in her life had she slept on the same sheets for a whole month, but then never before had she slept fully clothed for weeks on end, either. She cut her eyes around at Finn.

"Well?" Finn asked.

"Real money?"

"No, not real money. But whoever loses the most virtual money has to buy the first round in Dodge," Coosie answered.

"I'd rather be playing strip poker," Dewar whispered from his bed site.

"You'd lose then, too," she said.

"You talking to me?" Finn asked.

"Blackjack or Texas Hold'em?" she asked.

"Name your poison. Since you are the girl, you get to choose. But don't be thinkin' that we'll cut you any slack just because you are a girl," Rhett said.

"Blackjack, then. Granny taught me both, but I like blackjack better. Get ready to lose your shirts and your money, boys."

"Ooooh, I'm shakin' in my boots," Sawyer teased.

"That your Cajun grandm-m-mother?" Buddy asked.

Haley nodded.

Buddy grinned and stammered that he'd put his money on Haley to win.

"Thank you, Buddy. Aren't you playing?"

"No, he's the dealer," Coosie said.

"Why didn't you bring out the cards before now?" Haley asked.

Coosie put a bowlful of potatoes into the pot where he was making beef stew. "Y'all need something to get you through the tail end of this drive. Remember that when you're doing the show. Save a few tricks like cards till the end."

"So we're really on the tail end?" Rhett asked.

"Six more days," Dewar answered.

"You beat me, woman, and I'll buy you a cute little heart tat with initials in the middle," Rhett said.

"You beat me and I'll buy you two drinks of your choice," Sawyer said.

"I drink expensive and if I beat you"—she pointed at Rhett—"then you shut up about another tat."

His eyes widened. "Another? You've got a tat. For real!"

"Another?" Dewar asked.

"Where is it?" Sawyer asked.

"I didn't say another tat on me, did I?" Haley asked.

"No, but it slipped out and that's what you meant," Finn said.

"Dewar, did you know this woman has a tat?"

"I'm pleading the fifth." He grinned.

"Then she does?" Rhett asked.

"Truthfully, if she's got a tat it's hidden in a place I've never seen," Dewar said.

"Well, that don't mean jack shit. There ain't no way you've seen all of her. Not on this trip," Rhett said. "But you got a deal. You win, I won't tease you about a tat. That don't mean I won't still try to get you to spike your red hair though."

"You're on," she said. "Before or after supper?"

"Oh, you're eating first," Coosie said. "Hungry stomachs cause fights, and like I said, you're already a bunch of bitchy little girls today."

"Come on, Dexter." Finn rolled his eyes.

"Truth is truth. Don't matter if you roll it in chocolate or cow shit. And you owe me a dollar for calling me by Dexter instead of Coosie," he said.

Haley stretched out on the bed, propped her head on the saddle, and tried to remember everything about blackjack that her grandmother had taught her. It wasn't a difficult game and it had been a helluva long time since she'd learned the tricks of counting cards, but she had a knack for it. And by damn, she didn't intend to buy a single drink. The sore loser was going to pay for at least two top-shelf margaritas made with Patrón Silver instead of Jose Cuervo.

She licked her lips thinking of the taste of the salt around the rim of the drinks. The last time she had a margarita was the night that she and Joel broke up. He had taken her out to dinner and afterwards she'd broken the engagement. It was time for another margarita now because she was one hundred percent sure she'd made the right decision that night.

She turned her head slightly to see Dewar propped up on an elbow staring at her.

"What?" she asked.

"What were you thinking about? Your expressions changed from smiles to scowls in seconds."

"She's thinking about losing after bragging like that," Finn said.

"Dream on, brother," she said without blinking.

Dewar smiled. "This should be interesting."

When supper was over, Coosie broke out the cards and handed them to Buddy. He sat down on his bed and motioned for the players to gather round. Haley chose the spot beside him with the other four making a circle.

"Coosie?" she asked.

"Oh, no! I'm keeping my money. I'll buy my drinks but I'm not contributing to the delinquency of you young'uns," he said.

Buddy dealt the cards and just like riding a bicycle, Haley remembered her grandmother's tricks. They used dry beans for money with each bean representing one dollar. At the end of the night, Haley had a pile of beans in front of her big enough to make supper for them all. Rhett had two beans left. Sawyer had none, and Finn had ten. Dewar might have had a hundred.

"I like Patrón Silver in my margaritas," she said as she

pushed the beans back into the middle of Buddy's bed-roll. "Y'all just tell me where we're going to celebrate."

"Okay, how'd you do it? I thought when you messed with your ear it was your tell," Rhett said.

"I meant for you to think that," she said.

"And when you twisted your braids?" Finn groaned.

"I don't have a tell. I used to do both, but Granny made me wash dishes if I lost, so I learned real quick." She laughed. "Oh, I forgot to tell y'all that she bought her bright red Caddy with what she won in one weekend up in Mississippi."

"Does she play the ponies too?" Dewar asked.

"No, just poker, but she is very good at it. She won't even touch a slot machine. She's been tossed out of most of the casinos in Las Vegas so she doesn't go there anymore."

"Well, you won fair and square so I'll foot the bill for two of them fancy drinks," Rhett said.

Coosie yawned. "Bedtime, children."

The night was warm so Haley lay on top of her sleeping bag instead of getting inside it. A mosquito sounded like a jet airplane as it buzzed around her ears and she swatted at it twice before she smashed it on her cheek. Not a single cowboy sat up or asked why she'd slapped herself. It wasn't one damned bit fair to be camped by the river in a spot without a single tree when they were all passed out as cold as a bunch of drunks.

She looked over at Dewar and he nodded toward the river. She slipped her boots on and he held out a hand. She took it and he pulled her up and led her into the semidarkness outside the camp.

"I missed dancing with you on Friday, but we were

too tired to get out the guitar after that day. Then Saturday we went to the store," he said.

"Me too," she whispered.

He sang "The Sweetest Thing" quiet enough that only she could hear it as he two-stepped with her on the banks of the river. When the song ended, he pulled her down to the sandy bank to sit beside him.

"You are so pretty in the moonlight. It's even better than candles. Half your face is in shadow and half lit up. That's you, Haley. Part open as a book. Part a secret that I want to figure out," he said.

She moistened her lips with the tip of her tongue and wrapped her arms around his neck, tangled her fingers in his hair, and brought his lips to hers. He lay back in the sand, taking her with him. She snuggled up close to his side and threw a leg over his. She wanted him so badly that her insides were a quivering mass of liquid desire. She'd never been so turned on without any prospect of satisfaction.

"Mmmm," she mumbled.

"I know," he nuzzled her neck. "I feel like a sophomore out behind the barn after a dance."

"I never been behind a barn after a dance, and I don't even want to go if it feels like this. I'll never get to sleep," she moaned.

He unzipped her pants, ran his hand down inside, and she arched against him.

"That's not fair, Dewar. I'm already on fire."

"We could take care of your problem." His fingers were magic but she wanted the whole ball of wax, not just a sample.

She wiggled away from his hands. "No, not like that.

It's not fair to you. I'm going to roll over, butt to belly, and we are going to get a quickie. They're asleep and the frogs and crickets don't give a damn what we're doing." She undid his pants for him.

"Oh, God, that feels good," she said.

He kissed her on the neck and whispered sweet words into her ears with every thrust. The wild ride ended with both of them stuffing their fists over their mouths to keep from screaming out.

"Lord, Haley!"

"No, just plain old Haley. I don't deserve that kind of title." She giggled.

She righted her jeans, not even caring that she'd have sand in her underpants all the next day. The satisfaction was well worth whatever she had to pay for it. He tucked things away and zipped his pants.

"I am so looking forward to a hotel with a door and a lock," he said.

"And a shower afterwards and sheets instead of sand. But I will miss the stars. There's something sexy about looking up over your shoulder at the stars twinkling up there like diamonds on a black velvet cushion," she said.

He sat up and pulled her over into his lap. "Or seeing them reflected in your pretty eyes during sex."

"I'm hungry," she said.

Dewar laughed out loud.

She clamped a hand over his mouth. "It's sex. I'm always hungry afterward."

He leaned back. "Always?"

"I wasn't a virgin, Dewar. I've never had sex like it is with you and it takes a helluva lot out of me. I'm hungry afterwards but I never mentioned it before because it sounds crazy."

"And when it wasn't me?" he asked.

"Never was hungry."

His chuckle came out like his voice, in a deep Texas drawl. "Then I suggest we go raid the wagon, but we'll have to be very quiet. Coosie will wake up at the softest whisper of canvas being lifted."

She stood up and followed him back to the campfire. He raised the canvas flap at the back of the wagon and felt around until he had a flashlight in his hand. Keeping it inside the wagon, he turned it on and she stuck her head inside with his.

"Crackers and—dammit!"

"What?" Dewar quickly turned the light toward her.

"Oreos! He's got chocolate back here and he didn't tell us. I may eat the whole package," she declared.

She left the crackers and brought out the cookies. "Now let's go back to the river and have a feast."

"Something to wash them down?" Dewar held up a bottle of Boone's Farm strawberry wine.

"And wine, too. What was he saving that for? The last night we're on the trip?"

Dewar looked at it carefully. "We're having it with our chocolate cookies right now."

They snuck back to the river and sat down in the same spot. He opened the bottle of wine, took a swig, and frowned. "That tastes like shit! Give me a cookie to get the taste out of my mouth."

She exchanged the bottle for a cookie, ate a bite of the chocolate, and then sipped the wine. "Not too bad, but it's not as good as the real thing."

"And that is?"

"Chocolate-covered strawberries and champagne," she answered.

"Honey, you been on the trail too long. That is as close to strawberries and champagne as a quickie is to two-hour sex in a round bed with satin sheets." He grinned.

"Oh, and how do you know that?"

"Let's just say I wasn't a virgin when I met you, either. And when one of our horses wins the big prizes there's always chocolate strawberries and champagne right along with caviar, if you've a mind to eat that shit. Tastes like you ought to use it for bait to me."

She giggled. "Momma says it's my Cajun blood surfacing. I hate caviar and I'm not too fond of sushi, but I never thought of it as bait."

"Stick with me, darlin', and I'll make a redneck out of you yet."

"Is that an invitation?" She handed the wine back to him.

"Yes, ma'am, it sure is."

Chapter 24

AFTER MORE THAN THREE WEEKS ON THE TRAIL, EVERY-one had settled into their riding positions just like the sleeping arrangements. Dewar rode point alone unless they were going through a town and then he insisted that Haley ride with him. Buddy and Sawyer herded cattle on one side. Finn and Rhett took care of the other side. Coosie brought up the rear with the chuck wagon, and Haley and Eeyore usually rode behind the wagon or beside it if she was talking to Coosie.

"Are you tired of this constant moving?" she asked Eeyore.

The donkey's ears perked up at the sound of her voice.

"Won't you be glad to get back to Dewar's ranch and have a pasture to romp around in all day?"

"Donkey won't talk to you," Coosie called back. "Come on up here and ride beside me."

She clicked her tongue and guided Apache to the side of the wagon. "Will you tell me a story?"

"Not this morning."

"But I'm bored. It's not even midmorning and did you ever see that movie *Groundhog Day*?"

"Oh, yeah! Same thing happened every day for months because he couldn't get his head on straight. Is that what you feel like this is, Haley?" Coosie asked.

She nodded. "Some days the land is flat. Sometimes it is up and down, but it's all the same. Look at the back end of cows, talk a little to Eeyore, and hope you'll talk to me."

"It'll make you appreciate your rut when you get back to it." Coosie smiled.

"They've moved Dodge City. We should have been there days ago. I could have driven from Ringgold to there in less than a day."

"That's in a car. This is on horseback and we're making good time even with the rain. Speaking of which, it's going to rain tonight, darlin'."

"No! How do you know?"

"My leg hurts. Arthritis is the best weatherman in the whole world."

She moaned. "I don't like sleeping in the rain."

"Well, if we're lucky, there'll be a barn up ahead. If not, then I don't reckon the powers of the universe give a damn whether we like it or not."

"I'd sleep standing up in a broom closet if it was dry," she said.

"Be careful. You might have to do just that with that donkey of yours in there with you. And I'm not talking to you today. You don't deserve conversation."

Her big eyes widened even further. "What did I do?"

"You got into my cookies and my wine last night. I figure they moved Dodge City one mile further west for every cookie you ate and it's going to rain to punish you for drinking my wine."

She gulped. "I was hungry."

"There was peanut butter and a whole loaf of bread. And you ate a real good supper, so what made you hungry?"

She could feel his eyes boring into her face. She tugged her hat down. She had a stone face when it came to poker, but her grandmother said she could tell when she was lying by looking into her eyes. No way could she tell him that sex had given her a ravenous appetite.

"Poker. I'm always hungry after I win a big pot at poker and we didn't have a snack before we went to bed," she lied.

"Hummph," Coosie grunted.

"And besides, that wine tastes like shit so it shouldn't rain to punish me for drinking it. There should be a five-star hotel waiting up ahead for us to stay in to pay me back for doing you a favor and drinking that crap."

Coosie grunted again. "Me and Buddy like strawberry Boone. We was saving that bottle for the last night to celebrate two old men keeping up with the young bucks."

"Old, my ass, and I'm not talking about Eeyore. You're not a day over forty," she said, glad to take the conversation away from the reason she was so hungry.

"Darlin', me and Buddy will both be forty-eight if we live to see the fall. We was born six weeks apart. Me the first of October and him the middle of November."

She looked out from under the brim of the hat. "I'll buy you another bottle of that swill soon as we get to Dodge if you'll call off the rain."

He threw back his head and laughed. "Can't do it. It's already scheduled according to my leg, but you can buy me a bottle anyway."

"Now will you talk to me?"

"Nope. My cookies are gone. I'm not in the mood for stories. And there's no place to buy more so you're shit out of luck."

"You are mean," she said.

"You are the one who ate the cookies."

By nightfall she'd decided that hell was seeing southern Kansas from the back of a horse with no one but a gray donkey to talk to. She missed her cell phone and talking to her mother and friends. She even missed bantering with Joel, and that was really, really saying a lot. She missed looking at him across the boardroom table and arguing with him about everything from which show they'd run at what time to who would star in the show.

She and Dewar hadn't had a rousing good argument. Yet they circled each other like wary dogs at the beginning, but since the first kiss, they'd been so busy trying to figure a way to be alone that they hadn't had time for a fight. Would they weather it or would it be the undoing of them?

Lightning split the sky in the southwest and she counted, starting with one-Mississippi until she heard the faint clap of thunder. Ten minutes and it would be on top of them. Damn! She wished she would have never touched those cookies or that wine. They weren't even that damn good.

"Y'all see that old trailer ov-v-ver there?" Buddy pointed.

"Looks like it'd have rats in it." Haley shuddered.

"It's d-d-dry inside. I checked it out," Buddy said. "I'm takin' my bed in there. Y'all can get blown away if you want."

Coosie winked at Haley. "There's your five-star hotel."

"Looks to me like an old rusted-out trailer someone left behind," Sawyer said.

"Looks like a dry place to sleep to me." Finn followed Coosie and Buddy.

Lightning zigzagged through the air and she counted. Eight more minutes.

Eeyore brayed and hugged the back side of the chuck wagon. She hurried to his side, scratched his ears, and assured him that it wouldn't hurt him. She looked across the distance at the trailer.

"Don't even think about it," Dewar said.

"He's scared."

"Probably always will be and he'll always hunt up a barn or a wagon to hide behind, but there's no way Coosie will let you take him in the trailer."

"Just until the storm passes?"

Dewar shook his head.

"You are the trail boss. Make him let me take Eeyore inside until the storm passes. I'll be mad for days if anything happens to my donkey, and I mean it."

Dewar shook his head more emphatically. "And I'm saying no. He's a donkey."

She tilted her chin up at him defiantly. "Then I'll stay out here with him."

The next clap of thunder came three minutes after the lightning and Eeyore brayed again.

"You are picking a fight. Why?" Dewar asked.

"I am not! I just don't want to leave him out here alone when he's scared."

"I'm not taking him in the house when it storms. You'll be in Dallas and probably won't even think about him when it thunders. So why are you fighting with me?"

"To see if we can stand it," she said honestly.

"Well, pick another subject on a day when there's not a damn tornado on the way." He pointed to a wall cloud coming at them.

"A tornado looks like a funnel," she said.

"That's one kind but that one is worse. Grab your bedroll and saddle and run. We've got about two minutes," he yelled.

The stillness was so eerie that she ran toward the place where she'd tossed her bed and saddle, snatched both up, and was on the first step of the trailer when she heard the distant sound of a train.

"It's coming!" Dewar said right behind her.

"That is a train," she hollered above the din.

The door opened and Buddy pulled her inside, held it open for Dewar, and then slammed it shut. "It won't be v-v-very stable, but it'll beat stayin' outside."

Eeyore set up a pitiful braying right outside the door. The noise that went along with it said that he was beating at the metal with his front hooves.

"God almighty, Dewar, he's scared out of his mind. Either you open that door and let him in or I'm going outside," Haley declared.

"Let the damn animal in. I swear to God he's making more noise than the tornado," Coosie said.

She slung the door open just as a clap of thunder rattled not only the trailer but her very bones. Eeyore sprang straight up and into the trailer, shaking himself like a dog, sprays of water sending cowboys diving behind folding chairs trying to get away from it.

The wind whipped the door shut with a loud bang and she turned around to see them all wiping at their faces and slapping their hats against their thighs.

"See what you did," Dewar said. "Now we all smell like wet jackass!"

"You might as well smell like one. You've been acting

like one. He's scared. Poor baby." She grabbed him by the wet ears and hugged him.

He shivered again, threw back his head, and brayed at the ceiling.

"What do you intend to do with him now?" Dewar asked.

"You've hurt his feelings," she said. "You should apologize."

Sawyer roared with laughter. "Apologize to a jackass? You've got to be kidding."

Eeyore took a couple of steps away from Haley, backed up, and sat on Dewar's lap and then looked at Haley with a hangdog look.

"He's forgiving you." Haley smiled.

Dewar pushed at him with both hands and Eeyore let out a bray that rattled the walls even worse than the wind and rain. He got to his feet, farted loud and long right in Dewar's face, and trotted over to Sawyer.

Finn, Sawyer, and Rhett all covered their noses and backed into the kitchen with Coosie and Buddy. Dewar waved one hand around and held his nose with the thumb and forefinger on the other hand. "Damn, Haley, put him outside."

"I will not. That's what you get for being mean to him."

Eeyore lumbered into the kitchen, head butted Sawyer, and stomped on Finn's feet at the same time. Finn fell to the floor right beside Buddy, holding the toes of his boot and cussin' a blue streak. "Damn donkey does not belong in a house and he sure don't belong in a little bitty trailer. He's got his tail up and he's going to…"

"He just did," Finn said. "And it don't smell too good. Haley, it's your jackass. You clean it up!"

"I will!" She grabbed a broom that had seen better days.

"Just be thankful he's not big as an elephant," Rhett said.

Eeyore turned around and licked Rhett's face from chin to forehead with one big slurping motion. Rhett used both hands to try to get the slobbers from his face while Buddy guffawed behind him.

Eeyore's rear end started to wiggle like a calf playing in the pasture and Rhett took off for the room at the end of the hall with Sawyer and Finn right behind him. Buddy threw both hands over his face, but Eeyore wasn't thinking about licking. He wanted to play now that he was safe and warm.

Buddy hopped up on the bar and rolled into a ball. "Get this d-d-damned jackass away from me, Haley, or I'm going to shoot him and D-d-d-dex... I mean Coosie can cook him tomorrow."

Haley took care of the mess on the floor, tied the bag shut, and fought with the door to get it open just enough to shove the bag outside. She melted into a chair beside Dewar and wondered if there would be a single cow left when the wind stopped blowing. Eeyore dropped his head in a pout and stomped back into the living room area. He laid his head on her lap and looked up at her with big pitiful brown eyes.

"See, he is sorry. He was scared." She stroked his still-wet fur.

"Put him in the bedroom," Coosie said.

The tone in Coosie's voice said that if she didn't, he'd kick poor old Eeyore out into the storm and her right behind him, so she led him into the room right off the living area, took a rope from around her saddle horn, and tied him to the closet door handle. "You stay right here, sweet boy. That old, mean storm will pass soon."

When she backed out of the bedroom, Dewar was still fanning the smell away from his nose and Coosie had his hands on his hips.

"What?" she asked.

"He's not eating with us," Dewar said.

She cut her eyes around at him but didn't answer. A short bar separated the living room from the kitchen to the left, a doorway into the bedroom where Eeyore let out another pitiful bray was to the right, with a hallway leading to another bedroom past the kitchen. Furniture was scarce, limited to a few plastic lawn chairs, a couple of metal folding chairs, and an old chrome table with a yellow top in the kitchen area.

"Looks like a huntin' cabin to m-m-me," Buddy said.

Wind and rain pounded the outside of the metal building with enough force that it should have tilted over, but it stood its ground. Haley sat down on the floor in the doorway into the bedroom and put her hands over her ears. "If Eeyore wasn't in here with his weight, it would blow us away."

"Think it'll take us all the way to Oz?" Dewar asked.

She looked up and nodded.

One second it sounded as if a freight train was coming right through the middle of the trailer, the next the eerie quietness returned and sun rays filtered through the dirty windows to dance on the linoleum floor.

"Everyone okay?" Coosie asked from his refuge behind the bar in the kitchen.

"I'm alive," Dewar said.

"We're fine back here," Sawyer hollered from the other end of the trailer where he, Finn, and Rhett had taken off to when Eeyore lifted his tail.

"They m-m-must have anchored this thing into concrete. I was sure we really were going to blow away," Buddy said.

Dewar crossed the living room in a couple of long strides and opened the door. "I'll check the cattle."

Coosie joined him. "I've got to see about my wagon."

Haley jumped to her feet and headed out right behind them.

"Where are you going? Your donkey is in the house," Dewar said.

"And that's where he's going to stay. I'll muck out the room tomorrow morning. He's afraid of storms and I can see black clouds down to the southwest even yet." She pointed.

"And what if a coyote or a mountain lion comes huntin' a cow for supper?" Coosie asked.

The donkey heard her voice and kicked at the trailer walls. She went back inside, untied him, and led him outside. He tossed his head a few times and then followed Dewar to the edge of the fence where the cattle were huddled around the old longhorn bull.

"Just tore the tie-downs and flipped back the canvas enough to get some water inside, but it didn't reach the flour or sugar so we're fine. We only got the very edge of the storm. Just the wind and rain. If we'd have been in the eye of it, this wagon would have sure enough landed somewhere in Iowa," Coosie said.

"What are we going to do for supper?" she asked.

Coosie rubbed his bald head. "I'm thinkin' if that's a hunter's cabin, then the propane tank out back might have some fuel in it. We can check and, if it does, we could cook something on the stove in the kitchen. Electricity is turned off. I checked that first thing but the stove might work."

Sure enough the propane tank was half-full and the stove worked. Coosie was like a little boy with a brand new toy. He made macaroni and cheese from a box, heated up beans from a can, and fried potatoes with smoked sausage and onions in them. He tested the oven and found that it worked too, and put on a big roast for the next day's dinner and whipped up a lemon poppy seed cake from scratch.

"Five star ain't got a thing on us." He set the warm cake and the rest of the supper on the short bar.

"Damn straight!" Haley agreed.

He pointed a long-handled spoon at her. "You are still in trouble."

"What'd she do?" Sawyer asked.

Coosie drew his eyebrows down at her. "You tell 'em."

She raised her hand. "My name is Haley Belle McKay Levy. I am disgusting. I steal Oreos and strawberry Boone's Farm wine and I bring donkeys in the house when it storms, and if he's scared, he's coming right back in here tonight, too."

Buddy frowned. "M-m-my wine."

She tilted her head up and laid the back of her hand on her forehead in a dramatic gesture. "It's a disease. I couldn't help myself. I'd been clean for twenty-three days and ten hours but the Oreos called my name and I took them. Then I found the wine and stole it too. It tasted like shit but I drank it and pretended I was having chocolate-covered strawberries and champagne."

Sawyer glared at Coosie. "You had cookies in that wagon."

"And Boone?" Rhett asked.

"Yes, he did. And I found them and now he doesn't." She put her wrists together and held them out. "Lock me away. I'm an addict. And beware. If I eat lemon cake, I turn into a slobbering monster."

Buddy started the laughter and soon even Coosie was chuckling.

Haley bowed deeply and blew them all kisses.

Dewar started a slow clapping and the others followed suit. "Funny, but that damn jackass is not coming back in this house, Haley."

"That was an amazing performance. Now let's eat before this food gets cold. It's not every day you get cake on the trail," Coosie said.

"Am I forgiven?" Haley asked.

"Hell, no! You still owe me a box of cookies and Buddy a bottle of Boone."

"And I get your piece of lemon cake," Finn said.

Haley air slapped at his arm. "This ain't your fight, boy, but you touch my cake and I'll show you what a fight is."

The party mood lasted until she unfurled her bedroll and washed up behind a shut door with four walls around her. Buddy had brought in a small plastic pan of water for her and she was alone. She washed up, stripped down to her underwear, and crawled inside her sleeping bag. And it felt all wrong. The stars were out but the windows were too dirty to see them. The moon looked like a misshapen marshmallow, and the room smelled musty. She missed the clean smell of spring night air and the chirping crickets and frogs.

Stick with me and I'll make a redneck out of you.

Dewar's words echoed in her ears but she didn't want his words. She wanted his arms around her and his warm breath on her neck. She wanted the stars and moon above her, the noise of cattle, and even Eeyore's brays. She slipped out of her sleeping bag and opened a window. Eeyore lifted his head and trotted over to it and she swore he whined. She eased out into the living room and had a hand on the door leading outside when Dewar raised up on an elbow.

"It's not even raining," he whispered.

She dropped her hand. "He's lonely and scared and he's used to keeping watch over me."

"Leave a window open."

"I did, but it's not the same. He'll start braying if you don't let him come inside and then the boys will be mad because he woke them up."

"You are one exasperating woman," Dewar said.

She grinned and opened the door. As if he knew he should be quiet, Eeyore made his way from the ground into the trailer and into the bedroom as quiet as a Chihuahua instead of a full-grown donkey. He stood by the window and lowered his head as if telling Haley and Dewar that he'd let them know if anything dangerous threatened one of his cows.

"Damn woman." Dewar flopped back down.

Haley wiggled down into her bedroll. "Good night, Dewar."

Chapter 25

Purgatory.

Neither heaven nor hell but the limbo of hanging between awaiting the fate of a decision of a higher being as to whether snatched up into everlasting glory or slapped into the flames of hell.

Haley had never believed a place existed like that, not until they were getting very close to the end of the drive. She awoke that morning to the sounds of men's voices in the living room and kitchen of the trailer house, to cattle milling about outside and a little gray donkey staring right at her.

She could swear that he was crossing his legs. Not one little pile was on the floor, but he looked miserable. She quickly crawled out of bed and he followed her to the door. When she opened it he bailed outside and romped through the wet grass. He was back in his own world, his cows around him, and everything was right with no clouds in the sky.

It was in that moment that she wondered where her world was and the word *purgatory* came to mind. Nothing about her or what she did belonged in Dewar's world. And yet, she had changed since she left Dallas, and she wasn't totally sure that she belonged in that world anymore either.

"I'll be okay when I get back into my normal routine." She went back to her bedroom, folded the edges of the tarp over her sleeping bag, rolled the whole thing up tight, and expertly tied the knots to secure it. A knock on her doorjamb sounded as foreign as the room looked to her that morning.

"This is your wake-up call, M-m-miz Haley," Buddy said.

She smiled at him. "I'm awake. Breakfast ready?"

"D-d-dex… I mean Coosie says it will be soon." He grinned. "D-d-did you sleep okay in your little bedroom?"

"Like a baby," she lied.

She wasn't announcing that she'd have rather been outside listening to their snores floating across the campsite on the cool spring night breezes or that she had missed seeing the stars twinkling above her as she fell asleep. She couldn't even come to grips with the idea, much less put it into words.

They were on the trail again by the time the sun was fully up that morning. The rain had left everything a muddy mess, but it also brought a clean smell to the air. Eeyore had glued himself to her side most of the morning, leaving for only a few minutes at a time to check on the cows.

"Coosie," she got his attention. "I was wondering why Buddy only stutters on certain words?"

"His grandparents raised him after his momma and daddy died. Near as the therapist can figure that's the reason," Coosie said.

"I don't understand. Does he still see a therapist?"

Coosie shook his head. "That was back in our army days. She thought she could help him but nothing helped. He stutters on *D*, *M*, *V*, and *R*. Daddy. Momma. Vera. Richard."

"His mother was Vera and his dad Richard?"

"That's right. I don't even hear the stutter anymore. And the ladies think it's cute."

"What ladies?" she asked.

"Our Saturday night ladies. We usually pick out a bar that's got some dancing going on for our Saturday nights," Coosie explained.

"Didn't either one of you ever want to settle down and raise a family?"

"Oh, we might someday," Coosie said.

"You got a woman in mind?"

Coosie pointed a finger at her. He tried to look serious but she could see the grin playing at the corners of his mouth. "I ain't sayin' I do or I don't."

The wind picked up after dinner, whistling across the flat land as if it was romping and playing like a bunch of children on recess. Haley held the reins tightly in one hand and her hat on with the other. Poor little Eeyore's ears lay flat back against his head making his big, long face look even more ill-proportioned. The cows ducked their heads and followed the longhorn bull, but they bitched at him the whole afternoon.

A forest of wind turbines stood over to the east, lined up one after the other, the enormous blades whipping around generating electricity for dozens of farms. She wished for a turbine in the soul that could generate a good mood or settle the uneasiness about the unrest in her heart, but such things didn't exist.

They passed through a gate into a freshly plowed field. The wind whipped the black dirt around into tiny dust devils about belly high on Apache. High enough that particles filtered up to her face and nose and she started sneezing.

Coosie flopped a red bandana to the side of the wagon. She wrapped the reins around the saddle horn and quickly reached for it with that hand.

"Put it on like this." Coosie showed her how to fold it into a triangle and tie it around her head.

She jerked her hat off, shoved it under her knee, and held it there tightly while she followed his instructions using both hands. When she finished, she slapped her hat back on and retrieved the reins.

"Wow! I did it," she said from under the bandana. "Not that it means anything to most people, but it does to me. I can ride with no hands, keep my hat secure, and tie a bandana around my head. I may be a cowgirl yet."

∼∾∼

Dewar sat down on the edge of her bed that night after everyone was asleep. Stars twinkled in the dark sky and the quarter moon dangled among them as if it were a Christmas ornament on a tree.

His forefinger traveled down her arm to her hand. He clasped it loosely in his, the feel of her soft skin against his calluses like silk against burlap. "You looked like Annie Oakley out there today with that bandana on your face. I should've told you to tie one around your neck in case of dust storms."

"I thought they were just to make you cowboys look tough," she said.

"Well, there is that too. I missed you last night. We were actually closer than we usually are, but—" He paused.

"But there was a wall between us, right?"

"I didn't like it, Haley."

She leaned into his shoulder. "Me either."

He let go of her hand and slung his arm around her, drawing her even closer. She fit well there and things were right inside his heart and soul when there were no walls between them.

"Next week at this time we'll be back in Texas," he said.

"The world can sure change in a month, can't it?"

Dewar squeezed her tighter. He didn't plan on falling for a Dallas executive, but he had, and in such a short time. However, as he and the rangy longhorn headed up the drive that day he did some calculating. If he'd been dating Haley, going out even twice a week and spending a total of four hours each time on the date, that would be eight hours a week. He'd been with her twenty-four hours a day for twenty-five days. That added up to six hundred hours. Divide that by four to get how many dates it would represent and he came up with one hundred and fifty. Then divide that by two and he would have been seeing her regularly for seventy-five weeks, which was a year and a half.

When a man thought of it in those terms, it wasn't strange at all that he'd fallen for her. She was smart, determined, and she'd make a fine woman to ride the river with, as Grandpa O'Malley often said about the women his brothers had married.

"What are you thinking about?" Haley asked.

"You."

"Good answer. Now what were you thinking about me?"

"How far you've come since you fell off the horse on that first day," he said.

"Darlin', I did not fall off that horse. I would have had to get on him to fall off him and that never happened. I slipped in horse shit and fell before I ever got mounted."

"Are we arguing?"

"No, but I wish we were."

"Why?"

She leaned back slightly so she could see his face. "Because the first big fight is going to either make or break us."

He kissed the tip of her nose. "You really think so?"

She shifted her position so that she was sitting in his lap. "I do. Want to say something really stupid so we can see."

"Not tonight. I missed holding you and kissing you last night, and besides, I'm a lover, not a fighter," he said.

"That's what I'm afraid of. If you fight as passionately as you love, the fights could be hellacious."

He strung kisses from her neck to her eyelids and back to capture her lips in a kiss that proved that he did indeed know his way around the lover business. When he broke away he whispered, "But just think about how passionate the making up will be after we fight."

"Whew!" She wiped at her forehead.

"I'd give half my kingdom for an old trailer to appear out of the dirt right now," he said.

"I'd give half of mine for it to rise up from the earth like a mesquite tree," she whispered back.

"But here we are camped in the middle of a pasture without even a chigger, weed, or a wildflower," he said.

"I'll just keep my thoughts on that hotel room in Dodge City. You reckon the cowboys that ran the cattle up through here got antsy to see things come to an end?"

"I can't believe you just used the word *reckon*. You've been keeping company with Coosie too long.

But to answer your questions, I imagine they were very antsy that last week or two. Time was nearing when they'd have a paycheck and they could hit the saloons. Reminds me, we should see the Boot Hill Museum and have a drink at the Long Branch Saloon while we're in Dodge."

She cupped his face in her hands. "Darlin', I would rather spend every minute with you in bed. I can have a drink at any number of bars in Dallas."

Dewar hugged her tightly. "If we don't get some sleep, we won't have the energy for that kind of romp. So good night, Haley! See you in the morning."

—

The next day was Thursday and if all went as well as it had been going, they'd bring the cattle into Dodge City on Sunday afternoon. Dewar awoke that morning, stretched, and looked over at Haley, who was already sitting up, watching Coosie and Buddy put breakfast together.

The constant wind blew the aroma of bacon and coffee right to him and his stomach growled so loudly that Haley turned to look his way.

"Hungry," he said.

"Sounds like it."

He pushed back the sleeping bag that he'd used as a cover rather than crawling inside and zipping it, put on his boots, and poured two cups of coffee. He carried one back to Haley and sat down on the edge of her bed.

"Whoa! What's going on here?" Sawyer asked. "Man takes coffee to a woman before she ever gets out of bed means something, don't it?"

"Means that he's a nice man," Haley said.

Finn looked over at Sawyer. "What's the matter? You missin' your woman this morning?"

Sawyer's nods were emphatic. "You are damn right, I'm missing her. She's probably shopping for just the right lacy underwear for when I get home. I bet it's black and…"

"Shut up!" Rhett said.

Sawyer laughed loudly. "Why? You wishin' you had a girlfriend thinking about nothing but you when you get home?"

"How do you know she's not thinking about anything else? Maybe she's thinking about her job or her friends," Haley said.

Sawyer shook his head. "I'm an O'Donnell. When we fall in love with a woman, they never think about anything else."

"That don't hold water, Sawyer. You weren't thinking about her when you joined this trail drive. You were thinking about being out here for days on end playing cowboy. You were all excited about riding a horse for a whole month and eating campfire food at night. So don't give me that load of bullshit about never thinking about anything else," Haley said.

He narrowed his eyes at her. "I said our women don't think of anything else, not that we don't."

"That's not fair then. If she's that besotted with you, then you should have stayed home with her and kept her happy," Haley argued.

"You should have been a lawyer," Coosie said. "Now you kids stop your bitchin' and fightin' and come eat breakfast. We're headin' out in half an hour and there's no snacking. Dinner ain't until noon."

All morning Dewar wondered if Haley thought about him as much as he did her during the day when he rode point and she brought up the rear. Did she ever imagine him riding naked? He imagined such things all the time.

He looked over at the longhorn who was eyeing him suspiciously. "Don't look at me like that. You've got a bunch of cows following you. Don't tell me you never think about them."

The longhorn shook his big horns and trotted on up ahead.

"Just what I thought. Male is male, no matter what the species," Dewar said.

Sawyer rode up beside him. "Who are you talkin' to?"

"Myself. And that means we need to get this ride done and go home. When a fellow starts expecting a damn longhorn to answer him, it's time to go home," Dewar said.

"You got a thing for Haley?"

"What makes you ask that?"

"You took her coffee this morning."

"Last week I handed Buddy a cup of coffee. You didn't ask me if I had a thing for him," Dewar said.

"You going to answer me?" Sawyer asked.

"Don't know yet. We've got a date when we get back to Texas. We'll see how that goes before I make any rash statements."

"It won't work," Sawyer said.

Dewar looked over at him.

"You can take the girl out of the city, but you can't take the city out of the girl. Kiss her good-bye at the end and cut your losses, cousin. She's pretty but she'd wither up and grow bitter on a ranch."

"Thanks for the advice," Dewar said.

"Get yourself a country girl like I got waitin' on me. Grew up on the ranch next door and we been datin' for two years. She's a keeper."

"Congratulations."

"Just sayin', man. Just sayin'." Sawyer turned his palomino horse around and headed back to his post.

"You think he's full of shit?" Dewar asked his horse.

Stallone raised his head and snorted.

"I thought so." Dewar laughed.

Chapter 26

ON FRIDAY MORNING THE WIND KICKED UP AGAIN AND the bandanas were jerked up to keep out the dust. Dewar rode to the back of the trail to make sure that Haley had her face covered. Her strange aqua-colored eyes looked huge when that's all he could see. She rode with one hand and held her old straw hat on with the other.

"Pretty damn good cowgirl, ain't she?" Coosie yelled from under his bandana.

Dewar nodded and turned around. When he passed Finn he made a motion for him to pull up for a minute.

"Something wrong?" Dewar asked.

Finn pulled his blue bandana down so he could talk. "You serious about that woman?"

"Why are you askin'?"

"Just wonderin'. Seems like in the past couple of days you been ridin' to the back a little more than usual. I don't think it's to steal sweets from the wagon."

"And if I was?"

"I'd say you was a smart man. She'll do to ride the river with, man. I didn't think she was worth a damn when she first joined the drive, but she's done good, especially for a city girl."

"What about that old sayin' about takin' the girl out of the city but you can't get the city out of the girl?" Dewar asked.

"Hey, that girl is an exception. You'd do well to ask her out when we get home," Finn said.

"I already did."

"Smart move. Let me know how that turns out." Finn pulled the bandana back up and rode off to bring a straggler back to the herd.

When night came the wind had ceased and they were stopping in a pasture with a working windmill and a big, round galvanized watering tank. The cattle lined up around the tank for their first water of the day. Eeyore waited his turn, checking the trees around them for any varmints that might be eyeballing his herd.

As she brushed Apache's dapple-gray hair, she unfocused her eyes and pretended that the tank was a hot tub. The grass around it was hard wood and the trees beyond that were a steamy spa where she'd sit a while after an hour-long massage.

Two more nights on the trail and she could have all of it. When she got home, she'd make an appointment for a whole day at the spa complete with a massage, a facial, and mani-pedi. It actually was not an option. It was a pure necessity before she donned her power suit and high heels and walked back into the conference room.

She couldn't go in there with her hair in braids, no makeup, and freckles shining across her nose.

"Oh, no!" she whispered.

She'd completely forgotten what the sun did to the freckles scattered across her nose when she spent too much time without sunblock. She had a small compact mirror in her purse tucked in the bottom of the saddlebags, but she hadn't taken it out in days. She wondered just how much damage the wind and sun had done to her face.

One look at her arms told her that she now had a farmer's tan. Brown below her shirtsleeves and white as the driven snow above them. Would Collette, her masseuse, know how to take care of that issue?

Coosie said that Sunday afternoon the boys were going to hit a bar or two and she could do whatever she wanted. Join them or stay in her room. Then the next day, on Monday, they were sleeping late and doing some sightseeing. On Tuesday morning bright and early the plane would be there to take them home.

Haley was determined that she was not going to the office her first day back in Dallas. Her father could have a fit for all she cared. It was going to take a whole day at the spa to make her presentable. If Carl Levy didn't like it he could fire her because she was not backing down.

The next morning she awoke earlier than everyone else and picked up her notebook. The end was in sight and the contestants would be both grouchy and giddy. They needed something really big right there on the last two days to draw in the viewers. She tapped the pencil against the paper and tried to think, but nothing materialized. She rubbed her forehead and still nothing.

Then it came to her like a lightning flash. Someone was going to get sick and hold up the process another day. The cook could always pretend some illness that would prevent them from going on. Being so close and then to have to sit still a whole day with nothing to do would drive them all insane. She wrote that down and hoped the whole time that she wasn't creating an omen and that Coosie would stay well.

Coosie coughed a couple of times and then rolled out of his bed, shook out his boots, and crammed his feet down in them. Haley held her breath until he started whistling. He wasn't dying with consumption or he didn't have pneumonia setting in out there thirty miles from a doctor.

"Hey, what're you doing up so early? Gettin' anxious about the end?" Coosie asked.

She pulled on her boots and joined him at the back of the chuck wagon where he was busy making biscuits and lining them up in the bottom of the big cast-iron Dutch oven.

"I woke up trying to think of something that would put a twist in the works right at the end of the reality show," she said. "I decided that the cook was going to pretend an illness so they'd have to sit still right here for an extra day and then you coughed."

Coosie laughed out loud. "That's a good one. Or else one of the women could start throwing up. They could think it was food poisoning but it would turn out one of the men got her pregnant."

Haley opened the spigot on the bottom of the barrel and filled the blue granite coffeepot. "But we couldn't depend on that happening. It might, but it's not a for-sure thing. The cook will be a paid employee and not a contestant, so he could feign sickness easily."

"Who's sick?" Dewar asked.

Sawyer sat straight up and rubbed his eyes. "Someone is sick? Well, shit! And right here at the end. We going to be able to go on?"

"No one is sick. We were talking about the reality show and the last few days of it," Haley said.

"Well, thank God. I'm ready to go home to my girl-friend. I swear, I'll never leave her for thirty whole days again. Hell, I might not even leave her for a couple of hours on Saturday night to go into town to a honky-tonk for a beer with the guys," Sawyer said.

A stabbing pain hit Haley in the heart. She'd have to leave Dewar. Maybe not for thirty days but for at least a week. Probably two weeks before she could get away to see him again.

––––⁓⁓––––

Saturday afternoon they crossed the Arkansas River. It hardly seemed like a river at all since it was noth-ing more than a dry riverbed. The chuck wagon had forded rivers, creeks, and gullies since the day they left Ringgold without a problem, but that day the wheels buried in the sand and no amount of horsepower could budge them.

Coosie wiped sweat from his bald head with his ban-dana and glared at Haley. "You wanted a problem to hold your show up a day. Looks like you got it. I might have expected you to make us a day late."

Coosie motioned for Buddy. "Come help me unload the wagon. If it's lighter maybe they can get it across and then we'll reload it."

"Haley, you take Buddy's place with the cattle then. And you two can catch up with us when you're back on firm ground," Dewar told Buddy and Coosie.

She rode on ahead to Buddy's normal place alongside the cattle and in a few minutes Sawyer was right beside her. "Hey, are you serious about my cousin?"

She shrugged.

"I talked to him about you."

She raised both eyebrows.

"I like you, Haley. I really do, but you're not for him. He's not poor by any means but you can't make a silk purse out of a sow's ear, you know."

"I would think how I feel about Dewar is my business. And I'll have you know I'm not a sow's ear," she said tersely.

"I'm not talkin' about you, darlin'. I'm talking about Dewar. He's a cowboy. You are a city girl. You can't mix halos and horns."

"And which am I? Horns or halos?"

"Okay, then you can't mix spikes and spurs."

"Oh? I betcha I could get a pair of spurs on my spike heels. We have a date planned. You want to make it a double date with your girlfriend? She could wear that black lacy thing you were talking about," Haley said.

Damn, she wished he would have never brought that blasted cup of coffee to her bedroll. They didn't get all concerned about the day he'd held her hand on the walk to the church as they did about that cup of coffee. What made it such a serious gesture?

She kept turning in the saddle and looking back, hoping to catch sight of Buddy and Coosie. As cranky as Coosie was, she liked riding with him better than Sawyer. But the sun kept getting lower and lower and still the wagon didn't show.

Dear Lord, what if I jinxed it when I thought about the cook getting sick? What if he broke an arm or worse, a leg, trying to get that wagon out of the sand? Buddy could never pick him up, as big as he is. What if Buddy fell and hit his head while trying to get Coosie into the wagon? One of us should have stayed with them just to be a lookout. They aren't young anymore. With that much work, they could even have a heart attack and be lyin' back there dead.

Finally, when Dewar had called it a day and stopped beside a farm pond, she heard Coosie cussing not far behind them and shouted, "They did it! They got the wagon out of the sand."

Eeyore brayed and rushed to her side. She scratched his ears and told him that she was fine. "I was just worried about the wagon. Give me time to get Apache brushed and out to eat his supper and then I'll brush your coat."

"That jackass knows which side his bread is buttered on." Finn chuckled.

"What's that mean?"

"None of us would brush him or make him into a pet the way you have. I bet you want Dewar to take him in the house when it snows this winter."

"He *will* have a stall in the barn, right, Dewar?"

"Quit worrying about Eeyore and get the fire going for supper." Coosie hopped down from the buckboard. "Me and Buddy worked up an appetite back there."

Finn and Sawyer gathered sticks and Rhett started removing the harnesses from the horses and brushing them down. In no time there was a pot of stew bubbling over the fire and a pan of corn bread cooking above that.

"This will be our last supper on the trail. I'll cook up extra for breakfast and we'll have leftovers from that for dinner tomorrow," Coosie said as he prepared supper.

"Wow!" Dewar exclaimed.

Buddy nodded. "We've almost m-m-made it."

Dewar looked at Haley. "So you think you can put a reality show together with what we've done?"

"Oh, yeah!" she said.

He looked across the campsite at his cousins. "Are you boys ready to go back to Texas?"

Sawyer raised his hand. "I am ready for a hotel room to scrub the grime off me first."

"Trip has been very good for me. I'm glad I came along for the ride and I think I've faced off my demons. I'm ready to go home," Finn said.

"I'm tired of this and I'm ready for a job that lets me sleep in a bed at night and take a shower. I'm even ready to dance with a pretty girl. How about you, Buddy?" Rhett asked.

"Ah, me and old D-d-dex... I mean Coosie could do this forever if it was just chasin' cows and cookin' supper. But if we couldn't go d-d-dancin' on Saturday nights, then we'd just as soon be back at the D-d-double D-d-deuce."

"You got that right. I wouldn't mind this kind of livin' if we could stop at a motel, clean up, and go have a beer and a two-step with the ladies every so often," Coosie said.

"What about you, Dewar? You tired of the trail?" Finn asked.

"I think I am. Now let's roll out our bedrolls one more time. Tomorrow we'll send them all home with the horses."

Haley busied herself getting her bed arranged, keeping her head turned away from the cowboys so they couldn't see the tears streaming down her face.

Chapter 27

HALEY FIDGETED IN HER SADDLE. SHE'D PROVEN, BY damn, that she wasn't all fluff, high heels, and hair spray. She could go out into the field and do the job. The last ten minutes of the journey took them toward an enormous feedlot already brimming with cattle. Several semis were parked in front of the small office building, but two took her eye immediately. One was bright red with Double Deuce painted on the side and the other was shiny black with the O'Donnell Horses logo printed on the side.

Those would be the trucks there to take the horses and Eeyore back to Ringgold. She swallowed an enormous lump in her throat and leaned forward to kiss Apache between the ears.

"You've been a good horse. I'll miss you," she whispered.

Eeyore trotted along beside her and looked up at the sound of her voice.

She wiped the tears on the sleeve of the denim jacket Liz had loaned her. "You'll be happy on the ranch. I promise I'll come and see you when I can."

The first day she'd thought it was all a big April Fools' joke. Now with good-byes at hand, she wished it had been.

When she and Coosie reached the parking lot, the cattle were already in three big pens. Liz, Raylen, Tyson, and Lucy sat on the porch of the office in rocking chairs. Lucy left the porch and threw her arms around Coosie first and then Buddy.

Haley expected someone ten feet tall and bulletproof, but Lucy was a short, pregnant brunette. Haley didn't see anything outstanding about her until she dismounted and saw her crystal clear blue eyes. They sparkled like the ocean water on the Hawaii shoreline and absolutely looked like they could see under Haley's hat and right into the depths of her soul.

"I'm Lucy and I missed Buddy and Dexter something awful." She extended her hand. "I didn't even get to talk to them on the phone. That's just not right."

Haley shook her hand and then saw another person coming toward her.

"I'm Tyson. Lucy is my wife and she keeps us all in line at the Double Deuce."

Tyson was almost as big as Coosie. He had close-cropped red hair and the freckled complexion that went with it. His shoulders were square to match his face, and his arms looked like he was a professional wrestler.

"Lucy should not be riding in that truck," Coosie grumbled.

"That's what I said but you know how it is." Tyson grinned.

Lucy popped her hands on her hips. "It's six weeks until the baby gets here. I could ride that horse if I wanted to."

Haley liked Lucy immediately. The woman had enough spunk that she could have probably ridden a horse for thirty days even if she was pregnant.

"You tell him. He never listens to me. And he made

us call him Coosie the whole trip and, if we didn't, he said when the trip was done, we had to give him a dollar for every time we made a mistake," Haley said.

"Well, you are Dexter to me and always will be." She looked over at Haley. "You've got to be a strong woman to have survived a month with this crew. Come visit me. I'd love to hear the stories."

"Thank you!" Haley stuck her tongue out at Coosie.

"That piece of meanness comes on the Double Deuce, I'll hide," Coosie teased.

"You can run, but I can run faster," Haley said.

Dewar rode up from the pens and dismounted. "We did it! We made it on schedule and in spite of a stampede, the cattle weighed in really good."

Raylen gave him one of those man hugs that said he'd missed his brother. "Momma is of the same opinion as Lucy. You aren't going to be able to go very far for a long time and you'll have to be home by suppertime."

"No problem there," Dewar said.

"Well, unsaddle them and we'll load 'em up. We drove up yesterday and had a little sightseeing today. Now we've got to get these trucks headed toward home if we're going to get these horses in their stalls by midnight," Raylen said.

"You'll be takin' that sorry-lookin' little jackass home too," Dewar said.

"You've got to be kidding me." Raylen snorted when he laughed.

"Nope. It belongs to Haley. Stupid thing survived lightning and he's her pet, only the fancy apartment she lives in seems to have a thing about four-legged jackasses. They let two-legged ones walk through the doors any old time. Just because Eeyore doesn't own a three-piece suit or Italian loafers he can't go inside," Dewar said.

Haley poked him on the arm. "You better take good care of him or he'll tattle."

"I don't doubt it for a minute," Dewar said.

Liz looped one arm through Haley's and the other through Lucy's. "Come on, ladies. We only have a few minutes to visit while they load up."

Haley removed her hat and jean jacket and handed them to Liz before she sat down in a rocking chair. "Thank you for letting me borrow them. I had no idea that day what I was getting into."

"Your suit and shoes are at my house. I'll put them in the backseat of your car tomorrow," Liz said. "There's something different about you, Haley. What happened out there on the drive?"

Lucy sat down in a rocking chair and whispered, "Did something happen out there between you and Dewar?"

"We don't mean to be rude. It's just that both of us noticed the way his eyes were on you when he rode up," Liz said.

"I don't know. We have a date sometime in the future. He's taking me to the Chicken Fried."

"It's Dewar." Lucy sighed.

"Dewar wouldn't be taking you to our local restaurant for the whole area to see you with him if he didn't really, really like you," Lucy explained.

"Then it's a big thing?" Haley asked.

"Yes, it is. Put on your best cowboy boots," Liz said seriously.

Haley straightened a leg and looked at the only pair of boots she owned. They'd walked through mud, cow shit, and rivers for a whole month.

"This is it," she said.

Liz laughed. "I know exactly where you are coming from, honey. I was in your boots a couple of years ago."

Dewar let out a whoop that caused Haley's head to jerk around so fast that it made her dizzy.

Liz smiled. "Raylen just told him that we're expecting a baby in December. If you listen just a minute you'll hear another one. Yep, there it is."

"What's the second one?" Haley asked.

"Their sister, Colleen, is also going to have a baby," Lucy said. "The O'Donnells love kids. The more the better."

"Plus yours," Haley said.

"They're claiming him. In Kentucky we call it shirt-tail kin. Looks like the menfolks got the wagon in the trailer. And Tyson is motioning to me. Our gossip session is done."

"Have fun these next two days and we'll set up a girls' night to have a long visit. Does Dewar have your phone number?" Liz asked.

"He will before we part company," Haley said.

"Good. Oh, and go see the Boot Hill Museum. It's pretty neat."

"And get your pictures made at that old-time photography place," Lucy threw over her shoulder.

Just that quick it was over.

Cattle in the pens. Eeyore in the truck headed for the O'Donnell ranch. The chuck wagon and two horses in the Double Deuce truck. It reminded Haley of Christmas morning when she was a little girl. She'd looked forward to the day for a whole month, shook the presents, sat for hours watching the twinkling lights, agonized over what kind of cookies to make for Santa, and then in less than an hour it was over.

She stood there bewildered and confused. Would her contestants feel like that when their horses were loaded up and taken away?

"Oh, shit!" she mumbled.

"What?" Coosie asked.

"My things from the saddlebags," she said.

"Are in grocery bags in the trunk of that black car over there." Dewar pointed.

One small black Chevrolet and two large white mini-vans were parked on the other side of the office porch.

"We got the white minivan since there are three of us, and besides, we called it first," Finn said. "And we let Coosie and Buddy have the other van since Coosie would have to eat his knees if he got into that little bitty car."

She looked at Dewar.

He shrugged. "We got the short straw. Raylen delivered our money for the month. So here they are, folks." He passed out envelopes filled with twenty-dollar bills to each of the cowboys and had two left when he was done. "One for you and one for me. Where do you want to go first?"

Haley was stunned. "I get paid too?"

"You worked. You get paid."

She took the envelope with H. B. McKay written on the outside.

"I want to go shopping," she said.

Finn grinned so big that his eyes disappeared. "Well, that settles it. She's riding with you, Dewar."

"Y'all ain't going to buy new duds?" Dewar asked.

"Nope. I intend to do laundry at the hotel, take a bath, and put on my clean clothes and then go out on the town," Finn said.

"You can bet your sweet little ass I'm not shopping. Me and Buddy is going to get some good old hamburgers and take them to our room and watch television all night," Coosie said. "Lord, I missed *Law and Order*."

"Looks like you are with me. I suppose the trail boss should suffer through shopping and let the rest of the crew have a good time," Dewar said forlornly.

"Well, that's so nice of you," she smarted off.

"See, I told you. She's got a temper to go with that red hair," Sawyer said.

Haley held out her hand. "I believe one hundred dollars of what is in that envelope belongs to me."

He opened it up and counted out five twenty-dollar bills, put them in her hand, and said, "Don't spend it all in one place, darlin'."

"It'd buy a nice second tat," Rhett said.

She pointed at him. "Go get a haircut and hush!"

"We'll meet at the airport at twelve thirty, day after tomorrow," Dewar said.

Coosie and Buddy's van pulled out onto the road heading into town with the other cowboys right behind them. Dewar opened the passenger door to the small car for Haley and waited until she was settled before he closed it. He whistled on the way around the back end of the vehicle. He'd wondered how in the great green earth he and Haley would ever get to ride in the same vehicle and spend the next couple of days together without a problem, but she'd fixed it all by saying that she wanted to go shopping.

"So where to, m'lady?" Dewar asked.

She raised one shoulder. "I have no idea. Never been here before. I need a shop that sells underwear and clothes. Doesn't have to be fancy."

He backed the car around and pulled out onto the highway. "I haven't been here in a couple of years. We come up to the rodeo sometimes. I do remember a Walmart because we went there to buy food."

"That will do fine," Haley said.

"You'll wear Walmart clothes?" He gasped.

"I'd wear Goodwill right now."

"Okay, then Walmart it is. I think we turn on Fourteenth Street if I remember right. The hotels are all on Wyatt Earp Boulevard and Fourteenth comes right off that."

"There is Fourteenth," she said excitedly and flinched when a truck passed them.

"Trucks go faster than horses, darlin'." Dewar chuckled.

"Who would have thought it would be difficult to adjust back into the world?" she said.

"It spooked me too," he admitted.

"I see the sign. Wow! I'm getting excited about a Walmart. I think you've made me into a redneck, Dewar."

"Only for a little while. When we get back to Texas, you'll be the high-maintenance businesswoman you were when you joined up with this renegade band of cowboys."

He parked the car and she was out of it before he

could open the door for her. She grabbed his hand and practically pulled him inside the store and shivered when the cold air rushed out.

"I'd forgotten about air-conditioning. It wasn't a dream. It really does exist," she said.

"Yes, ma'am. Now where to first?"

"Underwear. Mine is threadbare and then a couple of outfits to get me home. And a pair of sandals, some fingernail polish, and hair spray and good soap."

He pulled out a shopping cart. "Guess we're going to need this. We might even need to call Coosie to come tote your things to the hotel in the van."

She grabbed the front of the cart and pulled him toward the clothing section. "Why did he get the van anyway?"

"Raylen said that there were only three cars left at the small rental company and he took them all. He'd hoped to get club cab pickup trucks for us, but he had to settle with what they had. The company did agree to come out to the airport and get them on Tuesday so we don't have to take them back and get taxis."

She tossed three pairs of lacy bikini underpants in the cart and followed those with two new bras and then pulled the cart in the direction of a rack of sundresses. She chose a white one with pink polka dots and a mint green one and headed for the shoe aisle. If anyone had told her six months before that she'd wear a pair of shoes from Walmart, she'd have ordered up a CAT scan for them.

She picked up a pair of pink sandals and a white pair and put them into the cart. "Now to the place where they sell sweet-smelling soap, bubble bath, and shampoo."

"I need some Stetson and a new razor. I reckon those will be in the same place," Dewar said.

She stopped and looked up at him. "I'm sorry. Did you want to buy new clothes?"

"I'm going to do what the boys are doing. Find the laundry room at the hotel and do some washing. I could probably use new socks. Mine all have holes in them."

She steered him toward the menswear. "Tube socks for boots?"

He nodded and she tossed in a bag with six pairs.

"Underwear?"

"Commando."

She shivered.

"Cold?" he asked.

"No, commando. That was not a weather shiver but an anticipation one."

He grinned. "It's going to be an interesting two days."

She stopped at the cosmetics section and threw in everything she thought she might need. While she did that, he picked up a bottle of Stetson, shaving cream, and a new razor.

"Now food," she said.

"We're eating in tonight?" he asked.

"Let's order pizza tonight in the room. And I need a nightshirt or…" She wiggled her eyebrows.

"Black and lacy like Sawyer said?" Dewar asked.

She did indeed find a black lacy teddy, but she put it back on the rack when she saw a flowing white gown trimmed in green velvet on a clearance rack. It was no doubt leftovers from Christmas, but she loved the feel of the cool cotton and all the little pin tucks on the yoke.

"That's pretty damn sexy, ma'am," he whispered.

She tiptoed and kissed him on the cheek. "I hope you think so when it's hanging on me and not on the hanger. And now to the food. We'll need snack stuff. Microwave popcorn. Beer. Cookies."

"We're only going to be here two days, darlin', not a month."

"Yep, and I plan to work up a helluva appetite in those two days."

Chapter 28

THE LADY BEHIND THE COUNTER AT THE HOTEL didn't snarl when Haley and Dewar pushed the door open, but they could see it took a lot of willpower for her not to do so.

"We'd like a room for two nights," Dewar said.

"Sorry. We're booked up except for one whirlpool king," she said.

"We'll take it. And could you tell me who makes the best pizza in town?"

"I'll need ID and a credit card," she said.

Dewar pulled out his wallet and laid both on the counter. "Pizza?"

"There's a folder in the room with all the restaurants in town, but this is my favorite. It's a little more expensive but it's really good." She handed him a brochure from under the counter with a menu and prices.

"Thank you."

She pushed a paper in front of him and handed him a pen. "Breakfast is from six to ten in the morning right through those doors. Here's your room key. Anything else?"

"That'll do it," Dewar said.

"Good," Haley said. "Let's go get our luggage."

A wicked grin played at the corners of Dewar's mouth. "You mean our saddlebags?"

"No, I mean our Walmart plastic bags."

The woman pursed her lips in a tight little line.

As luck would have it, the six o'clock news came on the television in the lobby and the anchorwoman said, "And today, six cowboys and one cowgirl finished up a grueling monthlong reenactment of the Chisholm Trail cattle run as a prelude to a reality show that will air next spring. We'd hoped to interview them, but they came in earlier than expected and when we got here all we had to talk to was one longhorn bull and ninety-nine head of cattle. However, Dewar O'Donnell, the trail boss for the operation, told the manager of the feedlot that it had been a wonderful experience…"

"Aren't you glad we got in early?" Haley said.

The woman behind the counter whipped the paper around and looked at Dewar's signature and picked up the phone.

Dewar threw an arm around Haley's shoulder and ushered her out to the parking lot. "I didn't know they were putting it on the news."

She was as fidgety as a sugared-up six-year-old after a day at Grandma's house by the time Dewar popped open the trunk of the car. They both looked like laden-down pack mules when they went back inside the motel's lobby.

"Do you need help with that?" the woman asked cheerfully.

"No, ma'am, we've got it," Dewar answered.

Haley could hardly stand still as he pulled the room card from his pocket. She'd waited for this for a whole month and, like Christmas morning, it had finally arrived. But suddenly she was terrified that she hadn't gotten the right cookies and the look on her face must have shown the fear.

"Is it not what you wanted? We can go somewhere else," Dewar said quickly.

"No, it's great. It's perfect. Even if it didn't have a whirlpool tub, it would be perfect." She crossed the room and unloaded several bags on the desk and sunk down into a chair.

"No bouncing on the bed?" Dewar asked.

"I'm too dirty to flop out on a bedspread, and the look on my face wasn't because this room isn't good enough, Dewar. I was thinking about Christmas."

He sat down on the sofa and propped his feet on the coffee table. "That's a helluva long way from the end of April whether you go backwards or forwards."

"I used to get so excited at Christmas. I couldn't wait for it to arrive. I loved the presents and the tree and the pretty decorations and the dinner afterwards. Then the next day we flew down to Louisiana and I got to play with my cousins for a couple of days and visit with Granny Jones."

"I thought your momma was a McKay?"

"She was. Granny is her grandmother. Her mother died when she was young and her grandmother raised her. But on Christmas I used to worry and worry about what kind of cookies to leave Santa Claus. That thought went through my mind when you opened the door. I wondered if I had chosen the right cookies at Walmart for us to snack on."

Dewar left the sofa and kneeled beside the chair. Without touching her, he leaned forward and brushed a sweet kiss across her lips. "Darlin', these next two days are going to be even better than Christmas, and Santa Claus is going to love whatever cookies you have."

Her heart skipped a beat just like it did when she had opened the first present under the tree or when she'd stepped off the airplane to find her granny waiting beside the big outlandish twenty-year-old Caddy. Who said Christmas had to be in December?

He stood up and kicked off his boots. "I'm going for a shower. You can have the whirlpool and they'd better have a lot of hot water in this place."

She jerked her boots off and tossed her socks on the pile of dirty clothing he was making beside the sofa. When he was completely undressed he padded naked to the bathroom. His nice firm butt was white, along with his legs, his back, and arms down to where his shirtsleeves ended. The rest, including his neck, was tanned to a rich brown.

She peeled her jeans and underpants down at the same time, then came out of her shirt and bra. She shut her eyes when she passed the mirror on the closet doors, but when she got into the bathroom she chanced a glance toward the mirror above the vanity and groaned. Her forehead had a line across it where the straw hat had sat day in and day out. Below the line was as brown as Dewar's neck. Above it was lily white. The same with her arms. The area below the shirtsleeves matched her eyes, nose, and chin. Above that she was pale.

"Shit!" she mumbled. "I can wear long sleeves, but even makeup won't cover this forehead."

Dewar's singing in the shower took her mind off the reflection in the mirror. It was an old Willie Nelson song, "You Were Always on My Mind." She didn't hear the words as much as she heard the deep timbre of Dewar's voice.

She leaned down and adjusted the water in the tub and poured in a double dose of bubble bath, laid out a razor for her legs, which were a fright, along with shampoo and conditioner, and set the lotion on the vanity. Then she unbraided her hair and sunk down into the warm water.

She leaned back in the water, bubbles and all, and got her hair wet then lathered it up. Leaving the shampoo in her hair to do its job, she hummed along with the next song Dewar sang and shaved her legs.

"Luxury," she said.

"What was that?" Dewar stepped out of the shower onto the bath mat. Dark hair plastered against his neck and hung in his eyes. He towel dried it and then combed it back with his fingers.

"Your hair has gotten long in a month," she said.

"I like you better as a redhead."

She looked at him with a question on her face.

"You're a platinum blonde right now."

She reached up to a head full of suds and smiled. "I'm glad you like the red hair."

"Always have. Must be the Irish in me. Want me to rinse that out for you?" He wrapped the towel around his waist and picked up a glass. He knelt beside the tub and held the glass under the water, filling it time after time and pouring the warm water through her hair as his fingers worked the suds out.

"My God, that is sexy," she said.

He kissed her on the neck right under her ear. "Yes, it is."

She turned her face up to find his eyes half-shut and dreamy. His mouth found hers and the hunger in his kiss came close to boiling the bathwater.

"You ready to get out of here?" he whispered.

"Oh, yeah!"

He stood up and reached into the water, scooped her out, and set her on the vanity. He picked up a thick white towel and dried her hair.

"Dewar, this is heaven," she said.

He leaned down and kissed her on the forehead. "Your skin is as soft as silk and I can't ever seem to get enough of you."

She gasped when he kissed her hard, picked her up, and carried her to the bed. He reached down with one hand and threw the covers back and laid her on the cotton sheets, then crawled in beside her, covering both of them with the top sheet and fluffy duvet. His lips found hers in another searing kiss and she snuggled as close to him as she could get.

Maybe if she melted her body into his he would never leave her, maybe the next two days would be the new *Groundhog Day*, and she could relive them day after day until she died.

Her body had gone from hot to blazing with his kisses. Now that his hands were everywhere, the noise that came from her throat was almost as feral as that mountain lion had been the first night he kissed her. She tried to hold it back, but it was impossible. She wanted him worse than she ever had.

The vibrations shaking her insides into hot overflowing lava had already knocked any sanity or dignity out of her. She wanted him inside her. Right that minute. She didn't want two hours of foreplay. She wanted to feel the heat of him on her and in her and she didn't want to wait.

Her hips arched against him, against a hard erection, and he moaned. "God, Haley, slow down or…"

"I don't want slow. I want fast, furious, and wild. Please, Dewar." She pressed harder against him. "I've thought about this for two days."

He drove into her but it only made things hotter. She'd never known such wild abandon heat existed. Not even a Texas wildfire could eat up as much pastureland as his thrust after thrust created in the pit of her belly.

Her wrists were above her head, held there firmly, and his mouth was on hers, demanding, tasting, and driving her to climax and then building another bonfire from nothing but ashes.

She squealed the second time the fire erased every thought from her mind except pleasure with Dewar. She heard him say something that sounded like her name and he let go of her hands, sunk his face into her neck, and groaned.

He ran a hand down her ribs and she instinctively arched against him again.

"More?" he asked.

"Not right now. My God, I have no bones. I'm just a puddle of satisfaction. I can't even think."

He started to roll to one side and she wrapped her legs around him to keep him where he was.

"No. Don't go. Five more minutes. I like the way you feel on top of me."

"You do have bones." He kissed her tenderly, nibbling at her lip.

"But they are weak, so don't fight me. Feel that warmth?"

"Need the air-conditioning adjusted?"

"No, it's that magical stuff called afterglow. Don't you just love it?"

"I thought the bed was on fire," he teased.

She reached around and slapped his bare butt.

"Are we going kinky?"

She giggled. "Not me. I can barely keep up with you in conventional sex. It don't get no better than this, darlin'."

"You got that right, honey."

His voice drifted off and his body relaxed. She felt him leave her as he rolled to one side and shut his eyes. It wasn't a disappointment because it wasn't a final good-bye. More like a wait-a-little-while and I'll be back moment. She cuddled up next to him and slept.

A hard knock on the door awoke her and she reached for Dewar only to get a handful of nothing but sheets and pillow. She sat up, tucked the sheet under her arms, and looked around. Something wasn't right. She didn't remember drapes over the windows in the trailer.

The smell of pizza filled the room. She must be dreaming. Coosie could cook in the trailer kitchen with the propane, but he wouldn't be making pizza for breakfast... and where did the bed come from?

The cobwebs cleared from her head when Dewar appeared wearing clean jeans and carrying a box of pizza in one hand and a six-pack of beer in the other.

"Sleeping Beauty has awakened," he said.

"How long did we sleep? What time is it?"

"I woke up an hour ago and did the laundry. I checked in on you a couple of times, but you weren't moving a muscle. I ordered pizza and offered the delivery boy extra money if he'd bring beer with it."

"Best sex I ever had. Better than sleeping pills." She smiled. "Give me five minutes."

She dropped the sheet and made a beeline to the bathroom. There was toilet paper on the roller and an extra roll behind that, so she wasn't sparing when she grabbed the cute little end folded into a point.

She took a fast shower, dried quickly, and donned the fresh lacy underwear and nightgown she'd hung on the back of the door before she got into the tub hours before. She looked in the mirror and whined like a two-year-old who'd lost her favorite blanket when she saw the half-white forehead. She drew down a feathering of bangs and sawed them off with the razor she'd shaved her legs with and looked again. They weren't even but at least she didn't look like a mutant skunk. She brushed out the rest of her naturally wavy hair and let it fall to her shoulders.

When she opened the door Dewar's eyes widened and he sucked in enough air to whistle softly. "My God, you are beautiful."

"It's just a cotton gown," she said.

"It's sexy as hell and you look like an angel."

"Thank you," she said. "But this angel is starving."

He twisted the lids off two bottles of beer and opened the pizza. "I didn't know what you liked so I got a meat lovers."

"My favorite." She sat down beside him on the sofa, pulled her feet up under her, and let the ruffled tail of the gown float down to the floor.

"Wow!"

She looked up.

"You really do look like an angel, Haley."

"Do you know what an angel is, darlin'?" Her eyes were more green than blue in the dim light of the lamp.

He shook his head.

She sipped the beer and said, "It's a woman who's had the hell screwed out of her. In that respect, I might be an angel."

He laughed out loud and handed her a beer. "You drinking that, looking like you do, seems wrong. You should be drinking pure water straight from heaven."

"Well, don't be getting that picture fixed too firm in your mind because after we eat and let it settle a bit, I intend to hang this gown on that chair over there along with my halo and put on my horns again," she teased.

Dewar laughed again and picked up a piece of pizza. He held it toward her mouth and she opened wide. He held it firmly until she'd bitten off a chunk at the pointed end and then he took the next bite.

"Food for the gods, so we might both be angels," she said after she'd swallowed.

"Pizza your favorite food?" he asked.

"No, but you can't laugh if I tell you," she whispered. "And you might have to sign in blood and put the document in the wall safe."

His curiosity was piqued. "Give me one of those napkins. I'll prick my finger."

It was her turn to laugh and it felt good to be sitting in a hotel room flirting with a sexy cowboy who thought she was beautiful. "It's hamburgers. Big old greasy hamburgers with mustard, lettuce, tomatoes, and pickles and french fries and a big chocolate malt."

"Onions?"

She shook her head. "Not me. Ruins a kiss."

"You are kidding me, aren't you?"

Another wiggle of the head. "No, sir! I love pizza,

but burgers are my favorite. Momma says it's my back-woods blood surfacing."

"Was your momma backwoods?" he asked be-tween bites.

She picked up her very own piece of the pie. "No, but her grandmother, the granny who is still alive in Louisiana, was. Goes like this. Granny lived out in the Bayou Teche on an island and only came to town a couple of times a year and they docked the boat at a ramp that a sugar plantation owner had built. Story has it that when she was eighteen her family came to town and the plantation owner's son was fishing off the ramp. The next month they were married. Momma met Daddy when he came to Louisiana to do a piece on sugarcane for his dad's magazine."

"So back there in the woodpile you've already got a few redneck genes?"

"No, darlin', I got Cajun genes. There's a big difference."

Chapter 29

HALEY AND DEWAR WERE BOTH IN THE PANTING stages of the grand finale of wild morning sex when the room phone rang. Simultaneously they threw back the sheet and sat straight up, eyes wide and stunned.

On the second ring, Dewar grabbed the receiver and said, "Hello."

Haley took several deep breaths. It had only been a month since she'd heard a telephone, so why did it scare the bejesus out of her? And who in the hell other than the front desk even knew where they were? If it was the snooty lady down at the desk, she hoped Dewar read her the riot act.

But his voice was all honey and sugar when he said, "Yes, ma'am."

She cut her eyes around to see the phone receiver coming right at her hand.

"Your mother," he mouthed.

She put it to her ear but couldn't say a word for a second because she was busy watching Dewar's fine-looking butt going toward the bathroom.

"Haley!" Jenny Levy yelled.

"Hello, Mother," Haley said.

"Who answered your phone?"

"Dewar, and you know that because the room is in his name, not mine," Haley said.

Silence.

"What are you doing in his room?"

"It's our room. He paid for it, so his name is on the register."

More silence.

"You want to explain?"

"Not right now."

"Have your fling, but you will explain when you get home tomorrow. We have a conference at five o'clock. We'll have a private one with your father, you, and me at four thirty. That will give you plenty of time," Jenny said.

"Tomorrow I'm going straight to the spa when I get home. Even a mother's love would be shocked at the way I look right now, and when you see me with freckles and a farmer's tan, you take it all up with Daddy. Wednesday I'll come to the house for supper," she said.

"It's dinner, not supper, and Joel is invited but not at home. We're going out that evening to celebrate you coming home."

Haley rolled her eyes.

"He would like a second chance," Jenny said.

"I wouldn't."

"Oh, I think you would."

"Momma, that boat has left the harbor. It wrecked at sea and there were no survivors. You can invite whomsoever you please to dinner but it ain't happenin' with me and Joel."

"We'll see. See you on Wednesday. Reservations have already been made at your favorite restaurant."

"McDonald's?"

"Don't be ridiculous! You've grown up past burgers and fries."

Dewar came out of the bathroom with a towel around his waist, water droplets still hanging on his hair, and smelling like Stetson. He dropped the towel and crawled up from the bottom of the king-sized bed like a big cat, his eyes twinkling in mischief.

Haley giggled. "Gotta go, Momma. See you Wednesday unless I decide to stay a whole week in Dodge City and hitchhike home."

She reached across the bed, put the receiver back on the base, and popped up on her hands and knees to crawl toward Dewar. She growled deep in her throat and he responded. The next sound out of her was a sexy purr that could have been heard all the way down to the lobby.

———

Boot Hill Museum covers a whole city block on land that once was Boot Hill Cemetery and still has a few of those ancient graves with rough wood crosses bearing the names of the folks lying six feet under.

Haley and Dewar bought tickets in the gift shop but they made out in the darkness through the fifteen-minute video presentation about the area instead of watching the film. They held hands as they started the tour, first in the cemetery, then in the exhibit hall, and finally down to the actual replica of an old-time Western town.

"First stop, the Long Branch Saloon," he said. "You'd have made a right fetching dancing girl in your short-tailed skirts and fancy shoes."

"And you'd have been the cowboy who came in and sat right up close to the stage, right?"

"Oh, honey, I'd have been the cowboy who snatched you off that stage and carried you over my shoulder back to my ranch so far back in the sticks no other man would have ever been able to take you away from me." He kissed her lips, still bee-stung from that morning's romp in the hotel room and the making-out session in the darkness of the tiny theater.

"Well, if that's the case, then buy me a beer. I might never get another one if I'm living on the backside of hell for the rest of my life."

He smiled, but a niggling thought surfaced that reminded him she would probably look at his ranch like the backside of hell after living the fast-paced life that Dallas offered.

She sat down on one of the bar stools and crossed one leg over the other.

He held up two fingers to the bartender. "Two beers, longneck Coors if you have them."

He turned his attention back to Haley while the bartender wiped the moisture from the outside of the bottles.

"You are beautiful in that pretty dress, Miz Haley." He ran a hand up her thigh and smiled when goose bumps rose up.

"That makes me hot," she whispered softly.

The bartender set the bottles down in front of them. "Two beers. Need glasses?"

"No, this is fine," Dewar said.

"Y'all on your honeymoon?" he asked.

"Yes, we are," Dewar said quickly.

"We don't get many honeymooners, but I sure recognize them when we do. You make a good couple. Bet you are a bull rider and you do barrel racing, right?" he asked.

"You nailed it," Haley said.

He whistled as he wiped down an already clean bar and waited on three elderly couples that had claimed a table close to the stage area.

"When did we get married? Did I miss something?" she whispered between sips of beer.

"Don't you remember? It was just before I made an angel out of you," Dewar teased.

"Do we have a picture to prove it?"

He whispered into her ear, "No, but there's a picture place right down the street from the saloon. Want to get one done there for your momma?"

She turned quickly and kissed him full smack on the lips. The bartender stopped whistling and three little ladies giggled behind their dark brown sarsaparilla bottles.

"Yes, I will definitely need proof," she said.

They carried their beers with them and meandered through one building after another until they reached the old-time picture place. Dewar tipped his bottle up and finished off the last drop before tossing it into a barrel just outside the place. He waited for Haley to do the same and then threw an arm around her shoulder and opened the door.

"You folks want a honeymoon picture made?" the man asked.

Dewar nodded.

"First a proper wedding picture and then we want one done where I'm a saloon girl and he's the sheriff," Haley said.

"Like Miss Kitty and Marshall Dillon?" he asked.

"That's right, but first the wedding picture of her in that outfit." Dewar pointed to a white dress and a lace veil hanging on the back of a chair.

"You are my second newlyweds today. Come right on over here, ma'am, and I'll help get you hitched up into this dress." He held it up like a backwards robe and she shoved her arms through the long sleeves, and then turned around to allow him to tie the back.

He fussed and muttered around getting the high collar to stand up just right and then handed Haley a handful of hairpins. "You've got such a good look for this picture. Would you mind twisting your hair up like they wore it in those days? There's a mirror behind you."

"You got a rubber band anywhere in this place?" she asked.

He handed her one from the desk behind the camera.

She'd seen her grandmother do her hair dozens of times. First she pulled her hair up into a high ponytail, fastened the rubber band a couple of inches from the scalp, then simply squatted it down to the top of her head, twisted, and held the loose bun down with a few pins.

"Wow!" Dewar exclaimed.

"Granny does it all the time. I figured I could copy what she does with a rubber band." She pulled a few strands down from the washerwoman hairdo to frame her face.

The photographer set the lace veil right in front of the bun and smiled. "Perfect. Now you are going to stand behind your groom. Give me a minute to get him in the proper suit for a wedding."

Haley watched as the photographer pulled out the right shirt and tied it behind Dewar's back. Then he set a hat on his head, handed him a jacket, and patted the chair for him to sit.

"Shouldn't the bride sit?" Dewar asked.

"No sir!" He laughed.

"Why?" Haley asked.

"It's not proper for me to say such things in front of an innocent new bride." He chuckled.

"After the picture is taken and I get into my saloon outfit, can you tell me?" she pressed on.

"Yes, ma'am. A man could tell a dancin' girl such a thing but not a new bride. Now you stand right here behind him with your hands on his shoulders, over to the side just half a step so we can see more of your dress; that's perfect, and now look this way. Oh, you two make the perfect newlyweds."

He shot three different angles and then motioned for them to take a look on the computer screen. "Which one?"

"I want all three," Haley said.

"I'll take that one," Dewar pointed.

"All eight-by-tens?" the photographer asked.

"Yes, sir." Haley nodded.

"Why do you want all three?" Dewar asked.

"One for my desk. One for my granny for proof, and one for Momma. Now put me in the saloon getup and tell me why I stood and he sat in the last picture," Haley said.

He quickly transformed her from a bride to a dancing girl and Dewar from a groom to a cowboy with chaps, a gun, a different hat, and spurs. "This time you sit on this stool right here, ma'am, and you, sir, put one arm around her shoulder. You look up into his eyes and you look down at her like you could eat her up."

Dewar put an arm around her shoulder and tilted her chin up with his fist. "No problem doing that. I could eat her up."

"Perfect. Hold it. Don't move. God, you two are so good at this."

He snapped three times in rapid order and then motioned for them to come take a look. "Would you sign a consent form for me to use this one as a display? If you will I'll give you each a copy for free."

"If you tell me your raunchy story about why I have to stand and he has to sit in the wedding photos," Haley said.

He shoved a paper toward them and Haley signed with a flourish. Dewar's handwriting was more cramped and tight.

"Okay, the story is like this. In the old days the photographer didn't go to the wedding to take the picture on the very day the couple married. Usually, they got married in the living room of a loved one's home or sometimes in the church, but it wasn't the big affair that it is today. So the newly wedded couple waited until the next day after the wedding and came to town for the picture."

"And?" Haley said when he stopped.

"Think about it," he said.

Haley shook her head slowly. "I'm getting nothing. Explain it to me."

"Okay, here's the deal. It's the next day after their first night together. Darlin', he's too tired to stand up and she's too sore to sit down."

Haley threw a hand over her mouth and laughed so hard she got the hiccups. "Damn, that's funny," she finally sputtered.

"And true." Dewar chuckled.

"You got that right. I'll take three of those too," Haley said.

"I want three of them also," Dewar said.

"For who?"

Dewar planted a kiss on her forehead. "One to hang above the mantel in our living room, honey. And one for my momma, and one for my granny. They'll like the hussy picture better than the wedding picture."

They paid the bill and told the photographer they'd pick up their pictures on their way back to the car. Then they wandered back outside, across the front lawn to the church where they sat down on a bench. Dewar carefully removed all the pins from Haley's hair and pulled it free from the rubber band to let it fall down around her shoulders. Then he tangled his fingers in it and kissed her hard right there in front of all the tourists and even God if He was looking out the church window.

"You ever had sex in an outhouse?" he drawled.

Her nose snarled. "I don't think I could get past the smell."

Dewar's face broke into a grin. "It's a real outhouse, but it hasn't been used in probably a hundred years or more." He pointed to a small white house with peeling paint not far from the church. "I don't reckon it'll smell like anything but fresh air."

She giggled. "I'm an outhouse virgin, but I'm game if you are."

He pulled her up by her hand. "Are you serious? I want you right now, Haley. Must have been the photo session. God might strike me dead or else that little old lady over there with the blue hair might call the cops if we have sex on the church bench," he said.

"Then outhouse, here we come." She pulled him in that direction.

It was barely big enough for them to get inside and shut the door, but they managed. Dewar pinned her against the door and she hopped up to wrap her legs around his waist. His hands went to cup her bottom and his mouth found hers in a kiss that sent steam flying out the customary outhouse moon cut in the door.

He tore the side of her panties trying to get his big hand inside them, and she reached down to help him. Then suddenly her other hand and his were battling to see who could unzip his jeans and undo his belt fastest.

Her back was braced against the wall, one of his hands was still fumbling with her underpants, and then boom, he was inside and thrusting. The excitement in the small dark place with her so solid against the wall all but knocked the breath right out of her.

"Mercy!" she said.

And then it was over, three thrusts later, as fast as it had started. In all her memory, that had to be the quickest climax she'd ever reached.

"Whew!" he said.

"I know! And in an outhouse! It was fantastic," she panted.

He eased her away from the wall and stepped back as far as he could, pulled a white handkerchief from his hip pocket, and handed it to her.

"Thank you. I was wondering about that."

"Guess I owe you a new pair of underwear." He chuckled.

"These will hold together until we get back to the hotel. Or I could leave them in that hole right there with this hanky and go commando the rest of the day."

"Not if you want to have dinner at that cute little

restaurant we saw. Just thinking about you commando will bust the zipper out of my jeans and we'll have to go back to the hotel."

She tiptoed and kissed him, rearranged her clothing, and peeked out the moon-shaped hole. "It's all clear. No auras floating around the church and the blue-haired granny has disappeared. I'm opening the door now."

"One more second!" he said. "Got to buckle my belt and kiss you one more time. Man doesn't do a slam-bam-thank-you-ma'am job and not even kiss the angel."

Chapter 30

HALEY LOOKED AT THE COMPANY PLANE ON THE SHORT taxiway and sighed. She'd had the perfect honeymoon but no marriage. Dewar hadn't even said the three magic words even though there had been plenty of opportunity.

"Miz Haley, it's good to see you again," Kyle, the pilot, said.

She shaded her eyes with her hand and wished for Liz's old straw hat. "You too."

"Can I get your bags for you?"

She laughed. "That would be my Walmart plastic sacks this time, Kyle. I think Dewar and I can handle them."

Dewar stuck out his hand. "Hello. I'm Dewar O'Donnell, the trail boss for the cattle operation."

Kyle shook hands with him. "I'm Mr. Levy's pilot, Kyle Massey. You are the last ones here, so if we can get your luggage, oh dear, she wasn't teasing." He gasped when Haley brought out several plastic bags.

"No, she wasn't. We sent the saddlebags home with the horses. I'm afraid Samsonite doesn't work on a cattle drive," Dewar said.

Coosie waved from the backseat in the plane when they boarded and the steps were coming up behind them. "Look who decided to fly with us. We thought maybe you two killed each other over that shopping trip."

Haley opened the one plastic bag she'd kept with her

and handed Coosie two boxes of Oreos and Buddy a brand new bottle of strawberry Boone's Farm.

"Are we even now?" she asked.

"We are even," Coosie said.

"Please buckle your seat belts," Kyle said.

Dewar and Haley sat down beside each other and buckled up. She glanced at the cousins. Rhett looked tired. Finn looked bored, and Sawyer's eyes were swollen.

"Leave you boys alone for two days with a month's paycheck and you don't even look happy?" she said.

"Sawyer didn't waste a bit of time using the hotel phone to call his woman, and he's been poutin' like a girl since," Rhett said.

"There's a big difference in pouting and having a broken heart," Sawyer said.

"He wouldn't leave the room. He's drunk a whole bottle of whiskey and we had to coax him to get him to eat," Finn said.

Haley touched Sawyer on the shoulder. "Tell me what happened."

"She was at a party the weekend after I left and it happened. She fell in love with someone else. They flew to Vegas on Saturday and got married and she's going to live in Greencastle, Pennsylvania. What Texas girl moves off to Pennsylvania anyway?"

Haley patted his shoulder. "I'm so sorry, but she couldn't have loved you as much as you loved her or that wouldn't have happened."

"I should have stayed home and she wouldn't have gone to that stupid office party."

"Put on your big-boy britches and suck it up. If you'd stayed home and y'all got married while we were all gone, it wouldn't have lasted," Dewar said as the plane took off.

Haley slapped him on the leg.

"What was that for? He's had mollycoddling for two days. He needs to man up. When he gets home he doesn't need to be whining around like a little girl. He needs for his friends and family to see him with his head up."

"Momma and Poppa havin' trouble with the babies back there?" Coosie called over his shoulder.

"What does Grandpa think he should do?" Haley yelled back.

"I'm not old enough to be his grandpa, but if I was I'd tell him the same thing that Dewar did. She's gone. Water's done flowed away under that bridge and it's time to burn the damn thing."

"Okay, okay! Enough advice. Lord, I'll be glad to be back home just to get away from all you meddlin' relatives." Sawyer leaned his head back and shut his eyes.

"What did you two do, Coosie?" Haley asked.

"Me and D-d-dexter went to that big m-m-museum. Boot Hill. We had us a beer at the saloon and looked around at all the stuff," Buddy said. "We went to a Western-wear store and bought us new boots."

He shoved a big foot out into the aisle to show Haley and she nodded.

"We watched some television and ate too d-d-damn m-m-uch food and D-d-dexter, he d-d-don't snore as m-m-much on a bed as on the ground. What did y'all d-d-do besides shop?"

Haley felt the blush crawling up her neck and didn't dare look at Dewar or it would have gone into full-blown crimson. What did they do? Well, they made an angel out of her—several times!

"Did you go to the museum or shop the whole time?" Coosie asked.

"We shopped for about an hour at the Walmart store. I bought this dress and shoes there," she said.

"And you look almighty pretty in them. I didn't expect you to clean up nearly as good." Coosie chuckled.

"We went to the museum yesterday and we ate at that Mexican place on the south side of the highway just down from the hotel where we stayed," she said.

And if you look closely there's a halo floating above my head because Dewar screwed the hell out of me.

"Did you go inside the church?" Coosie asked.

"No, we didn't know you could go inside."

But I'm surprised the outhouse is still standing.

"What'd you think of that stuffed buffalo?"

Haley smiled. "It was huge. Did you guys get your pictures made in the old-time photography place?"

"Hell, no!" Buddy exclaimed. "D-d-did you see the prices on them things? I bought boots and a new buckle with m-m-my m-m-money."

Finn leaned out into the aisle. "Me and Rhett had ours made to take home. I'm a Confederate soldier and Rhett here is a gambler. You have yours done?"

"I was a saloon girl with a tall plume in my hair."

"Dewar?" Rhett asked.

"The man thought me and Haley were newlyweds so we had a bride and groom picture made."

Sawyer groaned.

Finn laughed. "You going to show it to your momma? It'll give Aunt Maddie the heart flutters. I heard a while back the whole female population around Ringgold was out kicking the mesquite bushes seekin' a bride for you. Way I heard it was that they was about ready to put an ad in the newspaper over in Wichita Falls with a picture of you and then in big letters above it a headline that said, *COWBOY SEEKS BRIDE*."

Rhett picked it up from there, "And Aunt Maddie was going to buy one of them number machines and nail it to the front porch post. The women would be free to camp out in the front yard until she and your brothers' wives interviewed them."

"Y'all are full of shit! Of course I'm going to show it to her. Way she and the rest of Ringgold has been parading women past me, I might even tell her it's for real."

"Man, I'm cuttin' out of your place soon as we get home. Ain't no way I'm stayin' around for that party," Rhett said.

"Oh? Don't you think my new mother-in-law is going to be all smiles and sweetness?" Haley teased.

"My momma says that Aunt Maddie would probably go to war if anyone tried to take Dewar out of Ringgold," Finn said.

"But Dallas isn't that far for Dewar to move," Haley tested the waters.

"Honey, Bowie would be too far and it's less than twenty miles. Don't you tease Aunt Maddie about a weddin'. She'll have you staked out with a fire built up under your new skirt tail so fast you won't even know how you got burned," Finn said.

She wanted to slap the grin right off Dewar's face. "Is he right?"

"Oh, yeah."

"So you are a momma's boy?"

The smile disappeared. "I wouldn't say that. I'm a ranchin' man and Bowie is too big for me. It's got about three thousand people last I heard. How many folks live in Dallas?"

She squirmed and didn't answer.

"One point two million," Sawyer said without opening his eyes.

"Point proven," Dewar said.

In less than an hour the small plane landed at the Nocona Municipal Airport. Kyle was surprised when Haley stood up to get off the plane with the other passengers.

"I supposed I was taking you on home," he said.

"My car is at the O'Donnell ranch. I'll ride over there and drive it home."

"Yes, ma'am." Kyle ran a hand through his silver hair. "Drive safe."

When Haley stepped out into the hot sunshine, Liz waved. Lucy stood beside her and Raylen leaned against a club cab truck. She wasn't expecting such a big welcoming committee or to see her car sitting right there either.

"Hey, y'all made it!" Lucy yelled.

"I drove your car over here for you to save you some miles," Liz said. "If you go east on Highway 82 you can catch I-35 at Gainesville and be home in an hour."

Haley's heart spiraled down and she wasn't wearing boots to catch it.

"Well?" Dewar said.

"You've got my number and we've got a date," she said.

"Yes, we do." He walked her to her car and tossed her part of the plastic bags into the backseat. "Looks like your suit and shoes are all clean."

Dewar brushed a quick kiss across her lips. "Call me when you get home, H. B. McKay."

She smiled up at him. "H. B. McKay got lost out there on the drive. You call me later. And give my donkey a hug."

"You've still got the cutest ass in the world," he whispered.

Bright, blistering, red scarlet filled her cheeks and her neck. She ducked into the car. The keys were in the ignition, so she stuck her hand out the window and waved as she pulled away from the airport and headed home.

She was sitting at the second red light in Nocona when her phone rang. She fished it out of her purse and answered without looking at the caller ID.

"I'm still blushing," she said.

"About what?" Joel asked.

"Hello, Joel," she said tersely.

"What were you blushing about?" he asked.

"Nothing. Just something Dewar said about my donkey."

"Your what? Good God, H. B., you aren't bringing a donkey to Dallas, are you?"

"Sure I am. I'm going to potty train him and get him a diamond collar and a leash and I'm buying a special van next week so he can ride to work with me. I hope you like him because if you hurt his feelings we'll have to send him to jackass therapy," she said.

"That's not a damn bit funny," he said coldly.

Dewar would be in stitches, she thought.

"Well, it was at the time and that's what I was blushing about."

"You know I hate it when you joke like that. I've made reservations for dinner for two tonight and we're having dinner with your parents tomorrow night. I have some work to finish up, so I'll pick you up at eight thirty," he said.

"No thanks. I'm not even going home. I'm going straight to the spa and it's going to take them until closing time to get me in shape," she said.

"I insist."

"I said no."

"I'm willing to give you a second chance," Joel said.

"Thanks but no thanks for the second time. I don't want another chance, Joel. Have you changed this past month?"

"No, have you?"

"Tremendously, and you aren't going to like me at all," she said.

He hung up on her and that made her giggle even harder than the idea of taking Eeyore right into Joel's office.

She threw the phone on the passenger's seat and made it all the way to Gainesville before it rang again.

She pulled over in the parking lot for the Day's Inn motel and answered it after she'd checked caller ID.

"Hello."

"I really, really miss you," Dewar's drawl came through the line.

She shut her eyes and enjoyed the delicious heat flowing through her body.

"Me too."

"Turn the car around and come back."

"You get in your truck and come to Gainesville. I'm sitting in front of a Day's Inn."

"I wish I could but Raylen and Liz have held down my half of the chores this month. They're leaving in a couple of hours to spend the rest of the week down your way. I'll be down there for the Resistol Rodeo this weekend. Want to go with me?"

"Sure. What night?"

"Saturday night."

"Spend the night with me afterwards," she said.

"That could sure be arranged."

"I'm getting all warm and tingly thinking about it," she said.

"Hold that feeling. Eeyore says that he likes his new home and he misses you too."

She groaned. "You aren't playing fair. I miss him."

"All's fair in love and war."

"Which is this, Dewar? Love or war?"

"I'm not fighting. Are you?"

"It's going to be a long week."

He chuckled.

"I'm hanging up now. Call me in an hour?"

"You call me when you get home."

Chapter 31

SAMMY, THE DOORMAN, CARRIED HER WALMART PLASTIC bags from her car into her apartment building without so much as a raised eyebrow. But two of her elderly neighbors gasped when she lugged them into the elevator.

"That damned airline lose your luggage, Haley?" one asked.

"No, ma'am. I've been out on a field trip and my saddlebags went home with the horse, leaving me with nothing to pack in."

"Oh, my! Saddlebags? A horse?"

Haley nodded. "Yes, ma'am. I rode one every day for a whole month and herded cattle from a little town north of here all the way to Dodge City, Kansas. It was for a reality show we're working on."

"That is dedication to a job. I bet you had to stay in some nasty motels in those little bitty towns, didn't you?"

"That would have been luxury. I slept on the ground in a sleeping bag and ate food prepared by a cook on an open fire."

And fell in love with an amazing cowboy who is absolutely the most wrong man for me in the whole universe.

The second lady patted her on the shoulder. "Darlin', you deserve a medal."

The elevator doors opened on her floor and she shoved all her bags out into the hallway and waved at the ladies. She didn't want a medal, not unless it was a buckle attached to a belt around Dewar O'Donnell.

The bags looked out of place in her ultra-modern apartment full of enameled black furniture with lots of black leather and glass. She pulled back the drapes to let in the afternoon sun and see the magnificence of downtown Dallas. But she still felt like she did in the trailer the night they'd endured the tail end of a tornado. The air was fresh inside the apartment but it didn't have the faintest whisper of cows or sweaty cowboys or even beans boiling on an open fire.

She reached for her house phone and dialed the number for the spa located in her building. When the receptionist answered she said, "Mallory, I need the works. I don't care if it takes until midnight."

"Come on down, Miz Haley. We'll put you right into a room. Nails, toes, and everything?"

"Even the mud bath," Haley said.

"Honey, what happened?" Mallory asked.

"You'll see. I'll be there in five minutes." She stepped over the bags and heaved a sigh of relief when the elevator was empty. What in the hell had happened to her in just one short month? She loved her apartment, so why did it feel like the walls were closing in on her? The view out the window never ceased to amaze her, looking different by the minute depending on where the sun was hanging in the sky. That day it appeared to be a stylized print from a cheap picture and not nearly the real thing.

"Oh, no!" Mallory said when Haley walked in the door.

"Oh, yes. Thirty days out in the sun does have its effects, doesn't it?"

"You poor baby. Don't even sit down. It's going to

take until midnight for Collette to undo this mess. What in the hell were you thinking?"

"That it was an April Fools' joke," Haley said honestly.

She was sitting in a hot tub, bubbles popping all around her when she called Dewar. He answered on the first ring.

"Is this the sexy girl in the pretty white nightgown that I just spent two wonderful days with in Dodge City?"

"No, it's the sunburned, unevenly tanned woman who is trying desperately to look decent by tomorrow morning's conference."

"Darlin', you'd look good in a gunnysack roped up in the middle with a length of jute twine, and you look damn fine in nothing at all."

"Where are you that you can talk like that? I hear voices behind you," she whispered.

"In a tractor, doors shut, air-conditioning going, and the radio now turned down low. You are hearing the Bellamy Brothers singing about this being our secret, our own private affair. And you are either at Niagara Falls or in a hot tub."

"I'd rather it was Niagara Falls. Let's quit our jobs and go there."

"Sounds wonderful but I don't have a job."

"You quit?" She held her breath.

"No, it's not like that. A job is something that you go to from nine to five or whatever hours it demands and then you go home and forget it. I don't have a job like that. I have a way of life. It's here twenty-four seven, not totally unlike the cattle run. It's just the way I live. But with a little planning, I could take a few days to go to Niagara Falls if you want to quit your job."

She leaned her head back and an attendant brought

a rolled towel to go under her neck. "I don't think so. I just proved that I can do fieldwork. No way am I quittin' when I'm ahead."

"I see. Are you in the hot tub in your house?" he asked.

"I have an apartment in downtown Dallas, only a couple of blocks from the corporate building. The hot tub is in the spa on the first floor. I'm here for the works. I'm getting all fancied up for the rodeo on Saturday. And what exactly should I wear?"

"Your old boots, a pair of jeans, and a pretty shirt that's so sexy all the other cowboys will be jealous of me," he said.

"The spa manager is motioning for me to go to the next thing on the agenda," Haley said.

"And that is?"

"A warm mud bath."

"You've got to be kidding. You had one of those when Eeyore and the coyote locked horns and you hated it. I'll never understand women!"

She stood up and took the hand the assistant offered. "We weren't born to be understood, Dewar. We were born to be loved. I can't take my phone in the mud bath area. Rules of the game. We are supposed to listen to soft music and breathe in the aroma of therapeutic candles with tea bags on our eyes so that the toxins will leave our bodies. I'll talk to you later."

"Sweet Jesus! You are sitting in mud! It's putting toxins into your body more than it's sucking out," Dewar said.

"Later," she said and handed the phone to Mallory.

—∿∿—

Dewar was ready for work when he arrived home that afternoon, so Raylen gladly turned over the tractor to him and went with Liz to her doctor's appointment in Wichita Falls. He'd dumped his bags at his house, talked to Eeyore a few minutes, and then started plowing.

Everything felt right except that empty house. He was back on his home turf, among his own cattle, horses, and dirt. Eeyore was happy in the pasture with his Gypsy Vanner horses and Rye and Austin were coming to dinner that evening at his folks' place with Rachel and Eddie. They had two kids already. His sister, Gemma, got one with a marriage license instead of a birth certificate, but no one would ever know she hadn't birthed Holly, as much as she loved her. Now she, Liz, and Colleen were all expecting a baby.

If Dewar had been a woman he would have felt the ticking of the biological clock. But he was a man and all he could do was yearn for what all his siblings already had. Trouble was he wanted it with Haley and that was as possible as Lucifer setting up an ice cream store in hell.

He made a sharp turn to the left and started down the back side of the hay field. "She made it pretty damn clear when she said that there was no way she'd quit when she was ahead. So now what? The heart wants what it wants and it doesn't accept substitutions."

He imagined her in a big claw-foot tub filled with warm mud. It wasn't nearly as repulsive as he thought. Matter of fact, it was downright sexy seeing her breasts all covered with chocolate coating and her aqua eyes glittering as he drew pictures on the parts of her body that he could reach with his forefinger.

He put the vision out of his mind and concentrated on the classic country songs on the radio, but every single one reminded him of her in some way.

"Please Help Me I'm Falling," an oldie by Hank Locklin, talked about a man who was already married and falling in love with another woman. In a sense that was the case with him and Haley because he was married to his way of life and he was falling in love with her whether he wanted to admit it or not.

Charley Pride said it all when he sang that it would take a little bit longer to get her off his mind. He said that the lonely feeling would go away, but Dewar didn't believe it for a minute. Half of his heart went to Dallas in that little sports car with a woman that was as married to her way of life as he was to his. Maybe he should just cut the strings right now, today, and forget all about the way he felt in Dodge City.

"Walk Through This World with Me," a George Jones classic, started playing and it said everything in Dewar's heart. He asked her to go where he went, share all his dreams with him. He said that he'd searched for her and now that he'd found her, new horizons were in his world and all he wanted was for her to take his hand and walk through this world with him.

He turned off the radio at the end of that song, but the lyrics kept running through his mind on a continuous loop. When the day ended, he parked the tractor at the edge of the field and waved at Wilma, who was taking clothes off the line in her backyard. Wilma was middle-aged and took care of cleaning and cooking for Liz since she didn't like to do either one.

"I could hire a woman like Wilma if Haley wanted

to freelance. Lucy would know of a woman who would love to work for me, I bet," he said aloud.

Forget it! It's not the cooking and housekeeping that she'll shy away from. It's a whole way of life. She needs more than a cowboy.

His house was as empty as a tomb with only the noise of the shower beating down on his tired body. He leaned against the back wall and let the hot water massage the muscles in his shoulders. Riding inside an air-conditioned tractor wasn't supposed to stiffen him up worse than riding Stallone all day long.

Shower done, dressed, and a stuffed animal for each of the kids from the souvenir shop at Boot Hill in his hands, he closed the door behind him and walked the quarter mile from his place to the two-story farmhouse where he'd grown up.

Rachel met him at the door, hands on her hips and eyebrows drawn down over her blue eyes. "No more."

He squatted down to hug her. "No more what, baby girl?"

"No more go for Nunky Dewar."

"Okay, baby. No more go for Nunky Dewar. I promise, but I brought you and Eddie a present." He brought the stuffed armadillo and the horse from behind his back and held them toward her.

She grabbed the horse. "Star!"

"Pretty close, isn't it?" Dewar hugged her again.

"Lookee, Mommy, Star!"

Austin came from the kitchen, Eddie in her arms. "She's going to do Maddie proud. All she talks about is Liz's horse, Star. And he's just as addicted to her. The horse sense has skipped a generation and landed right smack on her."

"I believe it. Let me see that boy."

She put the baby in Dewar's arms and he headed for the nearest rocking chair. "Look at how you've grown. By the end of summer, you'll be riding bulls with your daddy and me."

"That's enough of that talk," Austin yelled from the kitchen.

Rye clapped a hand on his younger brother's shoulder and sat down on the sofa near him. "So the trip was good?"

"Great," Dewar said. "No problems except that crazy donkey of Haley's got a little jolt of lightning. And we faced a tornado and Haley had to bring the donkey into the old huntin' trailer we were holed up in. Oh, and between the jackass and Haley, we did have a stampede. But other than that, not much happened. Well, we did meet an old whorehouse madam who told us some funny stories."

"Well, shit! I wouldn't want to go with you on an exciting trip. Tell me about this woman who went with y'all."

"She did just fine. Hell, Rye, I thought she'd run back home an hour after she finally got into the saddle, but she was made out of tough stuff. She rode through rain and didn't even bitch about not having a bathroom. She did carry her own toilet paper." He laughed.

"Do I hear a little bit of missing her in your voice?" Rye asked.

"You hear a lot of missing her, but I'll just have to get over it. She's city. I'm just a cowboy. Be like..." He paused.

"Like me and Austin. It's doable if both hearts want

the same thing. If one doesn't, though, it won't work. Give it time, brother," Rye said. "When do we meet her?"

"She's coming to the rodeo on Saturday night."

"Oh, she is?" Maddie yelled from the kitchen.

"Yes, Momma, she is. You are going to like her."

"We'll see about that," Maddie said.

Chapter 32

HALEY REALLY DIDN'T INTEND TO GO TO WORK THE next day, but her mother called and asked her to come in for half a day, so that morning found her right back in her old routine. High heels and her best black suit with the red satin button-up shirt under it felt strange on Wednesday morning when Haley dressed for work. She picked up her briefcase holding her laptop and that day's printed agenda from her assistant, Joyce. She had a meeting with her parents in the conference room first thing that morning, after which there would be a larger meeting that would last until ten. From then until five she was booked solid with one thing and another, then there was that dinner with Joel and her parents that she couldn't figure a way out of short of crawling up in a casket and crossing her hands over her boobs.

The first person she saw when she walked into the ground floor of the business was Joel holding the door for her. She waltzed through with a nod but he quickly caught up, grabbed her arm, and spun her around to kiss her right on the lips.

"I missed you, darling," he said.

She wiped the back of her hand across her lips. "We'll talk later. I've got to meet with my folks before the midweek conference."

"Yes, we will. I'm looking forward to dinner tonight." He winked.

"Lord, put me back on a damn horse," she mumbled as she pushed the elevator button.

Her mother crossed the room in long strides and hugged her tightly. "Look at you. I expected a holy mess from the way you talked, but you look wonderful."

Jenny Levy was five feet ten inches tall without her high heels. Her Cajun blood showed in her jet-black hair, ebony eyes, and the angles of her face. She wore a gorgeous blue sleeveless dress with a short-cropped jacket over it and shoes dyed to match.

"Most of the mess is covered up. See?" Haley pulled back her bangs.

"What in the hell happened? Do you have leprosy? My God, Carl, what did you do to my baby?" Jenny shot daggers at her husband.

Carl wasted no time in setting his coffee down and getting to his daughter where he took a look at her snow-white forehead. "Hat?"

Haley nodded. "My arms are the same. White above my short shirtsleeves and brown as toast from there down."

Jenny pointed at Carl. "Look what you caused. I told you to send Joel."

"She needed the experience. Now let's talk. We've decided to trash the reality show after all. Joel has a new and fresh idea about country folks going to the city. Kind of like Crocodile Dundee when he came to New York, only with today's twist."

Haley's blood ran cold through her veins. She looked like a damn redneck. She'd lived through a tornado as well as a stampede, had almost gotten hit by lightning, and could have been bitten by a rattlesnake. She had spent hours and hours on notes for the show. And they were trashing it!

"Get a cup of coffee, darling. I promise your father will never ever do this to you again or I'll tell Granny to take him to the bayou and leave him there," Jenny said.

"I don't want a damn cup of coffee," she said coldly.

"Now, don't take that tone with us. It's like writing a book, honey. You get rejections. The reality show was a great idea, but it was a day late and ten dollars short when it came to the market."

"When did you make this decision?" Haley asked.

"Joel did the research while you were gone," Jenny said. "He brought it all to us two weeks ago."

"And you let me stay out there with the mosquitoes, the chiggers, horse shit, and tornadoes? You didn't even try to send a rescue squad to ask me if I wanted to come home?"

Her father shrugged. "We weren't sure where you were."

"I was on a freakin' horse's back going fifteen miles or less a day on the Chisholm Trail, which is marked pretty damned well. You could have found me," she shouted.

Carl held up a finger and narrowed his eyes. "Don't raise your voice."

She spun around and headed out the door.

"Where are you going? The midweek conference starts in five minutes," Carl said.

"Have it without me. Hell, you can make all kinds of decisions without consulting me. Why in the hell would you need my input in a little thing like a midweek conference? I'm taking the rest of this week and maybe next week off. Dock my pay if I don't have enough vacation time to cover the damn days."

"Hey, there's no need for this," Jenny said softly.

"Oh, I think there is." She kept walking.

"Where can I reach you?" Jenny yelled.

"In an emergency—and it had damn well better be an emergency—you can call Granny. I'm going to Louisiana."

—⁓—

Dewar was mucking out a horse stall when his phone vibrated in his hip pocket. He leaned the shovel against the stall door and smiled as he answered it.

"What are you wearing?" he asked.

"A damn suit and a damn pair of high heels, both of which I'm going home to change," Haley said.

"Whoa, darlin'. Who done pissed on your bagel this morning?"

"My parents, and I'm mad as hell and I'm not going to be fit to be around until I quit fuming and I won't be at the rodeo on Saturday and I won't be at my apartment. I'm going to Louisiana to spend a whole week with my granny and they can all slip in cow shit and fall right into hell."

"Whew! What on earth happened, Haley? Did they prearrange a marriage or sell you into slavery?"

"They decided two damn weeks ago to cancel the reality show and they didn't even have the decency to come find me. And Miz Sadie will be looking for us to film the whorehouse and don't you dare kiss me again, Joel. I swear I'll knock the shit right out of you," she said.

"I'm not Joel. What in the hell is going on there?" Dewar said.

"Well, he was coming at me with a big grin and he

already kissed me hello this morning. Joel, you can go to hell!"

"Haley? Are you all right?" Dewar asked.

"I'm fine and dandy and Daddy can adopt Joel's sorry ass and call him a son. I'm going to Granny's and we might just gamble the hell out of what's left of my whole paycheck from the trail drive."

"When are you leaving?"

"Soon as I go home, pack my suitcase, and get the valet to bring my car around."

"Drive safe and call me when you stop for lunch?" Dewar said.

"Probably before then, and thanks for not trying to talk me out of it," she said.

"Hell, honey, I'd leave too. Carl was out a wad of money for that project."

Haley hailed a taxi and then said, "He'll write it off as a tax expense. Give me an hour and I'll call you when I'm not ready to burn down the corporation. I'm in a taxi going two blocks when I could have walked that far even in these ridiculous high heels. Don't that make a helluva lot of sense."

"Cool down, darlin', and don't drive fast when you do get behind the wheel of your car," he said.

He stared at the phone for a long time before he put it back in his pocket. Life could turn on a dime and change in the course of a five-minute phone call. He'd been thinking about buying roses and champagne for after the rodeo on Saturday. Now he wouldn't even get to see her for two weeks.

"Your new girlfriend?" Maddie asked.

She didn't look old enough to have five grown

children, three grandchildren, and three more on the way. She had a few crow's-feet around her bright blue eyes, but her chestnut hair didn't sport even one gray strand. She was tall and slim, wore tight jeans and a chambray work shirt out over an aqua-colored undershirt, the same shade as her eyes.

"It was Haley. She won't be coming to the rodeo. She's going to Louisiana to visit her grandmother," Dewar said.

"Likely story," Maddie grumbled.

"It's the truth. She's mad at her folks. After all the money and time spent, they decided there would be no reality show and she really worked very hard on that trip thinking up ideas for the show. I'd be pissed too, Momma," Dewar said.

"Rich city people. No understanding the way they think. You going to exercise Glorious Danny Boy this morning?"

"Soon as I get this stall cleaned out, we've got a date. He says he missed me pretty bad," Dewar said.

"Not as much as your family did." Maddie led a saddled horse out of the barn and mounted up for a ride.

Haley whipped around a few loops and caught I-30 west toward Shreveport, missing all the morning traffic and getting through town before the lunch crowd found their way onto the streets. When she got there, she'd go south on 49 straight into Jeanerette and on out to the sugar plantation where Granny ruled the roost.

She slapped the steering wheel when her phone rang and the ID said it was Joel.

"What in the hell do you want?" she said.

"If I was your father I'd fire you," he said.

"Well, you aren't, and frankly I don't care if he does."

"He and your mother have worked their whole lives to…"

She did a head wiggle. "Don't you start that shit with me. They've worked their whole lives because they wanted to. Why didn't you come after me when they ditched the reality show idea?"

"I'm the one who said you should stay out there and learn to appreciate how good you have it here." He laughed.

It all came tumbling down on her in the confines of a small car and made her mad all over again. He had called the shots and her parents had let him. She hung up on him without another word, steam practically shooting out her ears and from the top of her red hair.

The phone rang again and she pushed the speakerphone button. If they wanted a war she could deliver it complete with weapons of mass destruction. She was a tough woman. Hell's bells, she'd just ridden a horse for a month. They couldn't win against her.

"Haley Belle McKay Levy, you turn that car around and come back to work. If you weren't my daughter, I'd have fired you on the spot. But if you are here by the time we go to dinner, I won't." Jenny's tone left no wiggle room.

"I'm just a stupid employee that you left out in the wilds for two weeks past when you knew you weren't going to run the show, so fire my ass. I don't care. I can find a job."

"Not without my recommendation," Jenny said sternly.

"Is Daddy standing right beside you?"

"Yes, he's here and so is Joel. You are on speaker-phone. What in the devil has gotten into you?"

If she told them that Dewar had gotten into her by the river, under a shade tree, in a hotel room, hell, even in an outhouse, they'd all three drop dead on the spot.

"I'll decide in the next ten days if I'm going to look for another job or work for you," she said.

"Young lady, you've got five hours, not ten days. If you aren't at dinner tonight, you are fired," Carl said. "You won't last a week in the real world."

"I just lasted a month in a world a lot more real than anything you can throw at me." She poked the button on the phone and kept driving.

When it rang again she looked before she answered.

"I'm still mad," she said.

Dewar chuckled in his throaty drawl.

She smiled and part of the anger floated away from her heart. "I think I just got fired."

"You what?" he stammered.

"My dad said that if I wasn't at the dinner tonight with him and Momma and Joel that I was fired. I'm not going, so I think I just got fired. Maybe Granny will put me to work at the sugar plantation," she said.

"Doing what?" he asked.

"Hey, I just helped herd cattle through three states. I can bring in a sugar crop if I need to," she said defensively.

"You can do anything, honey."

"So you think I could last a week in the real world?" she asked.

He chuckled again. "You just lasted four times that long. Don't argue with success. What do you really,

really want to do, Haley? What's been your secret dream that you never shared with anyone else?"

"Right now I want to own my own cable television company and do the reality show myself. I want you to be the trail boss and I'll go along and help produce it and we'll live under the stars just like we did on the trial run. But that's not a possibility so I'm going to Granny's and they can all go to hell. What are you doing right now? Tell me so I'll quit thinking about how mad I am."

"I've got to take Glorious Danny Boy back to the stable and brush him down. Want a job exercising horses? We pay minimum and you could have room and board at my house," he said.

"Hey, cowboy, don't offer something you can't deliver. I might take you up on that offer if Daddy is serious," she said.

"Talk to you later," Dewar said.

The next call was from her assistant at the corporation.

"Did you really quit?" she asked.

"No, ma'am. I got fired, or at least that's the threat if I don't go to dinner with Momma, Daddy, and Joel."

Joyce snorted. "Gossip has it that Joel had a girlfriend who just dropped him and he can't bear being rejected twice so he's put out the word that he dropped her because he's still in love with you. Joel is just a plain old gold-digging son of a bitch. Jenny won't let your dad fire you. Come on back home and let's get some work done."

Haley shook her head. "Ain't happenin'."

"What's his name?"

"Whose name?"

"Whoever you've fallen in love with."

"I'm not in love."

"You might fool some folks, Haley Belle, but not me. If you want to talk or learn the gossip, give me a call. And they aren't going to fire you. Don't worry about that. If they do, I'll shoot Joel for you," Joyce said.

She was through Shreveport and headed south before her phone rang again. She'd cooled down but still didn't want to talk to Joel, so she let it ring three times and checked the caller ID before she answered.

"Yes, Mother."

"Are you on your way back?"

"Who's in the room with you?"

"I'm alone and it's not on speaker."

"No, I'm still going to Granny's."

"I called her. She knows you'll be there in time for dinner this evening," Jenny said.

"And?"

A long pregnant pause followed, but Haley didn't say anything.

"She said that we did you wrong and you had a right to be mad at us. I didn't want your father to send you on that trip. Then I wasn't in agreement with him and Joel when they decided to let you finish the trip. We've been arguing all day."

"Want to go to the sugar plantation with me?" Haley asked.

"I'm not that mad, yet." Jenny's laugh always made Haley happy.

But not that day.

"Am I fired?"

"Hell no! I'll fight them all on that. *I'll* quit and go to the plantation if he fires you for real," Jenny said.

"Thanks, Momma."

"You'll be all right once you think about things. Now tell me about this trail boss that you spent so much time with," Jenny said.

"See you later, Momma."

Chapter 33

GRANNY OPENED THE DOOR BEFORE SHE KNOCKED. Her hair was as black as Jenny's, but it had help from the beautician she visited on a weekly basis. Her eyes were dark brown and she was only two inches taller than Haley.

"Come on in here, *chere*. I understand there's a war goin' on in Texas."

Haley hugged her grandmother. "Little bit. I love the way this house smells."

Mahalia's smile was like a candle in the back of a dark cave, instantly telling Haley that she'd done the right thing in coming to see her grandmother even if she had done it in the middle of a hissy fit.

"Like jambalaya?" Mahalia asked.

"Well, there is that. But down here everything is so much slower and it smells different and it's peaceful."

"Of course it's slower. If we flopped around like gators with their heads cut off like y'all do in the big city, we'd all drop dead in this kind of heat. Movin' slow is preservation down in our part of the swamp. And what you are smellin' really is jambalaya. I remembered it was your favorite so I made it when your mom called. I got boiled shrimp, too. That war make you hungry, did it?"

Haley put her purse on the credenza in the foyer and looped her arm around Mahalia's shoulders. "Fighting always makes a good Cajun hungry. You told me that."

"It's the truth, *chere*. Now come in here and tell me about the trail boss."

"Momma's been tellin' tales."

"She did but I see something different about you, *chere*. Something only a man can cause. You might as well tell me because I'll pester the shit out of you until you do," Mahalia said.

Haley sat down at the small table centered in the big country kitchen. There was a formal dining room, parlor, and an enormous living room, but Haley's favorite room had always been the kitchen with its delicious aromas and intimacy.

"His name is Dewar O'Donnell and he lives in Ringgold, Texas. He comes from this big family but the town itself is tiny. Only a hundred or so people, Granny, and he lives on and operates a horse ranch."

"Glorious Danny Boy and Major Jack," Mahalia said.

"Who?"

"Maddie O'Donnell is one of the most prominent horsewoman on the face of this earth right now. Dewar is her son, so I expect he's quite a cowboy."

"But who is this Danny Boy and Jack?"

"The most famous racing horses in history. They don't race anymore, but their offspring bring the big bucks. I bet on Danny Boy one time up in Mississippi when I went to place a little money on the ponies. Came home with enough to buy this diamond ring right here." She pointed to a two-carat solitaire on her right pinky finger.

"But he said he was just a cowboy," Haley said.

"Oh, yeah, *chere*! Does he look like Cash?"

"Who?"

"His father, Cash O'Donnell. Lord, honey, that man

is so sexy he'd make a holy woman take up hookin' just to get him in bed." Mahalia filled a bowl with jambalaya and stuck it in the microwave oven.

Haley blushed.

"Guess he does," Mahalia said. "Well, I'm glad you've come to visit and get out of the war zone. Let them fight it out. Your momma, she don't lose many battles. Now let's talk about what we're going to do. Tomorrow we'll go into New Iberia and eat at Victor's and do a little shopping. The next day is the party, and Sunday we'll go out to the island and spend the day reading, maybe take some sleeping bags, do a little fishin', and spend the night in the old home place."

The microwave dinged at the same time her phone rang.

"Hello, Dewar. I'm here," she said.

Her grandmother went for the microwave, took the food out, and set it before her, then busied herself in the kitchen whipping up a Cajun dessert while she listened with one ear to her granddaughter's conversation.

"Good. Still pissed?" Dewar asked.

"Not nearly as bad but yes," she said.

"I miss you."

"I miss you too. We need to talk when I get back."

"Yes, we do. But what I've got to say can't be said over a telephone. But you *could* tell me what color your panties are," he teased.

"Good Lord!"

"Does that mean you aren't wearing any?"

"Dewar!"

"I see a red glow in the southern sky. Is that you blushing?"

"You are horrible."

"Hanging up now. Call me tomorrow and let me know what is going on," he said.

Mahalia sat down beside her. "You are in love, *chere*. Your daddy is going to shit little green apples."

"Then Momma can make apple pie."

Mahalia laughed until tears streamed down her face. "You are my granddaughter for sure. You act just like my mother, even if you do look like the Irish side. Irish and Cajun mix. That boy hasn't got a snowball's chance in hell, *chere*."

"It's not him I'm worried about, Granny. It's me. I've lived in the city my whole life. I've always had people around me. What would I do on a ranch?"

"I'd lived on a little island in the bayou my whole life with only my family around me. I looked at the son of the owner of this plantation and asked myself, 'Can I live in such a big place?' and you know what my answer was, *chere*?"

Haley shook her head.

"The heart wants what it wants and I wanted your grandfather. So I learned to live in a town with five thousand people and I thought it was huge. Love conquers time and space and size. You think about that for a few days. Now let's gossip about all your cousins. I've already put out the word that there'll be a party here Saturday night. I called Bubba and the Gators to come play for us so there'll be dancin' and lots of food. Ain't nothin' a Cajun likes better than music and eatin'."

Dewar had supper with his folks that night and begged off going to midweek church services. When he went home to his empty, lonely house he wished he had gone with them. He showered and watched television until he realized he'd watched a whole episode of *Justified* and didn't even know what had happened. He picked up the remote and pushed the power button, wandered into the kitchen, and opened the refrigerator. He took out a beer and twisted the top off.

The first sip reminded him of Haley at the campsite the first time Coosie went for supplies and brought back candy bars and beer. She'd been so pretty sitting there in the moonlight in her little short braids. He dug his phone out of his shirt pocket and had his finger on the speed dial button when he stopped.

She needed time. She damn sure didn't need to feel pressured, or worse yet, stalked. He picked up a book from the coffee table and carried it and his beer to the bedroom. The beer went on his nightstand and the book got tossed onto the bed while he removed his jeans, shirt, and boots and donned a pair of soft cotton plaid pajama bottoms. He took another sip of beer before he stretched out on the bed and picked up the book.

When the alarm went off the next morning he was hugging the pillow, the beer was lukewarm, and the book was thrown on the floor. He groaned and slapped the snooze button. He didn't want to leave the dream about Haley. They were back on the trail and she was arguing with him about making Eeyore into cat food.

He grabbed the phone and sent her a text message: Is Sleeping Beauty awake?

Instantly he received one back: Not until the prince kisses her.

He poked the buttons with his big thumbs: Is that an invitation?

He fidgeted while he waited: Party Saturday night. Cajun music and food.

He was typing when the phone rang.

"Do you always get up this early in Louisiana?" he asked.

"When you are staying with Granny you do. She's says folks can sleep when they are dead and you need to get all you can done by noon because it'll be so hot after that you can't work."

Dewar propped up against the pillows. He could listen to her voice all day.

"So what's this about a party?"

"Granny is throwing one for the family so I can see all of them. It's been more than a year since I've been here. Last Christmas we didn't get to come for the holidays. Want to come?"

"It could be arranged. Tell me the truth. Were you just joking and now you can't back out of the invitation?" he asked.

"Hell, no!"

"Then you are serious? Just tell me what time to be there."

"In twenty minutes," she said.

"How about Friday night?"

"How about Thursday night?" she countered.

"If he comes on Thursday night you two can take a picnic to the island on Friday," Mahalia yelled from the kitchen.

"Granny, you're eavesdropping," she yelled back.

"Yes, I am and it would help a hell of a lot if you'd talk louder," she said.

Dewar chuckled. "I can't wait to meet her. I'll be there Thursday evening."

"I… can't wait to see you," she said in a rush.

"Me too."

———∿∿∿———

Haley had packed jeans, shirts, and even her old boots in case her grandmother insisted they take a walking tour through the sugarcane. That's what she was wearing when Dewar pulled up into the drive at dusk that evening. She'd been talking to him for fifteen minutes, ever since he got to Jeanerette, giving him directions about how to navigate the back roads and get to the sugar plantation.

Now he was here and the truck had stopped and he was getting out and her feet were plastered to the ground. She wanted to run to him, jump into his arms, wrap her legs around his waist, and kiss him until she couldn't breathe, but her feet would not take the first step.

Mahalia was on the porch swing and Haley heard her giggle. "Girl, he's even sexier than his poppa. What in the hell are you doing just staring at him, *chere*? Get your ass out there and make him welcome."

Dewar took a step and opened his arms. She wasn't sure if she'd sprouted wings and flew into them or what happened, but suddenly his lips were on hers and the world was right again.

"I'm never letting you out of my sight again," Dewar whispered. "I've been miserable without you."

"Me too," she said.

"Y'all goin' to stand out there in the heat all day or come in the house where it's cool? Supper is ready," Mahalia hollered.

Haley made introductions when they reached the porch and Mahalia stuck out her hand. "I'm right glad to meet you. I met your folks years ago at the tracks."

Dewar took her small hand in his, brought it to his lips, and kissed her fingertips. "It's so nice to meet you, ma'am."

"He's a charmer, Haley." Mahalia smiled.

"Yes, ma'am, he sure is." Haley tried to wipe the grin off her face, but she couldn't. Happiness had settled around her like the afterglow when she and Dewar had sex.

"Come on in here, Dewar O'Donnell. Tonight we're going to get to know each other over supper. Then tomorrow you two are having a day alone out on the island in Bayou Teche. Saturday we're having a party so you can know my world and see the other side of Haley's family. It will start right at noon and last all day, so wear your comfortable blue jeans and boots because you're going to dance with my granddaughter when dark settles." Mahalia talked the whole way to the kitchen.

The small foyer had a staircase going up to the second floor on the right side and doors opening on both sides after that.

"Living room." Haley pointed to the left.

"Parlor." Her finger swung around to the right.

"Dining room." The room right after the parlor.

"Kitchen!" Mahalia veered to the left. "It was built this way so it had windows on two sides that could be opened to cool it down back before there was air-conditioning. Got pretty hot in here when we was cooking meals for ten kids."

Dewar's eyes twinkled and Haley shook her head.

"Don't be getting any notions in your head about ten kids," she said.

"You go ahead, honey, and think like that. Then she'll think that she's got it easy with only half a dozen." Mahalia laughed.

———

The sun was barely peeking over the horizon when Dewar awoke the next morning. He reached across the bed for Haley and got an armful of feather pillow. That's when he remembered where he was and that she'd kissed him on the cheek after a delightful evening with her grandmother and sent him off to bed alone.

He didn't want to sleep alone ever again. He wanted Haley beside him like they were in the Dodge City hotel. He wanted to wake up with her in his arms and go to sleep with the taste of her kisses on his lips. He was in love with the woman and he was done with seeking all over the state for someone to share his life with. He'd found her! Now the big job in front of him was convincing her.

"Breakfast in fifteen minutes," Mahalia yelled up the stairs.

He bounded out of bed, got dressed, and made a quick stop in the bathroom to shave and comb his hair. He met Haley coming up the steps when he started down.

"Good morning." She smiled.

"Yes, it is now that I can see you." He stopped and kissed her hard and passionately.

"Putting it on the table," Mahalia hollered. "Quit kissin' and come on in here and eat before it gets cold."

"Granny!" Haley said.

"I'm old. I'm not stupid. You can kiss each other all you want out on the island. Right now my breakfast is getting cold," she said.

They were holding hands when they entered the dining room. The table was laid out with enough food for ten people rather than three. Beignets, eggs, grits, bacon, and ham and a big basket of hot biscuits.

"We expecting an army?" Haley asked.

"Didn't know if you was still mad."

"Well, it looks absolutely wonderful," Dewar said.

Mahalia smiled. "You wait until you see what I got in the picnic basket. Y'all stay out all day and have a good time. Me and the relatives are going to make a big party today and then Saturday the party starts in the middle of the morning and lasts until midnight."

Haley loved her grandmother but she couldn't wait to get out the door that morning. She wanted time alone with Dewar, and the island was the perfect place. He'd gone on ahead with the picnic basket and she was right behind him. Right up until her grandmother grabbed her arm and hauled her back into the foyer.

"Girl, you are a fool if you let this man get away from you. I don't give a shit if he's a rancher or where he lives. He loves you," Mahalia whispered.

"I know, Granny. I love him too."

"Well, don't drag your feet about telling him. Man can't read your mind, you know. You got to open up your mouth and your heart and tell him how you feel," Mahalia said.

Dewar held the door open for her and jogged around the front of the truck. When he was inside and buckled up, he leaned across and kissed her long, lingering, and hungrily.

"I love you," he said.

"I love you, Dewar O'Donnell. Now what do we do about it?" she asked.

"First thing is to find this island, right? Tell me how to get there."

"Well, first we drive a ways and then there'll be a boat tied up at the dock. It's got a motor so we don't have to row, which I should make you do after that monthlong horseback ride," she said.

"Would you do it again?"

She laid a hand on his thigh. "In a heartbeat, darlin'."

It took twenty minutes to go from the dock to the island, which didn't cover more than five acres all total. An old weathered cabin with a wide front porch sat right in the middle. There was a chicken house out back, and as far away from the house as possible the outhouse with a moon cut in the door still stood as a silent sentinel of bygone days.

"They had a garden over on the other side of the house and they ate a lot of fish," she said. "And don't be gettin' any screwball notions about that outhouse. Until a couple of years ago it was still functional, so it won't smell as sweet as the last one we were in."

He tied off the boat and picked up the basket. "Are we going inside or…" He let the sentence dangle.

"It's just an empty house. When we came out here as

kids we brought sleeping bags. See that tote bag in the bed of the truck?" She pointed.

"When did that get there?"

"Granny put it there while we were finishing breakfast. It's got a blanket and two pillows in it. There are fishin' poles on the back porch if we want to do anything other than lie back under the shade trees and make wild passionate love," she said.

"Pick the place and let's get that blanket on the ground, then."

She grabbed the tote bag and carried it to a big tree not far from the house. Once the blanket was fluffed out, she tossed the two pillows on it. Dewar set the picnic basket off to one side and pulled her down beside him.

Haley didn't care if her cute little cotton sundress was hiked halfway to her panty line when she stretched out beside him. She laid her head on his chest and listened to his heartbeat. Good and strong, just like Dewar.

"I really do love you," she whispered.

"Did you mean it about owning your own cable television station?" he asked.

"That wasn't the response I was expecting." She smiled up at him.

He kissed her again, soft that time but still hungry.

"I love you, Haley, but I'm a rancher. I don't know how to be anything else."

"Yes, I'd love to have my own station. I could start small and grow and in a few years I'd be running Daddy some competition, but what has that got to do with loving you?"

"I put in a bid for one in Wichita Falls. I've got a friend

up in Ambrose who has a lot of money and he wants to invest in it too," he said.

The words came out so fast that she wasn't sure she heard them right. "You did what?"

"I'm supposed to be on a knee when I ask you to marry me, but I don't want to get that far from you. I want to spend my life with you, Haley. I want to go to sleep at night knowing that you'll be right there beside me when we wake up in the morning. I want to ranch and raise horses, but it's okay if that's not what you want. I'll buy you a television station and you do what you love, starting with putting out your own reality story about a bunch of city slickers on a cattle run."

"Yes, yes, yes. Dewar, I love you." She rolled over on top of him and kissed him until they were both panting.

"Long engagement?" he finally asked.

"Courthouse closes at five. That too long?" She busied herself unbuttoning his shirt.

He deftly unzipped her dress. "I think I can live with that."

"Tomorrow's party just turned into a wedding reception," she said as she undid his belt buckle.

He hooked a thumb under her underpants and pulled them down. "Do you think your granny planned it that way?"

"She probably did. I love you. I love you. I love you," she singsonged.

Mahalia arose early the next morning and at seven she climbed the stairs to wake her granddaughter. Her hand was raised when she saw the piece of paper thumbtacked to the door with a note above it that said "Do not disturb" written in bright red lipstick.

She stuck a thumb under the marriage license and carried it back down to the kitchen where more than a dozen female relatives had gathered to help with the party plans. "We've got a lot of work to do, ladies. This party is now officially a wedding reception."

She picked up the phone and hit a speed dial button. "Good morning, Jenny. That cowboy is here that Haley fell in love with out there on the trail drive y'all made her go on so you can't blame nobody but yourself. And he's not in his bedroom but there is a do not disturb sign tacked on her door and it looks like it's written in red lipstick."

She slapped a hand over her mouth when Jenny screamed, "Dammit! Mama, what have you done?"

"Me, *chere*, I didn't do anything but plan a big party that starts in a couple of hours. Oh, I forgot to tell you, I'm holding the other piece of paper that was tacked to the door. It's their marriage license. Guess they went to the courthouse down in New Iberia yesterday. My party is a wedding reception now. Get in your little airplane and tell Carl to bring his allergy pills. And leave that pansy-assed Joel fellow at home. You bring him down here and I'll feed him to the gators."

"Shit!" Jenny said.

"Party starts in two hours. You better get things going."

Haley hugged her grandmother from behind and kissed her on the cheek. "Good mornin', Granny. I see you found my note. I'm taking breakfast up to Dewar on a tray."

"Put her on the phone," Jenny said.

"I'll see you before noon." Mahalia hung up.

"Who was that?" Haley asked.

Mahalia turned around and gave Haley another hug. "Someone wanting to know what time the party starts. Congratulations on your marriage, my child. I told you he was a keeper."

"Yes, ma'am, he sure is."

Chapter 34

Four months later

IT WAS A HOT AUGUST MORNING WITH THE TEMPERATURE already rising up close to the ninety mark at eight o'clock. A herd of bawling cattle roamed around in the ranch yard with one little gray donkey in their midst. The chuck wagon was loaded and ready with Coosie on the buckboard and Buddy on a horse beside him. Sawyer was the only cowboy they could talk into going with them again, but he was there along with a couple of other O'Donnell cousins who were eager to be a part of the reality show.

Dewar mounted up and looked down at Haley. "It's your show, ma'am. You get to tell us when to roll out of here and head for Dodge City."

Haley led Apache up to his side and mouthed, "I love you."

He grinned and whispered the words back to her.

She held up a hand and Eeyore brayed. "Hey, you don't get to start this." She laughed. "Cowboys and cowgirls, it's time mount up. Reality begins right now."

She was the proud owner of a television station and her first big production was going to be the Chisholm Trail reality show as well as her honeymoon. She was so excited that she could hardly wait to get in the saddle and be on her way.

Her contestants mounted up. Most of them had never even touched a horse before that minute. The camera crew was doing a great job of being inconspicuous. She'd chosen them well and it was going to be a fantastic reality show!

One cute little blond-haired lady looked at the big horse in front of her like it was a stick of dynamite before she finally slipped a foot into the stirrup. She grabbed the saddle horn, got off balance, and promptly fell backwards on her butt.

Haley handed her horse's reins to Dewar and started toward her, but Sawyer was faster than greased lightning. According to the name tag pinned to the front of her brand-spanking-new Western shirt the woman's name was Angelyn. Haley would bet dollars to doughnuts before the end of the month that Sawyer had shortened it to Angel because Miz Angelyn's eyes left no doubt that she felt a hell of a lot of heat when he touched her.

Sawyer let go of her hand, tipped his hat, and went back to his horse.

Haley took off her hat and set it firmly on the woman's head. "You'll be needin' this and…" She stepped forward, hugged her, and whispered, "don't worry, honey, you'll do just fine."

Read on for an excerpt from Carolyn Brown's
next Christmas cowboy romance,

The Cowboy's Christmas Baby

THERE SHE STOOD WITH A DEAD COYOTE AT HER FEET,
a pink pistol in her right hand, three bluetick hound
pups cowering behind her, and cradling a baby in her
left arm.

"Natalie?" He raised an eyebrow and blinked sleet
from his eyelashes. Yesterday he had awakened to
overbearing heat in Kuwait, and today Texas was colder
than a mother-in-law's kiss on the North Pole. Maybe he
was seeing things due to the abrupt change in weather.
She looked like the woman he'd been talking to via
the Internet for the past eleven months, but he hadn't
expected her to be so tall, and he damn sure had not
expected her to be holding a baby or a pistol.

She whipped around and raised the gun until it was
aimed straight at his chest. "Who the hell… oh, my
God… you are early, Lucas. Surprise!" she said.

"Yes, ma'am," he drawled. "I guess I am, but you
aren't supposed to be here for two more days."

"We were working on a big surprise for your home-
coming. Hazel was going to make your favorite foods
and we had a banner made and I heard a noise and the
coyote had the puppies cornered and…" She stopped
and stared at him as if she expected him to disappear.

She caught her breath and went on. "Why in the hell
didn't you tell us you were coming home early? You've
ruined everything."

"It's my ranch. It's my house and I can come home when I damn well please," he said.

He looked from the baby to the dead coyote, to the puppies, finally meeting Natalie's big blue eyes staring at him across the six feet separating them. There'd been more warmth in her face when there were oceans and deserts separating them than he felt with only six feet between them.

The whole scenario he'd played out in his mind was shot to hell and back. She wouldn't take two steps forward, hug him, and then share an intimate, passionate kiss that said that yes, they had become more than Internet friends.

A whimper came from the blue bundle and she looked down at it. "I know you are hungry, son. We'll go inside in just a second."

Dammit!

He'd thought he'd found the right woman. Hell, he'd even entertained notions that she was *the one*. He'd been right all along: people were crazy to believe what they saw on the Net or to trust anyone they met on there, either.

"Joshua is hungry. Can you put these pups back in the pen? Sorry little critters dug out from under the fence and the coyote cornered them up by the porch," she said.

She damn sure looked different in real life with curves and legs that went from earth all the way to heaven. She was stunning in those snug-fitting jeans, red flannel shirt, and thick brown hair floating in gentle waves down past her shoulders. How could he have not known she was pregnant?

Because you only saw her from the waist up and in

pictures that she posted. Man, you got duped real good this time. Sucker!

"Well?" She shoved the pistol into the waistband of her jeans, shifted the baby to a more comfortable position, and headed toward the porch.

He dropped his canvas duffel on the icy ground. "I'll take care of the coyote and the pups. Then we've got some serious talking to do. Where are Grady and Gramps and Dad?"

"Grady took Henry home after supper. You hungry?"

Yes, he was hungry. He'd foregone supper until he got home because he couldn't wait to have Hazel's home-cooked food. But the way his stomach was churning around he wouldn't be able to swallow. A baby boy, for God's sake! And she never mentioned him one time.

"Hazel in the house?" he asked stiffly.

She stopped and turned. "No, she is not. I've got to get Joshua inside, though. He's cold. Just take care of those pups."

"Don't boss me, Natalie," he barked.

"I'm going inside. You can stay out here and freeze to death if you want, Lucas. The way you are acting, I don't reckon it'll be much warmer in the house when you get there anyway," she said.

He folded his arms across his chest. "And that is supposed to mean what?"

"Figure it out for yourself."

"Shit!" he mumbled under his breath.

He gathered up three wiggling bluetick hound pups and stomped toward the dog pens. What in the hell did she expect—a big old passionate kiss with a pistol and a baby between them?

He opened the gate and set the puppies down inside the chain-link fence, where they made a beeline toward the hole they'd dug. One by one they scampered out of the pen and into the yard and ran helter-skelter back to the dead coyote. One grabbed its tail and the other went to work on its ears, all the while growling like vicious mean hunting dogs.

Lucas grabbed a piece of two-by-four and chinked up the hole, fought them away from the coyote, and put them back in the pen.

"Whole bunch of you haven't got the brains that one of you should have. That coyote could have killed all three of you if it hadn't been for Natalie." He could hear their whining all the way across the backyard.

He thought about carrying his duffel bag to the bunkhouse, hooking up his laptop, and telling her via Internet to get the hell off his ranch. It would serve her right for not telling him that she was pregnant most of the eleven months they'd been cyber-friends or even mentioning that she'd had a baby. Hell, they'd shared everything over the Internet, so why shouldn't they break up over it too?

He was supposed to be waiting anxiously on the porch for her to arrive in a couple of days and they'd fall right into a wonderful relationship that ended in a trip down the aisle to the altar. Well that damn sure wasn't going to happen now.

He'd been right all along. He'd never believed in all the Internet shit the guys talked about. Not until Drew Camp pulled out his laptop on the first night and there was Natalie on the computer screen with her big smile and twinkling eyes. He'd always been a sucker for blue eyes, and if it had blue eyes, it had brought him nothing but heartache in the past. So why did he expect anything different with Natalie?

He threw his duffel bag over his shoulder and started toward the bunkhouse. He'd almost made it to the back-yard fence when that damned niggling voice in the back of his head told him he was a coward. Lucas kicked the trunk of a pecan tree so hard that it jarred his leg all the way to the hip as he murmured cuss words under his breath. He wasn't afraid to face Natalie or to have it out with her. But he damn sure didn't want to do it in front of Hazel.

Still, it had to be done, and Hazel could just sit there and be quiet.

"Yeah right," he said.

Hazel was never quiet. She spoke her mind and didn't spare the cussing when she did. He whipped around and the north wind blew little sleet pellets in his face that stung every bit as bad as a sandstorm in Kuwait, maybe even more so because his jaws were set so tightly.

"Might as well get it over with," he grumbled as he stormed back across the yard.

About the Author

Carolyn Brown is a *New York Times* and *USA Today* bestselling author with more than sixty books published, and credits her eclectic family for her humor and writing ideas. Her books include the cowboy trilogy: *Lucky in Love*, *One Lucky Cowboy*, and *Getting Lucky*; the Honky Tonk series: *I Love This Bar*, *Hell Yeah*, *Honky Tonk Christmas*, and *My Give a Damn's Busted*; and her bestselling Spikes & Spurs series: *Love Drunk Cowboy*, *Red's Hot Cowboy*, *Darn Good Cowboy Christmas*, *One Hot Cowboy Wedding*, *Mistletoe Cowboy*, and *Just a Cowboy and His Baby*. Carolyn has launched into women's fiction as well with *The Blue-Ribbon Jalapeño Society Jubilee*. She was born in Texas but grew up in southern Oklahoma where she and her husband, Charles, a retired English teacher, make their home. They have three grown children and enough grandchildren to keep them young.